MALINALLI

MALINALLI

VERONICA CHAPA

PRIMERO
SUEÑO PRESS

ATRIA

New York Amsterdam/Antwerp London Toronto Sydney New Delhi

ATRIA
An Imprint of Simon & Schuster, LLC
1230 Avenue of the Americas
New York, NY 10020

This book is a work of fiction. Any references to historical events, real people, or real places are used fictitiously. Other names, characters, places, and events are products of the author's imagination, and any resemblance to actual events or places or persons, living or dead, is entirely coincidental.

First Primero Sueño Press hardcover edition March 2025

PRIMERO SUEÑO PRESS / **ATRIA** BOOKS and colophon are trademarks of Simon & Schuster, LLC

For information about special discounts for bulk purchases, please contact Simon & Schuster Special Sales at 1-866-506-1949 or business@simonandschuster.com.

The Simon & Schuster Speakers Bureau can bring authors to your live event. For more information or to book an event, contact the Simon & Schuster Speakers Bureau at 1-866-248-3049 or visit our website at www.simonspeakers.com.

Interior design by Jill Putorti

Manufactured in the United States of America

1 3 5 7 9 10 8 6 4 2

Library of Congress Cataloging-in-Publication Data is available.

ISBN 978-1-6680-0901-7
ISBN 978-1-6680-0903-1 (ebook)

For my grandmothers, Adela & Jesús Maria
my parents, Marcella & José
and my husband, Bruce

CONTENTS

BOOK I

BOOK II

BOOK III

BOOK I

A SORCERESS'S NAME BECOMES MINE

Long ago, our world, with all its mystery and magic, was carried on the back of a crocodile. One misstep and we would all plunge into darkness. By the time I was born, the earth had already been created and destroyed four times.

The land of my birth rested near a winding river called the Coatzacoalcos. Water was everywhere. Silty creeks. Clear streams. Turquoise lagoons. Our house sat within palms of green so deep with color that the leaves appeared blue.

My mother's pregnancy had been a difficult one, and my grandmother, mindful of the capricious natures of the gods, had requested that the wisest of the midwives tend to Mother. And so it was Toci who prepared the opossum tail broth for my mother to drink, who carried my mother into the sweat lodge. Bathed in sweat, the two women roared like Jaguar Knights on the battlefield, their war cries shaking me free.

But as I wailed my first damp breaths, my mother continued to scream. After swaddling me in a cotton blanket and setting me on the earth, Toci returned to my mother and guided my brother into the world.

Upon hearing the news of our creation, a few of the duller villagers ran into the jungle to hide. In small, faraway towns, parents were often so fearful of the power possessed by twins that one of the babies was put to death. In my village, most people believed that twins were the creators of order. We were the monster slayers. Quetzalcoatl—the Feathered Serpent, benevolent god of wind, had been born a twin.

I was the daughter of Jade Feather and Speaking Cloud, and the twin sister of Eagle. The blood of the Toltecs ran through my veins.

▲▲▲▲

My father, Speaking Cloud, a learned nobleman and warrior, believed it a sign of great favor that the gods had entrusted twins into his keeping. His ancestral line included magicians—the firstborn of every family attended the House of Magical Studies in Tenochtitlan—so he understood the deep meaning of such occurrences.

Toci had related all of this to me when I was old enough to understand. With her wrinkles, crown of silver hair, and deep-set brown eyes, she appeared older than time. I never tired of hearing the story or the prayer she invoked at my birth:

"My beloved daughter, my precious jade necklace, my treasure. You have arrived, captured by your brave mother, to live on this earth, this vast and lonely place. Let the gods hear your cries! You have come to tend the fire, to sit by the hearth. Your world is here, within these strong walls."

▲▲▲▲

It was our tradition that within days of being born, a child would have his or her fate read by Crooked Back, the town's calendar priest. After accepting my parents' offering of twenty lengths of white cloth, the old seer turned to his sacred books of names and destiny. The air crackled as the priest unfolded the stiff pages until they covered the ground. He then consulted another book of divination, then another, talking to himself as he studied the painted symbols, the figures of the gods and spirits that had been in attendance at the exact time of our births. He fingered some pages carefully and stabbed at others, turned the books this way and that, peering closely one moment and backing away wide-eyed the next.

When, at last, Crooked Back was satisfied with what he'd seen, he proclaimed that our formal name would be Malinalli, Wild Grass, and that due to godly influences and the position of the stars, my brother and I were doomed to be "carried away by the wind" and live "miserable lives" far from home.

Alarmed, Father challenged the priest. Old Crooked Back sputtered with indignation, for no one had ever questioned his authority before. Committed to improving our fate, and by combining their strengths of will and through magic, my parents moved time: they changed the moment of my brother's entry into the world so he could take the day-sign name Eagle, Cuauhtli. To shield me from my fate, my father decreed me Malinalxochitl.

In Nahuatl, it means Wild Grass Flower. A name filled with sunlight.

▲▲▲▲

For Eagle and me, the world seemed wide and open. In our home, white stucco rooms led from one into the next, with high-beamed ceilings. The finest rooms were decorated with paintings of gardens and colorful shrines dedicated to the gods—all faced a courtyard shaded by rubber trees. Pots brimming with epazotl and iztauhyatl and flowering jasmine and sunflowers colored the air with their scents. There was a sweat lodge and a granary, where we stored the harvested ears and kernels of elotl. Our house was an endless palace, and the wilderness beyond it was our empire.

We tumbled through cornfields, crawled in mud, ran between grasses that soared over our heads, and splashed through lagoons and swamps governed by mysterious forces and the beasts of our dreams. I was easily distracted. Butterflies, hummingbirds, snakes, croaking frogs, and birds in the trees all called me to come play. Eagle was never without a stick in his hands and a plan in his mind. He poked and prodded holes and dark crevices, waved that stick as if he had already achieved the illustrious rank of Jaguar Knight. He always took the lead, shouting, "Sister! Sister! Follow me!"

Seeing the light dancing in his eyes filled me with such joy, it was as if I were being lifted off the ground. Peering into still water at the river's edge, two reflections greeted us, two identical faces framed by dark hair.

Like most children, we played tricks on each other—sneaking up like shadows to scare, hiding a favorite toy, cheating at patolli, our favorite game. Eagle was always the honorable knight; his tricks were obvious and teasing. I, however, liked scaring him. Knowing how much he hated snakes, I hid their skins in his clothes and set loose live creatures beneath his sleeping mat. He was quick to forgive me.

We spoke a special language that no one else could understand, not even our parents, who spoke Nahuatl—the language of the nobility—and Popoluca. By the age of two, Eagle and I mimicked these sounds like parrots. But when we River Twins were alone, we preferred our secret words.

▲▲▲▲

Aside from Eagle's dislike of snakes, we were fearless. Much of that invincibility we owed to our father. Not even the shape-shifters on the darkest of nights frightened him. He was knowledgeable about demons and monsters despite the fact that he never attended the famous magicians' school; he wasn't firstborn. He said nighttime was the time favored by Tezcatlipoca, the trickster god, who enjoyed disguising himself as a shrouded corpse. That was when the Blood Drinkers emerged from the shadows with their sharp teeth bared. Whenever Father told these stories, he'd jump and growl at us, clawing at the air. He would open his eyes wide, then scrunch them up, contorting himself to make us laugh. My father wanted to put us at ease with the dark. Eagle and I would shiver with glee as he recounted tales about the horrors that awaited us outside. We desired nothing more than to venture into the night, but our mother forbade it.

My mother, Jade Feather, kept an obsidian knife in a bowl of water near the door to keep us safe from night demons. She believed that such an arrangement could destroy these creatures.

To distract us from our fascination with the dark, she would sometimes let us look at her amatl-paper books. The one Eagle and I favored most was a wondrous creation made up of large, many-folded sheets of crushed fig tree paper containing red-and-black paintings that represented our calendar's twenty day signs—crocodile, wind, house, lizard, snake, death, deer, rabbit, water, and so on—and images of the gods. We would tuck ourselves against her on a reed mat plumped with pillows and, holding our breath, wait patiently for her to turn back the cover. With each unfolding, the thick pages crackled like my grandmother's knees on a rainy day. Some of my mother's books opened into sheets so long, they stretched across the hearth room.

While snuggling against my mother and twirling strands of her rose-scented hair between our fingers, we discovered gods and goddesses dressed in all of their finery: feathered headdresses, nose rings, earspools, and thick-soled sandals. Eagle and I would carefully point to our favorite drawings. His was an Eagle Knight dressed for battle in a padded vest with feathery wings and a helmet with an eagle's beak. I favored an image—smaller than all the other pictures—of a woman in a long black cloak painted with stars. Underneath, she was dressed in a white huipilli and skirt, and her long hair was held back with a circlet made of heron feathers.

The first time I saw her, my mother said, "That is the sorceress Malinalxochitl." Hearing my name filled my heart with pride, but a harsh tone singed my mother's words. I leaned closer as my brother teased, "Look at *you*, Malinalxochitl," which I did, for as long as I could.

When I was young, I knew nothing about my name except that the villagers of my town spoke it with fearful reverence. Later I would learn that in the time of the ancestors, the first Wild Grass Flower was a mighty sorceress. She was the older sister of Huitzilopochtli—Southern Hummingbird—the god of war. She was his equal, the ancients said, who saw through the darkness of men's minds. And though the people in my village had stopped honoring her long ago, the memory of her avenging nature still lingered. She frightened them. Along with the stories, a question had taken root in my mind: What had she seen that upset her enough to make her seek revenge?

As if my mother knew that I longed to touch the sorceress's image, she'd whispered, "You are not the same." Then, turning to my brother, "Guard your tongue, my son. You, too, daughter. The gods don't enter human life." She'd pushed our hands firmly to our sides. "Malinalxochitl wears the Mantle of Magic and must not be disturbed. You must never make light of the divine ones, lest you provoke their wrath." She meant to show us that we were powerless to the gods' whims. I quietly repeated the words *this is the sorceress Malinalxochitl* as if they were a charm.

That book served my mother's purpose, discouraging us from running wild into the dark. But it also piqued my curiosity. I'd asked both my mother and father if the sorceress was able to overpower monsters and other scary beings. Surely her magic could make such creatures disappear, I'd said.

My parents shook their heads and claimed they didn't know. That's how they answered all of my questions about her.

Despite my parents' tales of the darkness, I was never frightened. Listening to my mother sing and being carried in the crook of my father's arm made me feel safe. At the marketplace, which teemed with people and sounds, and at the temples where priests with soot-stained faces prayed, I was at home. The sun rose every morning. The god of rain favored our land. The elotl grew, was harvested, and became food to fill our bellies.

We were blessed in many ways. My mother was the great beauty of our village, with her blue-black hair and amber-colored eyes. She was the descendant of a noble family. They were Tolteca, from the northern kingdom of Tollan, known for their art and wisdom. "My people invented the healing arts and read the secrets of the earth so well, they could uncover mines of turquoise, amber, crystal, and amethyst just by running their fingers through the land," she'd say proudly, her voice full of a feeling that drew me close.

▲▲▲▲

The rhythm of my days began to change when I turned four, when my mother taught me how to sweep the house and ground corn into cakes. Each day my mother, grandmother, and our servants gathered in the courtyard to spin and weave.

"Cloth is our treasure, more prized than gold," my mother often said to me. Our village was known throughout the land for the exquisite quality of our weaving. The women were required to create three hundred bundles of embroidered cloaks and blankets of diverse colors, and five hundred white embroidered loincloths. It was said that the tlahtoani Moctezuma, the Revered Speaker, wore white cloth that had been made and embroidered by my mother. I dreamed the cloth I wove and embroidered would someday be as prized, but my fingers, and my patience, felt too small to complete the task.

Wriggling and dreaming suited me much better. In fact, being still and silent while the servants moved busily around me was the hardest task of all. Luckily for me, I could always stare at the shrine that adorned our home. It was filled with idols carved of greenstone, wood, and clay set on a carved ledge of cedarwood. I would stare and imagine them sitting beside me: beautiful Chicomecoatl—Seven Serpent—the goddess of maize; Tlaloc, god of rain, google eyed and ever watchful; with Huehueteotl, the old fire god, guardian of the hearth and fire.

My mother had a way of knowing when my thoughts were leaping across a limitless sky. "Someday you shall have a home of your own, a hearth to tend, food to make ready," she advised as she paced the courtyard one day. "Your husband will expect much from you." Her voice was soft yet filled with thorns. I could not stop thinking, *What husband?* I was going to be a magician! As firstborn, in a few years I would be attending the House of Magical Studies, where I would learn how to turn bullying children into toads. Where I would learn how to protect my family. Where I would be invincible. But I dared not speak a single word of this. The silence I offered in response bore down on me like a mountain of stone.

▲▲▲▲

When we were five years old, my brother and I attended our first sacrifice at the main temple in our village. My lip was tender from a maguey spine piercing inflicted by my mother when she'd caught me staring at an extravagantly feathered Mexica tribute collector at the marketplace.

The sacred calendar of days was filled with rituals that honored the gods of rain and wind, and goddesses of the earth, corn, and rivers. The world had already been destroyed and reborn four times by tempests, floods, jaguars, and windstorms, and now we were living in the time of the Fifth Sun, which was destined to end with a rumbling of earth so great that it would swallow everything that lived, even in the sky. Our gods provided protection and guidance, and many ceremonies included offerings of blood to help strengthen Huitzilopochtli—the Mexica sun god of war—in his battle to light the earth.

After the Mexica invaded and subdued the regions along the river—in the time that preceded the birth of my grandparents—they placed

Huitzilopochtli above all other gods. He was responsible for keeping the sun on its course through the sky and victory in war. In return, he demanded offerings of blood and the human suns that beat within our breasts. He was the most bloodthirsty of all, just like the men who served him.

My mother and father taught us that life is precious and doesn't last forever.

I thought I understood what this meant.

On the day of the ritual, during the eleventh month, also known as the Month of Sweeping, we dressed in our finest garments. My beautiful mother held one of our hands in each of hers, and together with Father and Grandmother, we walked in silence to the temple precinct. We were one family out of many, hurrying to the center of our village. I noticed that people stepped aside to let us pass. At first, I thought it might be because we were dressed so finely, but that wasn't it at all: they moved for the twins, in case the stories of us possessing special powers were true.

I had visited the temple many times before this day, but now I felt the air shivering with an anticipation that made everything look new. Even the music of drums and flutes pounded overhead more loudly, and quickly, than I'd ever heard. The white stone pyramid and the temple that crowned its summit loomed in front of me. I let go of my mother's hand. Stepping carefully, holding the hem of my skirt, I moved to stand at my brother's side. Eagle was squinting up at the temple. I was not tall enough to see what had caught his attention. Just then, the music stopped, giving way to flights of whispers. As Father pulled us back, I felt a shift in the air.

Priests appeared along the western edge of the sacred precinct. As they walked toward us, their long dark hair and black robes reminded me of crows. They led a girl dressed in royal turquoise to the temple's stairs. Her hair swung in braids that brushed my skin when she passed in front of me. Her eyes were dark and shiny and closed off. I could smell her—a mix of copal incense, the perfume of marigold flowers, sweat, and what I thought was the scent of fear. Earlier that day, a friend from the village told my brother that the offerings were always given something special to drink to bind them closer to our gods.

Slaves or war captives were chosen for our rituals, but now and then, someone we knew walked the divine path. When my grandmother was little, her friend was drowned to honor the rain god. To be chosen was an honor, and the girl's family was highly regarded thereafter. However, people said something happened to Grandmother when she learned her friend had died. They said it was as if a hard rain had washed her spirit away. I was secretly grateful to not have known the girl about to be offered. But I still couldn't look at her face. I felt like my stomach was clawing its way to my mouth.

I swallowed the knot in my throat and squeezed my brother's arm. I could suddenly see in my mind what was about to happen. I felt the urge to go home or to somehow grab the girl by the hand and run to Eagle and Mali's secret hiding place, where we would share something good to eat.

In the gold light of the sun, I finally turned my face up and watched the girl climb the stairs to the top of the pyramid, where she was met by more priests. She lay on the stone that was there, her robes hanging over the edge.

I fought to control my breathing as the priests lifted and pulled the girl by her arms until her head hung back, off the stone. The music stopped. I squeezed my eyes shut and hid my face in my brother's shoulder. I knew one of the priests held a knife. In my imagining, the blade caught the sun as he raised it to strike the girl's naked chest to cut out her heart.

I clung to Eagle. I felt nauseated and could feel myself start to sink to the ground. *No, no, no. Stand up. You are the daughter of Jade Feather and*

Speaking Cloud. Eagle is your brother, and you are safe. But when I went to straighten myself, the looseness in my limbs threatened to give way to a faint, until I felt Eagle's arm tighten around me.

The pressing silence could have signaled the end of the world. I reminded myself that the ritual was to honor the sun and the renewal of light and life, not just death. This offering of a heart and blood was necessary.

But it was no use. My stomach pitched again, but now with a new thought: Could I be cut open like that, when my body grew as tall as the girl's?

I wriggled away from my brother, questions gathering into a storm cloud in my mind, until a light of certainty flickered: *I will never be thrown across a stone altar. It is impossible. I am destined for magic!* For assurance, I looked at my parents. My mother's face was smooth and calm, her eyes closed as if in prayer, and my father stood with his stone-faced stare. I interpreted their steadiness as a sign that I was right and had nothing to fear.

Everyone around me stood quietly, so I did, too. But even with my brother's hand around mine, I felt alone. I rubbed my temples to soothe the ache in my head, but the throbbing persisted. The heat and the smell of other people's sweat were making me dizzy again. When I looked up at the pyramid, the priest was lifting the girl's heart into the air. I held my breath. With great ceremony, he saluted the sun. Then he tossed the heart into a large stone bowl. I could not look away.

A drumbeat began, shaking the people out of their paralysis. With sighs of relief, they began to leave the temple precinct and return to their homes. I jerked my head around to get a closer look at their faces. Why weren't they crying? My neck flared with heat as if a knife had struck me, and water streamed like a great river from my eyes. I remained in place until my brother looped his arm around my shoulders and led me away.

The memory of what we had witnessed bound Eagle and me together in a new way. We picked at it like a scab. My brother assured me again and again that we were safe. I wanted to believe it, too. But just in case, my five-year-old heart made a sky-high promise: once I was at the magician's school, one of the first spells that I would learn to cast would be the one that would make us live forever.

BALANCED ON THE BACK OF A SLEEPING CROCODILE

You will be an Eagle Knight and win all of your battles," I pronounced one day as Eagle and I were playing in the marshes, in our secret spot near the giant stone head, "and I will sit at home and weave enough cloth to shield all the stars from the moon."

I was joking, of course. These days, we found time to escape to watch the constellations form in the night sky. Eagle would whisper their names to me, while I would imagine changing their shapes with my magical powers. Sit home and weave cloth? Never. My destiny shined brighter than that. But a bitterness tinged my words. Eagle and I had just celebrated our eighth year, and this seemed to be all I did with my time. But not for much longer.

At this age, the children of nobility always began their lessons in religion, astronomy, the calendar, and history at the school for noble youths. But I knew my life would soon be different. I wouldn't be learning anything as boring as that! At any moment, my father would announce that it was time for his firstborn child to journey to the House of Magical Studies in the magnificent city of Tenochtitlan, and I would be on my way to the magicians' school, where I would become a great sorceress.

I was destined to learn the spells that call the rain and stop the wind. I would hear the magical stories of the first Malinalxochitl and finally get answers to everything I wanted to know. After mastering the sorceress's spells, I would follow in her footsteps and enact justice by rooting out all those with dark intentions. I would be my family's shield. My life as a magician would not involve lying in wait.

Yet a special kind of magic was already mine. By this time, I could imitate everything from the noble speech of my father to the coos and soft murmurs of my grandmother, the strange dialect spoken by traders from the Hot Lands to the droning intonations of the priests. I could speak to the parrots in the jungle and howl and grunt greetings to white-tailed monkeys. At the House of Magical Studies, I would learn to command entire armies to do my bidding.

My brother said, "Yes, I can picture you, sister, at your loom with a few brats squalling at your feet."

I pushed him away. But then the thought of us turning old filled me with sadness.

"What will I do without you, brother?"

"What will I do without you?" He paused to lick his lips. "The time of my departure approaches. I am to go to Tenochtitlan."

"Oh, to the school there?" *Why was I not told?*

My brother shook his head. "Not that." He swallowed as if his throat had suddenly dried up. "The House of Magical Studies," he mumbled.

"Where?" I thought he must be confused.

"The House of—"

Oh, but I'd heard him. Suddenly, the sound of the ocean was roaring in my ears. "No!" I jumped to my feet. "Not you! I'm the one!"

For a moment, I saw my brother as my enemy. How could he steal my birthright? Rob the calling that had been singing my name since I was born? How could I learn the universe's secrets if I was to sew and rock babies for the rest of my life? His betrayal choked me, then set fire to my throat. I watched as his face knotted up, but I didn't want to hear whatever he had to say.

"I am firstborn. Me!" I shouted.

"But you can't," he said.

I took a step closer, and he shrank back.

"You're a girl," he explained in a small voice.

I leaned in. Had he gone soft in the head? I tried to laugh. "Yes. And so why—"

"You can't be a girl. They do not allow girls at the House of Magical Studies."

I felt as if my brother had struck me with a slab of stone. I rocked on my feet before regaining my balance.

I didn't understand. *How can this be? Where do the goddesses and sorceresses develop their crafts? The women magicians who heal hearts, divine fortunes, and conjure universes? Is there a place for us, for me, in this world?*

This isn't happening. I always thought I would be the one to cast spells, wear a special mantle, and guide Moctezuma and his people toward a righteous path. That I might become great, like . . . *her*.

I looked away and caught the flight of a bird in the trees, and for a moment I had a thought: Maybe both of us could go. Yes, why not? And since we were twins, our magic would be twice as powerful. Together we would be invincible.

Something inside me had softened. Apologies and my plan were forming on my lips, but when I turned back to my brother, the words died in my throat. I stared at Eagle but saw only an obstacle.

I screamed at him, a horrible sound, like a nightmare unleashed. The force of it knocked him off his feet. I couldn't stop. He ran. I continued until my voice grew hoarse and large white spots danced in front of my eyes. I felt my body whirling off into the dark, as if the power of my anger was propelling me into the Underworld to live among the dead.

▲▲▲▲

For the following three nights, creatures haunted my dreams, and I imagined holding everyone around me in a cage, or worse. Some of the things that I pictured terrified me, as if I had summoned the demons of the fleshless realm to rise up and rain terror on all of us.

But soon after my brother and father departed for the House of Magical Studies, I shook myself free of fantastical imaginings, preferring the relative safety of loneliness. Eagle and I had never been apart from each other. I felt as if I'd lost half of my body, and most of my heart and spirit as well. When I had to, I did my work, shuffling from one chore to the next, grinding the maize, fetching water, and sweeping. I was ready to collapse at any moment.

Who am I without my twin? What am I supposed to do now?

Upon his return, Father was shocked to find me sitting in shadows, haggard and listless. But he showed me great mercy by leaving me alone. The day I finally summoned the courage to leave my home to go to the market, whispers followed me everywhere, like the twittering of sick birds. I imagined they were saying things like *She should be ashamed to ever think she could study magic in Tenochtitlan. She is bewitched, and her mother should hold her face to a flame.* I did hear someone recall the calendar priest's promise that the wind would carry me far from home. They tossed my name around carelessly. Our neighbors and the townspeople, even the hairless little dogs gawked at me.

I searched for something to do that could help me forget my brother. My embroidery needle, untouched since that awful day of his departure, called out to me in a tiny, curious voice. I took a corner of the courtyard and set to work there. In the beginning, I was my usual all-thumbs self, but then it was as if the cloth and my needle had been waiting for me to join them. All kinds of creatures began to sprout beneath my tireless fingers—serpents with powerful jaws and teeth like jaguars, their bodies curled, green as bile. My hands could barely keep up, driven as I was by my anger over being left behind. I sat alone and sewed scales that looked like they could cut fingers and flaming tongues that scorched small holes in the cloth. If not for my embroidery needle and pattern of serpents, I would have choked someone.

I felt annoyed whenever the women's voices grew too loud or someone laughed, worried I might be tempted to look up and lose my way stitching. It didn't matter; they stayed away. My new skill frightened these women. I ignored the fuss, keeping my head down and my hands busy with needlework, bewitched. Still, during the following years, word of my strange ability with needle and thread spread throughout the surrounding villages and to places along the river.

▲▲▲▲

Where once I had roamed the wilderness with Eagle, golden and happy, I was now inside almost constantly. Sewing snakes all day made me sullen. Four long years had passed, and now I was twelve, a pale and bony creature with no friends, who spent her days embroidering cloth after cloth. Sometimes my mother had to take my needle away from me. "That's enough, Mali. You're squinting again," she'd complain. "A hump is growing on your back. Go with the servants to the market," she would command.

Oftentimes between stitches I would stare at the walls. Ever since my brother's abandonment, I had been having visions. It was as if I had drunk from a cup of sacred wine and been blessed with special powers of my own. I saw the magicians' place—carved with fifty-two serpent heads, mouths opened to bite the air. A blind hunchback stood guard, armed not with weapons but with a length of red cotton cloth in one hand and a broom made of heron feathers in the other. I watched my brother exchange his fine garments for those made of maguey fiber, and I could feel him trembling before he lifted his chin and followed the magician into the school.

Our bond was so strong that every now and then I could hear my brother explain what I was seeing. *Look there, sister, at the small boy on the sleeping mat next to mine. His name is Copil. He was born in the land of the Maya, and two of his teeth are pointy and sharp like a jaguar.* So went my brother's voice one night, not long after he had gone to the magicians' place. The hairs on the back of my neck stood on end. I felt his warm breath upon my cheek.

Look up at the ceiling. There is an opening for a hawk and an owl to fly through each night. I have heard that they are shape-changers, teachers with the power to turn themselves into birds. And there are ghosts, Mali!

I admit I was jealous. I grew up hearing tales about headless apparitions, skeletal spirits, and the woman in white who roamed the streets mourning her lost children. But to actually see one? Why had I been denied this?

Then lo and behold, through my brother's eyes I saw the specter of the ruler Axayacatl wander the halls of the House of Magical Studies, reciting poetry in gold sandals and a turquoise cloak.

The light shifted as I watched Eagle follow the magicians' instructions to catch and burn spiders and scorpions, then mix the ashes with tobacco, seeds, and handfuls of soot. A cold fear within me took root. The sorcerers smeared their skin with the paste, ready to embrace the shadows. The same mysterious and silver-infused glow held my brother as he shared spells with me for transforming river pebbles into beetles, conjuring tortoises to fly, summoning Underworld shifters to haunt dreams, and a trick that unleashed the gift of invisibility. Above all else, he gave me a charm that would unlock a power meant to be mine alone. *You must not tell anyone*, Eagle said, *for it is forbidden to give such things to mortals outside our walls.* And after a breath, *Seek the strength that awaits beyond your name and release your full powers.*

It was like a riddle, something to puzzle through, but I couldn't solve it no matter how hard I tried. Nor could I perform his spells with success. But there was strength in knowing that I had this charm and that someday its power would be mine.

▲▲▲▲

Our people believed that the world was balanced on the back of a sleeping crocodile, the oldest, mightiest, most spiny-backed of all caimans, to be precise. We all knew it was a precarious predicament. But I felt the beast shifting beneath my feet when, less than a month after learning about my secret charm, a fearsome messenger from the House of Magical Studies arrived with news about Eagle. Tall with froggy eyes and a voice to match, the man curled his dirty, stubby fingers around the edge of his black cloak as he told my mother and father that Eagle had developed a fever of mind and body and was close to death.

Liar. I turned to my father, ready to tell him that during one of my visions, Eagle had told me that a jaguar enjoyed chasing him through the halls of the school. Then I saw the beast. It crouched low, chin to ground. I heard my brother's heart beating, tasted blood when my brother bit his lip, and screamed as the jaguar leaped into the air with a mighty roar. As the beast fell upon my brother, it grew human arms and legs and took on the figure of a man, with a dagger clenched between his teeth.

But how could I tell Father this? I was never convinced that my vision revealed the truth. It haunted me with worry, but I couldn't accept it. It was only in that moment when I believed it. Back then, as soon as I opened my mouth, I hesitated. My visions were my secret. What could I say in front of this sour-smelling creature that wouldn't upset my family?

"You must come at once," the messenger said.

My father hugged and kissed me on my forehead, held my mother for a long, sweet breath, and left home on One-Dog, a poor day for a journey. I was so afraid for him and for my brother. Eagle had said there were magicians who could transform themselves into birds and animals. One of the sorcerers must have the power to change himself into a jaguar. Who was he? And why had he attacked my brother?

▲▲▲▲

Strange things occurred while my father was away. One morning, I saw a ghostly woman in white speaking to a hummingbird, but with a glance away and back, they were both gone. After that, one of the clay idols moaned. It was the old fire god, who sat cross-legged in a special place close to our hearth, keeping watch over the fire. I was alone sweeping when his mournful wail pierced the air. I grabbed hold of the pine torch affixed to the wall to cast light over the statue, but I never heard the sound again.

And the strangest thing of all: one day as I sat embroidering, a yellow snake I had stitched along the hem of the cloth seemed to come to life in my hands, slipping free of the threads and moving sinuously between my fingers. I shrank back, afraid of the snake. Then, thinking that my eyes must be playing tricks, I looked away. But there was no denying the slithering sensation stealing up my arm. Upon closer inspection, I found the creature beautiful. Somehow, I truly had brought it to life. The realization sent a surge through me. Invisible sparks darted from my fingertips. I wondered if I had solved part of the charm without my knowing it. After a few breaths, the snake seemed more like an old acquaintance rather than a shocking apparition. Something shifted deep inside. I had been feeling adrift and alone, but this magic brought me comfort.

THE OLD FIRE GOD CRIES

After three moons had waxed and waned, another stranger appeared in our courtyard. My heart fell when I saw him standing in the rain—wet yellow plumes stuck to his head, a drenched red cloak hung to his knees, and the gold-tipped walking staff flashed like a lightning bolt.

Inside, he stood near the warmth of our fire and addressed my mother in a curt tone. She stood regal and straight beside my grandmother, with all our servants at her back. With no embroidery needle to steady my fingers, I bit my nails. I should have melted into the shadows, but instead, I pressed closer. With a superior expression, he said he was from the office of the prime minister in Tenochtitlan. "I come at the command of the great Moctezuma himself to inform you that your husband is dead."

My knees buckled, and I fell to the floor. It was as if my insides had turned into a puddle, a shapeless waste skimming the ground. Images flashed through my mind. I saw my father, wiping my tears from my face. I knew he would never have approved of my lying in a heap. But I couldn't get up. Before my mother could form any words, the man grunted, "Your son, too."

I jumped up in shock, a dread in my stomach confirming my worst fears. My mother swayed and, for the briefest of moments, placed her hand on the wall for support. When her gaze caught mine, I wanted to throw myself into her arms, but I stood quietly, watching her breast rise and fall as the firelight caught the shine of her tears.

"Your husband filed a petition with us after learning of your son's death at the House of Magical Studies."

The bile rose up to my throat, hearing my brother's passing put so plainly as that.

After rubbing his hands together to warm them in the fire, the messenger pivoted to look at my mother. "It was a matter that should have been left to the school to investigate, but your husband refused." He lifted his chin and sniffed hard, making a face, as if the air was not to his liking. My fingers itched to pummel him and conjure an army of snakes to constrict his throat and limbs. He said, "Your son was plagued by ill health, is that not so? Caught chills easily?"

My brother never caught the fevers or bone-rattling coughs that blew through our courtyard during the month of Ceasing of Water, when the mountain gods blew their coldest winds. He always had the strength to draw water from the river and hunt with Father. No malady felled my brother. In my mind's eye, I saw the man with the dagger in his mouth, enveloping Eagle in darkness. This Mexica breathing falsehoods had lips like a fish, and I longed to spear them. Sensing my rage, my grandmother held me back.

The messenger carried on, oblivious. "A bad recruit for the House of Magical Studies, sounds like to me." He grunted. "If he had made more of an effort studying the magic spells for staying warm, and honoring the gods, then perhaps he would still be alive. Your husband meant to conduct his own investigation and petition to have his case presented to the tlahtoani himself. The fool! One does not trouble the mighty Moctezuma with such petty cases. Your husband paid for the disrespect—confined to a cage with no food or water. His body is still . . ." He drew a sharp breath, shut his mouth for a moment, then continued.

I could see my father standing before seated officials, eloquently calling for justice. It filled me with pride. But as the messenger recounted the events, I found it increasingly harder to breathe. I saw the spear point prodding Father to stoop from his great height and enter a wooden cage carpeted with fragments of stone. When I blinked, my father twisted between the bars and lay in filth. His once bright eyes were rimmed with shadows. Food scraps littered the ground all around him, unfit for a dog.

We were all crying silently by then, though we stood quietly and patiently until the messenger was finished. Then, with great composure, my mother served the man food and drink. She thanked him for traveling from the court of Tenochtitlan to share his news with us and commended his superiors for allowing him to come to her humble home. She bowed her head and prayed to the gods that they would keep the man safe during his journey back to the imperial city. A dark hope rose within me that he would not make it back safely, that something terrible would befall him in punishment for his callousness.

He could have stayed silent and gone on his way with his belly full of our food, but he had to have the final word.

"They are gone, and you will never see them again. Now, fill your days with weaving and sewing, sweeping and caring for your home, and pray to the gods, as always."

My hands balled into fists as I watched him walk away, his head proud, as if he were our master. I could have chased him all the way back to Tenochtitlan. *Liar. The gods are not to blame for this!* But my mother's cries turned me around. She bent low, as if to eat the earth, but instead of touching the ground with her fingers and pressing them to her lips, she laid her head down and cried. The other women joined, filling the air with their grief. Watching them, hunched and rocking back and forth in pain, I imagined my brother's body torn apart by the dagger. I hungered for pain. After failing to spy the flint knife my mother kept near the hearth, I began cutting my hands with a maguey spike, until my grandmother took it away from me.

I knelt on the floor and, shaking, opened the pack that held my brother's possessions. The Mexica had thrust it into my mother's arms as if it was tainted. I found a black cloak of coarse fiber, a white ribbon, a small lava-stone bowl that smelled of sage and frogs and wet bark when I held it to my nose, a boar bristle brush, and a book where he kept his painted words. I lingered over each treasure, but ultimately my fingers kept turning to the jade feather I'd once worn on a deer-hide string around my neck. I had given the feather to Eagle before he left for the House of Magical Studies.

Even the fire was moved by these objects, dancing and leaping one moment to get a better look, on the brink of dying the next. I watched the toothless old fire god raise his hands to his face and cry.

There was no packet of my father's belongings. It was as if he had simply vanished from the earth. All we had were words.

Through the fog of our grief, my mother and I wrapped Eagle's things in a length of our finest white cloth and perfumed the precious bundle with incense. Then she brought out a long sheet of blue embroidered cloth that bore the shapes of clouds and a gold sun.

There were no remains, and this worried me. How would their souls find their way if there was no ritual burning? The sacred rite protected souls and gave strength for the dangerous passage through to the Underworld. And what of the little dog that is supposed to serve as guide? How would it ever know that my father and brother need its protection and companionship?

To ease my distress, my mother, following the Toltec ways, embroidered cloth images of the god Quetzalcoatl with the hope he would watch after the souls of my family. She marked their eyes and mouths with gold thread and gave them headdresses of iridescent quetzal feathers. And as the rain fell, we placed all of the folded offerings to rest under the earth beneath one of the rubber trees. I prayed that my jade feather would find its way back to my brother and father, so they would have something to remember me by as they wandered for the next four years in Mictlan, the place of the fleshless.

▲▲▲▲

Lightning streaks of gray appeared in my mother's hair overnight. She refused to eat. The chatter that had once filled the courtyard died, and she no longer shared stories, gossip, or wisdom for us to live by. Instead, at the dawn of each day, she simply breathed into a handful of corn kernels to warm and prepare them for the heat of the griddle, then found refuge in her embroidery, stitching with a fury that surpassed my own. We were a sight, my mother and I, kneeling in the courtyard, bent over our cloths, needles flying. Silence was our constant companion as butterflies, stars, flowers, frogs, and snakes appeared beneath our fingertips effortlessly, maddeningly, adorning towers of cloth that rose ever higher, as corn cakes grew cold on the griddle and stews bubbled into dry lumps.

When I was not embroidering, and my mother wasn't looking, I cried to the walls, the birds, the statues of the gods . . . anything that would listen.

How could this be happening to us? Where was my father? My brother?

I got down on my knees and prayed to Ometeotl, the dual god, both a man and a woman. "Oh, Great Lord and Lady of All Created Things," I addressed the god formally, "remember me, Malinalxochitl, who works tirelessly at her loom, embroidering the cloth, tending the hearth and home? Behold, Lord and Lady, that I have lost a father and a brother to the god of the Underworld. May your heart take pity on me. May you help me, answer me, *why* . . ."

I burned paper that I'd painted with my blood to make it more worthy of their attention. But Ometeotl must not have heard me or seen the smoke of my offering, for no answer came.

"You must be brave now, Mali," the women whispered to me, so my mother wouldn't hear. I tried to convince myself that my brother was supposed to die like this. It was his destiny to serve the gods. Had not Mother and Father told me that the world is a place of great pain and sorrow? I dried my eyes and called upon what bravery I possessed to rise within me. But then I had only to look at the moon to be reminded of the night my father pointed to the rabbit in that silvery sphere. Near the swamp and marshlands where Eagle and I played, every rock and tree and lily pad held the memory of his voice. As I gathered water reeds, I could hear the cry, "*Sister! Watch me*," and I would turn and see him laughing, and tears would begin anew.

Nightmares sought me out, dug their claws into me, and filled my mind with images of my father's and brother's journey through the nine levels of Mictlan, crossing rivers and mountains, attackers without shape or form assaulting them with arrows. Once, I had envied my brother for being chosen to attend the House of Magical Studies. Now, more than ever, I wished with all of my heart that I could have been the one to go, for then my brother and father would still be alive. Curse the school's rules. I could have learned Malinalxochitl's spells and protected them from harm! The desire pressed heavily on me, and with it crept a hate for that school and for Tenochtitlan, source of all my woes.

THE PLACE WHERE SORROW IS LEFT

For eighty days, we mourned. Following tradition, I neither washed nor combed my hair. My face became crusted with dirt and dried tears. Spiders lodged in my tangles. At the end of this time, the priests came and scratched the filth from my face and wrapped what they had trapped beneath their fingernails in paper. These were taken away to the Place Where Sorrow Is Left and abandoned with other paper tears.

When these priests arrived, it was the winter month Feast of the Mountains. My mother's spirit found its way back to us, but I refused to celebrate the end of sorrow by bathing. I prized my dirty skin because the dirt was from the time before my father and brother died: How could I wash it away? I wanted to rub it in deeper and make it a part of me forever. The servants were diligent about keeping the incense burning to mask my pungent smell, but it was not enough. After one hundred and twenty days of breathing my stink, my mother lost her patience. I was so filthy, she forbade me to work with cloth, which only made my fingers ache with longing for the needle. I was grudgingly allowed to sweep the courtyard, which I was grateful for, as it was a sacred duty to keep our home clean.

"Let me wash your hair for you," my patient mother had offered on an overly bright day. The sun wasn't yet at its zenith, and I'd been pacing the courtyard, trying to ignore my mother, grandmother, and servants who were weaving and sewing in the shade. Poinsettias, hummingbird flowers, and angel's trumpets thrived in pots around the yard. I carefully averted my eyes, still smarting from our last argument.

"Don't you miss them?" I'd lashed out, grief loosening my tongue. I had been sullenly watching her move about the hearth room, placing fresh flowers at the feet of the clay idols. I thought I'd heard her humming. The house had been fresh-smelling and scrubbed clean, as if my brother and father were due to return any minute. I'd been standing close enough to smell the rose oil in her hair. It was like a slap in my face. "Don't you care?" I'd yelled. "Everyone walks around as if all is well."

"I know this is hard for you, child," she'd answered softly. "But there is work to be done."

Child. The word irritated like a patch of nettles, and I struggled to listen.

"Someday you will understand. Just as the snake sheds its skin and leaves a kind of death behind, so must we continue on. Until the gods say otherwise."

She was right, of course; we had no control. Life would continue. The rains would come and the corn would grow until the gods decided differently. I half-heartedly recalled the words my father had learned from a traveling court poet that we are not on earth forever but only for a moment. I pushed these thoughts away. While a part of me felt ready to carve a path forward, I wasn't ready to accept that they were gone. I wanted to turn my tears into fiery arrows to launch against Tenochtitlan and the emperor.

Her calming tone had continued. I longed to be carried along the soothing river of her words, but the poke of that word *child* made me want to refuse her. And yet . . . the promise of water moving against my skin—how rich and pleasurable that would feel—was hard to resist in the end.

▲▲▲▲

I was loathe to bathe standing in the pumice stone trough that we used for dyeing cloth, but Mother refused to let me walk to the shallow pool near the river where Eagle and I used to wash and play. I wasn't certain if this was because I was too old to be seen naked or too filthy. My scalp and skin itched fiercely from the dirt. My feet would require a good rub with a giant's portion of volcanic stone if they were ever to be smooth and clean again.

Shielded by a curtain of white cloth, I was lathered and doused with buckets of cold water. After my mother soaped my hair and washed it clean with rosewater, after the servants burned my clothes, then and only then, did my mother decide I was ready for the temazcalli.

The sweat house was a circular enclosure made of stone set apart from the main house, with its own hearth built into a section of its outside wall. It had an earth floor and a small opening in the roof. When the wall glowed red hot, I opened the little door, crouched down, and entered. My mother and grandmother followed.

Once we were all seated inside the temazcalli, Mother threw water from a clay pitcher onto the wall. The stones hissed. The steam enveloped me in waves. I closed my eyes to concentrate on the water and give thanks to it.

I licked the sweat dribbling off the tip of my nose and opened one eye. Dark curls of hair had escaped my mother's crown of braids. Her skin glistened. I opened both eyes. She and my grandmother were sitting comfortably, their legs stretched out in front of them. There was something noble in the way they held their naked bodies, as if works of gold crowned their heads. I, on the other hand, was doing my best to imitate a clam: I sat closed, wrapped my arms around my legs to hide my budding breasts and the scallop-shell pendant that hung low on my hips. All young girls from noble families wore them until they married.

I tried my best to relax, to embrace the feel of the hot mist on my skin, the smell of pine from the fire, and aloe. In the soft dark, I felt as if I were sitting on Earth Mother's lap. I tried to rid my mind of all thoughts and listen to the women's steady breaths, the hissing steam, the delicate ping of water droplets. Just as I was beginning to feel my shoulders soften, I thought I saw my brother's face in gathering wisps of steam. No mistake, for then I heard his steady voice forcefully say, *Release my heart from captivity*. I shivered, and the wisps slipped around me. His heart? But he was dead.

I pulled in tighter, rubbing the chill away, catching my mother, her arching brow, as if she'd caught me in a new lie.

▲▲▲▲

A crush of feelings fought for my attention like equally matched warriors. In the end, anger won my twelve-year-old heart. Where once there was this feeling of a birdlike softness inside me, always setting me to crying, it became a creature with fangs and piercing yellow eyes. It coiled beneath my breastbone and hissed. One day I stomped my feet and yelled, "What kind of people are these Mexica? What kind of place is Tenochtitlan that would allow a boy like Eagle to die like that? What kind of monster imprisons someone who wants nothing more than to learn how his son died?"

I raged against the gods. It was blasphemous, but my anger was limitless. I stood in front of them—Chicomecoatl, Tlaloc, and Huehueteotl—all carefully arranged in their places on the flower-decorated shelf, copal incense swirling, and spoke to them as if they were subservient to me. "How could you do this? My family has always obeyed and worshipped you. Did we not pray hard enough? Were our sacrifices too poor?" My voice made the clay idols tremble. "I know I am not the most accomplished of daughters . . . Is that it? Are you all punishing me? Tell me. I demand an answer!" But I saved my loudest curses for the ruler of the empire who wore my mother's cloth. Moctezuma.

"I will avenge their deaths! I promise you! You will curse my name."

Now I knew what vengeance was made of: a fire that starts low in your belly and reaches into your chest to engulf your heart. It fills your blood with hatred. It's a spearpoint in your back, pushing you to act. I wanted to destroy Moctezuma for what he had done. And I would need the strength of the mightiest sorceress of them all, Malinalxochitl, to achieve my goal.

I was more determined than ever to learn everything I could about her. I wanted to *be* her.

I was filled with heat. It felt better than grief. So as the women dyed the cotton threads, tending the great stone pots filled with their colors in our yard, I plotted a path forward. If I could not attend the House of Magical Studies, then I would create my own school. *I'll begin by teaching myself sword fighting and study all the things I imagine are taught at that sorry place that refuses girls.*

Every morning, before the sun rose, I snuck out and went to the marshes to practice my swordplay using a sharpened tree branch for a sword and a circle of pulled cloth and twisted twigs for a shield.

When I wasn't cutting down enemies, I practiced spells I'd learned from my brother and waited for the transformations that never came. I tried and tried his conjuring trick, the one with a brew of ground tobacco leaves and crushed snakeskin, guaranteed to mask me in a cloud of imperceptibility.

But in my mind, I was not failing. I had been able to see things through my brother's eyes, make threads come to life, surely it was just a matter of time before some other kind of magic was mine. And I had a plan, a thing of beauty: After sneaking into Tenochtitlan, I would wrap myself in my magical cloud and drive a dagger into Moctezuma's heart. Then I would wreak havoc on the House of Magical Studies and conjure giants to destroy that place that refused to share their learnings with girls. I prepared a cloth bundle for the day that I would run away to Tenochtitlan and hid it in the grass behind the stone head.

My long absences were noted by everyone at home. Not that I cared. It was as if I were living in a place far removed from the world, guarded by thick walls and patrolled by the beast with fangs and claws lodged inside me. One morning, I found my mother waiting for me at the hearth, with one of her books tucked under her arm. She took me gently by the hand and led me to the place in the marshes where Eagle and I used to play.

To my astonishment, the first thing my mother did at the site was pick out the cloth bundle that I'd hidden away in the grass. Without saying a word, she sat on the ground, and after drawing her blue-sandaled legs to the side, with the stone head at her back and my bundle serving as a pillow, she gestured that I sit with her. She drew me into her strong arms and held me as if I were a small child again. I played with her turquoise armband as she rocked me, her voice tender with lullabies to soothe the beast nesting inside me.

"It is good that your father named you Malinalxochitl," she said. "Your name will offer you protection from harm."

I adjusted myself so that I could look up at her face. "What kind of harm, exactly? Like what happened to Father in Moctezuma's imperial city?" I wasn't speaking out of fear—I was going to be goddess strong one day—but out of curiosity.

She placed her finger to my lips. "There must be no more talk about the tlahtoani, do you hear me?" Her voice was firm. "The walls of our home, even these rocks, have ears," she cautioned. "A woman's voice could be her undoing. If you're not careful, shame and sorrow will follow you, too." She did not move her finger away until I nodded. I swallowed the unease stirred up by her warning, nestled closer, relishing the feel of soft cloth and the warmth of her skin beneath my cheek.

"There is something important I need to share with you. On the day you were born, the calendar priest named you Malinalli, the sign of wild grass. He said you and your brother had a cursed fate—that you were destined for a painful life far from home. But your father and I refused to accept this. We changed your birth date and your destiny. You were born into the light of Malinalxochitl. You will summon her and do great things with your life.

"Always remember, you are my precious necklace and my creation. The blood of the Toltecs runs through you," she whispered into my hair, then tightened her embrace and kissed me. Once the shock of this revelation passed through me, I nearly sang with happiness. The richness of her voice, her hair, everything that touched her assured me that what she said was true.

Then my mother released such a sigh that I thought I felt the stone move with her breath. "There is so much for you to learn."

I sat up. "Teach me, then! Teach me everything."

"Look." My mother picked up the book she had brought with her. It was the size of her hand and had a jaguar skin stretched across thick paper. In the center was a turquoise stone. The pages opened out into one long, colorful strip made of deerskins that had been glued together. I'd seen parts of this book before; my mother had shown it to me and my brother many years ago. She had two others that were filled with black-and-red images.

Paintings of the gods, framed by the symbols representing days of the calendar, starting with One-Crocodile, covered the deerskins. The pictures had guided my parents' stories about how the sun was born, why the moon possessed the face of a rabbit, and where the wind went to rest.

I scanned the wide length of the book until I saw something curious. "Who is this?" I said, pointing to a woman in a running pose. She had tattoos on her cheeks, was armed with a wooden war club and a shield, and wore a gold nose plug shaped like a half-moon.

"She is Coyolxauhqui, Painted Bells, the Moon Goddess. And this . . ." my mother said, directing my attention to another figure standing beneath a colorful symbol of wild grass flowers encircled by a snake, "is Malinalxochitl."

Startled, I sat back. I had not seen these before. Not ever. She, too, carried sword and shield. She hadn't been armed in any of the other books.

"None of the goddesses we pray to carry weapons," I said. Did someone want to hurt Malinalxochitl?

"That is true," my mother answered. "The world is vast, and there are sacred rituals unknown to us here, in our village on the river. But in the time of our foremothers, in ancient Tollan, the people honored female strength and the generative dark and luminous aspects of Malinalxochitl."

I frowned. How could someone be dark *and* luminous? But before I could say anything, a flash of sunlight sparked the shield. I leaned in so close that I could see shiny speckles, like captured stardust. I thought I smelled the colors. A yellow like sunflowers, the black of a burnt pine torch, and the red of the dusty tang of crushed cochineal bugs.

"Do you see how the artist paints her with a collar of hummingbird feathers and jade stones around her neck?" my mother said, her hand smoothing my hair. I nodded.

"The adornments are sacred to Wild Grass Flower and to her younger half brother, Southern Hummingbird, the god of war." She shifted in place to reach Malinalxochitl's headdress and fingered the spray of white feathers that crowned her head. They, too, appeared to shimmer with movement, as if caught by a gentle breeze. "White heron feathers are special to her too. It has always been so. Feathers. Serpents. They are sacred to her."

But my attention was glued to the sword and shield. I was enthralled and a little terrified. "What did she need them for?" I had assumed that spells and magic were her only weapons. Then I remembered something about her being able to root out all those with dark intentions. I imagined that this might make some people angry. Especially those who were determined to destroy, armed with their obsidian-studded blades, bows and arrows, poisoned spears, and sturdy shields.

"Their mother was Coatlicue, Serpent Skirt, an earth goddess," my mother said plainly, as if that was enough to explain the mystery. I looked up at my mother, questions crowding my mind. But the armed figure of Malinalxochitl drew me back, and I kept my eyes on her. As I nudged the paper with my finger, I thought I saw her shield burst with sunlight.

"If her mother was a goddess, then that makes her a goddess," I said as I continued to make the image glow in my mind.

"Some think so. Most prefer to see her as the sorceress who tried to destroy her brother," she explained, her voice angry and tight. "But it is he who destroyed her." She paused. "He slaughtered Painted Bells."

Startled by such a gruesome thing, I jumped back from the book. "He killed his sisters?"

My mother shook her head. "Only Painted Bells. Wild Grass Flower survived."

How could a brother do such a thing? Puzzled, I sat back on my heels. "Why would he want to hurt them?"

"To us, it seems a mystery. Confusing. But in the time of the Great Mother, the world was different." My mother tipped my face up so that she could look me in the eye. "Long ago, women were the centers of all power. Noble blood ran through the mother." She dropped her hand and fingered a fold in her skirt, saying, "That is how the Mexica built their dynasty." Her voice was tense. Forgetting all about "stones with ears," she went on angrily, her eyes sparkling. "It was a princess from Tollan who gave them their power and established their royal line. Without her . . ."

I could tell by her angry tone that this was important. No, more than important, for here I was looking at a picture of Malinalxochitl! To see my namesake armed like this lifted my spirit.

Frustrated, I waited to hear more, though there was nothing but the sound of croaking frogs and whirring insects rising in the grass and banging into my face.

To break the silence and urge her to continue, I said the first thing that came to me. "The children still tease me about my name."

"I know," my mother said.

"They say I'm the seed of evil." I caught her gaze. "Was *she* evil? They say she cursed the land and turned her back on the people." I took a breath. "I would never harm my brother."

She nodded and started to smile, but I think she was remembering Eagle because her mood turned to one of sadness. "I know you wouldn't." My mother often used a fat silence to force me to be quiet. Usually, this was effective. But today I became gruff with her.

"So, is it true? Was she evil?"

My mother hesitated. "A woman with great power can be frightening. An adversary who can bring her enemy to her knees and hope for her people."

Her words hung in the air. I narrowed my eyes, as if this would make the words last longer. My mother knew how much I wanted to avenge Eagle's death. Was she giving me permission to seek out the enemy? To emulate the goddess Malinalxochitl, to be her, embrace evil if I had to, to achieve justice?

She must have read my confusion, because she said, "I understand how you feel. I really do."

I looked down, but not before catching a look of worry dart across her eyes as I fussed with the trim on my huipilli, then followed the flight of an orange-and-black monarch butterfly. According to our beliefs, he was a reincarnated warrior returning home. That's what I wanted—to return home to a brother and father. But that home was gone. When the monarch warrior fluttered out of view, I turned back to my mother. Her face was so calm and open that I felt ashamed to have spoken to her so meanly. Her eyes held more respect for me than I deserved. Before I could apologize, my mother said, "I cannot tell you more, but I know who can." She paused, and I held my breath. "You will go to a place where the learnings are limitless. You will be safe with them."

BOOK II

TEMPLE OF THE EIGHTEEN MOONS

The journey took Toci and me farther from the village than I had ever traveled before. The land was a tangle of palms and rubber trees that gave way to pines and cedars. We spent three nights bathed in blue-white moonlight. I lay awake most of the time listening to the murmurings of animals and Toci's soft snores. How could I sleep? My heart pounded with excitement. I was sure I was about to discover everything there was to know about Malinalxochitl, to learn her spells and the art of battle.

But on the fourth day, the moment Toci stopped, placed her walking stick on the ground, and began to chant a prayer, a curl of fear rose in my belly. What if I wasn't ready for this step? Adding to my sense of panic, a mist swirled into being, threatening to hide the earth and sky around us. The birds and insects of the jungle that had accompanied us were now silent. My mouth went dry. I tightened my fingers around the bundle that held everything I had been allowed to bring with me.

The mist grew thicker. As I considered asking Toci if something was wrong—*Perhaps we are lost?*—I remembered what my mother had said four days earlier: *You will travel to a temple in Quetzalapan, where you will study to be a priestess. Toci will accompany you. She knows this place well.*

A priestess of Malinalxochitl? Would I now learn sorcery to conjure an army of monsters to do my bidding? Master fighting with a true sword and shield? Study herb lore and learn how to vanquish people through subtle and not-so-subtle means? I could barely contain my joy.

My mother and I had been sitting near the hearth, and a steaming pot of tamales filled the air with the fresh smell of elotl. I'd been leaning so close to hear my mother's words that the flame nearly burned the edge of my huipilli. She did not say how long I would need to stay at the temple. And I did not ask. I knotted my hands in my lap and lowered my gaze. It had taken all my control to keep from needling her with my questions. I'd wanted to be the good, perfect daughter, at least for a while longer.

But during my self-imposed silence, I'd realized that I had never been away from my home or village before. What would it be like to live somewhere else? Then another truth took over: there was no one at home to take care of my mother and grandmother. My eagerness to leave had flattened like a cold tlaxcalli.

That was when my mother surprised me with a gift. It was a necklace of turquoise stones and crystal feathers, and it was the most beautiful object I had ever seen.

"My mother gave this to me in my twelfth year," my mother said, presenting the necklace on the bed of her opened palms. "It was given to her by her mother and has passed from mother to daughter since the beginning of time. It is yours now, Malinalxochitl."

My name on her lips sounded like a blessing. I sat up straighter, the way a fully grown woman was meant to sit with her noble mother. And now this jewel was mine? I'd felt a light shining within me, guiding me to her path.

She moved behind me and fastened the necklace around my neck, the stones feeling cool against my skin. She cleared her throat, and her voice trembled a little as she said, "Should you forget where you come from, who you are, you need only look at this to be reminded that you are the daughter of Jade Feather . . ." She paused, swallowing what I thought were tears. "Who is the daughter of She with the Sad Eyes, who is the daughter of . . ."

My mother had told me stories of how when the Mexica were little more than barbarians living off flies and pond scum, her people had been ruling the land for generations. As she spoke the name of the firstborn of all our ancestors, she finished with a great sigh, then kissed me on the forehead.

"I will never forget," I promised, looking her in the eyes. The pride—and was it sadness?—I'd seen reflected there made me drop my gaze.

As I remembered, I squeezed the bundle in my hands tighter. I had placed the turquoise necklace safely inside it. Knowing the beautiful treasure was close steadied me. *Whatever awaits*, I told myself, I am ready for it.

The mists felt cold, and I shivered. Just as I was about to ask where we were, Toci held up her hand. She stood quietly, then lifted her arms to the sky and gave voice to a string of words in an unfamiliar tongue.

The mists began to part.

I shrank back from the swirling air, as its fingerlike wisps seemed eager to touch me. When I felt that I was about to be enveloped by the whirling mass, the mists thinned and gave way to more trees, and slightly beyond that, a pyramid. Its white stones shimmered as if they were alive.

"Come now," Toci said, startling me. I looked at her, but I didn't move. "Malinalxochitl?" She arched her brow. "Come. They are waiting for us."

With her walking stick in hand, Toci led the way, moving with vigor toward a low white wall, which stretched before us. On the other side of it was the shining pyramid, and beyond that . . . I did not know. But my doubt, like the mists, did not linger. I jumped forward, eager to see what awaited me, relieved to once again hear the familiar sounds of monkeys and birds in the trees, to see hummingbirds slipping in and out of the throats of pink lilies. Butterflies moved over our heads in orange ribbons. The pyramid grew as we approached. *Is this the magic of Malinalxochitl?* I wondered.

We passed through an opening in the wall and entered a large courtyard, with the pyramid on the left and a long white building with a thatch roof and many red columns to our right. A strange, round-shaped building that spiraled like a shell sat beyond it. It was painted red, blue, and green, like the stone serpent heads that jutted out from the pyramid's base. There were pathways of cut white stone edged with giant scallop and conch shells. Jacaranda and silk cotton trees bloomed around the yard. Happy Goddess! Was this where I was to learn and achieve Malinalxochitl's powers? Her way of conjuring giants into being, moving mountains with a glance, eliminating enemies by use of a secret word? Everything I would need to make me feared? I glanced back and forth, absorbing it all. The place was far grander than the temple precinct at home.

But the most startling feature was the group of women, all dressed in white, who stood in front of the round building. They looked as if they had been expecting us.

Toci's steps quickened. Her mantle fluttered behind her. I ran to keep up, until I realized that the women were staring at me. I slowed my steps. I was the daughter of Jade Feather and Speaking Cloud and the sister of Eagle. I would show these women that I was not a peasant from the country.

I heard their voices on the breeze.

"Perhaps Toci has returned to teach us again," answered a musical voice.

Teach? I glanced at Toci. Was the midwife also a teacher for these women?

"Look at Toci's mantle," the same voice continued. "The embroidery work is exquisite. I must learn where it was made."

My heart soared. *I* had embroidered the nohpalli cactus leaves and five-petaled flowers that decorated Toci's mantle.

The women stood beside a shallow pool built of stone. The water mirrored the sky and thin clouds. It also shined with the women's faces and figures.

I stood at Toci's side, nervous that they could hear the excited pounding of my heart. I pressed my bundle to muffle the beating.

The women gathered before me seemed as different as birds in a forest: tall, short, young, and old. They wore their dark hair in long single braids, high on the head like a crown, or like my mother—gathered, with two strands crossed over the top with small tufts of hair pointed up at the sky. Their pure white huipiles and skirts bore very little embroidery. The lack of ornament did not lessen their appearance, for the simplicity of their garments and hair gave them a queenly richness. All save the eldest were barefoot. One wore a strange hat with flaps like wings. Her skin was pale as the tuft of a milkweed seed and shone as if it were lit from within by the moon. Small ovals of smoky obsidian glass framed in copper shielded her eyes.

I was glad I had taken Toci's advice and changed in the forest into a clean cotton huipilli and skirt, but now I felt that the blue garments, embroidered with stars and ocean waves, were too fussy. I thought my dark green mantle was too . . . green. My gold leather sandals . . . they were not right either. I pushed a loose strand of hair off my face and hoped my skin was not dirty.

The most regal-looking of the women stepped around the pool to greet us. Her silver hair was coiled atop her head. She was tall, and her fluid walk reminded me of my mother's. Her sandals were blue like the ones I'd seen in the book paintings that portrayed the royal women of ancient Tollan. Her deeply lined face was lovely and majestic.

The group quieted enough that I could hear the gentle lapping of water and wind.

"Welcome to the Temple of the Eighteen Moons," the woman said, then continued with great warmth, using an elaborate courtly manner of speaking. I knew it well, for I'd heard my father use it whenever he gave speeches. It was a very refined tone that made me take time with my words, made people feel respected and important. "You are weary. Rest now. Your journey has been long, but now you have arrived." Then, with a smile so giving that I could not help but return it, she said, "Thank the gods and goddesses you are here safe and sound. Tell me, dear Toci, what was your latest journey like? How you love to come and go! I can't wait to hear all about it."

Toci beamed, then stepped forward to hug her much taller friend. Toci pulled away slightly, enough to look up at the face of the priestess. "Greetings, Flower of the Night Sky. Too much time has passed since our last visit, yes? I brought you some of the flowers and herbs you are so fond of," she said, tapping the jaguar pouch that hung at her side. "You have said that ahuehuetl bark and marigold blossoms make a nice remedy for tired feet."

"Oh, thank you for thinking of me! You are a gift." Flower of the Night Sky turned her full attention to me. "And this is Jade Feather's daughter?"

"Yes, this is Malinalxochitl," Toci answered.

Some of the younger women gasped. The littlest one had covered her face with her hands and was now peering warily through parted fingers. Though most seemed too well-mannered to allow such a thing as a name to take them by surprise, their whispers filled the air.

I swallowed the little knot in my throat, then forced a smile. Flower of the Night Sky cast a look over her shoulder, silencing everyone, before turning back to me.

"I see. Just like the daughter of the Earth Mother." She nodded approvingly. "Welcome, Malinalxochitl. Welcome home."

My smile died. Home? *My home is with my mother, near the grave sites of my father and brother.* I clutched my bundle—my few possessions, the turquoise necklace—tighter to my breast. *Just wait until they say my name a few more times; they will not be so welcoming then.*

▲▲▲▲

We moved toward the building framed by red columns carved with butterflies.

"Is it true? You have a twin?" a voice teased. I looked down into the serious face of a priestess with slanted, sparkling eyes. The voices of the women around us faded.

"Yes," I said. "But he is—" Though I detected no malice in her gaze, my throat swelled, and I could not say it.

"Cloud Song?" Toci called to the priestess. My observer would not stop staring at me. "Priestess? How go your observations of the night sky?" Toci asked. "Have you seen the stars that scatter sparks and breathe fire?"

This final question abruptly ended the girl's study of me. "In the northern sky? Moving between the Evening Star and the crab?" she answered. "Yes, I've seen them." The girl ran to Toci's side. "The stars erupt often, and violently. These are very different from the sightings of four years ago," she said urgently. "Those were calm and had grace. These new eruptions disturb."

A deep crease appeared on Toci's brow. "What do you mean?"

"They tell of two great powers meeting. And one fading beneath the other."

"You have not seen this before, priestess?"

Cloud Song glanced away, then back. With everyone's eyes on her, she bided her time. "No, danger comes. But the power that will fade will eventually gain back strength and overpower the other," Cloud Song said. "This will take place long after all of us here have found peace in the Underworld." She turned to me then and gave me a smile. "Long after."

The look was unsettling and made me feel as if she were going to lead me to the Underworld right now. *I'll have to keep watch on her*, I thought as I moved away. I would soon discover that this sharp-eyed priestess was the Temple's astronomer.

Standing inside the red-columned building was a revelation of another kind. The High Priestess took me by the hand and led me deeper inside. "This is the temple of Quetzalpapalotl, Feathered Butterfly," she whispered reverently.

Over us was a broad ceiling set with beams of cedar. Murals painted with a garden of beasts and strange glyphs decorated the walls. A throne of pure white stone sat low upon carved jaguar paws, an altar beside it. I noticed flowers upon its surface, but no blood, neither fresh nor dried. It appeared that this goddess, whom I'd never heard of, did not demand sacrifices.

Behind the throne, the goddess's likeness commanded the painted wall—a woman's figure, dressed in a white huipilli and skirt, with giant red-and-green butterfly wings extending from her back, and a crown of emerald quetzal feathers on her head. Her face was as round as the moon, with softly closed eyes. A speech scroll emerged from her mouth to show the importance of her words. A curious assembly of bee-shaped incense burners guarded her and released a mild fragrance sweeter than copal.

How I yearned to tell my brother about this elegant temple—its markings, the paintings, and this curious goddess. Eagle had been the finest listener in the world. And with that, memories of him pressed against my heart. Despite the beauty of my surroundings, the warm welcome I'd received, and the hope that I would soon be learning about my namesake, sadness pulled at me. I would have dissolved into a heap of tears if not for the attention of a trio of young priestesses who fluttered to me, whispering all at once. They seemed nothing like the people at home, who regarded me with unease and distaste. These young women came to my aid. In this moment, these three priestesses—all with long dark hair, some with deep purple tones—became as dear to me as sisters.

Rabbit, at eight years, was the youngest and deeply afraid of the dark. Jeweled Laughter possessed the charming shyness the women from the eastern coast are known for. And Hummingbird, with the crossed eyes that were a sign of beauty among her people, the Maya, was the one with a voice like music. A sensible girl who would prove to have more wisdom in her little finger than wise men had in their whole bodies.

"Oh, everyone, look at her huipilli, the embroidery work! Did you create this?" asked Hummingbird. Her gaze, so open and accepting, put me at ease. I nodded, proud of my stitchwork. I lifted the hem slightly so she could get a better look.

"What magic!" she exclaimed as the two other girls marveled at the spiraling silver stars that I had mixed with curling blue waves, and the small diamond pattern of snakes made with a special green thread that caught the light.

I felt a tug on my skirt and looked to find Rabbit with tear-shaped eyes looking up at me with a big grin on her face. "Do you know any riddles, Malinalxochitl?"

"Riddles?" A note of laughter bubbled in my throat. My sadness and seriousness seemed to melt off my shoulders. I shook my head. "No, I'm sorry, but I don't."

Hummingbird explained, "Young Rabbit likes to tell jokes and play with words."

Jumping up and down, Rabbit said, "I have one for you! What is like a little mirror in the middle of trees?"

"I do not know, what?"

"Our eyes, of course!" she crowed victoriously. The girls, including me, joined Rabbit in laughter. The priestesses' happiness surrounded me like a warm embrace.

I felt acceptance watching their joyful faces and listening to their questions and giggles. Maybe knowledge of the sorceress Malinalxochitl would not be all I would gain here.

▲▲▲▲

Even the sunlight was different at the Temple of the Eighteen Moons. It was clearer. Warmer. Brighter. The place was a shield of calm. Thick mists enveloped the temple precinct in the early morning, but as the sun rose, the light burned the haze away and the temples seemed touched with gold. As part of my initiation, I was given nothing but water and a corncake to eat. No sooner was my thirst quenched than I was taken to sit in the temazcalli's steam as part of the required purification ritual for women who served at the temple. Silent priestesses rubbed my skin with laurel leaves and dressed me in soft garments that held the shimmer of dragonfly wings.

I eagerly waited to learn more about Malinalxochitl, and what her power might mean for me. But first I would have to learn to harness the wild natural world that surrounded me. On the first day, I was given the dried leaves of the piciyetl plant to smoke.

After leading me to a mat of woven seagrass, in a room beyond Feathered Butterfly's throne room, the High Priestess lit a pipe of clay and placed it in my hands. I coughed and sputtered through my first try, then inhaled the smoke deeply. I felt a fire behind my eyes. The priestess then left me. I continued to smoke as I admired the beautiful murals of painted jaguars and butterflies, when I noticed the quetzales and serpents seemed to be moving. I exhaled as quietly as I could and removed the pipe from my mouth. I stared, bewitched by the sight of animals freeing themselves from the walls and circling the air around me.

I listened to the quiet hum of their movements. The soft rhythm lulled me to sleep. I dreamed that I was standing alone on a bridge that stretched like a ray of white sunlight over a lake of pale blue-green water.

The immaculate square stones glowed with a fiery opalescence and led into a magnificent city where temples stood as proud as mountains. In the near distance, I could see paper and feather banners, bright as jungle birds, flying from the summits and garden rooftops of grand houses. A light wind was playing in my hair. A cloak stitched with white heron feathers fell in downy folds from my shoulders.

Since my talk with my mother, the calendar priest's prediction had infected my spirit. So many nights, I had dreamed of standing alone, forgotten, in a barren wood far from home. But *this* dream felt like a beacon, a new vision of my fate. In the days after, the worry slowly eased out of me as I pondered what the dream meant. Was I truly meant for greatness after all? For a long time after, I would remember the feel of the air and the soft feathers against my skin. And the heavy, affirming weight of the large shield that flashed with light in my hand.

▲▲▲▲

Each day began with the mournful cry of a conch trumpet calling us to prayer. After wiping the sleep from my eyes, I would join the priestesses in the courtyard. We were twenty-four in number, and when we stood together and lifted our palms to the rising sun, the forces of earth, sky, and wind joined with us to create a perfect oneness. We moved with surging invincibility tempered with a quiver of humility. In unison, we would then turn to pay homage to each of the directions and bow to the gods and winds that ruled there. After laying offerings on the altar, the High Priestess would lead us in a prayer.

Unlike in my village, where prayers were made with offerings of hearts and blood to Huitzilopochtli to encourage the birth of new corn and to mark the harvest, the Temple of the Eighteen Moons was a center of learning dedicated to worshipping the gods Quetzalcoatl and Feathered Butterfly, who brought life, not death. They stood for light and art, knowledge and beauty. We paid them homage with incense and flowers, honey and corn, and colored streamers made of our finest paper.

Every priestess-in-training had duties to perform after prayers ended, from lighting fires and fetching water to caring for the temples and weeding the gardens. I was tasked with sweeping the pyramid's 120 steps. During those first days, I was more than a little shaky as I made my way across the cold stone, afraid that I might fall or drop my broom. But I never did. In time, I learned to climb up and down easily. Even when the mist was thick and I could not see, my feet were sure and steady. To feel the wind in my hair and to gaze out at the world beyond filled me with joy. I felt both humble and tall as a giant perched on the top of its peak. It was capped with a simple stone altar and a three-stone hearth we kept always aflame for the god Quetzalcoatl. There was nothing to steal attention from the majesty of the sky and surrounding hills and land. I felt like I was standing at the center of splendor, joined to a force that connected me to the earth, the heavens, even the world below.

▲▲▲▲

At the beginning, I had a difficult time finding my way to classes. The red-columned House of the Priestesses had more passageways, courtyards, and rooms than I had ever seen before. One day, I couldn't resist the pitch of a set of narrow, winding steps and found myself stuck inside the Divination Labyrinth. The walls were painted shades of blue, from the palest hue to a deep-sea color. I should have paid special attention when the High Priestess warned me to not attempt the path on my own.

I prided myself on my keen sense of direction, but the more I walked, the more it felt as though the blue walls were pressing together, as if I had drifted into an underwater cavern carved out by a cenote. *Should I turn right or left?* All paths forward looked the same. A pyramid-shaped iron lantern set above my head emitted the glow of tired stars. The heavy humid air made it hard to breathe. I tried feeling my way around, but my palms and fingers met nothing but slabs of cold, damp stone.

I was ready to beat the walls with my fists, as if this would help, when I heard footsteps.

"There you are," Hummingbird said, moving toward me. Her white huipilli and skirt glowed in the murky blue. "I've been looking everywhere for you! Surely the High Priestess warned you not to venture in this direction." Her eyes brightened. "Not fond of restrictions, are we?" Her smile disappeared.

Goose bumps covered my arms and relief washed over me. I was sure she'd keep my secret.

"I run toward them," I declared, trying to mask the fact that my breaths were coming fast and I was desperate to get out of there. With my hand on the wall for balance, I moved to close the distance that separated us. "It angered my mother."

"She was worried about you, not angry. As a girl, I begged the gods for someone to keep me safe. But all that answered was the cold wind. You were lucky she cared."

I felt my shoulders softening at the touch of her words. Hummingbird's sudden sadness, an undertow as subtle as the flash of anger behind her eyes, clung to me. I marveled at how she'd elegantly crept around the corner, so quietly that even the gods would have startled to see her. They would have been as intrigued as I was by the jadestone that adorned her throat—a deep green, polished like starlight. Her long dark hair was caught in a thick braid that crowned her head. The shock of white at her temple and her confident stride made her seem taller than the blue walls confining us.

"Yes. I think you might be right," I said. For the first time since my brother's death, I believed that I had finally found someone I could talk to.

"Come, I will show you the way." She held out her hand, her firm grip and cheery smile making me doubt she was ever sad. "*They* say that the tombs of past High Priestesses are buried somewhere around here," she explained with a shiver. I took solace in her small show of fear. "*This* path is meant to promote meditation and calm, but the first journey must be done under the guidance of another priestess. You got quite close to the center of the labyrinth, and the secret to its design, all on your own. Not bad for a first-timer. You would have found your way before nightfall."

Before nightfall? Surely I would have found my way out sooner than that.

▲▲▲▲

After guiding me to freedom, Hummingbird took me on a quick tour of the House of the Priestesses: the throne room and adjoining chambers with painted scenes of gardens, narrow cells with butterfly lanterns nestled on the walls that overlooked idyllic courtyards, spaces without ornament, and rooms lavished with mosaic work and bursts of colors. There was even a strange space that seemed upside down, where embroidered tapestries floated up from the floor instead of down from the ceiling.

"And Malinalxochitl used her sword and shield to cut and carry the stones you see throughout here," she said.

Wait, what was that? I felt pride and awe—exactly how did Malinalxochitl manage to move the stones? I wanted to look more closely, but Hummingbird seemed in a hurry. I had to run to keep up with her as she pointed and talked. She explained how the lanterns were made of copper and had flames that never needed tending, talked about the special white lily that only bloomed for one night out of the year, showed me a courtyard tiled with pink-and-orange seashells from the faraway Divine Eastern Sea.

"Xochiquetzal, the goddess of beauty, assisted Quetzalpapalotl in its design."

We paused to admire it.

"Did you know that a priestess of the Temple of the Eighteen Moons is regarded throughout our lands as a *knower of things*?"

"Does the goddess Malinalxochitl know about me? Can she tell me my destiny?"

"Ha! That is for you, not her, to discover," she said. "But here, you will learn how to read the night sky and summon your animal guardian. Have you found yours yet?"

"My what?" I hopped forward and caught the smile on her lips.

"I thought not. Here at the Temple we call it a nahual. It is your ally in the animal world. Everyone has one. Mine is a red fox, a wily hunter who shows me where to look for dahlias at night."

I pictured Hummingbird's vixen digging in the black of night as we cut through a field of high grass and stopped a fair distance from a group of priestesses gathered beneath a shady cypress tree. Hummingbird nodded toward an elderly priestess barely tall enough to see over a wooden table strewn with bowls, cups, dried leaves, an old beehive, and birds' nests. She wore a winged hat with fisherman's netting to protect herself from the sun. Tiny obsidian ovals, held with copper strands, shielded her eyes.

"Soon you will have the honor of learning healing and herbal remedies with Priestess Morning Star. Plants, the trees, even the wind bend to her wishes." Then Hummingbird leaned in and whispered, "You want to stay on her good side. She has no patience for lazy thinkers or know-it-alls." She paused for a moment, then looked directly into my eyes. "I have heard that she spent many years of her life living as a caged oddity in Moctezuma's Palace of Curiosities. Her family sold her to his officials"—she widened her eyes—"due to the strange pale coloring of her skin and blue eyes. A warrior who had fallen in love with her set her free."

My stomach swooped and my breath shuttered. Moctezuma and his cages.

Hummingbird must have seen the worry in my eyes, for she quickly explained, "I am telling you this so you will not stumble and make a spectacle of yourself as I did in my first days." She turned on her heels and launched us in a southerly direction. "Now, Priestess Rose Petal—who is the most beautiful of them all—teacher of languages and the study of Turquoise Books, is very forgiving and doesn't mind if you slip in your pronunciation of the Puuc and Chontal tongues and want to show off your grasp of glyph writing." She played with the hem of her huipilli. "She used to be a concubine. One of her patrons released her from that life."

A concubine at the temple? I froze in place and stood there, gaping. How interesting. I had never met one before, but I had seen an ahuiyani sauntering through my village's marketplace. Her red-painted face, tzic—tli chewing, and shoulder-baring blouse made her hard to ignore. My mother had tried to shield my eyes from her, but I was fast and always wiggled away. Concubines were different, but I had not expected to find one here. Rose Petal, from what I had seen of her, seemed innocent of ever having anything to do with the buying and selling of flesh.

"We all have stories," Hummingbird said, as if reading my mind. "Mine is that my mother brought me here before my father could use me to pay off a gambling debt. She planned it in secret." Hummingbird's face was stone as she continued. "She studied here when she was my age. But she left as soon as she got here. It was not her fate to be a priestess."

She was so matter-of-fact, but a sadness in her eyes told a different story. How did she handle the loss of her mother? Was she advising me not to miss mine? To let everything that came before my life here go? Being with Hummingbird felt monumental, like something had shifted inside me. I wanted to experience it fully beneath this indigo sky, in this sacred land smelling of sunflowers. I wanted to freeze in my memory the way the corners of her eyes crinkled when she was recalling a fact. It was all so perfect that I almost forgot—who was going to teach me how to conjure monsters or, at the very least, snarling coyotes and venomous bats? How to make myself disappear and appear at will? How to vanquish my enemies with one word? But I didn't want to ruin the moment by asking her about magic spells and sorcery work, the kind Malinalxochitl would have practiced. Eager as I was to learn, I would wait.

Looking toward a meadow abloom with small yellow flowers, toward a forest thick with close-set trees, I wondered aloud, "What's over there? Does the land belong to the Temple?"

She shrugged. "All I know is that we are not allowed to go beyond this field and enter the forest."

"But why?" A heron with majestic white wings made graceful strokes through the air. My eyes swept the stand of trees from east to west. The forest piqued my curiosity, just as the labyrinth had.

"It is forbidden," Hummingbird answered. I met her studying gaze and smiled.

▲▲▲▲

From that moment forward, I threw myself into my work, the first to raise my hand with the correct answers even in those classes attended by the older priestesses who desired to refresh their knowledge.

I thought I knew all there was to know about healing and herbal remedies since I had watched Toci many times as she prepared the potions and poultices for my mother and the women of our household. She'd grind seeds and add this flower petal and that dried root as she whispered the appropriate prayers. But Hummingbird was, by far, the most talented of all of us. Plants, leaves, and seeds seemed to jump into her hands just at the moment a recipe called for their addition. I had a quick memory, but hers surpassed mine. She was generous with her knowledge, though, and helped me, reminding me often when my fingers began to stray to the wrong plant. "Be careful with those morning glory seeds," she warned more than once, "for they'll have you seeing visions and walking off cliffs!"

Despite my efforts, I struggled to get through mathematics and astronomy. I was only decent, at best, at divination and dream interpretation. But when it came to the study of languages, I was magic. My mouth embraced words with ease. From the familiar-sounding to the new, from delicate to throaty sounds, commanding constructions and serpentine requests, not a word was ill-formed by my lips. My tongue explored the in-between places of hard and soft interpretations. Sometimes, in classes with Rose Petal, and when I practiced on my own, I felt as if my body were floating on pure sound. We studied the more formal and courtly form of Nahuatl—which I was familiar with due to my father's gift for speechmaking—and Yucatecan and Chontal Maya languages. I understood books without ever opening them or studying their glyphs and symbols. They spoke to me!

Alone in the amoxcalli, after arriving early to class, I often heard the books' scribes talking to each other. Their voices varied, some pitched like a flute, others deep and full of rumbles. They discussed the sacred calendar, gave advice about the best time to plant the tomatl, and whispered incantations to heal a broken heart and call the dead back to life. They talked fast, but I understood. After two months, I probably could have talked circles around even our illustrious teacher Rose Petal, but I held back out of respect for her and for gentle Jeweled Laughter.

"She lost her voice," Hummingbird confided when I asked about the girl's steady and complete silence. "Eight months ago, when she arrived at the Temple, the High Priestess told us that Jeweled Laughter witnessed an act so vile and torturous that her screams drove all sounds out of her body." I was shocked to hear this, as I had never heard anything like it before. "She speaks eloquently with her hands, drawing symbols in the air," Hummingbird said.

I did not know anything about Jeweled Laughter's life, could not fathom her past and the horrors she had suffered. All I understood was my corner of grief, and how it could drive every other sensation from your being.

▲▲▲▲

When I learned there was a class called Centering the Goddess, taught by the High Priestess, I thought, *Now, at last I'll discover everything I want to know about Malinalxochitl.* I thirsted for knowledge about her. That was why I was here, was it not? To learn the spells that would make me as strong as her so I could bring ruin to Tenochtitlan and make Moctezuma pay for taking Eagle's life. For ensuring we'd never speak our private language again. An anger washed over me, sending sparks across the bark paper, smooth and ready to receive my notes, startling me.

So far, none of my studies had been devoted to such dark pursuits, and the omission had been making me restless and frustrated. Though I hid my true feelings, people had only to look at my embroidery work, at all the bile-colored snakes I was stitching along the hems, to know I was irritated. I thought this new class would reveal everything about her to me and, in some way, help me solve the charm that would unlock my power.

Our gathering place was one of the chambers adjoining the throne room. During the first lessons, most of what I learned I already knew from my mother. The High Priestess said that many people believed Malinalxochitl was no more than a mighty sorceress, but, in her opinion, Malinalxochitl deserved to be honored with the other goddesses. "She is revered and feared. Her dark powers had to be tightly controlled and balanced. If left unchecked, they overwhelmed her and led to chaos and reigning darkness." I sat forward on my mat, puzzled by this conflict with good and evil, but expecting deeper revelations. They didn't come, for in her next breath, the High Priestess went on to talk about Mayahuel, goddess of maguey. I had to be careful that my face didn't give my disappointment away, but the feeling passed. An unexpected revelation soon came, so strong that it pushed my craving for dark spells aside.

Over time, I learned that Centering the Goddess was also about looking. I was taught that the goddess was embedded deeply within, and I'd have to mine the cracks of heart and spirit to find her. As if this news wasn't shocking enough, one day the High Priestess showed us how we could achieve this. All it took was our voices and the regular act of breathing. When she demonstrated techniques meant to achieve calm and ease introspection, I thought I saw her lift herself from her kneeling pose into full levitation. Then I saw Jeweled Laughter rise, followed by Rabbit and Hummingbird. Everyone was able to float in the air—except for me. I fretted. Had I missed an important step? Was I breathing incorrectly? When I swept my arm beneath me to test for air, I felt my sturdy self firmly attached to the earth.

"You're trying too hard," Hummingbird whispered.

I took a deep, steadying breath and let it out gently, following the High Priestess's instructions to empty my mind of all thoughts. But nothing. Not even a wobble. My fists pounded my legs. I was never good at sitting silently in place and keeping still.

After a few minutes defying the pull of the earth, the High Priestess returned to her feet and moved on to reveal another path to gaining insight. She instructed us to say our names out loud in a high, clear voice.

Here was something I knew I could do.

"Trust your voice," she instructed, motioning for us to stand. "Fill the room with the might of your breath and the force of your spirit, and welcome your goddess."

I jumped up, closed my eyes, and shouted, "Malinalxochitl." I did it again. "Malinalxochitl." Disregarding my mother's warning that a woman's voice could be her undoing, I unleashed my name. I could feel it in my toes. "Malinalxochitl!" A storm started brewing inside me, as if answering my call.

"You too, Jeweled Laughter," the High Priestess said. "You have breath, force, and spirit. Come, your goddess awaits." She gestured to our sister to take her place with us.

As we shouted our names to the heavens, bodies vibrated with breaths and the unexpected joy that comes from setting your name free. Then, Jeweled Laughter finally placed her hand on her breast and raised it to her lips. Her fingers unfurled delicately. I watched her for a moment—thinking she might be scribing the symbols for her name in the air—before gently closing my eyes. Saying my name alongside my sisters, I felt a wave surge around us, its energy akin to what I felt standing alone at the top of the temple of Quetzalcoatl. This was the force of young priestesses shaking the essence of the world.

BREAKING THE SPELL

Time passed. Snakes shed their skins, grew them anew, then shed them again. Over the following years at the Temple, my desire for vengeance weakened into a dull ache that was easy to ignore in this peaceful place.

One day, in the middle of my third year at the Temple, Rabbit spied an eagle in the sky and claimed it was following me. We were weeding beds of squash plantings, heavy with their yellow treasures, when she saw the eagle, gave a shout, then dived into the dirt to hide among the broad green leaves.

"Tell it to go away!"

Confused, I watched her burrow into the earth a little deeper before looking up to see what had frightened her so. As the eagle circled us, I stayed still, held rapt by the sight of the magnificent bird. Gold-tipped feathers. Noble head with a white cap. I couldn't understand Rabbit's fear.

"What are you afraid of? It is a good omen," I said gently, brushing aside the leaves.

An eagle was a sign of favor from the gods; we had learned this in our divination classes. I reminded Rabbit of this, but she kept clawing her way through the dirt, throwing clods behind her.

"You must tell it to go. It means to do harm. It wants to eat me."

"Oh, Rabbit"—I rolled my eyes—"it does not." I crouched down and reached out my hand to pull her away from the leaves and stalks.

She scratched me, bared her teeth, and growled in a hoarse, twisted voice, "Leave me alone."

How could such a sound come from someone so small and innocent?

It gave me such a start that I did precisely what she wanted. I shook the sting from my bloodied hand and returned my gaze to the sky.

As I shielded my eyes from the sun and contemplated the eagle soaring on waves of wind, I attempted to "see beyond the power of sight." This was how Rose Petal had explained the importance of calling up all senses, including the needling feelings inside your gut, to uncover the truth.

I closed my eyes for a moment and tried to free my mind and open myself to the sun and wind. After a few minutes, the garden slipped away and a surge of cold air buffeted me, sending prickles racing up my spine. I opened my eyes. What if my brother had discovered the transformation spell to unlock his power to turn himself into his nahual ally? I opened myself a little more. What if this eagle was a sign that it was time for me to turn to the dark magic necessary to destroy Moctezuma?

More questions flowed. I conspired to understand the merits of each one as Rabbit continued her guttural screams and dug her trench. I vowed to press my teachers for more discussions about animal companions and acts of transformation. And for dark spells.

▲▲▲▲

The eagle disappeared eventually, but my thoughts about it remained. And whenever I brought up its appearance, Rabbit glared at me. I imagined she was embarrassed by her behavior and did not want to talk about it. Shortly after this, Toci arrived. I would have traded her visit for an animal sighting of the darkest kind had I known what was about to happen.

My meeting with her began well enough. The midwife's eyes lit up, and the way she clapped her hands reassured me that she was pleased with my training and how I had grown, for I was now fifteen. Toci had long conversations with the High Priestess and sat with me afterward.

"I knew you would excel at languages and place-finding. And your knowledge of the stars has improved a great deal, I hear."

Then her tone lowered, and she shared the news: my mother had remarried and was with child. A deep cold came over my body, freezing my feet to the earth.

Has she replaced me?

Then, I met Toci's pleading eyes and came to my senses. I let myself imagine a new brother or sister, a little one with my mother's sweet smile or gentle laugh. Slowly, the warmth flowed back into my limbs. I was so happy for our new family. My mother was beautiful and kind; I knew she would remarry at some point. She would never abandon me; I was her special creation.

"Well, then, my mother will need me," I said. Nothing would give me more joy than to see her again. "You've come to take me home! I can return to the Temple after the baby is born."

I waited for Toci to agree, to say that we had to hurry. The silence grew heavier and heavier between us. Finally, she spoke.

"Your mother has gone away with her husband."

I shook my head. "What did you say?"

"She is gone, Malinalxochitl," she answered gently. "She has gone to the home of her new husband. To live with his family."

His family?

The freeze washed over me anew, locking my gaze downward. I couldn't look at Toci. Her pity could easily unleash the tears threatening to pour down my face.

"Where is this place? I must go there. *We* must go," I said, my voice shaking. "My mother will need you, too. Grandmother must have gone with her. Please draw it on a map for me!"

I began to pull away, so that I might go to my chamber and prepare for our journey, but the slight touch of Toci's hand on my arm made my blood boil, trapped in a body that had gone stone still. With my next step, I stumbled, my limbs thrown off-balance by the crushing weight of my confusion. Why hadn't she sent a messenger to tell me this news earlier? Why wait until she was . . . gone?

"It is far, my dove, my precious one."

"Far?" I laughed uneasily, gave a little shrug, but I still would not look at her. I felt as if I'd been burned alive, as if my ashes could easily blow away with the breeze. No distance was too great, I thought. Why would it matter to Toci? I pulled my arm away and, straightening my shoulders, said, "We will go now." I met her eyes anew. We would do this together. I was ready to cross mountains to see my mother.

But my words did not have the effect I wanted. Toci's gaze softened into a look of such profound sadness that I could not hold back my tears. Finally, they broke over me like a dirty rain.

"It gladdens your mother's heart that you are safe and pursuing knowledge at the Temple. She sends her love and will tell you all you need to know soon. But not now, Malinalxochitl."

Not now?

"Then when?" I snapped, slamming my fist into a nearby tree. Toci did not flinch, and I did not apologize.

My mother has abandoned me? It couldn't be true! "Is that why she sent me away, so she could remarry and start a new life somewhere else? Far from me?" Tears burned in my eyes.

Toci shook her head.

"Let us be clear. Though my mother is with child and I could help her, she has no need for me, her own daughter," I said. I caught her eyes darting behind me, where Hummingbird now stood, which enflamed me all the more. Ignoring Toci's protests that none of this was true, I waved her off, turned, and took a step to run away.

After everything that had happened, how could she leave me behind? How could she have told me I was meant for greatness, when it was clear from Toci's expression that she never wanted to see me again?

"Malinalxochitl! Wait!" Hummingbird cried.

"Tell her, Toci. Explain it to her."

I ran into the cornfield, up and down the rows, and did not stop until I stumbled into the garden. Spent and shaking, I bent over to catch my breath. A light feather brushed against my leg, and I turned around, suddenly noticing a row of sunflowers standing behind me, tall as soldiers. They seemed so proud with their raised yellow heads drinking in the sun. The sight of them had always delighted me, but now I hated their height, their haughtiness. I lunged and ripped their prickly stalks out of the ground until their roots screamed. The petals crumbled in my hands and were crushed under my feet as I stomped on them. Stalks were torn and earth flew in the air as the garden dissolved around me. Then, upon this bed of destruction, my knees buckled and my head hung as if I were ready for someone to strike it off.

"If only I had been a more dutiful child," I cried to myself, a thundering ache building inside my head. "If only I had obeyed my parents in every way and not fussed about the House of Magical Studies, then none of this would have happened."

I did not know how close Hummingbird was until she was crouched down next to me.

"I'm sorry, Malinalxochitl. What do you mean?"

"Everything has changed," I said to Hummingbird. She had once guided me out of the labyrinth, but even she could not steer me out of this feeling. "The home that I love, and all the people in it, have been taken from me." A sob caught in my throat. "I am cursed. First the gods destroy my brother, then my father, and now they take my mother, too? The calendar priest was right. I am cursed and useless, ordinary Malinalli, not Malinalxochitl. How can she abandon me? Why?"

Hummingbird sat down. The sound of the wind rustling the standing flowers mixed with that of my labored breaths and the maddening pounding between my ears. After a long while, she said, "Tell me what happened." Her voice somehow cut through the noise, the hurt and pain. "It's just me," she said.

I met her gaze. She smiled encouragingly. Yet I felt a dark need to shock her.

I told her everything. Up until then, I had guarded my story. Sharing it made their deaths new, and I felt I was losing them all over again. I could hardly speak, for the pain was like a rope of knots caught in my throat. My cheeks burned with tears. Hummingbird's attention was ever constant, betraying no change in mood, no shifting from calm to horror as my story unfolded. She listened intently, nodding now and then. When I told her I felt abandoned by my mother, she placed her hand over mine.

"Your mother and father aren't here anymore. We're your family now."

By the end, I sat hunched, my body spent, voice hoarse. A part of me wanted to tell her about the charm and the mysterious vision. But I felt that I would be breaking a vow with my brother, and so I pushed the thought away. Hummingbird lay beside me quietly, upon the broken flowers, sensing I couldn't leave their nest quite yet. Her hand rested on my curled back as she watched over me through the rest of the day and night.

▲▲▲▲

The next morning, with rage still burning within me, I gathered a few things I needed before heading to my divination class in the green chamber. Toci had left a cloth with markings indicating my mother's new home, but I packed it away somewhere where I could never see it. Now that Rabbit, Hummingbird, Jeweled Laughter, and I were advanced students, we would be putting our knowledge to the test. In today's class, Jeweled Laughter was set to act as if she were under a spell. Already she had planned every twitch and contortion, and we would be charged with deciphering the nature of the spell and which of the many monsters—bloodsuckers, nightcrawlers, and headless ghosts—had cast it.

In the narrow anteroom off our sleeping chamber, I filled a clay bowl with water from the pitcher, then reached into my palm-leaf trunk to remove what I needed: a white square of cloth, a handful of corn kernels, and a bit of hemp rope. Just as I was about to leave, I heard someone whimpering, then a shout for help. Clutching everything to my chest, splashing water everywhere, I ran into the room and saw Jeweled Laughter sprawled on her mat and Hummingbird hunched over her. I thought they were practicing for class, though Jeweled Laughter seemed awfully still for someone who was supposed to be playing a role. Then I noticed Hummingbird—usually elegant and neat—was flushed, and strands of her hair were plastered to her cheeks.

"Malinalxochitl! Something's wrong."

I darted across the room, set down my bowl, and dropped to my knees in front of Jeweled Laughter. I felt that at any moment she would bounce up and gesture at what fools we were to be so worried. But when she didn't move, I placed my hand on her back, then quickly drew away in alarm: the girl's body felt on fire!

"Mother of the gods! What's happening?"

Hummingbird's hands fluttered to her mouth. "I don't know. We were gathering the things we needed for our class when she stumbled and lost her balance. I told her to rest. We had time . . . so she lay down . . . and then . . . and then—this. I've been trying to wake her. Now she's burning."

Could the sudden illness be due to a snake or spider bite? I bent over Jeweled Laughter and carefully examined her arms and hands, then her legs and feet. Her skin was clear of all marks and wounds. What could it be, then? I continued my inspection of Jeweled Laughter and placed my face close to hers and sniffed. Her breath had an odd smell.

As I sat back on my heels, Jeweled Laughter grabbed my wrist. I jumped. My flesh felt singed by flames.

This is no ordinary fever, I said to myself.

Jeweled Laughter moaned. I feared she was going to die. I had to take her to the High Priestess. But when I tried to lift her in my arms, she beat me off, scratching and biting, and knocked me off-balance. Her strength was uncanny.

Hummingbird's eyes met mine before darting back to Jeweled Laughter. "She's possessed, isn't she?"

Someone had cast a spell on my sister priestess. But why would someone want to hurt her?

"What should we do?" Hummingbird asked—there was an urgency in her tone.

We do not sit and wring our hands.

I cleared my throat. "Our classes have prepared us for this," I assured Hummingbird. "We'll learn who cast this spell and why."

She nodded hesitantly.

There were many methods that could help, and they came easily to mind: one required a length of rope; another called for seven corn kernels; the other asked for the seven kernels and a bowl of water.

"We can do this," I said. "We'll start with the corn and water." I looked at Jeweled Laughter. Her breathing was growing more shallow and uneven. I felt the fever burning inside her.

Everything we had set out—the water, corn, cloth—looked so puny and weak that it caused cracks in my plan. Did we really have time for this? Time for the prayers and incantations and testing to see if the water changed to red or yellow, or if it moved in waves. Did we have time to study the pattern of corn kernels, or to see if they floated in water? Hadn't we learned that these methods were not completely dependable? Jeweled Laughter's life was in our hands. We had to do something bold.

"There's another way," I whispered.

I ran back to the anteroom to look for the small jar Rose Petal kept on a wooden shelf, high and out of reach. If mixed with drops of water, its contents would safely clean a wound. Experienced diviners used this special octli to cure illnesses and banish evil spells. Skilled magicians drank it to gain access to the Underworld.

"What are you doing?" Hummingbird pleaded, running after me.

"We're going to help Jeweled Laughter." I tested the lowest shelf to make sure it would take my weight, then hoisted myself up and extended my arm as high as I could. I was careful not to upset the jars and urns that were jammed into every nook and cranny. "One of us is going to visit the Underworld to consult with supernatural beings about this illness." I breathed heavily as my hand searched for the jar, but it was no use; it was still out of reach. I found purchase on the next shelf and pulled myself higher.

"Go to Mictlan? But that's not possible."

Her point had merit, but not enough to stop me. Hummingbird and I were unskilled in this method, for it was forbidden. The High Priestess had warned us never to drink it, as it was sure to lead to unfortunate events. To sharpen her warning, she said that it could make a human think they were strong enough to stand up to anything, even death. But it was a risk worth taking. I would do anything for my sister.

Seeing that I was struggling, Hummingbird moved our trunks and stacked a few close to me. "Here, Malinalxochitl, come this way." She tugged at my skirt and gripped me securely as my foot sought the top trunk. "I beg you to come down. Remember the time you ignored the warning about the labyrinth and got lost?" Her face was knotted with worry.

I did remember. "That was the day we became friends." I grinned. She shook her head. "What do you think the Underworld will be like?" I wondered aloud. "Dark and misty, I imagine. Scary with skeletons, more than likely. But someone will help us."

"You can't be serious." In spite of her doubts, Hummingbird continued to hold on and keep me steady when I returned my attention to the shelf. With her help, I was able to reach the jar easily.

"Octli!" I shouted triumphantly, my hand clutching the small jar.

"Goddess save us!" she swore.

"Exactly!" I jumped off the tower of trunks, landing easily on my feet.

"You know we can't drink that," Hummingbird cautioned. "And even if we could, we don't know how much to drink or how to control it. How will we even know that we've arrived in Mictlan?"

"I'll go." I knew I'd be the one the moment I went to look for the octli. I placed my hand on her shoulder. "You stay with Jeweled Laughter."

Her eyes grew wider with fear.

"I can do this." Before she had a chance to stop me, I took a sip, and when nothing happened—that is, nothing I could physically feel—I took another swallow, then another.

▲▲▲▲

The octli was not entirely unpleasant. It tasted like sunbaked earth and was as thick as honey. The effect was almost immediate. It seemed to have tripled my courage, for I felt no fear, not even when the chamber's walls fell away and icy blasts of wind swooped around me and turned pond scum green. Streams of many-legged insects darted across my feet, and shadowy beings reached out from behind pillars of rock and towers of skulls to touch me. Step by step, the creeping sensations deepened, drawing me to explore further, sparking shivers of excitement. Unseen wings whispered in the dark.

Mictlan. Realm of the Skeleton Lord.

"Finally. I have you."

I spun around to see a figure stepping out of the whirling green fog. I was not so far gone that I didn't feel the hairs on the back of my neck stand on end. I struggled to breathe and see clearly. The courage I'd felt seconds ago seemed to have disappeared into the fog. What was I doing here? How could I get back? The creature would have the answers. I stepped closer to get a better sense of it. A body slowly came into focus. A womanly shape. No, a girl, with a liquid pouring from her hands. The face looked familiar—was it Rabbit? I froze, barely breathing. What was a young, innocent priestess doing here? It couldn't be. But I could see her clearly: my sister's hands dripped with blood, which shimmered and refracted through the multi-mirror lens of the octli.

Shaking with terror, I looked down at my own hands just in time to see a strange glow, like a flash of moonbeams, pass between them when I opened my arms in the green dark. Somehow, I knew I had to connect to that light. I tried to remember the words the priestesses shared just before they levitated.

I slowed my breathing and tried to focus on the light, to identify its source.

Breathe. Wait. Listen.

My mother's soft voice. Hummingbird's hand on my back. Rabbit's fearful eyes charting the eagle. Feeling it about to strike.

No, the light said. *This is not right. It will not stand.*

I pulled it into my throat and barked out a command.

"Let her go."

I remembered the day the eagle appeared. Rabbit had been convinced it wanted to eat her. And her voice . . . sputtering from her since then, between a growl and moan. The sounds of a walking corpse. I had thought she must have had a deep fear of large birds. But all this time, she had been a monstrous shape-changer, posing as a little girl.

The beast's laughter was a sharply cracked whip that pushed me back a step. "I will happily let her go! *You* are the one I want, Malinalxochitl," she said, pronouncing my name as if it were a filthy oath. "Join us. Come into the shadows, where you belong."

The octli emboldened me to step closer, though my heart was sinking. What if the calendar priest was right, and I was cursed all along? Was I Malinalli, the girl marked to live in the shadows? Would this thing swallow me up in one gulp? I forced myself to move toward it.

If this was the end, I'd accept my fate. A young girl's life was at stake.

The creature leered at me, raising her arms to the sides, and, after a quick thrust of her hands, talons emerged from her fingertips. Yellow, sharp, ugly things, as if from some overgrown monster bird reaching out to grab my hand. Her eyes widened like an owl's and protruded from her face. Her head swiveled twice around. Her feet became enormous, with blackened nails and sparse hairs that stood out like thorns.

A chill ran through me as the octli pumped through my veins with a cold, searing liquid fire. I was being eaten alive, from the inside out. My body started to levitate as I writhed and the monster that was Rabbit rose into the air and swooped back and forth in green streams of billowing smoke. Her skirt was in tatters, and small grizzled birds were growing out of the tears. Back and forth. Gray worms crawled out of her hair. Back and forth. My body stopped seizing and I suddenly felt still, almost sleepy as I stood, weightless, in the ether. Then, with a thunderous flap of her arms and a mighty shriek that rattled my bones, she pushed through the air toward me. For a moment, we were both mighty goddesses of the sky. She reached out farther with her hand, and a strange sensation came over me. I found myself wanting to slip my hand into hers. What damage could we do if we joined forces? Maybe, if I could get a little farther into her world, I could learn to be faster, stronger . . .

The next thing I knew, I was on my back in the sleeping chamber, staring up at the concerned faces of Hummingbird, the High Priestess, Rose Petal, and Morning Star.

▲▲▲▲

The High Priestess pulled Hummingbird to the side. After an exchange of whispers, the regal woman rejoined Rose Petal and Morning Star and carried Jeweled Laughter away. My sister's arms dangled lifelessly at her sides. Her hair, white with frost, hung in clumps.

"Is she—" I gasped.

"She lives, but she is very sick," Hummingbird said somberly. "The High Priestess would like to speak to you before the ritual tonight." She paused, and her eyes met mine for a moment. I already knew what the High Priestess wanted to talk to me about. I had broken a sacred rule, *and* I'd nearly killed Jeweled Laughter in the process. I was certain that I was going to be expelled from the Temple of the Eighteen Moons.

My octli-laced stomach twisted. I burned with shame. To be shunned by these gentle women . . . turned away from this center of knowledge and beauty that had given me so much . . . I couldn't bear it, especially since what I'd seen in Mictlan made me feel more powerful by the minute.

Hummingbird took my hand. "I thought you had died." I looked at her. "But then I heard you say Rabbit's name," she whispered, panic in her eyes.

I nodded, though it hurt to move my head. "I saw Rabbit transform herself into a monster, an owl creature." I shuddered, recalling how the beast had swooped back and forth.

Hummingbird swallowed nervously and patted my arm. "The High Priestess says we have one last chance to save Jeweled Laughter."

"*I* should be the one to save her! I'm the only one who understands . . ." I blurted out, jerking away from her touch.

The shock in Hummingbird's eyes forced me to take account of what I had said. I stiffened. *Who am I to think that I have the ability to venture into the Underworld? To think that I alone can get close to evil? To understand it and reach within it to channel its power? But do I really belong in the darkness?* As if my thoughts smelled, I moved apart from Hummingbird and scolded myself for being so conceited.

"I'm sorry," I said.

Her response was quick. "It's all right."

I felt ashamed of myself, and yet . . . I had really believed that I could do it. I still did. I felt the truth of it beating faintly, Malinalxochitl's essence throbbing inside me, in the center of my being. I would do it all over again.

But I was willing to admit a few things to my friend. "I should have known better," I explained, though Hummingbird, standing quietly, didn't seem to require an explanation. "I really thought I would figure out a way to help Jeweled Laughter. And to tell you the truth, being in the Underworld was thrilling. Terrifying but exciting." I stopped, catching a flash of concern in Hummingbird's eyes. Had I said too much? Then in a much more subdued voice, "But I've failed everyone."

"Nonsense." Hummingbird brushed a cobweb from my shoulder. "You didn't fail anyone." She clicked her tongue. "Oh, Malinalxochitl. Sacred octli?" She shook her head. "But then, who am I to judge? I did nothing. And I know how you are when it comes to restrictions. I should have followed you!" She pulled me into her arms. "I was so frightened that you would become trapped in the Underworld and we wouldn't be able to help you." She paused to take a breath. "You are the bravest girl I know."

Such relief swept through me that I broke into tears.

Hummingbird drew back to look at me. "You confronted an owl priest!" she whispered excitedly. Her eyes shone with admiration. "It may have been rash, but because of your courageous act, we know how to help Jeweled Laughter. Do you really think that you were in Mictlan?"

With my body spent, my head throbbing with pain, I nodded and had hoped to leave it at that. But she wanted to know more.

"It was thrilling? Do you mean you liked it? Goddess in Heaven!" she exclaimed. "I want to hear everything, you know. But first you have to meet with the High Priestess and tell her what happened. What you've learned will help us break the spell tonight. I am sure of it."

▲▲▲▲

I rushed to her chambers, sidestepping priestesses hurtling through the palace's corridors, bearing white cloth, clay bowls, and flickering copper lanterns. But at the entrance, I shrank back. I knew I deserved to be expelled, but to actually hear the words . . . I steadied myself.

The priestesses moved in a controlled chaos, obeying the quiet commands of the High Priestess standing in the center of the room. Her silver hair hung free, with strands plastered to her face with sweat. A priestess held out a long black robe, slipped it over the High Priestess's head, then smoothed down the mantle's folds. Another presented strands of turquoise beads. As the High Priestess bowed to allow herself to be draped with the jewels, she motioned for me to enter.

Gold flames flickered in the clay braziers and in the torches set along the walls. My shadow grew and shrunk as I moved deeper into the chamber. I would have preferred facing two owl monsters to this.

"Was it not explained to you that the drinking of sacred octli is forbidden?" She leaned forward to allow a priestess to set a gold and three-stone turquoise diadem on her head.

"Yes, I knew." I shifted uneasily from foot to foot, waiting for the dreaded words.

"Do you think rules do not apply to you?" She fixed me with her gaze. "Do you think your name Malinalxochitl puts you above our rules?"

"No!" Everyone's eyes flicked to me. I looked down at the floor.

"Such a name bears the heavy weight of responsibility. It must be hard for a little girl."

I looked straight into her onyx eyes and corrected her. "I am fifteen, Your Grace. Hardly a little girl." Everything went still, even the firelight stopped mid-dance.

She raised an eyebrow, opened her mouth to say something, then appeared to reconsider. "Much has changed for you, I hear."

Everyone went back to their tasks. The flames sighed.

I swallowed, thinking about my mother. "Yes." The pain in my soul was still there, though sharing it with Hummingbird had made it hurt a little less. "But I am better now," I assured her. I squeezed my hands at my sides and thought of something else: When should I tell the High Priestess about what I saw in Mictlan?

Bedecked with jewels and her flowing black mantle, the High Priestess stood erect and motionless. The flamelight glowed around her, a nimbus of gold and orange. I wondered if she would grow as tall as the ceiling to try to frighten me. She had done that once in one of my first classes with her, when my sister priestesses and I were unruly. *Please don't turn me away!*

"Good. I am glad to hear it," the High Priestess said. "I need—"

"I saw the beast in the Underworld!" Another hush fell over the room, and looks of blank shock followed me. Closing my eyes against their stares, the rest of my body braced for her stinging order and the words that would cast me out of the temple. I chanced opening one eye. The High Priestess was looking at me intently. A deep breath later, heat began to gather in my palms, as if they held fire. "I was there."

A long pause followed, then a soft sigh. "Very well." The turquoise stones flashed as the High Priestess nodded. "I need to know what you saw in Mictlan. We will address the fact that you drank a forbidden substance and overstepped boundaries long established between the worlds at a later time. That you did this and raced into the dark with such ease are matters of great concern." She peered at me as if I were a specimen caught in amber. "But this is hardly the first time a priestess of the Temple of the Eighteen Moons has committed such an infraction," she said with a slight smile.

Grateful that I was not going to be expelled, I could not help but wonder how many others had broken these sacred rules.

"What form did it take? Was it a bat with skeleton wings?"

"It was an owl with a head that spun around," I answered, twisting my hands above my head, "and with vulture-like talons. There were icy winds, but the air around it was green." I paused. "And it was dressed like one of us, like Rabbit."

"One of the Skeleton Lord's owl guards? Posing as a priestess? It must have slipped past the Temple's defenses . . . Icy winds, you said? Then you were in the fourth valley of Mictlan. We'll have to act quickly. Your act was impetuous. And brave." The High Priestess held her hand out to me. "We will speak more of this, but for now, we must work together to save Jeweled Laughter."

▲▲▲▲

It was the evening of One-Wind, a good night for a sorcerer to be born, but not one for breaking this owl guard's magic. Nevertheless, beneath a watchful moon, after my meeting with the High Priestess, I joined my sister priestesses in the Temple of Feathered Butterfly to perform the ritual that would free Jeweled Laughter. She lay in front of the altar on a bed of white cloth, as if she was sleeping.

My head was pounding, and my mouth was dry, and though I was a bit shaky, I stood beside my sisters. The only one missing was Rabbit.

I could feel tears gathering and fiercely blinked them back as Rose Petal entered the chamber bearing a wide and shallow copper bowl filled with water from the sacred pool. She placed it on the altar. I tried to calm myself by remembering that Earth Mother herself had crafted the shining dish as a gift for the Temple.

The High Priestess bowed her head over the water and prayed. Her robe was black and gold and embroidered with the goddess's symbols. We called it the Mantle of Magic. Strands of gold and turquoise beads glimmered around her throat and wrists. She beckoned me forward. Following the High Priestess's instructions, I lifted the bowl to my lips and drank from it. I felt Rabbit's presence, a shadow creeping in the corners and clinging to the beams above our heads. I could smell her, too—rot and mold and burned feathers. This was good, because for the spell-breaker to work, this evil imposter had to be nearby.

Rose Petal threw sage upon the open braziers. As the aroma spread, she cried, "Oh, Mother of the gods, listen, come, behold this girl." Her voice softened to a whisper, then grew strong again in prayer. I joined hands with the High Priestess, and as we looked into the water, I could feel the owl creature circling, daring me to cower or magnify its power. I fought the sensation. I could not fail again.

The High Priestess raised her arms to the ceiling, spread her fingers wide, and began speaking to the vision forming on the water. The braziers crackled as more herbs were cast into the flames. A great wind howled, scattering the light. The High Priestess's voice sounded far away.

Breathe.

Steeling myself, I stepped closer to the water. Out of the corner of my eye, I caught the fluid appearance of a majestic blue heron, with a sword-beaked face, emerge from the feathered shoulders of the High Priestess, who was enrobed and bejeweled just as before. As I struggled to catch my breath, I saw the owl-eyed monster staring out of the water. Plumes of smoke rose from the glassy surface and hissed.

The wind stopped, and the room became still. A gnarled, taloned hand stuck with fragments of sharp feathers rose from the water. No one moved. I felt the opalescent heron creature beside me stiffen, as if it had the power of sight and was looking for something. The hand turned to the right, then to the left. The fingers curled, and I could see in the next instant that the hideous thing was pointing at me, making me feel as if I were the monster that needed to be cast out. I reflexively lunged forward to grab hold of its wrist before it could harm me. I was ready to fight.

Just as my hand touched the beast, bright chaos erupted in my mind. I saw the shape of Malinalxochitl, and a wide, luminescent desert expanding before her crawling with beasts ready to do her bidding. Startled, I jumped back. A shriek erupted from the bowl, followed by a great fluttering of skirts and an odd whirling sound. A dank and putrid smell filled my nose. In that moment, I knew that the spell had been broken. Rabbit was dead.

All that remained of the girl and the creature from my octli-laced journey to Mictlan was in a pile in a corner of the room. The sweet, tender explorer was reduced to charred skin and bones, with very little left of her—long matted hair clotted with blood and bits of yellow and brown feathers. A nub of a talon. Thickened nails from a claw. An eye like an owl's, still open and bright. The little girl who laughed and enjoyed telling riddles. Who reached her hand to mine when she felt afraid of the dark. The joy I related to when she shouted her name when we were discovering our inner goddesses. The sadness I felt with her when she had a nightmare. It was as if she had been murdered in front of our eyes. The dreams she represented, cold and lifeless at our feet. Hummingbird and I stood with our mouths open.

It was most certainly a devious owl guard and shape-changer, the High Priestess explained to us. She lifted her arms, ready to comfort us. I stood a little apart, still in shock, wondering if I should say something to the High Priestess, until Hummingbird reached for my hand.

"I think we . . . *you*"—she turned directly to me, her voice slick with disbelief—"scared it."

But as we continued looking at each other, she grinned. A smile twitched at the corners of my mouth, almost involuntarily, as I was troubled to hear that I had scared something to death. Especially since that thing was a little girl I cared about. *Also, was it really me? Surely it was fear of the towering blue heron that blew it to bits.* Then I remembered how the villagers, even the women in my own home, sometimes flinched when they heard my voice, how they ran and hid when I entered a room. Now, I'd learned even some monsters were afraid of me. Despite myself, pride bubbled inside me. I was an adversary, one that should be taken seriously. But what would I, or could I, do with this power? My mind whirled.

"He penetrated our temple and tried to steal our secret teachings," I overheard the High Priestess say. "The monster, one of the lord of death's henchmen, nearly succeeded."

Ignoring the thing's repugnance, the priestesses wrapped the remains in white cloth, and he was cremated outside the Temple's gates with talismans to ensure his spirit would never roam the earth again. Hummingbird secretly followed them to watch the ritual. When she came back, she looked pale and shaken, and motioned for me to follow her.

"Mali," she said, walking quickly toward the labyrinth, "when the priestesses started the pyre, the flames turned green, and a voice cried out, 'You cannot escape what's coming. She who walks among you will bring your ruin' before burning out. Do you think he was talking about . . . what happened?" Hummingbird said, her voice barely a hoarse whisper.

"Of course not." I pulled her back toward the temple. "It's a trick, something the Skeleton Lord and his malevolent fiends take delight in executing. It just wants to throw us off-balance."

Inside, I wasn't so sure.

▲▲▲▲

Jeweled Laughter's health improved in the space of a few days. I was overjoyed when she became strong enough to rejoin our classes. Though a well of sadness and confusion sat low and cold within me, a constant companion. The loss of Rabbit, my mother, and the certainty of who I even was had taken a toll. Was I a danger to my sisters? Or was the owl demon's prophecy just a bid to divide us?

But caring for Jeweled Laughter felt healing for me, too. This, plus Hummingbird's support and the High Priestess's gentle counsel, sustained me. I was with my sisters, and it felt right, natural. No one had mentioned the pyre's prophecy, and it seemed like my indiscretion had been forgiven. In fact, walking the labyrinth with me one day, the High Priestess had even acknowledged that, sometimes, the perspective gained from standing outside the rules was worth the retribution that followed.

"Our powers are rarely clear, or simple," she'd said.

Hearing this, I believed she understood me. I wasn't a threat or a goddess. For now, at least, I could just be a student.

Or so I thought, for what came next half removed me from this world: the High Priestess and I were standing at the center of the labyrinth, before the turquoise Xiuhcoatl, idol of the Fire Serpent, when she said to me, "Be careful, Malinalxochitl." Inside a breath, a flash of blue heron feathers and the blade of a beak transformed her face.

Then she was her calm, beautiful self again. "Power can be brutal, the dark unforgiving," she said, brushing a shoulder where feathers lingered. "But sometimes the only opening is through darkness."

THE SORCERESS'S SHIELD

On the mountain of Coatepec, Malinalxochitl's brother tricked her into believing that he would change." We were in a special temple of Malinalxochitl, set deep within the forbidden forest, and the priestesses were telling her story. Finally, after years of wondering, the time had arrived to understand my namesake. Was I really destined to shine in her light? My heart was racing as I hung on every word Morning Star shared.

As she waved her hand, a bright glow illuminated a roughly painted mountain on the far red-striped wall. Her throaty voice became strained. "He had already destroyed their half sister, Painted Bells. The death had eaten away at Malinalxochitl's spirit and soul, but she foolishly believed him, not knowing that jealousy had long ago caged his bilious heart."

I bit my lip, remembering my mother telling me Huitzilopochtli had killed the moon goddess.

"Malinalxochitl trusted her brother. She had faith in the promise that he had made to her and to her followers—that they would rule together. But on the mountain, his magicians cast a spell that made her fall into a deep sleep," Morning Star said, dropping her arm and casting us back into the gloom.

The High Priestess continued then, the sound of her pacing footsteps echoing in the temple. "When she awoke, she found herself alone. He had abandoned her and taken most of their followers with him, the ones who were drawing closer to the bloodlust. Only a few supporters remained with her."

My mouth was dry. Bloodlust. This revelation took me aback, though it shouldn't have. How many times had my younger self imagined Moctezuma's smashed body and skull spraying the sky red?

"But then Malinalxochitl discovered that the sorcerers had diminished her strength. It is said that her roar of anger—her final act of magic—was so great that it created a chasm through the chain of volcanoes that stand to the east of the valley of the lakes." Squinting, I could make out ribbons of blue flowing from the High Priestess's mouth. "She put aside her sword and shield, but not before vowing to destroy her brother, to avenge the brutal death of her son, Copil, and to reduce to ashes the city of Tenochtitlan, built by the Mexica upon her son's sacrificed heart."

I wrapped my arms around me, not only to ward off the chill but to also control my anger. My mother had told me some of this, but now the story sounded personal, as if the god had attacked my family. *He murdered them all?* His malevolent deeds cut me to the bone. *Tricked her and killed her son. Then they built Tenochtitlan . . . upon his heart!*

All at once, more torches flamed and lanterns flickered, filling the space with warmth. Yet I still felt cold. Gutted. Looking around me, I noticed the flames had revealed something that instantly overcame my anger. A painting like the one in my mother's book—a woman in goddess raiment brandishing weapons. On the earthen wall above her, Earth Mother with the gnarled roots and the crown of a blossoming tree. And something else . . . a stone bench shaped like a standing jaguar—Or was it a throne?—stood at the center of the room, and its head was turned as if it was looking at something. I followed the animal's gaze, which led me toward a large round shield hanging on the wall. Instantly I could see it wasn't a painting, for it was curved and wondrously assembled.

I turned to the priestesses for an explanation.

The High Priestess nodded. "Magnificent, isn't it? It is the sorceress's shield. It guarded the people's protector."

The people's protector. I realized that I'd always heard of her described as the Avenging One, even the Destroyer. But . . . Protector? Never.

"The obsidian pattern captured light and held its power," the High Priestess said. "Rays of sun. Beams of moonlight. The glow of stars. The shield absorbed all. Morning Star and I have heard that it had the ability to freeze enemy warriors in their tracks, repel evil spells, and calm savage beasts. It could even stop time itself. The shield bearer wielded it as she saw fit." She paused. "It was up to Malinalxochitl."

It was up to Malinalxochitl. Sparks went off in my mind.

"She vowed to keep them safe from harm," the High Priestess added in a near whisper. I turned to her to make certain I had heard her correctly. What did this mean? Keep who safe? Safe from what? But her nod was as elusive as her words.

I moved to take a closer look and didn't stop until the shield was within my reach. It was round like the moon and made of white deer hide that had been stretched over a reed and wooden frame. To the east of the mosaic of broken volcanic glass was her name sign—Wild Grass Flower—and to the west, a serpent, both made with various shades of white and black beads. Long white heron feathers dripped from the lower rim, which was studded with turquoises.

Its beauty was spellbinding. But its splendor was secondary to the thrill I felt over my need to actually hold it, to feel its weight in my hands. *It would make me so strong that I'd be invincible. It's magical. It belonged to HER.*

Though I clasped my hands behind my back, the beast inside me lusted after this shining shield. I moved to grasp it and remove it from the wall, but at the last moment, I drew back. *Wait! Are you thinking you can just run off with it? After one trip to Mictlan and a few sips of sacred octli, you think you can use this to make war against that monster Moctezuma? Think, Malinalxochitl!*

Patience. I still wanted Moctezuma's head, but I also had other aspirations. Now I was a priestess of the Temple of the Eighteen Moons, a knower of things. I'd been to Mictlan and come face-to-face with a shape-shifter. I did things differently now. From this point forward, everything I did would be with my sisters.

While staring at my broken reflection in the shards of glass, the shield seemed to ask, *Who are you?* I was quick to answer: *Malinalxochitl, the daughter of Jade Feather, who is the daughter of She with the Sad Eyes, daughter of . . .* And then I stopped. My blood pounded in my ears. As I placed a hand on the wall to steady myself, I could sense Morning Star leaning toward me to catch me should I fall. Something pushed against my palm then, something deep inside this earthen cave, this shrine deep in the forest. An energy reached out to me.

This is what my mother wanted me to find. This shrine, this story, told by these women . . . To think that for the past three years the sorceress's shrine has been practically right outside my door. Hidden away. Here! Guarded by the Temple of the Eighteen Moons.

For a moment, my heart silenced my gnawing grief. It was a sensation that lifted me; a mix of strength and grace flowed along my spine. My mother had sent me here to learn my power. She had not abandoned me. She was here with me. I could feel her.

Then tears came.

Thinking about my mother, my Tolteca ancestors, and now this story and this place, how could I not cry?

The sound of a priestess delicately muffling a cough broke the fierce pull of my thoughts and feelings. I turned around to face the High Priestess and Morning Star and bowed my head.

"Thank you for bringing me to Malinalxochitl's shrine." The silence held us, and for a little while, that was enough for me.

But my mind was still on fire with questions, and the moment I looked up, they all tumbled out. "Why is the shield here?" I asked. "You're guarding it? For how long? Since her brother defeated her? Does everyone at the Temple know about this place?" My voice echoed, sounding strange and rough, but I couldn't stop myself. Nor was I concerned about angering anyone. I locked my arms over my chest and waited for the answers I felt I deserved.

The High Priestess tilted her head to the side, while Morning Star grumbled at my impertinence.

"Her brother stripped her of her goddess stature and forbade the people from recognizing her," Morning Star explained. Her wisdom halo glowed brightly now. "He did not act alone. Many gods and goddesses helped him. Her teachings have been forgotten by all save a few."

"But why?" I could no longer stand still. "I don't understand. He's the one who killed everyone," I pointed out, pacing back and forth.

Morning Star peered at me above the rim of her eye shields. "Power," she answered simply. "He blamed her for his murderous behavior. He called her wicked, evil, and cunning. Said she had used evil arts to bewitch him. And everyone believed him and his thunderbolts. By then the people, the ancestors of the Mexica, had grown accustomed to his demands for bloodier sacrifices. The offerings of beating hearts." She paused for a moment. "They enjoyed these spectacles. Perhaps the people were concerned that another ruling deity, Huitzilopochtli's sister, might force them to control their bloodlust."

I wanted reason to rule my thoughts, and I fought to make it so, but the more the priestesses talked, the more upset I became. When I had first entered this sacred place, I was reverent and quiet, but now I was furious. I noticed my hands were clawing at my skirt, pulled away as if I were on fire.

Morning Star continued, as if both of them did not notice my increasing temper. "There are other shrines to her. One in Coatepec, another in Tollan, and in the mountains outside Tenochtitlan. But her shield is here," she said with a gesture toward the magnificent design. "The priestesses of the Temple serve as its guardians."

"But we also keep watch over this." The High Priestess moved her hand, and flames sparked in more butterfly lamps, setting beams of light dancing among outcroppings of crystals, illuminating a strange altar of copper set against a wall previously cast in shadow.

The altar looked mangled and ill-formed, as if it had been pushed out of the earth or hammered into place by someone forced to mold it in darkness. It stood as high as my hips and had four legs as sinewy as snakes. Set in its middle was a large oval of obsidian glass. I took a step—*patience*—then stopped. As I took a deep breath, I felt a wisp of cool air sweep around my shoulders, lingering for a moment, before darting away. I reached out to try to bring it back, but to no avail. I turned to the priestesses to see if they had felt it. Clearly, they had not.

The altar seemed to shine brighter now, casting orange ribbons that gave my white skirt a coppery glow. I drew nearer to it, but not close enough to see into the mirror's surface. I recalled my classes in the healing arts and divination, how a priestess could depend on an uncloudy piece of obsidian to learn the causes of afflictions and to see into someone's future. Water, too, worked in this way. But a shiny piece of obsidian glass was what the master seers and healers prized most. Since this one was hidden with Malinalxochitl's shield, it had to be especially powerful.

Long ago, I was able to see the world through my brother's eyes. Could I use this mirror to see as I once did? To peer inside the House of Magical Studies, behold mysteries and unmask secrets? Would it permit me to see the future?

I felt the priestesses watching me carefully as I picked up one of the lanterns and set it gently on the altar. I pressed myself close to the glass, expecting to see my own reflection. But the shiny surface bore the quiet image of the lantern's flickering flame and nothing more.

▲▲▲▲

The moment we returned to the Temple of the Eighteen Moons, I wanted to go back to the shrine. Disappointed that I hadn't seen anything in the mirror, I was convinced that all I needed was to feel the shield in my hand. But a few days later, we received word that a woman in the village a half day away had died in childbirth, and I wanted to be one of the priestesses to journey to the burial site to guard her body. For four nights, we would sit with Music of the Wind's husband and his family to protect her.

One of the greatest of all of our teachings is that women in childbed are as courageous as warriors on the battlefield. Women who die as they give birth are "valiant warriors." Their destiny in the hereafter is to meet the Sun Lord at his zenith and march in procession, carrying him on a litter made of feathers. She is a bearer of magic, hence the need to protect her grave. Warriors and sorcerers coveted the middle finger of the dead woman's left hand and her hair. They would attach them to their weapons and staffs to make themselves invincible.

More than anything, with my sisters at my side, I wanted to defend this woman's soul so she could rise, be reborn, and march before the sun, guiding it through the western sky. I had to go. And I swore that I would carry Malinalxochitl's shield.

VIGIL AT A WARRIOR WOMAN'S GRAVE

The sun had set when we began our march to the sacred burial site. Were it not for the torches held aloft by the High Priestess and the astronomer Cloud Song, the dark would have swallowed us. The High Priestess had given me beautiful blue sandals, but the new shoes cut my feet with each step. I was thankful that I'd been chosen for this important role, but I was also disappointed because I wasn't allowed to bring the shield. When I asked if I could carry it, both the High Priestess and Morning Star had fiercely denied me. Instead, I held in my hands a splintered wooden war club and a battered shield shorn of all its featherwork. At the fine ceremony that had been held to see us off, during which Morning Star placed these weapons into my hands, all I could think was that they looked plain and not very protective.

My grip on sword and shield was firm when the low, keening wail of a shell trumpet split the night. I knew it must be one of our priestesses from the Temple announcing the position of the moon. I sighed into the dark and clung to the familiar sound.

▲▲▲▲

We approached our destination. There, a cluster of people, lit by a bonfire, huddled around a fresh mound of turned earth. All were plainly dressed, but the men wore quilted cotton armor and were armed with spears, swords, and clubs stuck with shards of flint. One man wore the orange mantle of a distinguished warrior.

The High Priestess and two elderly priestesses offered a prayer and invoked the goddess Feathered Butterfly's protection and power. They then turned their palms to the sky and called out to the moon and the earth, and all the spirits that moved between them, beseeching their protection. From between the folds of her cloak, the High Priestess removed her sacred jaguar pouch and cast herbs and copal into the fire. The smoke burned blue. After kneeling, I focused my gaze on the ground and held myself with pride, and even though I didn't hold the weapons I wanted most, for the next four days and nights, I was ready to defend the body of the woman buried in front of me. I would prove to everyone that I deserved the right to carry the sorceress's shield.

▲▲▲▲

The world fell into a deep sleep, and by the fourth night, it appeared that we would not need our weapons. Guarding a grave is a very quiet act. Boring, to tell the truth. I could no longer feel my legs, and my arms felt heavy, even though I had placed my sword and shield on the ground. My stomach rumbled, and for a moment I allowed myself to imagine a table set with my favorite foods. Any priestess who guards a valiant warrior woman must abstain from eating anything more than a few swallows of corn gruel, so I was very hungry.

As my mouth watered over a plate of frog legs cooked with tomatl, I heard a noise. A sea of darkness stretched beyond the circle of firelight that surrounded us, and as hard as I tried to see into it, I could not. I caught Hummingbird looking at me. She raised her finger to her lips. The other priestesses had heard the noise too, and they held their weapons close. They had already risen to their feet and removed their mantles, and the warrior in the orange cloak stood armed and ready.

Someone was coming toward us.

As I rose and shifted my weight to the balls of my feet, I heard people moving, then running. *Body snatchers!* I gripped my sword, taking deep breaths to calm my pounding heart. I had taught myself how to fight long ago. I held only a branch then, and the enemies were giants only I could see, but I had learned how to move the weapon from side to side and deliver blows from above.

Five men came screaming and running out of the dark. They were naked and painted with yellow stripes, waving swords and spears. I dropped my shield so I could hold my wooden sword with two hands. My knees began to tremble, but hearing an eagle circling above cry out strengthened me, and I prepared for their attack.

The monsters hurled themselves at us. Because the priestesses were the closest, we bore the brunt of their charge. I heard the crash of weapon against shield. The High Priestess was the first under attack. With a cry, she raised her sword arm and struck a man down. Not too far away, Cloud Song was shielding Hummingbird from another man. I turned and saw Rose Petal defending the grave as one of the defilers kicked the earth aside.

It was only seconds, but I looked back just in time to see a blade barely miss my cheek. I spun around to face my enemy, and as he struggled to lift his sword again, I lashed out with my weapon but missed him by leagues. He smiled at me with red-stained teeth and raised his sword until it was level with my eyes. He would have separated my head from my shoulders had I not tripped on my cloak and fallen out of the way.

I scrambled to my feet, tearing the cloak off, and darted away. My enemy's grin had become a sneer. His head moved as I moved, following me like a snake.

The leaves and sky glittered through my field of vision as I ran through the trees, my heart bursting from my chest as he advanced, quick on my heels. A hillside jumped out from the forest and blocked my path. There was nowhere to run. I squeezed my sword between my hands and turned to face him. Then, I attacked. By the time he shook himself into action and lifted his sword and shield, it was too late. My sword entered his body, and blood spurted in an arc, catching my chin. I stumbled backward as I watched his eyes widen, then the warrior in orange cut him down to the ground.

Panting, I wiped the sweat from my eyes and forced myself to look away from the body. Was he truly dead? What of his soul? Then the sounds of fighting to the east drowned out the questions and took my mind off the dead man's blood. I ran back and watched Music of the Wind's family surround and strike out at the two remaining men. Our attackers were tiring, and I knew that victory would be ours. For a moment, I allowed myself to relax. But then came a steady and loud thumping, and suddenly we were surrounded by more men, five . . . no, six, with stiff feathers in their hair, outfitted like soldiers I had never seen before. They wore blue loincloths and jaguar-skin leg guards and sandals. Their shields were folded on their backs. Black stripes made their faces frightening.

I cried out, and before I knew it, Rose Petal stood on my left and the High Priestess on my right. Their hair had come undone, and their blouses and skirts were stained and bloodied. I felt their strength. They were warriors now.

"Protect us, Mother. Protect us now," Rose Petal prayed. She stood hunched and sweating, shifting her weight from side to side as she held her sword in front of her. The High Priestess and I raised our swords, too, and together we moved forward to charge these new intruders.

One of the men stopped. Throwing up his empty hands, he yelled a short string of strange words that made the High Priestess and Hummingbird respond with a shout.

"Wait!"

Music of the Wind's husband and his men came up behind us to throw themselves at these strangers. More words flew back and forth, and then I recognized the richness of their voices. They were Maya.

Hummingbird and the High Priestess lifted their arms, and everything came to a halt. After placing their bodies between us and this new threat, they turned to us and said, "These people wish us no harm. They are from coastal lands of the Divine Eastern Sea. They were on their way to the Temple of the Eighteen Moons, when they heard the attack."

I felt my body go limp. Weapons thudded to the earth as one by one we let them go.

"Sweet goddess of all!" someone breathed.

Fingers wisped across my cheek and, startled, I turned to slap them away. "Be still now, Malinalxochitl," Rose Petal soothed as she studied my face. I wiped my cheek and looked at the blood on my hand. I was wounded? "No harm. It will heal soon enough," Rose Petal said.

As she removed two small pottery jars from her jaguar pouch and began to wash my cheek with a bit of water, I watched Hummingbird and the High Priestess talk to the man who had spoken. He wore a jaguar pelt over one shoulder, the head of the beast hanging at his hips.

I had heard his Maya language from the traders who traveled down the river to our village, at the Temple, and from Hummingbird's own lips.

Music of the Wind's family dragged the dead bodies out of the way. Someone fed the fire, so it surged and crackled. Cloud Song and the elderly priestesses began to chant over the grave site. Their voices rose as they spoke to Music of the Wind's soul and assured her that she was safe and that soon she would find herself in the company of the sun. I heard the eagle beating its wings, circling the sky.

My gaze wandered back to Hummingbird and the warrior. She was speaking to the ground, for it is always improper for a woman to look a man in the face. He was slim, yet broad-shouldered, and with a great many tattoos, including twining serpents around his wrists and arms, and constellations of stars sprayed across his chest and shoulders. The jaguar pelt, the jeweled cuffs around his arms, and the green feathers suggested wealth. The sharp, carved planes of his profile displayed a severity of character, until he turned to me and I determined that he was more inquisitive than severe. But that was not what held my eyes. Even in the orange light of the fire, I could see that he was far more muscular than any of the men who had attacked us.

"You are staring," Rose Petal whispered in my ear.

"I was just . . ." I blathered, then gathered my wits and held my tongue.

"His name is Shield Jaguar." She smiled. "Pakal Balam," she pronounced in the Maya tongue.

Pakal Balam. "How do you know that?" I whispered back.

She stepped away and regarded my cheek with keen interest. "Oh, he has been to the Temple before. At first, I did not recognize him. He was just a boy when he came to secure a love potion for his father, the ruler of Mayapan. He is much changed. I wonder what brings him back to us now?"

I looked down and pretended to study my sandals, wishing that Rose Petal would turn away or, better yet, *move*, so that I might take my time studying this Maya.

NOBLE MAYA

Pakal Balam.

His name was a burst of sunlight upon waves of foam.

The earth trembled when I caught him studying me. He stood apart from his men, and the flames of the fire flickered over him, pulling him out of the shadows. I studied him and felt Earth Mother set the ground to rocking. She was warning me. I know that now. But there was nothing I could have done to stop what was happening.

With as much modesty as my curiosity would allow, I followed the Maya back to the temple. Pakal Balam and his men served as our guards, for even though we had all proven ourselves in battle, the dawn could still be treacherous. The High Priestess carried her torch higher than before and walked with a bearing that made me proud each time I looked at her.

We trudged along in silence. I was sure everyone could hear my heart thumping, most especially the astronomer Cloud Song. Now and then she would glance at me over her shoulder and whisper, "Watch where you are going, Malinalxochitl."

The sound of the trumpet shell signaled our arrival at the gates of the Temple of the Eighteen Moons. I do not know how news of our victory had arrived so quickly, but there we were, bloody and filthy, our hair in tangles and our weapons in our hands, being greeted by the cries of the priestesses as we walked the petaled path that had been prepared for us. The Maya looked around, their mouths agape as if they had never seen such a wonder as our temple. Or perhaps the sight of so many women cheering startled them. I heard excited screams and claps, the shout of Hummingbird's and my name. I sensed Jeweled Laughter standing nearby. I rose onto the tips of my toes and tried to spot her waving in the crowd. In my eagerness, I snagged Cloud Song's hem. She turned and gave me a stern look. I fell back in step, but I refused to let anyone crush my mood. For the second time, I, Malinalxochitl, had stood up to evil and struck it down.

▲▲▲▲

Later that day, I hurried to the red-columned temple, with the steam of the sweathouse still warming my cheeks. In a few hours it would be awash with the colors of the sun god, blushing from the presence of so many courageous warrior women leading him to his sleeping chamber on the horizon. Soon I would prepare for the evening meal, then prayers. But for now, at the High Priestess's request, I was expected to join the other priestesses to welcome Pakal Balam.

The great Maya entered the temple and made the gesture of respect we called kissing the earth.

The High Priestess greeted him. "Welcome, dear friend."

He answered, the sound of his voice moving through the room like a wind that held the promise of hard rain. The High Priestess replied in his tongue. I listened closely as their voices played back and forth, but I was frustrated that I could not understand them. I vowed to myself that I would redouble my efforts to master the Maya tongue.

The High Priestess presented a book to him. He accepted it as if it were made of precious jade. He had changed his garments since I last saw him and now wore a deep blue mantle and a cloth of emerald green wrapped around his hips, edged with gold shells. His body was bare of jewels and the leopard skin. He needed no ornaments to tell me he was noble born. I felt a blush bloom in my cheeks.

Hummingbird leaned close to me and whispered, "How curious."

"What is?" I could not take my eyes off him.

"He says he is here on behalf of his sister, who would like an escort of priestesses to accompany her to the shrine of the goddess Ix Chel on the island of Ah-Cuzamil-Peten. He's come to escort the priestesses, and the first stops in their journey will be Komchen and Mayapan, in the lowlands of Mayab."

I knew of Ix Chel. She was the goddess of rainbows, childbirth, and beauty. Her shrine on that island was sacred to all the Maya.

"The Lady Six Sky is eager to visit it and make sacrifices to the goddess in the hopes that it will make her womb more fertile," Hummingbird said. "She believes that being in the company of our priestesses will aid her in this and make her feel at peace."

"Ah-Cuzamil-Peten is a long way in the turquoise sea," I said.

"Yes," the High Priestess added, walking up behind us. "It will be a dangerous journey. Just the kind of mission for two priestesses who have proven themselves able with swords and shields," she said, her eyes glinting.

▲▲▲▲

The very next morning, the High Priestess began instructing me on the *proper* use of sword and shield.

"You will be traveling through difficult territories and will need to know how to defend yourself," the High Priestess said as she hitched up her skirt.

I scowled. Hadn't I defended a warrior woman and killed a grave robber? I didn't think my sword-fighting skills needed improvement, but I kept my mouth shut and followed her outside, hitching up my skirt, too.

With the weapons I'd used the day before firmly in my hands, I assumed a basic stance, checking to make sure my feet were placed just so and that my weight was perfectly balanced. She approached and struck with her sword, but I stopped her thrust with my shield and countered her attack with one of my own.

"Well done," the High Priestess said.

I nodded. My arms screamed with pain. The weapons seemed so much heavier today.

Unlike me, the High Priestess was tall, lithe, her arms strong and muscular. She held her round leather shield with no more effort than if she were holding an ear of corn. After my next hit, which was very weak, she stopped and shook her head.

"I was focused on my feet," I lied.

"Try it again," she ordered.

I would hear these words a hundred times during our lesson. *She's the High Priestess. I can't get mad.*

She pushed me to my limit and showed me how to spin out of the way of a surprise thrust; how to fall without hurting myself; and how to flip and land on my feet. The latter maneuver I enjoyed so much that, gasping for breath, laughing even, I asked, "Can we do that again?"

She drove me so hard you would think she was evaluating whether I deserved to wield Malinalxochitl's shield. But what if I no longer wanted it? I'd been doing a lot of thinking since my visit to the shrine. I admired the sorceress's bravery, the protector side of her. I wanted to fight for my sisters, gain the power to strike down anyone who would hurt me or those I loved. But the vision of the snatcher I'd killed had come back to me in my sleep. The way his skin had opened against my sword. The sight of blood and entrails leaving his body as his eyes went blank. The stench of human life, decaying, as I wondered if I even had the right to take his soul.

Watching Eagle get attacked at the House of Magical Studies.

The young girl's heart being pulled from her chest on the pyramid.

The creature called Rabbit exploding into feathers and dust.

So much blood and darkness.

The cruelty and ruthlessness it took, from the ugliest root inside me, to lift the sword.

It wasn't for me anymore. The Temple was my home, with my sisters. I would do what I must to protect the shrine, but I didn't necessarily want to be pushed into a battle that I wasn't ready to fight.

I swung my sword, resisting and delivering blows, as the sun charted its course through the morning sky. I was sticky and my limbs trembled, but I held my own. By the time the wind decided to pay us a soft visit, Hummingbird had appeared and now watched quietly from a distance. I saw her out of the corner of my eye, and I was careful lest the High Priestess take advantage of my inattentiveness. But I couldn't stop my thoughts from veering to the night before, when I heard her slip out of our sleeping chamber. As my limbs had been restless, my mind awake and flooded with images of the grave site, the fighting, and Pakal Balam, I followed her out. I had observed her tiptoeing away in the night before, many times. But I had never been this sneaky.

Just a quick check to make sure she's all right, I'd said to myself. *Maybe she'll transform herself into a vixen and hunt dahlias!*

Winding through the stalks in the cornfield, trying to be quiet, I found Hummingbird near the place where she had found me that time after Toci's visit, though now there was a small, cleared path marked with a stone idol of the goddess of maize. The moon had been generous with her light, so I could see my friend clearly. She'd been sitting back on her knees . . . and smearing her face with dirt. I stopped dead in my tracks.

I shouldn't be here. I thought back to the day she had rescued me from the labyrinth, the sudden sadness on her face. I saw it then, and it made my heart cry.

She glanced up, had caught me staring. She tried to smile, and I knew then that she, too, had lost someone she loved. I took a deep breath, approached, and sat down beside her, and when she clawed another handful of earth and began to lift it to her face, I pressed my palm gently over her hand. The earth had been cool, but not as cold as her voice.

"The story I told you about my mother saving me from my father, who wanted to use me to pay a debt? It was a lie." Her expression had changed; her eyes burned like hot coals. "I killed him. I killed my father."

The heavy, humid air seemed to crash upon my head, and I felt a whirling in my stomach. How could she kill her father? I thought of my father caged like an animal. She must have seen the horror on my face, but she retreated behind a face of stone.

"He was using me the way a man uses a courtesan."

An ahuiyani? The whirls in my stomach were pushed aside by a sharp physical pain. I didn't know what to say. I didn't know anything save that I hated myself for having judged Hummingbird.

"No one cared that he was hurting me." She stopped, looked down at her hands in the dirt before continuing. "My mother brought me to the Temple, that part is true. But there was no debt." She threw a clod of earth and looked back at me. "My family wanted me dead. My father was a powerful man, you see. No one would listen. No one believed an eight-year-old girl." Tears welled in her eyes, but the force of her will, a power I'd felt emanating from her at the grave site and felt in that moment, kept them from spilling. I was not as strong and had to brush a hand across my eyes. *I'd kill him myself if I could.*

Hummingbird looked away, then tilted her face to me. "Have you ever felt like you just want the earth to swallow you up?"

It took not even a heartbeat to answer her. "I have."

She drew her hands to her lap and wiped them against her skirt, then reached for my hand. "Yes. You bravely told me your story," and I thought her eyes had changed, softened, as she looked back to another time.

"I couldn't bear the idea of living without my brother and father."

To which she replied, "Sometimes I just want to forget so badly . . ."

If only I had a charm for this, a spell to make it better and take the pain away.

"May I sit with you?" I whispered. In a small voice, she answered yes. But I hadn't brought a spell to share, so before we returned to our chamber, I brushed my fingertips along the edge of my huipilli, and after focusing my attention on the embroidered threads, brought the white vines and leaves to life. All of my sisters had seen me do this many times, and their reaction, like Hummingbird's then, had always lightened my heart. Hummingbird clicked her tongue and shook her head disbelievingly as I coaxed and twined the embroidery first around her wrist, then mine.

"You are my family, and I will always believe you," I promised, tapping her wrist bone gently. "You will always have Malinalxochitl's protection." I knew as soon as I said the words that I would fight any battle for her, punish the world if I had to. Protect her for as long as I lived.

Seeing the white threads streaming around my sword arm now, as I fought the High Priestess, sent a spark, doubling my strength. I released a beastly yell as I twisted and turned, delivering blows. My sudden change in momentum nearly toppled her. She righted herself quickly, lowered her head, and pinned me with a fierce stare. I intuitively rebalanced my stance and raised my shield, just the way she'd taught me, but she proved I still had much to learn. I ended up on my back and as helpless as an overturned beetle. The High Priestess reached down to help me up, and the lesson should have ended there. But I wasn't ready to quit. Perhaps I was showing off for Hummingbird. Or maybe I wanted to prove something to myself. For I shook my arms out, steadied myself on solid ground, and raised my sword. "Let's try it again."

BOOK OF MAPS

Several nights after Rose Petal marked me with the sign of the Temple—a tattoo of a butterfly poised on a crescent moon—I joined my sisters and all of the priestesses in the library to behold something so rare and mysterious it could only be looked at when the moon was full. On the long table rested a book five fingers thick, with a cover of tanned deer hide, set with a giant turquoise stone. The dust motes floating around the book reminded me more of stars than dirt, though it looked very old.

We stared at it, waiting. *Maybe it reveals another story about Malinalxochitl*, I thought excitedly. The High Priestess sat in front of the book, murmuring prayers to the goddess. Then the book groaned. It thumped, and the cover flew open.

The High Priestess clapped her hands together. "Ah, here we are," she sang. The crackly page was covered with a pattern that resembled a maze, all painted red, but before I had a chance to study it, the High Priestess delicately touched the upper corner and turned the page. After the next page, the book began to flip and unfold. One page became two, then four. She drew the paper out more and more, until the table was covered from end to end.

It was a map.

I sat back on my heels, transfixed. It was wondrous, painted so realistically with mountain peaks, rivers and lakes, villages and cities that I could practically see each individual blade of grass and crystal of snow. Flower heads drooped with the weight of their beautiful blooms, and cornstalks lifted tassels in search of the wind.

We huddled over the table, trying to find the point that signified the Temple of the Eighteen Moons. When at last I spied the site, I moved to place my finger over it, but just then, Morning Star said, “The map speaks,” and I froze. Morning Star waved her hand over a brown mountain peak rubbed with soot. It rumbled, and the table began shaking. As the sound grew louder, the mountain began rising out of the map. I heard it straining, and what sounded like trees creaking and falling.

“This is Popocatepetl.” Morning Star nodded approvingly. It grew so tall we had to stand to see everything clearly.

“And here is Iztaccihuatl.” As I caught my breath, she put out her pale finger. Snow began to fall. The second mountain pressed upward quietly, escaping the paper.

“The full moon awakens the map,” the High Priestess said, gesturing toward the moonlight falling through the high windows.

“Go now, Malinalxochitl, and place your finger over the marking of Feathered Butterfly,” Rose Petal encouraged with a lift of her chin.

I nodded dutifully.

She had surprised me at our final language lesson, pulling me aside to tell me that she needed to talk to me about “a language art never discussed at the Temple.” As everyone filed out of the class, she’d whispered, “Let me be plain: A woman who is ingenious and wise, who knows the intention of others, can outwit any evil. And survive.”

Dumbfounded, I’d stared. What was she talking about? She’d smiled slightly and crooked her finger, signaling that I should follow her. I did and soon found myself stuck listening to her drone on about matters of no concern to me then, having to do with feminine forces. I could feel my face flush red.

"It would be remiss of me to see you leave the Temple on such an important mission without sharing this with you," she'd said. I'd thought something was afoot. First, the High Priestess needed to improve my sword-fighting skills, and then Rose Petal wanted to speak about feminine forces? How strange. I was courteous and listened, but as soon as she was finished, I hurried away, mystified, and slightly embarrassed, by her talk regarding these forces. I'd wondered if she'd had some kind of vision in the obsidian mirror? In the end, I had talked myself into believing that it had all somehow been for my own good, as it would be the first time I would be venturing far from the safety of the Temple.

I forced these thoughts aside and focused on the map in front of me. I took care not to awaken another mountain. When I brushed the goddess's symbol, a blue butterfly rose from the map, and to shouts of delight, it fluttered over our heads. We hushed, watching silently as the butterfly flew about before returning to the map.

I wondered if I could find the secret temple hidden in our forest, but before I had a chance, the High Priestess said, "I wish to show Potonchan and Mayapan to Malinalxochitl and Hummingbird. Then we will mark the other places where Feathered Butterfly is worshipped," she said. I looked at the High Priestess, thinking about Malinalxochitl's temples. She'd said there were several.

She squinted at the map for a moment. Her expression brightened. "Ah, here is the place." She traced a path from our temple, down the river, to the Divine Eastern Sea. As she moved her fingers, I heard the sound of water and wind in high trees, then the chatter of monkeys and the shrieks of birds.

"Ten days by river, I think." The High Priestess turned her gaze to me, then Hummingbird. "Six more by sea."

I swallowed, realizing the distance to be very far.

I found the place marked with the symbols for Teotihuacan, the Place Where the Gods Were Born, and placed my hand over it, but the map did not respond.

"Alas, nothing can awaken Teotihuacan." Rose Petal sighed. "It fell silent after the time of darkness. But there among the ruins you will find signs of the first temple to Feathered Butterfly. What was once a beautiful and sacred place is now grown over with grasses and hidden."

I returned my attention to the map. Near Teotihuacan was an island city surrounded by lakes and mountains and marked with an eagle. Curls of fire and water rose from its beak. Following my gaze, the High Priestess said, "That is Tenochtitlan, home to the Mexica and Moctezuma."

The moment the High Priestess touched it, the pounding of drums and the sound of flutes erupted, then a plume of blue smoke unfurled, carrying with it the odor of fire and the incense copal.

The House of Magical Studies. For a moment, I allowed my anger to rise and throw its heat around in this peaceful place of knowledge and books.

I drew a deep breath to steady myself, then returned my attention to the eastern coast, specifically Mayapan and Ah-Cuzamil-Peten. I looked again at Tenochtitlan. Back and forth I went as I tried to imagine the distance between the cities. I noted the range of black and snow-capped mountains, the desolate deserts and cool, green forests. How long might such a journey take? Perhaps I could travel to Tenochtitlan after my time with the Maya.

"In the Divine Eastern Sea, something of great mystery has been sighted," the High Priestess said, interrupting my thoughts.

As she brushed her fingers over the eastern edge of the map, where land met water, the sea shimmered and moved. I heard the sound of waves. The water could have been lapping against the library's walls, for how loud it was.

"Pakal Balam told us he has seen mountains floating in the sea," the High Priestess said. "They're crowned with white banners, marked with strange symbols, that move with the wind."

All my sisters and the priestesses began speaking at once. Hummingbird watched Jeweled Laughter's hands spin the air with symbols. After nodding in agreement, Hummingbird said, "It sounds preposterous. Mountains? In the sea?"

"But Pakal Balam *says* he saw them," I said.

Hummingbird huffed. "What power could make a mountain float?"

"Perhaps it was an enchantment of some kind?" I offered.

"Then where are these floating mountains?" Hummingbird asked. "Why have they not appeared on the map?"

The High Priestess withdrew her hand from the sea and silence fell.

Morning Star's throaty grumble disrupted the quiet. "This is neither magic nor the work of a goddess. I do not doubt what Pakal Balam has seen, but it is not a mountain. It is a thing made by man. A new tribe comes, a dangerous—"

"Morning Star?" the High Priestess interrupted, stopping the elder priestess. "We are not sure what these sightings mean." She continued. "But this we know—we will not spread falsehoods or fear. We will guard our emotions until we know for certain the meaning of this unusual apparition."

The elder priestess was staring up at the ceiling. Both she and the High Priestess wore frowns, and the air between them felt cold to me.

The High Priestess looked straight at me. "Malinalxochitl?" Then, "Hummingbird? You will learn all you can about these strange sightings when you are with the Maya. Perhaps when you return to the Temple, you will understand this mystery better. Until then, we will ask the gods and goddesses for help. And I"—she narrowed her eyes—"will consult the painted books to see if there is an explanation for this strange occurrence."

▲▲▲▲

After two full moons, it was time for us to begin our journey to the land of the Maya. At sunrise, on the day known to us as One-Serpent,

Hummingbird and I oversaw the packing of ten tall and sturdy wicker baskets with various supplies, including the Book of Maps, and gifts: there were thirty lengths of embroidered cloth, jars of our honey, a book that told the story of the Maya Hero Twins, and a mix of the same night-blooming jasmine and copal that gave our temples their fragrant scent. Rose Petal carefully wrapped clay and crystal jars of remedies meant to cure everything from weak stomachs to cold hands and feet, along with mecaxochitl, rope flower, to help stimulate Lady Six Sky's womb, and a packet of powders to prolong her husband's potency.

To calm myself, I fingered the jaguar-skin pouch Toci had given me that hung at my waist. Inside I had placed my mother's turquoise necklace, a boar bristle brush, a clay inkpot, a handful of earth from the Temple's garden, and a leaf I had found while sweeping Quetzalcoatl's temple that morning—talismans that would both protect me and bring me comfort as I traveled.

Hummingbird and I turned to our sisters to say our farewells. Jeweled Laughter's left eye twitched. She took a quick, settling breath, then looking straight at me, placed her right hand over her heart, and tapped gently before sweeping me into her arms. Her hair smelled like sunlight and marigold blossoms. "May the goddess keep you safe, too," I said.

My sister. Will I ever see her again? I tightened every muscle to fight the tide rising inside me.

Jeweled Laughter pulled back and pressed a red shell into my hands. She pointed at the jaguar pouch, touched her face, and beamed a smile to rival the sun. "I will remember you," I promised.

Then the High Priestess took me by my shoulders and penetrated me with her fierce gaze. "Never forget who you are," she commanded. "Greet every dawn with the cry of your name."

From now on, I'd be on my own. Not the legacy of a goddess or a disciple of the mighty Temple of the Eighteen Moons or the fierce warrior who killed a man or the young girl who lost her family. Just . . . Malinalli.

For a moment, I considered studying Toci's cloth map. I should find my mother. Remind her we were a family. As soon as I thought it, I knew it was wrong. She had forsaken me, hadn't she? I would be just another woman walking, blindly, toward her future. My body suddenly felt small and listless. I thought of curling up in a comfortable bed. Playing in my secret place with Eagle. Standing anywhere but here.

The High Priestess tightened her hold on me. She closed her eyes and whispered a prayer. "Malinalxochitl, I bless you in the name of Feathered Butterfly," she breathed against my skin. *"When you are ready, it will be here for you."* She kissed my forehead.

It was time. *I will return.* But for now . . . I felt the force of the sacred pyramid's shadow on my back as I faced the opposite direction. My legs were leaden, but I knew I would move forward. I would be a guide, a supporter, and a protector, where I was needed. My sisters needed me to be their light.

As I took my first steps from the place that had been my home for three years, I promised myself that I wouldn't cry. But at the gate where the Maya stood waiting, I had to avert my gaze as Pakal Balam bowed to kiss the earth. That is, I tried to look away from him but caught his eyes on mine just as I turned to look back at the temple. I know he saw something more than my strength and determination. As we say in my land, he had "a polished eye." He saw everything.

BOOK III

THE RIVER

The march from the Temple's gate to the river had been quick, as if the Maya could hear their canoes calling to them. Hummingbird and I were strong from work in the gardens and from caring for the temples, so at first it was easy for us to keep up. By the time we reached the water, however, we walked with our arms roped along the other's back, like two grandmothers making their way home after enjoying octli at a feast. Pakal Balam had been far in front, leading us, the green feathers tied to the dark knot of his hair fluttering in the breeze.

I missed those green feathers now. Hummingbird and I were sitting in the center of the canoe beneath a thatch canopy that shielded us from the sun, and the noble Pakal Balam sat far behind me, behind Hummingbird, paddling with two of his men. Another five Maya were seated in front of me. I counted eight massive crafts with eight men in each.

Within moments of stepping into the canoe and beginning our journey down the Coatzacoalcos, Hummingbird and Pakal Balam began to converse in an easy manner. I listened as intently as I could to my sister, hoping my studies of the Yucatecan and Chontal languages had made me fluent enough to keep up with the conversation. I was able to unlock many words, but I was so anxious that most of the sounds vanished like mist. If

Pakal Balam's men were surprised to hear Hummingbird speaking in their presence, they did not show it. Because of the high esteem in which we were held, our priestesses moved about with more ease than other women.

Hummingbird's words were so proper you could have repeated them to your father, though now and then Pakal Balam answered Hummingbird's voice with a throaty laugh. I longed to laugh and speak with them, but I was too shy to insert myself and too afraid that I would make a shamble of their pleasant talk. I was no word dragger. Pakal Balam must have thought I understood very little, for he kept explaining everything slowly in his language. Still, his kindness wasn't enough to dare me to speak. I was relieved when the cries of birds and the chatter of monkeys finally made it impossible to hear their voices.

That first night, we camped on the shores of the Coatzacoalcos. Hummingbird and I slept side by side beneath a fawn-colored mantle the High Priestess had given us. The fire was to our backs and the wide river before us. I fell asleep to the sound of rippling waves, flames feasting on wood, and the low murmur of Pakal Balam's voice.

Every night thereafter, Pakal Balam and his men built a lean-to of sticks, with a roof of woven palm leaves beneath a sturdy tree, so Hummingbird and I could have privacy and sleep shielded from the rain. They spread mats of plaited grasses over the earth floor for us. Pakal Balam insisted on covering the opening with a fine mesh, a Maya custom that protected us from the insects.

On the second night of our journey, as Hummingbird and I gathered wood for the fire, twelve of Pakal Balam's men came to me and placed ten dead rabbits, handfuls of cacao beans, blue and green macaw feathers, and seashells at my feet. They touched their fingers to the earth and raised them to their lips in a show of respect. After righting themselves, they waited, motionless.

I stood, gaping, and would have remained so had Hummingbird not given me a good poke.

"Say something," she said quietly. "Go on."

"Thank you?" I whispered in Nahuatl. They appeared to understand. I added a short prayer, the same words we always offered to Feathered Butterfly as the sun set. They seemed content with that, for they bowed their heads, turned, then walked away.

"What does this mean?" I looked down at the treasures gathered in front of me. "This must be because they revere us as priestesses."

"This is for *you*," Hummingbird answered. "It is your name."

"My name?"

She looked at me, with that sparkling cross-eyed stare I had come to love, and said, "Remember how my sisters and I almost fainted when we heard it for the first time? These men must think you are that sorceress, or a follower of hers. Maybe they think that if they're not careful, you will put a spell on them and turn them all into lizards."

I playfully pushed her away. She narrowed her eyes at me and scrunched up her mouth in a serious expression. "They know that you were chosen for this task. They look up to you because they see you as someone who should be honored. And they are correct."

I waved her off. I was devoted to honoring Quetzalpapalotl and Malinalxochitl and their teachings. I was committed to one day avenging the wrongs that had been enacted against my family, but I was not ready to have tribute laid at my feet.

"What do they expect from me?" All this fuss made me uneasy. I wasn't used to people bowing and giving me gifts. "They can't expect me to call the winds to make it easier for us on the water," I said. "Or magically start a fire."

"They recognize your strength and courage," she said reassuringly. "Do I have to remind you of everything you've accomplished at the Temple? At the grave site, and with that foul owl priest? Are you not the only young priestess who was taken to see *her* shrine?" she reminded me without a hint of jealousy, then, "Get used to this kind of attention, my friend." She patted my arm before walking away.

LANGUAGE OF THE MAYA

By the third day on the river, my mind was humming in Maya. Pakal Balam would point to things of interest—a turtle resting on a log, an eagle circling in the sky, an armadillo drinking at the water's edge—and call out their names. I lapped up his words hungrily. Now I spoke without fear, my voice rising above the songs of birds and the shouts of monkeys. Yet there were still times when words fell in torrents, and I could not understand. Pakal Balam would un-hurry his words, pronouncing them in a deep, rich voice that caressed.

My mother had always been afraid my quick tongue would be my undoing. But her fear never stopped me from imitating those proud men from Moctezuma's city, or from commanding rocks to speak and urging birds to converse with me. Father used to take pride in my ability to imitate various voices and sounds.

I relished the magic and felt the power between my lips.

▲▲▲▲

Hummingbird described Pakal Balam as a "great cypress that shields his people with shade." Each morning and evening, before he accepted a bite of food, he would walk about the camp to see that his men had plenty to eat. Only when he was content that his followers' needs were being met did he sit with them and rest. And each night, while his men gathered around the fire, he would sing. Hummingbird and I would listen from our shelter, holding our breath as he sang the tale of the Maya Hero Twins and the story of Chac and the flood. A few of his men played flutes as his voice rose and fell in the night. Even the firewood crackled in rhythm to his words.

As I grew more at ease speaking in the Maya tongue, so, too, did my ability to set their picture words to paper. It was my habit in the evenings, as camp was being made, to practice my skill with the brush. One night, as I admired my work, Pakal Balam approached. Even without looking up from the paper spread across my lap, I knew it was him and, as always, I panicked over whether I should meet his eye. How many times had my mother punished me for doing the same? Too many to count! And yet all of the temple women—the High Priestess, Rose Petal, even Hummingbird—had gazed at Pakal Balam's face. How could they not? His features were exquisitely drawn, his handsomeness redefined the soul of what it was to be so . . . beautiful.

I glanced at him, then quickly back to my hands. But it was long enough to catch his smile.

"Forgive my intrusion, priestess." He gave a little cough and looked everywhere except at me. His green mantle was pushed back off his shoulders, and his skin was slick with sweat. The tattooed serpents on his arms were close enough to touch. He cleared his throat. "I know you keep this time for your words," he began. I leaned forward to hear him better. "And I would understand if you desire to be alone . . ."

I fluttered my hand, gesturing for him to please continue.

He reached into the pouch at his waist. When he opened his hand, I nearly cried out with delight. Sitting on his palm were two small wooden figurines, a monkey and a rabbit, each holding a brush very much like my own. These were the Maya guardians of writing. I'd often heard the scraping of his knife as he carved pieces of wood in the night. I reached out to touch them when the image of my mother's most disapproving look surfaced in my mind. I dropped my hands and lowered my eyes.

"I made them for you," Pakal Balam said.

I felt the heat rise in my cheeks as his words washed over me. I took a figure in each hand and turned them this way and that to admire them.

"They are very fine likenesses. I humbly thank you, most noble sir. I will treasure them always."

He surprised me by squatting down in front of me. This set my hands to shaking, and the figures toppled. They would have fallen to the ground had he not closed his hands around mine.

Even in the fading sun of that day, I could see the gold light in his eyes.

▲▲▲▲

Each morning as the Sun Lord rose, Pakal Balam walked down to the water to wash and pray. Save for the men who guarded the camp, everyone was asleep. I should have been, too, but I was spying on him. Quietly, I would part the curtain of netting that covered the lean-to's opening, then crawl out after him, keeping my distance but staying in sight. At the riverbank, through a curtain of reeds that reached past my head, I watched.

The dawn of the sixth day, I followed him to the river in a low crouch, taking care not to make a sound.

From my hiding place, I could see the serpent tattoos on his arms, even the feathers that crested their heads. His loincloth was white, unembellished save for a thin ribbon of red around his waist. He moved with grace, bending to cup the water to his lips.

Did the sun begin to shine more brightly just at that moment? Did I hear Earth Mother draw in her breath in admiration of such perfection? Did I see the river goddess stare?

The noble Maya knelt and sat back on his heels. I held my breath as he began to pray. His deep voice set the river water in motion. Then, from the waist of his loincloth, he withdrew a small knife. He held the blade's tip to his ear, and with a flick, pierced it. Blood began to flow, and he caught it in a small bowl. When he was finished, he placed the knife on the ground and lifted the bowl of blood in offering. His voice grew urgent. Blood trickled down his shoulder. I could smell the coppery tang rising above the river. I was not able to understand everything he said, but of this I was certain: he was offering his blood to the god Kukulkan, the god I knew as Quetzalcoatl, the Feathered Serpent.

Pakal Balam began to chant, when suddenly the air around him broke into glittering shards of light. Blinded, I looked away. As I turned to him again, I saw a green serpent rise out of the bowl, twisting and turning, with great fangs and eyes as round and deep as black lava pools. I bit my lip to keep from shouting. My hands and arms shook the grasses so hard I feared I would be found out, but the Maya's voice, now even louder, drowned out everything.

He held the bowl steady as he prayed. The Vision Serpent shone with scales of gold and spirals of red and blue. It towered far above Pakal Balam and turned its head, until finally it steadied and looked down on the man who had called it into the world.

My muffled cry drew the attention of the Vision Serpent and Pakal Balam. Bearing the might of their gaze, I toppled over, sending the tall grasses that surrounded me swishing and swaying as they closed in. The next thing I knew, he was standing over me.

Rising onto my elbows, I looked up at the sky and peered around the Maya. The serpent had vanished, if it had ever existed.

"What are you doing, Priestess Malinalxochitl?" Pakal Balam said, smiling.

I dropped my gaze, my cheeks hot with shame. "My apologies, noble lord," I said, rushing my words. "I have overstepped my place and committed a crime so grave that I will not stop you should you decide that I am unworthy of your sister's company and deem it necessary to return me to the Temple of the Eighteen Moons. In fact, I believe you should act immediately."

"First, answer me this," he said, crouching down in front of me. Flustered by his attention, the physical proximity of his body, and the droplets of blood scattered over his shoulders, I shuffled back and tucked my legs to the side. "Just one thing, little spy," he teased. "Did you see it?"

I didn't hesitate. "The serpent?"

He beamed. "Yes!" He shook his head as if I'd told him marvelous news. "No one else has ever set eyes on the Vision Serpent that visits me. No one," he murmured.

He cocked his head as he studied me. Anxious to return to Hummingbird, I rose to my feet.

The Maya shifted onto his knees, and before I understood what was happening, his hands were on my hips, pulling me toward him. I could not resist. Not even when he pressed his face into my skirt. Nor when I felt his breath through the embroidered cloth.

It was as if the threads of my skirt had decided to unravel, for it suddenly billowed around me and drifted down to my ankles. The river air felt cool, but lovelier still was the touch of Pakal Balam's hands and the heat that poured over the scallop shell that hung from the beaded belt around my waist—a shell as small as my little finger that I'd been wearing since the time of my first bleeding. I felt myself begin to fall, so I gripped his shoulders to steady myself. Then his fingers touched my place of joy. Before I had time to react, his mouth was there, nuzzling at first, followed by his lips, his tongue. I cried out, and he stopped to quiet me, shushing me against the skin of my thigh. I pressed my hand over my mouth as I moved against his lips, hungry for him to continue. His mouth breathed fire, stroking a flame, until I felt myself falling up to meet the sky.

▲▲▲▲

At the river's edge, I learned to love. I discovered how to stand breathlessly, my body trembling with want. And when he showed me how to touch him, I wanted to stay by his side forever. I imagined us becoming rooted to the earth, leaves unfurling from the crowns of our heads. I saw into the future, when canoes would pass us, and someone would point and say, "There stands the mighty Pakal Balam and Malinalxochitl. They loved each other so well, Earth Mother turned them into a mighty flowering tree."

Yes, I wanted that.

As Hummingbird and I turned to the east to say our prayers, I thought of him. As his men laid iguana eggs, orchids, and copal at my feet, and the world turned twenty shades of green, my heart turned to him. My thighs felt caressed by feathers each time he looked at me. The blue sign that marked me as a temple woman became hot to the touch. Every word he spoke enrobed the air with precious jade. His feet stirred the grass to music. His face appeared in the sky every time I opened my eyes.

I was certain that Hummingbird could read my love and need on my face, but if she did, she never told me. Even my improving skill of the Maya tongue did not give her pause to wonder. Instead, she shouted with delight after an entire day spent speaking in Maya. "If only the High Priestess could hear you! Your skill would delight her."

Now when I spoke, I did so as if my tongue had always favored the rhythm of the Hot Lands. Had the press of Pakal Balam's lips against my body imparted this new mastery? Had he breathed an incantation as powerful as the one that summoned the Vision Serpent to make my speech as fluid sounding as his own?

WORDLESS

The twelfth day began like all the others. In the stillness before dawn, I crawled out and made my way to the river, but Pakal Balam wasn't there. I rose to my feet to search, and suddenly he was standing in front of me, appearing out of the reeds. Before I could smile or whisper his name, he pressed his hand over my mouth and pulled me down into the grasses. The look in his eyes was as cold and slit as a snake's.

What have I done?

Then, I looked down and realized he was ready for battle, for he was dressed in a quilted cotton tunic and jaguar-skin leggings. A wicker shield and obsidian-spiked club sparked on the ground at his feet.

I struggled in his grasp, but his hold tightened. He cupped my chin and drew me closer. He did not speak, and yet his warning came to me, the word slipping into my mind.

RUN.

Over Pakal Balam's shoulder, I saw the painted face of a warrior with strange markings of red and yellow, the headdress adorned with feathers, and the weapon that was about to crash down upon us. The Maya gave me a mighty push. "Run!" he thundered. "Run!"

But I could not move. Terror seized my legs. I watched the strange warrior howl and bring his blade down, cutting Pakal Balam's face and arms. His blood drowned the grasses beneath us.

A high-pitched wail coming from a great distance overwhelmed me, until I felt my throat burning and realized I was the one screaming.

I moved to join Pakal Balam, to help him fight, to save him, but it was as if he had called the wind to come and keep me away from the fighting. A gust lifted me and turned me in the opposite direction. It pushed hard against my back, forcing me to run, unraveling my braid and whipping my garments. I tried to look behind me, but the wind was too strong. Whenever I felt myself trip and start to fall, it would yank me upright again.

The gale finally let me go in a field of reeds. I struggled to catch my breath, staggering through the grasses, my hands grasping at them for support. Visions of Pakal Balam's shattered face played in my mind. Eventually the sound of my blood pounding in my ears was replaced by the biting clash of weapons, cries, and shrieks. I stopped. Listened. It was coming from our camp.

Hummingbird.

Panting, the fear resettling into my bones, I ran back for my sister. I smelled blood, smoke, and burning flesh, but I never caught sight of the camp again, because suddenly three warriors sprouted from the earth in front of me.

Again, I was faced with cruelty and blood, but this time, I understood that there was no walking away. It would be theirs, or it would be mine.

I turned and lunged away. But an arm shot out, grabbed me, and hauled me back. I thrashed in the warrior's grip. *I'll cut you into pieces for this.* He laughed, and they tossed me like a ball from man to man. Their fingers bit into my flesh. Within moments, my captors locked a wooden collar around my neck. My knees buckled beneath its heavy weight. It felt like an entire tree had wrapped itself around me. I clawed at the collar, tried to pull it off, but it held me fast. It was as if the skeleton god himself had come to drag me down to the Underworld.

"Take her!" someone shouted in Nahuatl, my birth tongue. I was prodded by spearpoint and led away from the river and into the jungle, where a swarm of red- and yellow-painted warriors was making camp. Rough hands shoved me into a line with other captives—four women, seven men, and a young boy. I recognized a few of Pakal Balam's men, but as I strained to look, I saw neither Hummingbird nor Pakal Balam among them. I briefly closed my eyes and prayed that my sister had escaped and found refuge in the jungle. Hummingbird was strong and fast; she could take the pyramid's steps two, three at a time. She *had* to be safe.

But this feeling of certainty vanished as soon as my thoughts turned to the last moment I saw Pakal Balam. Where was he? Had he been taken captive, too? My breath was coming in sharp gasps, and my heart was in my throat.

Pakal Balam cannot be dead. This can't be happening.

A light rain was falling, and a humid wind brushed the ferns and palms, so I knew Quetzalcoatl, road sweeper to the god of rain, walked among us. Stiffly, I looked around me. Beneath the fronds of giant ferns, a group of men sat watching us. They were more richly dressed than the merchants of my village, with headdresses sparked by parrot plumes, and mantles that draped the way fine cotton does, in bold colors and patterns. They wore necklaces of gold, jadestone, and coral. Their gold ear spools so heavy, their earlobes brushed their shoulders.

My stomach stirred with uneasiness as one man studied me. He was old, with craggy, sagging skin the color of unpolished mahogany. He was squatting on his heels, puffing on a carved wooden pipe shaped like a parrot. His arms were showered with gold, and a gold labret pierced his lower lip. His eyes wouldn't let go of me, so I did what my namesake would have wanted me to do—I stared back and called upon all of the anger at my core.

I growled beneath my breath. There were twelve of them, along with the twenty warriors I had already counted. Merchants often traveled with armed guards, but why had these men attacked us? And why were we unable to fight them off? We had outnumbered them by more than twenty men. Could a surprise attack be so successful?

The beast that had awakened in the tall forest of reeds burned inside me. *If only I had the sorceress's shield and a good sword with me! If only I had command of her magic and spells . . . knew the charm to release my power . . . I would destroy them. What pleasure—to see this old one run for his life.*

I welcomed the raw edge of my fury, but I could do nothing but stare angrily at the old pipe smoker as he puffed away, watching me. Finally, he turned, elbowed the man seated next to him, and whispered in his ear. This other merchant kidnapper was young, with a great belly and a snout like a possum's. Listening to the old man, this possum creature nodded, then rose to his feet and lumbered toward us. He stopped when he was an arm's length away from me, then reached out and fingered the edge of my huipilli.

"Tell me, girl—how did you come by such lovely clothes? Steal them, did you?"

Steal? I slapped his hand away, alarming everyone around me. His nose flared. Then something caught his eye. So accustomed was I to the blue designs on my skin, I no longer thought about them. The edge of the crescent moon and butterfly must have shown above my collar, for he lunged at me and yanked the blouse down, nearly tearing it apart.

"She has the markings of a Temple woman!" he screamed. "The gods will strike us dead for this."

"Stop fussing!" the old man grumbled. "*She has the markings of a Temple woman*," he parroted in a squeaky voice, waving his hands. "You sound like my wife."

In spite of his years, he jumped to his feet and walked to a pile of cast-off garments that lay on the ground. He pulled two lengths of cloth free, then dropped the rags at my feet.

The gold frog hanging from his lower lip jumped when he spoke. "You will put this on," he commanded.

The blouse and skirt were made of the coarse maguey cloth that marked slaves and commoners. *By the goddess, how dare he?* I gripped the wooden collar, desperate to speak up, but had trouble removing it. As swift as a striking snake, he grabbed my blouse and ripped it from my body, causing me to lose my balance and fall. Angry and ashamed, I released a wail that shook the heavens. Everyone backed away from me then. I struggled to my feet and covered myself as best I could. Just as I stood upright, the old man scooped up a handful of mud and slapped it over the tattoo, knocking me back to the ground.

He crushed the white cloth in his hand. "Temple girl." He snorted, then threw aside the garment and shot a stream of spit after it. "Be sure someone covers the mark with dirt," he ordered the younger man. "They will be afraid to touch her if they know where she is from." The old man leaned down and put his face so close to mine, I could feel the coolness of that gold frog against my skin. "I expect to get a high price for you . . . priestess!"

▲▲▲▲

For four days we walked in a single line, a human chain, through the jungle, our collars secured to a long pole. My cut and blistered feet made every step painful, but I did not falter. Woe to those who could not keep up, or who tripped, because the collar and pole that kept us tethered were unforgiving, dragging you until you could right yourself again.

As the sun set on the second night, I watched my captors eat their fill of the armadillo and deer meat that had been hunted down for their meal. I was sitting, bound to the other captives. Some slept. I could not.

I listened to the rumblings of my neighbors' bellies, smelled the stink of bodies. The woman behind me picked through my braid and eliminated the nest of spiders and other insects that had found happy lodging there. I welcomed her touch. It kept me from crying.

I had overheard someone say the old man was taking us to the market in Xicallanco.

Everyone born on or near the Coatzacoalcos knew of the famous market on the island that sat with the Eastern Sea on one side and freshwater lagoons on the other. It is where the merchants of the Maya and those of the Mexica, Tabascan, Cholulan, and other peoples gather in peace to trade. There is a saying that anything in the world can be bought in Xicallanco for the right price. Cloth as sheer as a sigh with a sparkle to rival the moonlight. Parrots that could recite the story of the Hero Twins or any tale you liked. Concubines skilled at performing the Twenty-Four Arts of Pleasure. Emeralds the size of iguana eggs.

And now I, too, would be traded.

Where once I was the girl with the charmed tongue, now words withered in my throat. The merchants were so entertained by my refusal to talk that they gave me a new name: Wordless.

But what good were words to me now? Could they help me gain back my freedom? Encourage the gods and goddesses to release me? And even if they could, it would not really matter. The people I loved were gone.

I was afraid that if I closed my eyes, I would see my mother or Toci, Hummingbird, or Pakal Balam at the moment he was attacked. I convinced myself that as long as I remained awake, I would be safe. I concentrated on the mumblings of the frightened dreamers around me, the unceasing hum of insects, and the mild murmurs of birds and creatures shifting in their sleep.

Often, I recalled the High Priestess's teachings, and her strength and wisdom restored my spirit. *A priestess of the Temple of the Eighteen Moons observes the stars and knows their names. She studies the eighteen moons. She studies the symbols and painted words and the practices of other temples. She is a light, a flame, a mirror . . .*

I murmured these words to myself nearly constantly. When the old man stuck his nose into my face and yelled at me, I thought of a priestess's courageous heart. And I thought of Malinalxochitl, wondered how she would have used the dark's secrets to destroy this man.

When we stepped out of the jungle, my prison's shadowy green gloom opened up to a blinding light. The heat, bearing down like a crushing mantle, made it hard for me to keep my eyes open. But the fresh air and the crash of the water against white sand awakened something inside me. My breath caught at the sight of the Divine Eastern Sea. Here was a blue as vibrant as my mother's necklace, stretching out far and wide. I stopped to stare, before the pull on my collar forced me to continue walking.

The traders released my collar from the pole and prodded me with their spears to move toward a canoe at the water's edge. Drifts of hot, soft sand gave way to packed wetness that cooled my blistered feet. I stood silent, relieved to be untethered, as the warriors pushed twelve large crafts into the sea. Shrieking seagulls and pelicans circled the sky, competing against the shouts of the traders commanding us into the water. The warriors took care to settle us into the vessels, as a drowned slave was only food for sharks.

▲▲▲▲

With land always in sight, we journeyed south. I knew what awaited me, but for stretches of time, I felt free. There was a sameness to our days, a rhythm that I welcomed. Each morning began with the cries of gulls. Cold corn porridge, which had been mixed with a quantity of chiles, was fed to us at dawn. Then we took our places in the canoes. When the weather was favorable, we traveled by sea until sunset. I never tired of traveling over the water. The freshness of the air, the splashing of the waves, and the freedom of moving unhindered by the pole were all gifts. I slipped my hand into the sea and counted the fish that flashed beside the canoe.

Every day as the sun sank beneath the horizon, the traders pointed their canoes toward the shoreline. Soon we were making camp on the beach. The captives were heavily guarded, as were many large, woven baskets and trunks. These were filled with treasures meant for trade in Xicallanco, their contents unknown to me, though my nose detected the scents of vanilla and copal. The prisoners were also kept a good distance away from the fire that provided the old man and possum-looking creature with light and the means to cook the fish caught at sea.

Each night I huddled with the other prisoners against the chill of the wind off the water. With the sand serving as my bed, a pillow of coconut shells to prop me up so the collar wouldn't pull on my head, I lay awkwardly, but I could still see the stars. I wanted to stay awake and called upon the warrior in me who had defended a grave site to come to my aid. But sleep always overwhelmed me.

Thus, we continued for eight days and seven nights. Our journey came to an end on the day number Three-Death. Turquoise water turned to green, and I saw trees and mangroves rising out of lagoons. When we landed, my little freedom was over. The old man led us to the center of a city framed by temples, and at the foot of the grandest of all divine dwellings, he ordered us into a cage that smelled of animals. It was so small that the only one who did not have to stoop to enter it was the young boy. For two nights, it would be our home.

▲▲▲▲

All day and night, the whispers of the other prisoners brushed against my skin.

"They are going to sell us here. Some of us may be sacrificed."

"Food for the gods," whimpered a girl with dull eyes.

One of the captives, an old woman, let out a feeble sigh. "If no one has use for me, I will die on the sacrificial stone."

"Hush now!" said one of Pakal Balam's men. Just hearing the man's voice, friend to my noble Maya, was enough to send thoughts of him whirling in my mind.

"Look at her." My flea-picker glared at me. "Wordless will make a good slave. Everyone favors the ones who do not speak."

I ignored them. I thought I heard the skeleton god's bones rattling in the shadows. I struggled to put aside the idea that Death himself had come for me. I pulled my knees into my chest and rested my head on my arms.

Were my father's last days like this?

Green pus oozed from my blistered feet where insects had bitten and burrowed their way in. But my arms and legs, back, and breasts did not torment me as much. At the old man's orders, I had been covered with mud and dirt, and the woman ordered to do it was overzealous. I was grateful now. The mud had protected me from the torture of insects, and now it shielded me from the sun that poured in between the cage's poles. My skin was chafed from the coarse cloth I wore, but these were small discomforts in comparison to the pustules that tortured the other captives.

One day my blisters and scars would heal. The bruises around my neck would fade. There would be no sign marking me as someone who had spent time in captivity. But the wounds invisible to the eye would never disappear. The memory of the attack, the cage, the feeling of being trapped and a bony arm's length away from death would haunt me forever. They filled my spirit with an endless rage—the fuel I would burn to fight for my life.

LORD CURL NOSE AND THE ARTS OF PLEASURE

After two days, we were ordered out of the cage and led to a market, which looked like the one in the village of my home. Well-ordered displays of everything from mud bricks and logs to baskets of tomatl and ahuacatl, flint knives, and pots of honey lay arranged on the ground. The old trader pushed me with his cane to step away from the others and stand upon a platform set between a young woman selling monkeys and a boy with caged birds. Then beneath the full glare of the sun, he cried, "Attention, good people! Look here, at this fine offer! A female slave. She is young, strong, with good, healthy teeth. Take a look for yourself." He winked as he stuck his cane beneath the hem of my skirt and lifted it.

A small crowd gathered. A sweaty Maya stuck his fingers into my mouth and tugged my lips this way and that as he studied my teeth. Then others stepped up, men and women. One by one, they turned away, wrinkling their noses. I could not fault them, for I smelled the foulest of odors, strong enough to spoil the air of all of the eighteen heavens.

"Filthy, I grant you," the old trader admitted with a mocking shrug.

"But she will wash up nicely. Attractive she is, beneath the dirt. She would make a fine concubine." He blew a plume of smoke into the air. "Or an extra pair of hands for the wife. To spin cloth, sweep the hearth, cook, and care for the children. Come now. Only two hundred cacao beans for her. A modest sum. I am a reasonable man." The moment the old trader shrugged and claimed that he would accept a lesser amount of cacao beans for my sorry body, a nobleman in a litter chair motioned with his jeweled hand, bringing the sale to a halt. The old trader bowed his head. The nobleman then passed a deerskin pouch to one of his servants, who dropped the jingling bag of beans into the withered man's hands.

With a sharp nod, the old trader hissed at me, "Go now, pathetic creature." A thin trail of spit landed at my feet. "Priestess!" he snarled.

I lifted my skirt and glided around the stream of spittle. The crowd parted for me. But before I took another step, the possum-looking creature and one of the other traders approached me. The fat-bellied oaf was shaking with fear as he unlatched the thick collar around my neck. Free of that chokehold of wood, I became so light that I thought I might rise in the air. Standing straight and tall, I watched him out of the side of my eye, mentally scarring him with the burn of my rage. If only I'd learned to master the sorceress's spells! I would have bludgeoned him to death with that collar. I turned and looked at my fellow captives waiting for their turn. I raised my hand in salute just as one of Pakal Balam's men lifted his.

Not knowing whether strips of white paper would be threaded through my pierced ears to mark me as a future offering to placate a god, I fell in step behind the Maya lord's litter. After weaving our way past green lagoons and streams, we halted at a two-storied palace on the outskirts of Xicallanco. Silently, a young girl led me to a room that overlooked a courtyard, where a ceiba tree grew filled with birds and flowering vines. Two women appeared and immediately turned their attention to my garments. Without a moment's hesitation, they peeled my huipilli and skirt away and kicked them into the courtyard.

An older Maya woman with a flat forehead and crossed eyes oversaw everything. I took account of the fineness of her blue embroidered mantle and skirt. The noblewoman ushered someone forward, a man of middle years who carried the staff and sage leaves of a healer. He appeared not to notice my shameful filth and stench. With quiet eyes and cool fingers, he carefully inspected every inch of my body, even the female parts hidden from view.

After exchanging a few words with the healer, the noblewoman left me in the care of the gentle Maya women. They washed the dirt from me, then led me to a steam bath in an adjoining chamber, where I was massaged head to toe by a woman with fleshy, soothing hands. She took care not to enflame my skin any further. After a shower of warm water, I was pronounced fit enough to lie upon a length of white cloth and rest quietly in the steam.

Despite my gentle treatment, my fear persisted. It was our tradition to bathe slaves before we offered their hearts to the gods. Was this the first of many steps on my way to the sacrificial stone? *Are they going to perfume my skin with copal and marigold oil?* I wondered, as that memory of the young girl flooded my senses.

The garments presented to me did not ease my distress. The huipilli and skirt were a rich blue, like the deepest part of the sea, with shell designs embroidered with gold and silver threads, fit for a goddess or a woman chosen to represent one in sacrifice.

The quiet women dressed me and braided my hair with a length of gold cloth. They brought me food on a tray arranged with delicacies presented on black-and-red plates, but I could not eat. For long minutes I sat staring at the tray as the women watched and waited patiently. Finally, they slipped away. There was nothing to do now but wait for someone to tell me if I would live or die.

▲▲▲▲

The gold light in the courtyard dimmed, and still, I waited. My rage over being kidnapped and traded for a sack of beans simmered, but my fear was stronger. It made me dizzy and sick. I clasped my hands tightly to keep them from shaking. Images infiltrated my mind: my father being thrown into a cage and starving to death; my brother being stalked by a jaguar, the beast licking its lips in hungry anticipation. I saw myself, too, my body flung atop a blood-soaked offering stone, a soot-stained priest standing over me, raising the flint blade that would cut open my chest.

I did not want to die.

No one wants *to die, Malinalxochitl,* went a voice in my head. I ignored it, telling myself that I had to live so that I could find Hummingbird and Pakal Balam. I had to return to the Temple and prepare myself for the day when I would take command of the sorceress's shield. I had to right the wrongs that had been done to my family. A long journey stretched before me, and I could see the path. I could smell the jungles and the forests and mountains and taste the rain and cool streams and snow-laced air. I heard the voices of these places, their cities and people, an angry rush of sounds colliding in my head, never frightening, but sweeping, embracing. *I have to live.*

I collapsed onto the reed mat and cried out for my mother. I wanted her more than I have ever wanted anyone or anything in my life. I wanted to see her running toward me, shouting, "My precious girl! My bracelets of gold!" extending her arms to take me home.

Yet as the light continued to dim, I grew more certain that this was not the time of my death.

▲▲▲▲

It was dark when I heard a voice.

"Hush now, you must not cry."

Cool fingers were smoothing back my wet hair, touching my cheek. For a moment I allowed myself to believe that my mother *had* come for me. It sounded like her—that deep and pleasing voice, the soothing words. I turned into her touch, wanting more, until I realized her speech was laced with the golden cadence of the Maya.

I sat up with a start and found myself looking into the face of a young woman. Even in the shadows, in the pale light filtering in from outside, I could see she was beautiful.

"My name is Resplendent Quetzal, my lord Curl Nose's fourth concubine," she said. "You have been chosen for the flowery mat."

I breathed out with relief. At least my body would not be impaled on the pyramid by morning, bleeding vitality for everyone's sport. But I was still unsettled. *The flowery mat?*

I opened my mouth, but no sounds came. As I clenched my hands in frustration, I felt fresh tears wetting my eyes.

Seeing my distress, Resplendent Quetzal became distraught. "Oh, you must not worry, lest lines mark your brow and detract from your beauty. Our lord would be most unhappy to see deep furrows here," she said, smoothing my brow with her fingertips.

I looked closely. There was an air of honest authority to her gaze.

"You are most fortunate to live in the house of Lord Curl Nose. It has come to my lord's attention that in a former time, you lived as a priestess." The woman delicately patted her skin above her right breast. "You bear the markings of the Temple of the Eighteen Moons. The priestesses of that sacred place are much admired in our lands. My lord is much pleased with this and will desire that you continue your studies, for he holds wisdom in high esteem. But for now"—she paused and took my hands in hers—"your only task will be to learn the Twenty-Four Arts of Pleasure. It will be my duty to instruct you in the ways of a concubine."

I stared at her in shock. I was relieved that my life had been spared, but to now spend my days locked away? I was no man's plaything designed for his pleasure! My mother and father did not raise me for this!

I sat stunned, reeling with humiliation and anguish. Resplendent Quetzal placed her hand lightly on my shoulder. Compassion and a kind of understanding filled her dark eyes. For a moment I thought she knew how I felt. Then she hurried from the room, and I sat there, feeling wave upon wave of shame.

I remembered that Rose Petal had been a concubine and had lived in Tenochtitlan's House of Joy. Only now did I understand how frightened she must have been, why she had tried to teach me "a language art never discussed at the Temple." She had been warning me about what might await me out in the world. "Survival is everything," she'd said to me. She talked of "placating men" and things like feigning a docile appearance, complimenting constantly, marveling at their strength and wittiness. I had thought her mad. She had whispered a head-spinning list of behaviors and "feminine forces" that I needed to tuck away in my mind, just in case. And here I was, no longer free. My fortunes had changed, so now I had to change. Or die.

You will try to find a way to escape, at least at first, until you realize how far away you are, how little you know. Then you adapt to feeling numb, went Rose Petal's voice in my head. I clung to her words. And as the air cooled, and the dark deepened in the courtyard, I drew strength from them. I told myself that if Rose Petal could survive such a life, then so could Malinalxochitl. Perhaps Lord Curl Nose, like Rose Petal's patron, would set me free. Or maybe . . . one day . . . I would find a way to free myself.

▲▲▲▲

Who was this man I was destined to join on the flowery mat?

At my first quick, panicked meeting with him, I learned that Lord Curl Nose was a Maya merchant prince. Looks could be deceiving, but he appeared quite tame. Along with bulging eyes and fleshy lips, he had a nose shaped like a lavish gourd that had seen too much sun and rain and cultivated in earth far too rich and dark.

The first time he said my name aloud, we were sitting in the shade of the great ceiba tree that grew in a courtyard, and the sun was just beginning to bid farewell to the sky. The lord was dressed in a cape and breechcloths of blue woven cotton embellished with shells. Like most noblemen, he wore a towering head wrap of cloth and had a fondness for jewels. Strands of gold and turquoise beads hung around his neck and wrists. He had a nose plug of amber, inside of which I could see small bugs and leaves. A belt of jaguar skin set with crocodile teeth engulfed his small belly.

There I was, a girl of fifteen years, air pouring over me as his servants waved their feathered fans, newly bathed and perfumed with oils I didn't recognize, my body perched, as if I knew all the world's secrets.

"And what is your name, lovely one?" Curl Nose said.

I hesitated. My name might frighten him.

Tell him it is Wordless, a voice in my mind laughed. I shivered, recalling the old slave trader. Lord Curl Nose must have thought I was suffering from a chill, for he motioned to stop the fans. It was such a simple request. I knotted my hands together, suddenly angry. Why had the goddess not protected me? The High Priestess promised that the Temple's markings would keep me safe. And yet here I sat. Perhaps my mother was wrong. I could not evade my fate by adopting the name of a goddess. It was time to come to terms with the destiny the gods had written for me before I was born. I was alone now . . . I was just Malinalli.

"Malinalli is my name," I said finally, lifting my chin, wondering if he'd shrink from a cursed woman. Would he recognize my fate and sell me off?

"Malinalli," he said with a simple nod. He locked me in his gaze, and

I saw in his eyes a flicker of recognition. I braced myself, but he simply called to hear music.

A voice laughed cruelly in my mind. *Your curse is his blessing.*

The flute player answered with a low and beautiful sound that climbed through the silence.

As servants lighted torches, I listened to Curl Nose speak about his lands and his accomplishments. His wealth came from trade in honey, pottery, minerals used in the creation of pigments for paints and dyes, cacao and copper bells. But what made him rich beyond imagining was salt. On vast coastal lands near the port of Emal, following a tradition set by the gods, pools of salt water were enclosed, then allowed to evaporate. Lord Curl Nose held great leagues of these saltpans in his name and traded the purest grains throughout the land between the two seas.

"Even that rascal Moctezuma kisses the earth in praise of my salt," he admitted after looking about to make certain no one was listening.

Moctezuma? Hearing his name set my bones on fire. I struggled to keep my face calm.

Unaware that the name meant something to me, Lord Curl Nose continued to describe his land, speaking Nahuatl so that I could understand him more easily. I nodded courteously, changing my position slightly to mask the distress I felt building inside. Moctezuma. It surprised me a little that I could still hate him so much after all this time.

Curl Nose kept talking, and I was grateful for his chatter. I smiled now and then, but I could tell from the little furrows deepening his brow and the concern in his gaze that he thought something might be wrong. I didn't want to dwell on Tenochtitlan and anything linked to that city, so I followed his words, a lifeline out of my thoughts.

Curl Nose's courteous manner and gentleness calmed me. I was interested to hear that he excelled in languages. He spoke Nahuatl, Chontal, and Yucatecan Maya and was familiar with the Mixteca and Olmeca tongues. He enjoyed discussing a variety of subjects. In the next days, I would often wonder if he had been born on the day we call One-Wind, for such persons are known to have great minds.

Before leaving, he clapped his hands, and an enormous birdcage was set in front of me. "I present . . . Balché!" Perched inside on a tree limb was a parrot, a boisterous fellow who flapped his crimson wings, squawking, "Curl Nose loves me. Curl Nose loves me." There was a part of me that wanted to laugh. And I could tell by the imploring look on Curl Nose's face—a vulnerable need to please—and by the showy antics of the parrot, that man and bird were performing with the aim of dispelling some of my fear and unease. But I couldn't give in to that part of myself.

In a way, that girl was already dead.

▲▲▲▲

Pleasures of the flesh sweetened a fragile existence in a hard and cruel world where at any moment a god might decide to end your days. My mother never talked about this or the attentions between a man and a woman. I had heard my parents in the night. The Temple's priestesses had created a powder to increase Lady Six Sky's husband's potency. But I truly had not understood what *might* take place on the flowery mat until I met my noble Maya, Pakal Balam.

Now here I was, learning how to master this craft. It was not a very respectable course of examination, but did Feathered Butterfly not teach the priestesses to study "the practices of other temples"? Perhaps I could approach the Twenty-Four Arts the way a conscientious student might learn a lesson. What was the harm in learning to survive? If I might return to the Temple? Rose Petal had said it plainly, "Survival is everything."

Lessons took place at the hour of day when the fountain in the garden sat in a bit of shadow, in a room that adjoined mine, decorated with mounds of soft pillows, jaguar-skin carpets, and clouds of curtains that rippled in the breeze. The walls were painted with murals of a forest, where figures of men and women performed sexual acts while leaning against trees, lying on the ground, even suspended in the air.

Resplendent Quetzal explained that, according to the Arts of Pleasure, there were six kinds of kisses. Judging by the modest way she held her hands clasped in front of her, a solemn look on her face, she could have been talking about stomach ailments.

"There is the Soft Kiss, the Exchange of Breaths, and the Touching Kiss, where you use the tip of your tongue to explore Curl Nose's mouth. To incite passion," she continued, "there is the Pressing Kiss That Knows No Limit and the Fiery War of Tongues. There is even a kiss to tease. For this, the concubine turns away and leans back, like so"—she demonstrated, tilting away and lifting her chin—"to present her mouth to her master." She stayed in the position until I nodded in understanding.

"Good." She faced me calmly. "To feather someone is to give a great variety of these kisses. There is no proper sequence. It is up to you to determine the appropriate course of action."

I nodded again, though in truth, I was feeling a little overwhelmed. But this was a small, trifling thing compared to what came next. Resplendent Quetzal told me how a woman wise in the Arts uses her fingertips and nails to bring about pleasure. Then she ordered me onto my back, and with the softest breezes parting the curtains, she gently traced her fingertips up and down my body, setting jolts into my skin. I discovered that the places most eager to be pressed are the stomach, thighs, breasts, throat, and waist.

After reviewing the power of my sense of touch, instruction in the mating positions began in earnest. There were standing poses and arts less taxing, some so powerful that Resplendent Quetzal claimed they could rule even the most arrogant and selfish of men. After a few days of Captured Butterflies and the Cascade of Flower Petals, I was relieved when she returned to lessons regarding the kiss. In case I had forgotten, each one was explained to me again and demonstrated for me by Resplendent Quetzal. A woman had never kissed me in this manner before. It was lush, a different sensation entirely from Pakal Balam. More soothing and less insistent. A caressing wind compared to my noble Maya's piercing blaze. It had been a long time since I had been embraced. It was comforting to feel held, gently, in someone's arms again.

CONCUBINE

After my daily lessons in the Arts of Pleasure, I would return to my courtyard and sit beneath the ceiba tree. There I was free to study picture writing, astronomy, the Chontal and Yucatecan Mayan languages, and other diverse subjects with the most illustrious teachers in that region. But when the sun was at its fiercest, drawing the air up in shimmering waves, I was alone. As a new concubine, I was not permitted to meet with the other women.

The parrot was my closest companion—until the eagle appeared. Balché spotted it first, calling out, "The thunder rolls, the waters rise" to get my attention. From that point forward, it circled often. I spent my time praying to Feathered Butterfly, practicing my picture writing, keeping up my fighting skills—always pretending I was facing more owl priests—and thinking. This last activity I often did with a broom in my hand. Sweeping was a balm to my spirit because it created order out of mayhem and dirt. I could have left this chore to the servants, but a good broom made me feel at home in the world. It rooted me to my mother and village, to the place of my birth, and the Temple of the Eighteen Moons, home of my enlightenment. Lord Curl Nose was much dismayed to learn of my devotion to freshly swept floors—none of his women had touched a broom in many years—but after I assured him that I enjoyed it, he fashioned a special broom for me of mahogany. It was carved and painted with flowers and vines, with bristles of fresh straw and brush latticed with sweet-smelling herbs.

The knobby roots of the giant tree that sheltered me spread along the ground, clutching the earth like claws. Because of my studies at the Temple, and my parents' teachings, I knew that trees—like all living things in our world—possessed spirits and souls, a life beyond what was visible to the eye. This giant felt solid and sure against my back and beneath my hands, and I knew it held secrets. The Maya believed that a great ceiba united the twenty-two levels that made up the Heavens, the Earth, and the Underworld, and that the trunk served as a passage for magicians to travel in and out of these worlds. This tree was as fissured as an old man's face, and I found myself staring at it for long spells, waiting for a human shape to appear.

▲▲▲▲

After a fortune teller divined that the rains were destined to fall early, all of the members of Lord Curl Nose's household moved to his estate in Potonchan.

The travelers included Curl Nose's five wives and seven concubines—each of us borne aloft in a litter chair—and thirty servants, some holding large fans, others with musical instruments to entertain Lord Curl Nose. In addition, there were forty guards and one hundred porters bearing willow baskets filled with plain and embroidered cloth, looms and spindles, clothes and jewels, fifty of Lord Curl Nose's favorite headdresses, and provisions for our journey.

Like a giant snake, we wove our way. *How easy would it be to escape to freedom?* I wondered. But the treetops were so vast, I could not see even a sliver of sky. I had no idea where I was. Clouds of humid air moved like an army of ghosts. And when swamps and lagoons barred us, we took to the water in canoes. Mangroves sheltered us when we camped, and we ate, talked, and slept to the sound of fans and feathered whips beating the air to keep the mosquitoes away.

This journey was very different from the one I had spent in the company of the slave traders. I traveled supported in a cushioned chair. I was surrounded by people whose sole purpose was to fan the air and shade me from the sun. I was never beaten for looking up from the ground; my hungry eyes scoured every new town for Hummingbird, Pakal Balam, or any of my sisters. But Lord Curl Nose never admonished my quiet searching. He treated me as if I had been royally born.

Potonchan sat on a river. Its homes were made of mud bricks that had been whitewashed with lime, and they stood on wooden legs. Already I could spy wooden footbridges set up around the temple precinct in anticipation of the coming floods.

Lord Curl Nose leaned as close as our chairs would allow and told me about a merchant whose house had a marvelous fresco of cranes and flowers that I must see. How every spring the trees on his estate sprouted lavishly petaled blooms. That the lovely little fish in the streams were especially delicious when prepared with tomatl and chilli and the tender meat of frogs. I heard his joy that Potonchan would now be my new home.

▲▲▲▲

On the night when I turned sixteen and was able to see the figure of a rabbit on the full face of the moon, I joined Lord Curl Nose on his flowery mat. When he held out a gold chocolatl cup, I raised it to my lips, closed my eyes, and drank deeply. Chocolatl was known to stir the passions.

Quietly, we drank. When he set down the cup, I removed my garments with great care, for I had been told that the goddess Ix Chel—

the Maya's patron of all weavers and embroiderers—had embroidered them. Then, to the sound of a light rain falling on the earth outside his rooms and on the palms that grew there, I released the scallop shell that symbolized my purity from the gold cord around my waist.

My body was no longer my own.

STORIES OUT OF AIR

Women gather around children, food, and cloth. It is our way, and Lord Curl Nose's household was no different. I had little success preparing meals that were edible, but when it came to the creation of cloth, the goddesses had blessed me with talent. In my first year with the Maya, however, before I could officially take my place in the blue chamber with the magnificent courtyard that was used for clothmaking, I had to prove my artistry as an embroiderer and weaver of cloth. Now that I was officially able to be with other women, the first one I had to win over was Lady First Wife, Crescent Moon.

Crescent Moon was tall for a woman from these lands, and when she wore the lavish headdresses of wound cloth and feathers that she was fond of, she stood nearly as high as a Maya basalt carving. Fine scars pricked the skin around her mouth, a mark of beauty that was much admired. Her eyes were crossed, like all noblewomen's, and as gold as the honey produced by the bees on her lands.

The skill that finally captured Lady First Wife's approval was not so much artistic as it was magical. On a steamy day, as beads of sweat were falling into my eyes and dripping onto the cloth, dampening the edges, a bee I had been embroidering flitted its wings and, with a rushing humming sound, twirled out of the cloth. The twenty women who were gathered around me, sewing and weaving cloth, shouted. Lady First Wife jumped to her feet. Silently, we watched the creature zig and zag its way around the flowers that were in bloom throughout the deep blue courtyard, its loose orange and yellow threads floating in its wake. After many heartbeats, it circled back to me and took its rightful place in the cloth.

Emboldened, I began to speak. This raised more than a few eyebrows as, up until now, I had never shared more than a complimentary observation about the weather. While the threads beneath my fingertips continued to pulse with life, I said, "As a priestess, I have studied the eighteen moons; I know the sky and the stars, and can call them by name." As I started to reveal my learnings, my heart filled with life! For the first time since I'd been traded for a sack of cacao beads, I felt free.

When those twenty shocked faces softened, and Lady First Wife resumed her seat in her willow branch chair, I picked up my story and told them about the teachings of Feathered Butterfly. Long ago, Rose Petal had told me that a good story could be a lifeline—a way to root you to times past, even the future. I had been too young to fully understand, but now I could see, and feel, the wisdom of her words.

Feathered Butterfly's lessons came easily. It was as if I had been speaking about the goddess since the day I first learned to talk. I moved my hands the way my mother and Rose Petal had when they wanted to bring graceful emphasis to phrases. The needles and looms fell silent. The sun approached its zenith, and still I went on. Once I had finished, the women began to talk all at once, asking for more. Their bodies turned to me, angled like flowers toward the light, encouraging me to tell them everything about the Temple and my life there. Their reaction led me to wonder if I could call this place my home. *Perhaps I could learn to be comfortable here? Live happily with these women?*

So, over the following days, which turned into months, then years, I spun my past into stories about the Temple of the Eighteen Moons, the

High Priestess, Rose Petal, Morning Star, and Jeweled Laughter, each telling seducing me into thinking I was becoming less dependent on hopes I would get a chance to return.

The Maya were a gossipy group, with a few whiners, but they were good listeners, and they brought me news about oddities they'd noticed at the marketplace, as I was rarely permitted to leave the palace. They were much intrigued by my tattoo and the ritual surrounding its creation. When I told them about the time I spent guarding a grave site, they turned white as gardenia blossoms, chewed their fingernails, and shrieked when the suspense became too much for them to bear.

Each day I looked forward to telling my stories. But in my three years with the Maya, I never spoke about the secret shrine or the shield, the journey down the river, or uttered the names Pakal Balam and Hummingbird. One word would have loosened all my tears.

▲▲▲▲

Life changes: I was on the cusp of nearly accepting this and my new existence, when signs appeared to warn me that the world I knew was about to be torn apart. It was there in the icy shift in the wind that struck my cheek when I was sitting under my ceiba tree. Obvious when an owl crossed my path during a walk to the marketplace. On the day called One-House, a fiery blaze shaped like an ear of corn appeared in the eastern sky. Lord Curl Nose assured us that it meant nothing, but his sorcerers believed otherwise. I distinctly recalled the High Priestess saying to me, "The earth and sky, stars and moon, beasts large and small will show the truth of things." Although I was the only one who was not frightened, the sight troubled me. To be honest, it excited me a little, too. I wondered if it might be related to another strange occurrence that I had recently witnessed.

The next morning, after a sleepless night, all of the women drooped over their looms and embroidery. The lady and I were embroidering a length of yellow cloth, but that morning, even I couldn't work. My hands were like wet clay. I was peering closely at my stitches when one of the women came running into the courtyard.

"Floating mountains have been sighted on the sea," she cried.

At the sound of those words, all of the women turned and looked at me, for one of my stories was about the night my sister priestesses and I looked for these strange apparitions in the Book of Maps.

I could not even open my mouth to speak.

Then it is *true. It is not magic. The floating mountains exist.*

I rose to my feet, clutching my embroidery to my chest. Alarmed by the look on my face, Resplendent Quetzal set her loom aside. "What is it? Tell us, Malinalli. What does this mean?"

"Yes, tell us," Lady First Wife said. "I recall it was a delightful story, the Book of Maps."

I looked from face to face, saw the excitement in Lady First Wife's eyes, the fear in Resplendent Quetzal's.

"I do not know," I said.

But Balché had a different opinion. "They have arrived!" the parrot cried. "They are here."

TWO CUPS OF CHOCOLATL

I was pacing in my chamber, wondering about the appearance of the strange floating mountains, listening to the birds in the ceiba tree, when Resplendent Quetzal rushed in and announced, "Lady Six Sky is here—" and in the next heartbeat, the world outside the palace's walls came crashing in.

Lady Six Sky. Pakal Balam's sister. For a moment, the room was a blur, the wall of clay beside me seeming to cave in as I leaned on it for support.

Could he be here with her? Or any of my sisters?

"Our lord and lady's noble friend from Mayapan has arrived," Resplendent Quetzal continued, oblivious to my inner turmoil. "She will be joining us for the ceremony." The bold sun shining with orange heat had announced that it was time to honor the fertility of the earth and the ripening corn.

Will I see his face again?

"You must attend the ritual for the goddess Yum Kax. You are expected."

In my haste to get ready, I forgot to wash the ink from my hands and remove the brushes and paint quills I had stuck into my braid. Silently, I followed Resplendent Quetzal through the corridors, willing my feet not to run.

The sound of chanting and the aroma of incense greeted me before I stepped into the room and saw Lady First Wife and Lord Curl Nose, the wives and concubines, and Lady Six Sky's people. My knees trembled, but I pressed on into the crowded room painted yellow to honor both sun and corn.

The smoke burned my eyes. Chanting softly, I pored over and between every living creature in the room, hoping to catch sight of Lady Six Sky. But all I could see were warriors wearing green mantles embroidered with thunderbolts.

They stood still as statues. I felt my tattoo prickle as I waited for one of them to move. I blinked and looked away. The sensation passed. I looked again, peering around shoulders, but the warriors had shifted in their places. Now all I could see was a woman looking at me over a spray of pink feathers. As I met her gaze, her eyes grew wide.

My heart caught in my throat.

It can't be!

As her name leaped to my lips, Hummingbird lowered her fan and smiled.

▲▲▲▲

Later that day, I found myself in Lady First Wife's chamber, standing before her and her guests—Lady Six Sky and Hummingbird. Hummingbird's dark hair flowed down her back in a single braid, a red flower tied at the end. A white embroidered bracelet encircled her wrist. Resplendent Quetzal was kneeling quietly beside me, her hands cupped in her lap.

It took all of my strength to remain calm, to fight the tears brimming at the sight of her beautiful face, the bright dahlia shining in her hair.

I longed to take my sister's hand and run with her to my chamber, where I could finally share the thoughts that outran my spirit.

"So, this is the woman you spoke of, Hummingbird?" said Lady Six Sky. "The priestess who was with you on the journey?" Her voice boomed with the rumble of thunder. She was a small woman of ample hips and wore a collar of jade beads and wrist cuffs of gold. Her headdress was fashioned with gauze wings that swayed from side to side as she cooled herself with a spray of flamingo feathers. She tilted her head and examined me. Her stare lingered on the brushes I had stuck in my hair and at my stained fingers. I gripped my hands behind my back, ashamed at myself for having been so careless.

Hummingbird nodded, her eyes locked onto mine, as if to share a secret message. *Stay calm. Wait.* "Yes, noble lady. This is Malinalxochitl, my sister priestess from the Temple of the Eighteen Moons."

"The woman the eagle seeks? The woman who knows about the floating mountains?"

Another shock wave ripped through me as I willed myself to stand still, my hands fluttering back to my sides.

"Perhaps it is not me," I whispered, shooting a look at Hummingbird. "I now use the name Malinalli."

"I see." Lady Six Sky leaned back against the pillows, her eyes troubled.

Why are we talking about the High Priestess's vision? Is Pakal Balam alive?

"Our priests say that the floating mountains are a sign that the god Kukulkan will return to us soon," Pakal Balam's sister explained.

The Maya's white god, who sailed away from these lands on a raft of snakes?

Disregarding her hostess's surprise, Lady Six Sky continued. "Malinalxoch . . . eh, Malinalli? Hummingbird has told me that you spoke of this strange sight at the Temple. Could this be a sign from the god Kukulkan?"

I looked into the noblewoman's face, at the pricked tattoos marking her high cheekbones. Her eyes were the same chocolate brown, the lilt of her accent the mirror of her brother's. My body ached for Pakal Balam.

I was silent.

Lady Six Sky pressed on. "Tell us, what did the High Priestess make of these mountains?"

I focused and took command of my voice. The memory was clear. "The High Priestess did not know what they were. But Morning Star believed the floating mountains were created by men. She didn't think they were the result of some kind of magic or the work of a god or goddess."

Lady Six Sky leaned toward her hostess. "You see, it was my brother, Pakal Balam, who informed the High Priestess of the Temple of the Eighteen Moons of these mountains. These two priestesses," she said with a slight nod, "were journeying with my brother to my home to accompany me to Ah-Cuzamil-Peten and the shrine to Ix Chel, when their party was attacked."

Lady First Wife threw her arms up with such force that she startled Lady Six Sky, who jumped and catapulted her fan of pink feathers into the air. "Goddess in heaven, Malinalli! But why have you never spoken of this?" Lady First Wife said. A deep furrow appeared between her brows.

I looked down at my hands, at my fingers moving in the air as if embroidering cloth. What could I say? That the slave traders had handled me as if my body didn't matter? That no one had ever asked me what had happened?

Lady First Wife continued, sadness marking her voice. "All of your stories . . . but no mention of—"

It pained me to see everyone upset, but I never intended to tell the wife of my owner the entire truth of things.

"If I may, esteemed lady," Hummingbird interrupted. She rose to her feet then and came to me. She took my hands in hers, and at her touch, I felt my spirit lift, as if I were meditating at the temple and had learned how to float. I wanted to drift back to Pakal Balam, the Temple, and the world my sisters and I had built without men. Hummingbird turned to the noblewoman and said, "I have done all in my power to forget that fateful day on the river." She looked at me. "I believe Mali . . . nalli has tried to do the same."

"I feel that a great deal is about to change," Lady Six Sky pronounced. "It is a matter best left to the gods. But of one thing I am certain—I rejoice to meet you, Malinalli."

When I raised my eyes to her, she smiled.

"It was on my account that you left the safety of the Temple," she said. "And I am sorry for all that you have suffered because of me." She paused. "Sorry for us all."

Tears filled the lady's eyes, and in that moment, I understood. My heart flooded. The noble Maya Pakal Balam was dead.

A benevolent nod from Lady First Wife was my signal to take my leave. I calmly led Hummingbird away, and when I knew no one was looking, I grabbed her hand, and we ran through the corridors back to my chamber. My tears flowed freely as I took her into my arms.

It was curious, but for the next minutes, we just stared at each other and said nothing. All my thoughts were a jumble. Where to start? I was afraid; perhaps it would not be so easy to speak as friends again. And I think I was ashamed because I had failed to protect her. But I need not have feared, for she gave me that classic Hummingbird all-knowing head tilted to the side, dark-eyes-studying-me stare, and I knew everything would be all right. *My sister is here.*

She noticed right away the strange sounds coming from a set of willow trunks pushed up against the lime-washed wall. "What is that? It sounds like cloth coming undone." She moved closer to investigate.

"I know, it's strange. It started a little while ago," I answered, steering her away, "and I'll tell you soon. But for now"—I gestured to towers of pillows arranged in the courtyard—"come sit with me. I want to know what happened."

"What are you hiding? Why are you calling yourself Malinalli?" she stated simply, eyes keen on me as I strolled into my courtyard and did my casual best to plump a pillow.

There was so much I wanted to tell her. I felt dizzy, off center. Her attention latched on Balché as he showily flitted about in the trees, before resting her gaze on the shrine I had created to honor Feathered Butterfly.

After murmuring a short prayer, she said, "It's pretty here, but I know this hasn't been easy for you." It was so personal that I flushed.

"No," I answered tersely and to the point. I knew she genuinely cared and was worried about me, but I was ready to go back to that day on the river. I gestured to a cozy spot beneath the ceiba tree. "Tell me everything."

As she curled up on a pillow, I got a closer look at the carved box she had been carrying with her. It looked like I wasn't the only one with a secret.

▲▲▲▲

I'd been wrong: I wasn't ready to go back to that day on the river. All she needed to say was "Our last morning, when I awoke to find you and Pakal Balam gone . . ." With that, the air shattered. I attempted to smile and encouraged her to continue, which she did, dropping her gaze.

"I had not walked very far before the world erupted into fire," she said. "It all happened so quickly . . . I would have died instantly had I not gone to look for you, because our dwelling was set with flames. And I saw men with red and yellow markings, feathers cresting their heads, sweeping through the camp, throwing torch sticks as they attacked. I ran to warn you," she exclaimed with wide eyes, "but when I reached the grasses, a monster swooped down and threw me over his shoulder. I screamed, but all was crashing thunder, yells and drumbeats so loud . . . How could anyone hear me?" She nodded vigorously. "So I hit him! With my fists and feet. He dropped me then. As I gasped for air, he turned to me and lifted his weapon." She drew her arm back to show me and swiped the air with a vicious strike. "But he missed! He roared and reached to grab me, but I bit his hand. Harrrrrgh," she growled with a shake of her head, mimicking tearing a tough piece of armadillo flesh. "Suddenly, I became filled with the goddess's power, for I scrambled to my feet and escaped into the jungle."

For a moment I saw the warrior-priestess who had carried a sword and shield. How brave she was!

I studied my sister intently, soaking in her words, feeling my heart rise and fall as her tale spun on.

"I ran until all I could hear was the sound of my blood pounding in my ears. I stopped in a grove of trees, chose one with low-hanging boughs, and climbed it. Only then did I rest and allow myself to cry.

"I did not know whether you were alive or—" She swallowed and glanced away. "I prayed to Feathered Butterfly, to Chac and Feathered Serpent. Asked all our gods and goddesses to protect you." Hummingbird looked at me, hesitant. "I was not alone."

I held my breath.

"One of Pakal Balam's men, his right arm cut and torn, entered my little forest. Then another. Then three others." I bit my lip as I tried to keep my disappointment hidden. "I did not need to ask what had befallen you. The man who used to bring us treasures, do you recall him?"

I swallowed hard and forced myself to remember the man she was speaking of. "Yes," I answered as a shadowy figure rose in my mind. *I think he believed I was the sorceress-goddess Malinalxochitl.* My heart lifted a little, remembering. But my body thrummed with nervous energy being fed by her harrowing tale and my wish to hear about my Maya.

"He claimed that one of the attackers had captured you. He saw the eagle circle and fly out over the grasses, following the river east. He told me it was a sign that you still lived."

The light was fading, and yet I could see that her face brightened a little as she spoke.

"Four days later, we walked out of the jungle and saw the sea. How the goddess smiled on us that day! After so much darkness and green shadows, the water brought such relief."

I nodded, for I remembered the water, too. I clung to the image: a turquoise as deep in color as my mother's necklace. Hummingbird went on to praise the men's skills, their ability, with their few weapons, to fell a tree and make a canoe out of it. Their journey by water was fraught with peril in the form of sharks, fog, and fierce storms. "But our prayers were answered, and we prevailed," she said, lifting her arm in triumph.

But after telling me this, she sagged a little, as if the gesture had suddenly drained her of energy. She looked across the garden. Someone had come to light the torches in my chamber, as well as one in the courtyard, and the light spilled over us. Hummingbird was watching Balché as he tried to crack the hull of a seed. Then I noticed it was not Balché she was studying, but something in the distance.

I let her be. Together, we sat quietly.

After a while, Hummingbird broke the silence and continued her story. "The last day, there was such a sudden rising of wind and water that I was sure we were about to die. But it turned out to be a blessing, for it brought us closer to Mayapan. The husband of Lady Six Sky found us clinging to life at the water's edge.

"I told that esteemed lady what had happened, Mali." She continued. "And I told her stories about you," she added with more enthusiasm. "How gifted you were with needle and thread. The way you came to Jeweled Laughter's aid and helped to destroy the owl priest."

My eyes spoke to her directly: *But I failed to protect you.*

Hummingbird shook her head vigorously and looked away. "Lady Six Sky treated me kindly, and I grew to love my new home in Mayapan. Then two months ago, an eagle appeared." Her eyes made their way back to mine. "The bird was a noisy creature. The first time I saw him I thought nothing of it. But it kept returning," she said with a tilt of her head. "Days went by before I realized the eagle was the same one that used to fly above the temple, watching you." She leaned toward me. "I knew that he would lead me to you."

I leaned forward, too, mirroring her pose. "We must thank the cagle the next time we see it."

She smiled, though her mood changed to one of great seriousness. "But no one believed me!" She sat back. "Not Lady Six Sky, her husband, the nobles, and especially not the priests. But over time, the lady came to agree with me. Quietly, she planned our journey, and in the end, our numbers grew to include twenty, and more runners were charged with taking daily messages about our progress to her husband. By tomorrow morning, he will know that we are safe in Potonchan, and that I have been reunited with my sister priestess," she said, firmly clasping her hands in her lap.

I tried not to let my doubts steer me away from sharing my story. "My soul feels full," I said, tears in the back of my throat. "You are safe, and we are together again. Perhaps I can tell you what happened to me another time?"

I couldn't continue, until Hummingbird moved closer and took my hand. The softness in her eyes, and her touch, quickened the waters I'd been holding back for months. "Tell me now." And with that, the dam broke.

I spared nothing. I did not falter or try to paint a brighter picture of what had happened. I told her why I no longer felt the power and presence of the goddess and that I could not evoke Malinalxochitl's name. As I spoke, I felt as if a great stone were being lifted off my heart.

▲▲▲▲

It was late when we moved inside to my chamber. The sight of it aglow, arranged with freshly plumped cushions, filled me with quiet happiness. A servant entered bearing a tray with a pot for the making of chocolatl, a delicate red-and-black pitcher, and two cups. Silently, we watched the girl pour the chocolate from the pot into the pitcher at her feet to create a thick froth. Alone once the chocolatl-maker left, Hummingbird and I were two young girls again, sharing our thoughts, telling stories.

Not until our voices were raw from talking did Hummingbird pick up the carved box and open it. I blinked and wiped my eyes, thinking at first that the drink must have affected my mind, for I saw within the folds of yellow cloth my jaguar pouch, with my mother's turquoise necklace and the Book of Maps.

I pulled the pouch to my face and breathed deeply. I smelled copal, marigolds, and a touch of smoke. Traces of home. We would never be separated again, if I could help it.

▲▲▲▲

After stretching the strap of the pouch across my body and draping the necklace around my neck, I took the book into the garden and opened it on top of the yellow mantle. With the light of the moon and a small torch guiding us, Hummingbird and I unfolded the pages until we found the map the High Priestess at the Temple of the Eighteen Moons had studied in the hope of seeing the floating mountains.

Our wait was not long. The mysterious apparitions appeared on the Eastern Sea, blowing back and forth in an invisible wind. I listened to the sound of waves and rolling surf, but this was not as strange as the voices rising from the map. I heard men shouting in a strange tongue. Who were they?

One by one, as the floating mountains touched the painted shore, they disappeared. Eleven times we watched this occur, and when the last mountain vanished, we sat back and looked at each other.

Were they coming to fight a war? I nervously ran my mother's turquoise beads through my fingers. "I think they will be here soon," I said.

"Here?" Hummingbird shuddered.

I nodded and pointed to the place on the map where the images had disappeared, not far from the mark where we were. Hummingbird leaned forward to peer more closely at it.

"In the morning, I will tell Lord Curl Nose. Something must be done," I said.

"I have more news—" Hummingbird piped up anxiously.

"As do I," I interrupted. "I need to show you something," I said, jumping to my feet. I returned to my chamber and the set of willow trunks. Impatient, I gestured for her to follow me. "Come and look inside," I directed as I removed their lids. And as the odd sound we'd heard before circled the air freely, at first faint, then with more intensity, Hummingbird peered inside the closest trunk.

"Mother Goddess!" She pressed a hand to her chest and stepped back. But then she took another peek, as if she couldn't resist. "All of the embroidery work is coming to life."

I looked over her shoulder, nonchalantly noting what I'd been experiencing for the past weeks—the stars, flowers, rabbits, butterflies, and snakes, the clouds and moonbeams, stepped patterns and zigzags, *all* of the threads I had stitched were moving freely. There was a slight popping and an occasional unpuckering slither, sounds individual stitches make when they're being pulled out of cloth. Hummingbird watched a long vine twirl right in front of her nose.

She rose abruptly to stand straight. Her gaze flew across all of the baskets. "I take it that this is all your handiwork?"

"Oh yes." I nodded. "Apart from telling stories, nothing gives me as much satisfaction and sense of purpose as my needlework," I explained as I allowed a snail to inch along my outstretched finger.

She raised an eyebrow. "But don't you usually have to touch the stitches, focus your attention"—she twirled her fingers—"or something like that, to get them to move?"

I nodded again, smiling at the pink creature's opalescent shell. I had used special threads, made from bird feathers, gifted to me by Lady First Wife.

"But not now?" she cried shrilly. "You don't have to do that now?"

"You mean like this?" I touched her bracelet, one I had made for her long ago; the white vines and leaves twirled round like a living circle.

She smiled. "What do you think this means, Malinalli?"

I had prepared for this moment. Hands on my hips, I told her. "After a great deal of thought, after centering myself and finding the goddess within—as we were taught to do—I believe this means my power is growing stronger. *My power*, not Malinalxochitl's!"

The words to unlock the charm were still elusive, but the threads . . . It must be a sign that a great magic, a fulfillment of my own identity, was coming to life inside me. I was sure of it. What else could it be? Great strength would be mine. Freedom must be near at hand.

"Everything is about to change. There was a moment when I thought I might be able to accept this life . . ." I shook my head—I couldn't even finish the thought. "Then the threads came to life in this new way. And there have been other signs, like these mountains on the sea. Now is the time for me to escape Potonchan. Come with me! We can go back to the Temple!" I had packed a small bundle many days ago.

But it was plain that my friend was not as excited. She was looking away, and when she shook her head, my heart sank.

"What's wrong?"

"I can't go with you."

"You think Lady Six Sky won't allow it?" Lady Six Sky appeared to be a kindly ruler. Surely she would understand that to keep two friends apart a moment longer would be cruel. She might even help me.

"I—" Hummingbird began, then closed her mouth. I felt tense, as if a mighty spell was about to be revealed. Her gaze darted around the room. Then, after a breath, "I have a daughter in Mayapan."

"What? How wonderful!" I scooped her into my arms, joyous to hear this blessing. But I was puzzled. I pulled away and looked into her face, noticing a certain wisdom about her, different from before. "Why didn't you tell me this sooner?"

"I tried to tell you, but you—"

"I cut you off with my ramble about the baskets," I said. Ashamed, I looked down at my feet. "As you can see, I still behave rashly and unmannered." I lifted my gaze and apologized. In the next moment, the path forward became clear to me. "I will go to Mayapan."

Hummingbird beamed.

Do I hear the embroidered threads in the baskets chiming with approval?

But we shouldn't have bothered with our plan-making. There *were* changes brewing, vile acts. Even the trees would not be spared.

ON FLOATING MOUNTAINS

A disruption had been foretold. The Maya Star Gazers chronicled the upheaval in their ancient books. The priestesses at the Temple of the Eighteen Moons saw it in the Book of Maps. Even Lord Curl Nose's priests and magicians warned of its coming.

And so it was that on the day the Maya call Bacab, in the year the Mexica referred to as One-Reed, white invaders arrived in Potonchan on floating mountains.

The White Men appeared on our shore and ventured up our river in their canoes to pummel our warriors with their four-legged, smoke-breathing dragons and exploding spears. The attack threw Curl Nose's household into turmoil, inspiring me and Hummingbird to take advantage and sneak away in hopes of seeing these strange men for ourselves. Hiding in the mangrove swamp, we saw they were covered in hard shells that sparkled in the sun. Their swords were sleek, like liquid fire, and carved the air deftly. I wanted to hold one in my hand. And if only I'd had Malinalxochitl's shield, I would have joined the battle, confident the obsidian-mirrored beauty would prove superior to the invaders' designs.

Lost in my imagination, I must have raised my shield arm, for Hummingbird held her finger to her lips, signaling that I be utterly still and quiet. Black clouds of smoke smashed the sky around us and would have drowned out the loudest cry, but I heeded her warning and settled down. Balling my hands into fists, I observed the invaders lumbering in circles, as if in a delirium from too much octli. One of the men, balancing an overturned shell on his head from which a long blue plume waved, terrorized the trees, slashing the ancient ceiba that stood in the center of the square. The defilement launched me to my feet. Those of us who saw the spectacle gasped so forcefully that we sucked the clouds out of the sky. The Great Mother herself had nursed this tree from a seedling. She, along with all the gods and goddesses between the Heavens and the Underworld, wept. Even the ancient tortoise that lived among the trees cried.

That was the moment the peoples' power began to slip away.

▲▲▲▲

In a cornfield near the village of Cintla, where over a thousand men died, Lord Curl Nose and all the noblemen and their followers, as well as the highest-ranking war leaders, approached the pale men in peace, bearing gifts of cloth, gold, and food. The women remained in their homes, tending their hearths. In Lady First Wife's courtyard, tongues wagged about the strangers, but no one asked me what I thought about these men.

The rumors were nonsense, mostly. Many of the women believed that the pale men were gods. I knew this could not be true, because of one thing: they smelled. There were reports about the odor that these beings gave off when they removed their shells, an alarming stench like crocodile's breath and rotted meat. No god smelled of anything other than incense and sweet flowers and fields of gold corn standing proudly in the sun.

▲▲▲▲

One day, in Lady First Wife's courtyard, as we talked of the strangers' godliness—a talk that elicited snorts and cackles from my person—a large shadow was cast over us. I looked to the sky, and there was the eagle. Seeing it always brought a smile to my face, but as I watched, I became filled with horror. Even with my bleary eyes, I could see that the bird carried something in its claws. Shielding my gaze from the sun's glare, I struggled to determine what it was. Then the bird let the thing go, and it fell right into our midst. Or, I should say, *he* fell, for it was a boy. But as my eyes became used to the sight, I saw it was not a boy, but a man, a small man. I watched this curious person who had fallen from the sky pick himself out of the hibiscus and jacaranda plantings and dust himself off.

Panic followed. Even though the women had come to accept the presence of the pale stranger-gods, they were not ready to see a small man fall into their laps. To great yells and flailing of arms, the wives and concubines scurried to stand behind Lady First Wife's chair. Their befuddled gazes flew up and down between the sky and the man. The younger women huddled together, as if they feared another body was about to land atop their heads.

As I stood removed from their party, I was able to study the little man. Even though his legs were short, they were attired in a fine cotton breechcloth. His head and shoulders were slightly cocked, like an attentive bird. His cloak was deep black and embroidered with stars that appeared to move if you stared at them long enough. Rings of gold were set in his earlobes, and jewels flashed on his blunt fingers.

He looked around, blinking, as if he, too, were surprised by his strange and sudden entry into our courtyard. But he quickly gathered himself up, lifted his chin, and swept his cloak aside with a flourish.

"Greetings, most noble lady," he said, speaking Chontal Maya. He bowed gracefully in the direction of Lady First Wife, who had remained seated in her chair, then made the gesture of kissing the earth.

"I come from the great city of Tenochtitlan and seek the one named Malinalxochitl."

The women turned to stare at me. The man followed their gaze. "It's Malinalli," I said as his round, dark eyes brightened in recognition, despite my correction. He gave a brief smile, revealing crooked teeth, then looked down and placed his hand over his heart. In a strong voice, he announced, "My name is Copil. I bring you news of your brother."

▲▲▲▲

Under Lady First Wife's and Lady Six Sky's watchful eyes, I walked with Copil in the garden. They need not have feared. The man was very calm for someone who had just fallen from the sky.

"You say you have news of my brother," I said, looking down at him, "but it has been many years since he walked the earth."

The man nodded. "The brother you knew is gone, yes. It is true."

I continued my pace, as if we were speaking about nothing more than the blue sky. My head felt heavy and light all at once.

"He attended the House of Magical Studies and died there," I said, waiting a beat. "He was murdered."

I cleared my throat. The memory of a vision—when my brother confronted a jaguar—stirred.

"Yes. I, too, attended that esteemed school!" He stopped briefly, running to catch up to me. "We were friends, your brother and I," he said breathlessly. "He told me about you. My grandmother often told me stories about great and powerful twins, monster slayers that lived during the time of the ancients. All true, of course! Alas, I have no brother or sister."

I looked down the quiet path stretching before me. Sweat slipped down my neck. Gone were the blasts of the invaders' weapons tearing holes in the sky, setting fire to the air, but I would have welcomed them now.

Copil gave so great a sigh that it snagged my attention. He began shaking his head from side to side. "Oh my." Pressing his palm against his chest, as if some pain had suddenly come over him, he said, "It is time for you to know. He who sits on the jaguar throne had many of our novices and magicians put to death the year your brother turned ten years of age. Imprisoned and starved some of them. Fed others to the animals," and in a voice I could barely hear, "your brother was among them."

I let out such a scream that it brought the women running to see what had happened. I put up my hand to stop them, then returned to stare at Copil.

"Oh, dear lady! Please forgive me for bringing you this news," he cried into his hands.

I shook my head. My beautiful Eagle. Mauled by an animal as if he were dead meat. I would not, *could not* picture it. A thickness in the air suffocated me, as if I was the one trapped under a wild animal. I fell to my knees and covered my face.

Copil took a steadying breath and knelt beside me. He moved my hands and met his eyes with mine.

How dare you come here with this news? I wanted to lash at him, tear the limp expression off his face. But I was silent.

"For one so young, your brother's gifts were powerful. Eagle foretold the arrival of the invaders from the east. And he spoke of the defeat of the Mexica and the ruin of the great Moctezuma." Copil swallowed. "For this reason, he was destroyed. Moctezuma then imprisoned your father and starved him to death. Your home no longer exists, for the leader of the Mexica ordered it robbed, razed to the ground, all plantings rooted out and leveled to leave no trace of your family's existence."

The scene rolled over and over in my mind—my twin attacked by a murdering jaguar. I saw my mighty father, shackled, confined to a latticed cage so small that it seemed the reed poles were growing through him, poking out of his skin. I could feel my mother's fear, like a cold, nauseating liquid spreading through my body—up late at night wondering how she would keep me safe.

Then it hit me. This was that monster's fault, all of it. Eagle. My father. My mother. My Pakal Balam. Moctezuma, and his sick warriors, had stolen my entire life.

The sensation was not something I could swallow away.

▲▲▲▲

In the days that followed Copil's revelation, I haunted the halls and gardens, talking to myself, grieving for my family. I fell into madness, spending hours in the courtyard swinging my broom against phantom enemies and coaxing the painted trees, yellow-eyed frogs, and herons to free themselves from the walls. Copil had shone a bright scalding light on the sufferings endured by my brother, mother, and father, and now I felt completely unmoored by these revelations. The past—the awful truth of what had been done to them—was present in every breath I took. So twisted was I in my mind that for a few breaths I luxuriated in my cursedness.

The calendar priest's warning about me was a plush robe that I held tightly to my chest. This wasn't only about Moctezuma. *Blame me, too.* I declined all food and drink and refused to sleep. Hummingbird had to wrap a blue strand of cloth around my waist to keep my skirt from sliding off, but the embroidery threads kept coming undone. There was a mutiny of stars and flowers. A small bit of cotton hung loose, and I worried it into pieces as I admonished myself for believing that my power was gaining in strength.

GIFTS FOR THE CONQUERORS

Lord Curl Nose held a feast to celebrate peace with the invaders. My lord did not go so far as to invite any of these pale men, for their stink made his stomach turn, but nevertheless, it was a celebration. At the start, with great pride, my lord presented the trove of gifts he had received: strands of sparkling beads, a yellow blouse made from cloth that moved like water and felt as slippery as the flesh of a peeled tuna fruit, and a red covering for the head, flat as a corn cake.

After presenting these treasures, my lord invited me to sit by his side. It had been some time since I had the honor. Lord Curl Nose complimented me on the painted blush in my cheeks. If he was distressed to find me thin, he did not show it. He filled my cup with chocolatl and my bowl with bits of roasted quail and a warm maize cake dripping with honey. There was no talk of the little man or even the strangers. We traded pleasantries regarding the food and the acrobats, the singers and mischief-makers performing for our amusement. And yet my heart beat as if I were running away from something.

Lord Curl Nose took my hand and squeezed it gently. He leaned close so I alone could hear him.

"Dear heart, beautiful girl." He cupped my chin, then smoothed my hair. "We have all been asked to provide something of value to these strangers from across the sea. It is our hope that in return for our generosity, they will go away from here. They are draining us of food and, more horrible still, have cut more than one hundred of our trees for wood to light their fires and build their cloth houses. This cannot go on much longer before the Mother Goddess becomes angry." He shuddered, as if he had already witnessed her wrath. "There is much I intend to offer their leader, but the most precious of all my offerings will be you, Malinalli." He clasped both of my hands in his and held them tight. Had he not done this, I would have slipped into the pit I felt opening beneath me. "As their leader's purpose lies in Tenochtitlan—that is, I believe that is the story—you will serve me by teaching him the elegant speech spoken in that great place," he said, seeming to forget that I did not understand this stranger's tongue. "And in so doing, I grant you your freedom. You belong to Curl Nose no more."

At first, I could do no more than stare at the cluster of coral dangling from Curl Nose's ear, red as a spray of blood. Then I gathered my wits about me, and before he could continue his pretty speech, I stood, knocking over clay cups and dishes. *Enough.* The voices of the crowd, jeers and taunts of the mischief-makers, the sound of rattles and flutes, faded away to a soft murmur in my ears.

I should have escaped this place long ago. So what if I had lost my way in the swamps? Anything would have been better than this.

"You will be treated well," Curl Nose exclaimed hurriedly, eyeing the angry concubine standing over him. "I will see to that. Provide you with fine garments . . . jewels that befit your position . . . whatever you desire," he said as he turned his attention to his chocolatl cup.

There came a roaring sound into my head, like an angry sea, as I stalked away. When I felt the ground shifting beneath me, the press of Hummingbird's hand on my shoulder steadied me. Linking her arm with mine, she led me away to my room. When we got there, I understood my feelings.

▲▲▲▲

"I am done playing the docile maiden. I will fight Curl Nose with my bare hands, the White Men, anyone if he so much as looks at me!" I raged as I stumbled into my chamber.

Alarmed, my sister enfolded me in her arms. I repeated Curl Nose's words to her. The torchlight cast meager flickers as she rocked me and pressed cool hands against my brow, whispering that all would be set right.

"Surely the goddesses will not allow you to suffer any more. They will find a way to mend all of this. I am certain of it."

"It is as the priest warned at my birth—I am Malinalli, the wild grass that never ceases to roam and burn. Destiny declared that I'll always be miserable and far from my home," I said in a sudden moment of self-pity.

"Hush," Hummingbird soothed. "You are Malinalli, priestess of the Temple of the Eighteen Moons." Her fierceness helped recenter me, though we both knew it was Curl Nose's right to offer me to the White Men. It was the way of the vanquished to provide gifts of women to the victors. Our world was filled with tales and songs about daughters, concubines, even wives, awarded to the conquering armies.

"Do not feel anguish, sister. I will be at your side when you face these men!" Hummingbird declared, giving me a start.

I did not even have to think on it. "No. You must return to your child."

But Hummingbird's defiance was equal to mine. "There is nothing you can say to stop me, Malinalli. You are my sister, and I will not lose you again."

Irritation iced through me, followed by fear. *But you have a child!*

A long argument followed. Like two old crones, we were fixed in our convictions. Neither of us would budge. The fading calls of insects in the garden filled the silence when we finally lay down to rest. But even with Hummingbird slumbering beside me, I felt too unsettled to sleep. My thoughts veered wildly from one idea to the other.

I will not go! I will defy Curl Nose. Let the Maya and these White Men hunt me down. I'll fight them to the death.

One thing was certain now. Hummingbird's words proved true: the home and family I once knew were gone, forever.

▲▲▲▲

The next morning, the impossible happened. After we had accepted their terms, the invaders attacked Curl Nose's palace. No enemy upon entering a peace agreement had ever behaved so treacherously. I would hear later that they believed our halls and chambers were lined with gold. They circled in on Lady First Wife's blue courtyard, where we had gathered for safety. The invaders, many Maya, too, climbed over walls, scurried across the floors, rattling in their cumbersome shells, though some were dressed more plainly. One by one, our guards fell. Hummingbird and I did what any warrior woman would have done, we picked up the weapons and fought the attackers off.

With a flint-studded sword and a decent enough shield in my hands, I felt the spirit of the woman I had been at the Temple flooding back. The shrine's painted image of the sorceress flashed in my mind, and I imagined her strength racing through my arms. I roared with delight over the heft and might of the weapons, at my body moving in rhythms I had not forgotten. I needed to stop this evil, these pillagers attacking defenseless women. I felt my submerged anger and vengeance rise—a dark maelstrom of power. I caught a reflection in a mirrored plate that decorated the wall—unbound hair, fiery face, determined grin.

In a flash of time, my nahual animal guardian rose. My breath stopped. Snakes twined around my arms. *What is happening to my head?*

A white soldier screamed, breaking my vision.

I chanced a glance at Hummingbird, a warrior-priestess transformed—her arms, legs, and torso that of a human, but everything else . . . a fox. From a strangely long neck, a new jaw and forehead had emerged around her face. The Hummingbird I knew now had the jaws and the wily, feral fierceness of a red-furred vixen. I froze in awe, then had to react to an incoming blow that could have sliced my head off. I darted and weaved, withstanding the attack of powerful blades. Shielding myself, my arm vibrating, I nearly buckled beneath a rain of blows.

After Hummingbird and I cleared the courtyard of the defilers, sending one man crying and running away, the women remained frozen, pressed against the walls, their eyes wide and changing from awe to fear. Hummingbird's vixen had already returned to its human form. Ignoring my fatigue, breathing heavily from exertion, I approached Lady First Wife and offered to escort her away. She shrank back and stared at us as if we were not human. I smiled through my breaths for air.

"Come, Lady First Wife, please rest yourself. All of you," I said over my shoulder.

"Yes. They're gone now. You are safe," Hummingbird said, and though her voice was more pleasing than mine, they remained hesitant.

I was able to coax a few to sit in the shade of the trees. There was no part of me that wanted to join them. I had caught a glimpse of my nahual ally. I was a different Malinalli, neither concubine nor priestess, but something new. A rush of power raced through my limbs. My new fate reflected in the pools of blood. I may never return home, but I would skewer these white monsters. From this point forward, anyone who threatened my sisters would pay.

Once Hummingbird and I had settled the women, we raced out of the chamber ready to fight where we were needed. Out past the exterior wall of Curl Nose's palace we headed—straight into another wall, this one of unsheathed silver blades, gripped in the hands of White Men.

▲▲▲▲

They had been waiting for us. An army of men, still as stone, stares so wide the whites of their eyes glowed. They could have turned us into twin puffs of smoke if they'd known the spell for annihilation. I knew the one, but the power to make it real was not my particular talent. Still, I felt a fever of strength rising inside me, along with the possible solution to the charm. Odd that it took a battle with these invaders to make me feel that the answer was close at hand.

In spite of the danger I now faced, I smiled. This seemed to fluster some of the men, who looked away and shifted in place nervously.

I fixed my gaze on the shell-covered invader at the apex of this band of marauders. I knew him—the blue feather gave him up as the attacker who had slashed Earth Mother's ceiba tree. He uttered what sounded like a command. Made a gesture to suggest that Hummingbird and I release our weapons.

A quick turn of our heads, one look, and we knew what needed to be done. We were Temple-trained. *We are two against twenty. Surrender. Choose life.*

After we dropped our swords and shields, the man crooked his middle finger, motioning for us to get closer. We didn't move a muscle. I swallowed the dry knot in my throat. I was not afraid. But I needed to be careful.

Hummingbird leaned in close and whispered, "What do you think? Does he possess the magic of an owl priest?"

"No," I whispered back. His weapons revealed special powers, but this was just a man. An evil man, to be sure. His self-important stance and the way his rain-cloud eyes bored into me reminded me of the slave trader. *He looks at me as if he already owns me.*

A man standing among them, overhearing us, shouted out in Yucatecan Maya, startling us, "You are in the presence of Hernán Cortés, lord of the seas, captain of His Excellency the Emperor, and true defender of the people of this land."

We had not expected to hear anything that resembled our tongue. The man didn't look Maya, rather he struck me as a servant of some kind by the appearance of his plain garments. I would soon learn that his name was Jerónimo de Aguilar, a White Man, who had been storm tossed onto our shores when his ship became lost at sea many years ago. The Maya had saved him and made him their slave. His skin was brown from the sun and as weathered as a dry leaf. He had pointy bat ears, bloodshot eyes, and a bat tattoo marked his right hand. Cortés said something to him now, and then this Maya speaker pointed at me. "What is your name?"

"I am Malinalli," I announced without hesitation. Save for the man called Cortés, all of the men looked at one another rather stupidly and nodded, as if they knew me. As if they had nothing to fear from two warrior-priestesses.

They aim to see Tenochtitlan? They will be dead by Small Festival of the Lords, when the priests offer hearts to Tezcatlipoca, the trickster god, that bringer of fortune, creator of disaster.

▲▲▲▲

But I was possibly facing a disaster of my own.

I was eighteen, and already I had yielded to the will of the powerful and accepted my brother's and father's deaths, submitted to my mother's plan to send me away to the Temple, and accepted the High Priestess's charge to travel to the land of the Maya. I had survived an attack and the shame of being sold into slavery. And now this.

It is always better to bend than to break.

You would think the gods would have grown tired of toying with me, but no.

Now they wanted to push me into another new life.

A life of sorrow and pain. How else could this end for me? There was death, of course, but that no longer frightened me. It would reunite me with my brother and father, and there was nothing to fear in that. I did not need courage to face the skeleton lord.

Though I would need it to live. To survive among these strange men and journey to Tenochtitlan, to Moctezuma, to make him pay for what he did to us would take the combined valor and cunning of the eagle and the jaguar, the spirit of my nahual guardian, and the protection of the sorceress's shield.

▲▲▲▲

Twenty women had already been chosen to go away with the white conquerors. Not long after, that number increased. They took whoever they wanted, including mothers who refused to be separated from their daughters. And Hummingbird. When it was time, we were led down to the river and made to stand in front of the strangers. Their shells glinted in the sunlight. Mutterings rose from the crowd of pale men. Although we did not understand their language, the meaning behind their stares was clear.

The threads of bravery I was depending on to see me through began to break. It was horrifying to see Hummingbird with her wrists tied behind her back and to once again know that I was being traded away, as if my life never mattered. It was an experience I would never forget. Like the stench of the slave market, the smell of the cage, such an action had a stink to it. And it covered me now.

One by one, the women were forced to kneel in front of these men. A holy man who wore white robes muttered strange words as he moved his hands in the air, then he poured water from a large shell, wetting not only the crown of our heads, but drenching us until our garments clung to our skin. Many cried with shame. This appeared to entertain the strangers. Even their blue-feathered leader Cortés looked amused. With his helmet tucked under his arm, this coward stood quietly as his men gawked at us. The White Robe behaved as though the women's tears were signs of joy, because he continued to bathe us as if we were young thirsty corn plants casting roots in a dry and unforgiving land.

BOOK IV

MARINA

I was renamed Marina.

Marina. Like Malina, but with a slight rolling of the tongue, caught as if by rocks, there in the middle. A sound neither I, nor any of the women, could make. We tried and tried, but Malina was all we could give voice to. Their name for me was a bludgeoned version of Malinalxochitl, which I'd heard their plumed leader pronounce and mangle more than once. Cortés reduced all of our names to grunts and squeaks. Maya and Nahuatl are languages of pure music, but the White Men's coarse, lazy tongues were lost inside our flowing rhythms. Marina meant "of the sea." But I did not care for it. The people of my land did not accept it. Just as they didn't accept my given, true name, Malinalli. "Malinalxochitl," they all continued to say.

▲▲▲▲

The invaders' floating mountains bore no resemblance to our canoes but moved across the water just the same. The vessels rocked and plunged, creaking mightily, making it seem that Earth Mother and the goddess of the sea were dancing out of step to the Lord Wind's songs.

Displayed on all the ships were expanses of white cloth, with the symbol of two crossed sticks and a strange line of figures embroidered in gold on the largest piece. The one above my head held all of my attention. As the fabric snapped in the wind, I wondered how many women it had taken to weave such a magical thing.

After being herded onto the ship, the women huddled together. A few cried, chewing strands of their hair, and many prayed. From time to time, the waves would lift the ship high and send it flying through the air before slapping it down again. The planks and ropes complained. Hummingbird refused to cross the unsteady wooden planks, even when I offered to take her hand and lead her to my favorite place at the front of the ship. Even Copil, who had been carried aloft a vast distance, gripped in the talons of an eagle, would not join me. Balché's robust cries of ridicule and cackling laugh had no effect on them.

I was not afraid.

Whenever the ship plunged, I would grab hold of the jaguar-skin pouch at my waist and draw strength from it. I could feel the brushes and the inkpot I had placed inside. It also held rose petals, a small stingray spine, a disc of obsidian, a handful of earth from my courtyard, an eagle feather, and my mother's turquoise necklace. Thinking about my mother made my heart cry, but I tried to steady myself with the thought that this journey, this ship, these pale and filthy men, would lead me to Moctezuma.

I lifted my chin, filled my lungs with air, and turned my face into the wind.

▲▲▲▲

When we arrived at a white sand beach, Cortés chose an invader for me to lay with—a pale, clumsy fool the Maya would name Turquoise Eyes, who struggled to manage his fire stick. He was even worse with his tepolli. I countered his pulling and tearing at night with whispers and feather touches, everything I could think of to speed his release and get him off me.

From that point forward, I spent my days watching.

As I left the cloth house where they kept me in the mornings, I would catch Cortés "swallowing me with his eyes." And I would study him, too. How his men shoved their way forward in the hopes of gaining his attention. How even the dogs would leave their masters' sides and go to him. *How can I get this foul, powerful man to do my bidding?* The thought crawled into a remote corner of my mind, a dark place I couldn't yet reach.

▲▲▲▲

My second meeting with this spirit swallower Cortés did not go well.

It was a strange interrogation. Hummingbird and I were forced to attend Cortés in his cloth house. Aguilar, with his faded bat tattoo, serving as interpreter, asked, "Where did you learn to fight?" Many of the soldiers had witnessed my sister and I with our weapons in the blue courtyard. "What a strange custom you have here—allowing women to engage in battle."

I stared at Cortés. "We were taught to defend ourselves at the Temple of the Eighteen Moons. Warrior women are not uncommon in our lands. They are—"

But he wasn't looking for answers, for he and the interpreter cut me off.

Cortés then braced his hands on a wooden table covered with paper. His stare was cold, eyes gray like a coyote's. He was sweating. "You killed two of my men."

As soon as Aguilar spit this out, I answered, my patience frayed, "You killed six of our women."

Cortés looked back down at the table. Ignoring us, he unrolled a map. "Tell me, what do you call yourself?" he said, looking up at me. "I hear the people. They call you Ma—"

"Malinalxochitl. But I was born Malinalli." I paused, watched him chew my names. In all the time it took Aguilar to form words back and forth, I never dropped my gaze from Cortés. "I am named for a sorceress." I spread my hands wide so the fabric under my arms would wave in the wind like his grand fabrics. "A goddess," I said with a polite smile.

He nodded as his wrinkled mouthpiece spoke. Cortés's grin grew slowly, as though he was listening to something amusing.

"And which one are you today? Goddess? Or sorceress?" He paused. "Do you mean to bless me with riches or turn me into a fly?"

Aguilar snickered, and they both laughed.

Hummingbird gasped when his meaning became clear.

I am the one who could send you to the Underworld, you loathsome creature. But I was the model of decorum. "Whatever you wish," I said.

▲▲▲▲

According to Copil, we were in the land of the Totonacs, near the Place of the Luxurious Green Growing Plants, a strange name given that the only tree ornaments were a few stands of dusty-looking palm trees. The air that first day—and for many days thereafter—was thick, heavy with water, and filled with clouds of mosquitoes. I saw that a cooking area had been arranged between two trees, beneath the shade of a stretched-out piece of white cloth. Many women worked there, a mix of young and old, and even a few of the White women from the east. They hunched over metates grinding corn, slapping corn cakes between their palms, and stood stirring pots of simmering beans and stews, roasting fish and small plucked birds. They were intent in their work, and yet there seemed to be a peace about them.

I joined the Maya preparing skewered fish over the fire. But I was shooed away for allowing a fat-lipped sea creature of appealing succulence to slip and fall onto the bed of white coals, causing flames to leap and singe a bounty of other foods as well. I had always displayed little skill at the cooking fire, so I happily left those relieved women and went in search of Hummingbird, slapping at the mosquitoes feasting on my flesh along the way.

I walked quickly, my gaze lowered. Yet, now and then, I could not help but sneak glances at the sights around me. These men seemed to delight in emblems and banners as much as our people did. A large flag of blood red and gold flew from a pole in the ground outside Cortés's cloth house. Next to it, another banner bore a painting of a chalk-faced woman wearing a blue mantle. She held a naked baby in her arms, and even though there was no tepolli peeking between his chubby thighs, I was certain it was a boy.

A wooden cross three times the size of the tallest man stood a short distance from the captain's shelter. I thought it might be a symbol of fertility, for the Maya had stone carvings similar to it. I had seen a smaller cross like it in the musty place I shared with Turquoise Eyes. The cross had a dead man pinioned to it, dressed like a slave in nothing but a rag. It was just like the one I had seen during a ritual with the ringing of bells, held on the sands. There had been chanting and singing. I had assumed there would be an offering, yet no victim prepared to receive the sacrificial knife had appeared. The White Robes, I noticed, had crosses on their walking sticks. One also hung from the end of some dark and pretty beads that the holy men liked to rub between their fingers. I thought the beads served to calm the White Robes, for these men seemed as excitable as wild birds.

I was careful of where I stepped as I continued toward my destination. There were piles of cast-off garments, soiled clothes, and mounds of bodily waste everywhere. Pocking the sand were skins of the avocado and papaya topped by clouds of flies. Many of the invaders gathered around water casks and on cloaks spread over the ground, playing at games. Others sat polishing their weapons, exploding sticks so strange I reasoned some powerful magician must have created them.

I found Hummingbird ensconced in a pavilion that her white captor had built for her, close enough to the water's edge that I could hear the surf above the clamor of the camp. Somehow, she had convinced the man to let her gather shells and seagrasses nearby. She kept my mind and hands occupied that day, and for many days after, making elixirs and poultices.

"Three more of our people and ten more of the White Men have fallen sick," she confided to me as we crushed dried flower seeds, which she had brought from Potonchan on a metate. "It is the heat and insects that sicken us," she said, pounding her grinding stone.

The insects? Could that possibly be?

"Why their leader insists on staying in this vile place, living like crabs on the sand, is stranger than strange." She let out a little curse that surprised me.

As we worked, I kept glancing at the sky, hoping to spy the eagle. I had not seen him since Potonchan.

A sudden crash and howl of thunder, followed by waves of excited men's voices yanked my attention from sky to sea. In the distance, along the beach, I could see the strangers demonstrating the might of their weapons and what they continued to call horses before a group of Totonacs. Cortés enjoyed parading his men about and making fire and smoke appear in the air. I assumed Copil was keeping watch over them. He followed the invaders' movements closely and told me everything. He'd gotten in their way many times and been warned he'd end up chopped up and fed to the monster dogs if he wasn't careful.

Hummingbird reached for a cracked coconut shell and passed it to me. It was filled with a white sap-like cream, and it smelled like dead mice. I made a face.

"Rub it on your skin," Hummingbird directed.

I studied the sap in the shell. "What is it?" This was one substance even I did not recognize.

"A Maya remedy taught to me by my mother. It will keep the insects from biting you."

"Oh? Perhaps it is strong enough to repel Turquoise Eyes's attentions as well." I dipped my hand into the shell and began to rub the cream onto my arms.

Hummingbird leaned in close. "I know of other remedies that can safeguard you." Her gaze caught mine.

I knew from our days at the Temple that Hummingbird was skilled in the herb lore that rendered a woman's body incapable of bearing children. Even in Lord Curl Nose's household, the concubines knew whom to turn to for a special draught to ward against the swelling of the stomach. In that time, men left womanly mysteries in the hands of the women.

▲▲▲▲

Hummingbird and I were walking near the water's edge one day when I spotted Fray Bartolome, the holy man who had performed the strange bathing ritual on us. He was running toward us, arms flapping wildly, calling out, "Doña Marina! Doña Marina!" I groaned, for kicking his way through the sand beside the priest was Jerónimo de Aguilar.

"Look at their holy man, Malinalli, how his chin thrusts and his head wobbles!" Hummingbird giggled. "Does he not remind you of a partridge hen?"

She was right. Fray Bartolome's face was also red from exertion and the sun. He held the skirt of his garment bunched in one hand, exposing pale feet in sandals made of rope. He was excited about something. But I could not say the same of Aguilar, who trudged along, glaring at us. I wished this man no harm, yet he seemed eager to cause pain. His bilious eyes were filled with a sorcerer's brew of hatred for me. Copil had shared a rumor that could have explained Aguilar's animosity. He said that Aguilar had spent his first days with the Maya imprisoned in a cage, plied with food to fatten him up for the gods. He had escaped sacrifice only to live as a slave with various tribes, where he learned the Yucatecan and Chontal tongues. It was Copil's belief that the man had suffered such a fright that it made him ill-tempered and his words fall out in fits and leaps. It was a good story, but it did not make me any less wary of him.

Upon reaching us, Fray Bartolome took a moment to catch his breath, and then began speaking so loud and fast, he gave us a start. He stepped closer, pulling at Aguilar's sleeve and gesturing for him to speak.

"Fray Bartolome begs a few minutes of your time, Doña Marina," Aguilar began.

Hummingbird and I stood still for a moment, trying to make sense of the further words spoken in Chontal. While the holy man continued to smile at us, Aguilar looked as if he had sucked something foul. His pronunciation was passable, but it had none of the grace that the Maya language was known for. The White Robe clapped his hands with excitement before launching anew.

"Fray Bartolome rejoices in your devotion to the Almighty God," Aguilar interpreted. Eyes closed, as if he could not bear the sight of me, he listened to the holy man's next words and continued. "He offers to instruct you in the teachings of the Father Almighty, the apostles, and all the saints in heaven."

He must have seen me during the ringing of bells ceremony. Intrigued by the talk of this Almighty One, I cleared my throat. "Tell me, will this god you speak of protect my people?"

Eyes agog, Aguilar sputtered, "Of course! If the people renounce Satan." He then turned to the priest to tell him what I had said. The man's eyes widened, and I thought for a moment he was going to throw his arms around me in happiness, but he composed himself and stroked his beads instead. I wanted to know more.

"Holy One?" I bowed my head in reverence. This seemed to satisfy the White Robe, and he nodded for me to continue. "How many men must be sacrificed on your altar to earn the protection of your gods?"

When I said these words, the look of horror on their faces would have made you believe that the Skeleton Lord himself had suddenly taken my place. It was Fray Bartolome who gathered his wits about him first, and with some manner of decorum spoke out.

"There is but *one* God, the Almighty God, creator of heaven and earth. And there will be no such sacrifices," Aguilar interpreted. "The Father Almighty does not approve. He only wants you to renounce Satan. He desires nothing from you but your salvation."

How curious. One God? Had he defeated all the others? And no offerings of beating hearts? How could this God offer his protection without the spilling of blood? I was suspicious. I studied the wood beads hanging about the holy man's neck. *What spells and magic are required from these White Men to appease this God who has no need for blood?*

Hummingbird cleared her throat. "Is their god in the image of Kukulkan?" she whispered behind her hand.

I did not know. The Maya Kukulkan, like our Quetzalcoatl, was not as bloodthirsty as the sun god of war Huitzilopochtli. In the worship of Feathered Butterfly, only flowers, honey, butterflies, and corn cakes were offered. But this priest's Almighty One was all riddles and confusion. Nevertheless, I told Aguilar that since it was my greatest desire to learn more about his God, I would gladly come to Fray Bartolome for instruction.

The holy man moved his hands in the air, making the sign of the directions. He said something, after which Aguilar mumbled, "Peace be with you."

Peace? What a strange thing to say to two female captives. But I just smiled at the partridge as he wobbled back to the camp. It was my aim to understand this God and his words. Earn his favor, to help me in the battle brewing under my skin. Make him mine.

EMISSARIES FROM MOCTEZUMA

A group of noblemen and hundreds of their attendants arrived at the camp on the day the White Robes' Son God rose from the dead. Curious, I set aside my embroidery and moved away from the women to observe the procession more closely.

Each dawn I wondered if this would be the day we fell victim to an attack by a tribe of warriors, but these White Men, "Spaniards" they called themselves, must have been born under favorable stars because that had not happened. The people who had been coming to meet the strangers arrived not with weapons but with food and tribute. I could see that these banners and flags bore the insignias of gods and the emblems of noblemen. Shielding my eyes from the sun, I noted red- and pink-feathered cloaks. Embroidered mantles. Tunics as brightly colored as flowers. Sandals of orange and blue leather protected their feet. The musicians among them played flutes and rattles and shells. Porters followed at a slight distance, bearing overflowing baskets of provisions and wooden cages filled with turkeys and ducks.

A sudden gust of wind unfurled a banner with the insignia of an eagle perched on a cactus, a stream of fire and water curling from its beak.

I recognized it as the emblem for Tenochtitlan, Moctezuma's city. My heart raced. It was a monster's army. I moved closer.

The Spaniards had noticed the procession too, of course, and the White Men who were mounted on dragon-horses breathing smoke began to approach. As soon as they did, the party stopped. The music fell off into a spasm of squeaks. A few of the porters even dropped their baskets and fled at the sight of the snorting, bellowing beasts. Most of the noblemen did the same. The earth shook as the creatures lumbered near.

When I realized these Mexica men were afraid, a flicker of excitement ran through me. Had the "mighty" Mexica met their match? *Could Moctezuma lose everything to these invaders?* The dark thought made me shiver, and I liked the icy heat of it, the jolt of power. I sensed an opportunity, a vulnerability that could bring my lifelong enemy to his knees. *Watch and listen.*

The only dignitary who had not run away waved his arm in an attempt to scare the dragon men. After the creatures halted, he recommenced his stately walk.

I moved close enough to hear one of the ambassador's underlings greet Cortés and the Spaniards in Nahuatl. But since Aguilar knew not a word of that elegant tongue, there was no reply.

I learned that the ambassador's name was Teudile, his face all sharp angles and planes. The steward wore two rich mantles—one red and the other green—edged with gold fringe, both loosely crossing over his shoulders, falling in folds down to his ankles. A gold headband with a tuft of blue parrot feathers encircled his head, and green stones dripping with gold beads hung from his ears. Draped around his neck were collars of gold decorated with bells. Even his sandals glittered.

Did this feathered and gold-encrusted minister have anything to do with the deaths of my brother and father? My stomach roiled with anger.

Teudile's nose flared with the slow intake of his breath as his gaze swept the White Men gathered to receive him. He pursed his lips and tapped his foot impatiently as he waited to be showered with the courtesies he was accustomed to. When he realized none were coming, he lifted his hand, and five of his noblemen rushed forward to kiss the earth at Cortés's feet. After a royal nod, drums, conch shells, and flutes broke into exuberant song. Reed chests opened, and we gasped as, one by one, treasures were lifted high into the air.

▲▲▲▲

During Teudile's third visit, Cortés paraded his steel soldiers and fired off the cannons. He let loose the dogs and ordered his mounted warriors to display their skill by riding forward and back on the packed sand. What a clamor! And after Cortés presented a few gifts to be awarded to Moctezuma, the captain reached into the latest mountain of treasure that Teudile had presented and drew out a mask of gold. I watched Cortés slip it over his head briefly before the mask caught the sun and blinded me. It wasn't until I shielded my eyes from its brightness that I noticed it was in the shape of a crocodile.

Curious, I squeezed my way through the crowd so that I might see and hear all that was happening. Not long after the invaders appeared on our coast, I had a dream where I danced with a crocodile man. We vaulted over flames, until the room caught fire. I fled, but the human, beastly thing continued to jump in and out of the fire, laughing.

So, when *this* crocodile man began to dance, I could scarcely breathe. The men began to laugh as their captain pointed his feet and jumped about. But I did not. Neither did Teudile and his noble escorts. For the Mexica, the mask was a holy symbol, fit for a god.

Cortés, still wearing the mask, presented Teudile with a strangely built chair, a clumsy thing with crossed legs, pocked with wormwood holes, and topped by a blue pillow as flat as a poor man's corn cake. Dressed in mantles and gold more glorious than those worn on previous visits, Teudile stared at the chair for a long while. Then he made a joke. The arrogant nobleman, who had stood sniffing a flower cone filled with roses throughout most of the day, looked at the gift that the captain had just presented to him and said, "This stinking fool can sit his behind on that contraption, but the great Moctezuma will not. He will feed it to the fires that warm his animal house. In fact, I will advise him to do it."

The spell was broken. I laughed.

I regretted it instantly and felt a sickening in my stomach.

The crocodile man and Teudile stopped and looked to find the source of that unexpected sound. Up until now, everyone had assumed that only Teudile and his escorts understood Nahuatl. None of his men would have been so foolish as to laugh.

Teudile flung the roses to the ground. His voice scorched the air. "Who dares to be so bold?"

There was only one way to handle this. I stepped forward. "I dare."

I felt the old spiny-backed caiman that supported the earth grumble awake. The crowd backed away, revealing me to the two men.

"You understand Nahuatl, slave?"

Slave? I stood straight and, keeping my eyes lowered, brushed my skirt to call attention to the finely woven and embroidered cloth.

"Well?" he thundered.

A simple shake of the head would have sufficed, but instead, I answered him.

"Yes, my lord. I speak the noble Nahuatl. I am a priestess educated in many languages. Not everyone enjoys the same blessing, I'm sure."

The noblemen seemed to draw in their breath all at once. Teudile stepped forward and raised his hand to strike me.

"Marina!" Cortés quickly removed the mask, standing between us. "Doña Marina," he pronounced, bowing even. He held out his hand for me to take, but I did not move to his side.

I looked at Cortés and said in steady Nahuatl, "My name is Malinalli." To be certain everyone heard, and recognized me, especially Moctezuma's man, I clarified, "I am also known as Malinalxochitl." I drew myself up and, slowly, turned to face Teudile. He blinked, closing his eyes slowly, as if he'd suddenly fallen asleep on his feet. In the next breath, he was on his knees, kissing the earth at my feet.

The goddess's power raced through me as I invoked our name. I felt filled with light and goodness, but it roused something darkly defiant, too. How could I use it to get close enough to drive a spear through Moctezuma's heart?

Overwhelmed by conflicting feelings, I moved to disappear into the crowd. I needed to collect my thoughts. I needed a plan. But Cortés grabbed my arm before I could make my escape. He mumbled something to Aguilar, who approached and addressed me firstly as "Marina," then "*Doña* Marina" when Cortés cleared his throat.

The captain glanced at the ambassador kneeling in front of me. One thin, fair brow arched. Then Cortés began speaking rapidly. In the Maya language, Aguilar said to me, "Will you be so kind as to tell our distinguished guest that I—that is, Capitán Cortés, *Ambassador* Cortés—am the subject of the Most Powerful and Invincible Prince and Emperor, Don Carlos." Aguilar stopped to take a breath and load his mouth with more words. His eyes narrowed with concentration, and his brow furrowed as he pressed on. "The king looks forward to learning more about this place and its people." He cocked his ear as Cortés filled it with more sounds. "His Majesty has known about you for many years."

My heart jumped. How was this possible? Was this majesty man a magician? Was Cortés? Could they see the world in a bowl of water or piece of dark obsidian?

I looked more keenly upon Cortés. The magical power these men possessed was even greater than I had thought.

I stifled a snort as Aguilar's stumbling voice intruded my thoughts. Obviously, this man had no magic at his command.

"The King has ordered me . . . uh-hem, Capitán Cortés," Aguilar said, "to share various observations and words with the esteemed gentleman, the great Moctezuma. The capitán has the desire to discover all there is to know about this land."

I could hardly think. I closed my eyes to focus my attention. *Can I weave something from this man's stumbles?*

I rubbed my throat with my hand. Sometimes I still felt the choke hold of the wooden collar. *But I am no slave today,* I reminded myself. *I can influence these men. I can control their words.*

I gripped the edges of my mantle with both hands. After a long pause, I drew a deep breath and attempted to turn Aguilar's Maya words into Nahuatl so Teudile would understand.

"The leader of these men from across the Divine Eastern Sea says his name is Cortés." I kept my eyes lowered and waited for my words to take hold. I could feel the Spaniards sigh with relief at the sound of their leader's name. But Teudile showed no sign that he understood me. "Their leader is the subject of a powerful ruler." I heard the tremble in my voice and stopped to calm myself.

Remember who you are, and that this emissary serves a murderer. A murderer who is within marching distance of this land.

When I began again, it was as if another, stronger person was speaking through me, and when I finished, Teudile nodded with a respectful air and opened his arms as he replied. I closed my eyes for a moment and offered a silent prayer of thanks. I then took the ambassador's comments and turned them into Maya for Aguilar to translate into Spanish for Cortés.

Cortés was so happy to be speaking with Teudile that he clapped his hands and looked ready to dance again. Cortés exchanged more words with Aguilar, who then turned to me and said, "How does the noble Moctezuma look? He is young, or an old man? Is he very tall?"

I studied Cortés, then Aguilar, thinking them both very dense. Young? Old? What did it matter? He was Moctezuma! The Revered Speaker could squash the Spaniards like bugs if he wanted! Kill them as easily as he had ordered the deaths of my brother and father. But I made it seem as if it was the most intelligent question ever phrased and turned the words into Nahuatl.

The ambassador's response was quick. "Moctezuma is our master, lord of all these lands. He sits on the jaguar throne. He is neither young nor old."

Back and forth it went, until Cortés asked, "Does Moctezuma have much gold? Gold is a good thing, for our hearts are made sick without it."

As I repeated the words for Teudile to understand, I wondered about the nature of their heart malady. Was it the one we called Plummeting of the Heart? Or a Turning Around of the Heart?

Teudile answered that Moctezuma had rooms filled with gold, enough of it to heal all the men from the east. After Aguilar translated my words, Cortés looked as if he had cornered a plump pigeon to gobble up.

FEATHERED QUILLS AND PAINTED WORDS

Only ten days had passed since Curl Nose's fateful decision to give me away to these Spaniard men. And now a slip of my tongue had changed my life again.

Cortés's aim was to journey to meet Moctezuma, but few of our people actually believed the man would reach Tenochtitlan. As much as I wanted to go there, I had my doubts too. Men enjoyed the sound of their voices, especially when they were speaking about grand plans and dreams. They fell in love with their words. But when Cortés explained that he was going to meet with the most powerful man in the world, he meant it.

In the course of time, I would understand that Cortés believed words were tools, like sowing sticks used to prepare the earth for seeds. His pride was his weakness, the language that enunciated most of his actions. I would have to learn it well, to shape it as artfully as a cook handles warm masa. But could I survive this dangerous man long enough to reach the great murderer of Tenochtitlan?

▲▲▲▲

It was the month we called Drought. Cortés sent Turquoise Eyes away on a ship filled with treasure for his king. I was glad to be rid of him, until another man moved to take his place.

"La lengua," Cortés called me. The Tongue.

On a night so hot that even the mosquitoes were too tired to move, the captain got it into his mind to see what other feats his "Tongue" was capable of performing.

Cortés worked and slept in a thatched pavilion draped with lengths of white cloth. It was a palace in comparison to the other men's shoddy quarters. Woven mats and rugs covered the ground. His sleeping place was atop a bed of plush mantles. Strange sticks that burned slowly called candles, a marvel from Cortés's lands, illuminated a wooden table strewn with paper covered with flourishes of ink. I recognized brushes, feather quills, and an inkpot for word-making, a clay cup, and a magic-making object filled with sand.

Cortés stood behind the table, as if he had just risen from his chair. He wore a white shirt that tied at the neck, with sleeves like clouds. He gestured for me to step closer. When he spoke, it was barely above a whisper.

"The captain says," began Aguilar, "that he is a fortunate man. He has someone both beautiful and skillful to aid him." He stopped for a moment, cocking his head to listen to Cortés's softly spoken words. "You need not fear, he vows. You are not alone. You will be safe with him."

I glanced up then and saw something in the captain's eyes that made my breath jump. I felt as if he were already touching me.

"I do not look on you as a slave, but as a *free* woman," Cortés and Aguilar continued. "You are free, Doña Marina. Free to return to your people, if you like. Free to stay. To venture forward with us."

The Spaniard's voice sounded more slippery than usual and put me on guard. But I couldn't control my heart, which pounded so loudly, I felt like I'd already started running. Copil and Hummingbird could help me navigate the long, treacherous journey back to Potonchan. But would Curl Nose help us? Was there any chance we could find our way back to the Temple?

I was already planning the journey in my mind: long nights of walking. Sleeping by day in trees, under brush. Bundles of cloth to cover our feet and our bodies. I would walk until my legs were stumps if I needed to, if it meant I could see my sisters again. But the excitement drained out of my body almost as soon as it appeared. What if the Temple was no longer standing? What about all the women at the camp? If I went away, what would happen to them? I had the power to keep people safe by blunting this White Man's words. And only I could make the mighty Moctezuma pay. To shove his hateful actions back down his throat.

I heard Cortés cough. I looked up.

He said I was free. Just like the other men had. But they used my body and my voice as they pleased. They took my sisters and made a mockery of my people. No, I was not free. Not since they murdered my father and my brother. I would never taste freedom until I made Moctezuma pay for what he took from me in blood.

The wail of a shell trumpet, coming from one of the villages nearby, broke the silence. The sound was meant to guide the sun back to us, but as if it were a signal to me, I took my leave, backing away from Cortés. I ran to Turquoise Eyes's tent—my tent now that he was gone.

▲▲▲▲

The next morning, I awoke to find small butterflies woven from plaits of palm leaves and a clay bowl filled with shells at the entrance to the tent, and then a parade of Cortés's men brought the baskets that Curl Nose had given to me, filled with garments, my loom and all of my embroidery things, and my broom. The soldiers placed rugs across the reed matting and set down armfuls of mantles. It was an extravagant display of cloth, designs and colors fit for an emperor.

Was this Cortés's attempt to please me? To make amends for taking the Maya and me captive? For his ugly, disrespectful behavior? To lure me close so I would open my mouth for him?

I knew how to charm, too. I'd had years to perfect the feminine wiles Rose Petal had talked about at the Temple. I could place Cortés under a spell just by following Rose Petal's instructions. Though no magic would be required to flutter my eyelashes and giggle, to blush a coy, rosy hue. Another key to my survival had been my performance of the Arts of Pleasure. Curl Nose had been clear about what he expected from me. But Cortés . . . there was more than a touch of malice in his cool, appraising gaze. It might be worth finding out, if it meant being able to use him to defeat the usurper sitting on the jaguar throne.

THE SHAPE OF REVENGE

By day, Cortés spoke through the mouth of Malinalxochitl. At night, he pressed endearments onto my lips, guided my hand in the painting of symbols, and spilled his seed into my place of joy.

The night I performed the Art of Pleasure known as the Circle of Fire, he wept in my arms and asked me to show him more. I did not understand his words, but a man begging for attention and caresses acts the same no matter what tongue he speaks.

Everything I had learned from Resplendent Quetzal, I brought to those nights with Cortés. I felt no shame. Not then. Beneath the sun's watch, Cortés was cool and courteous, his voice calm with everyone he encountered. Even in anger, he rarely raised his voice. But in my tent, with the candles illuminating the dark, he moaned and roared and growled.

There is a song that is sung by the Cloud Women that begins with the words "I long for the flowery mat, I long for the songs. I am a blossom. He is my jaguar warrior. I have come to pleasure him and wrap myself in flowers." When I was with Cortés, however, I thought of wrapping him in thorns and shoving him through Moctezuma's heart. This was how I conjured passion every time.

▲▲▲▲

My nights spent with Cortés worried Hummingbird. She thought he might try to subdue my strong nature with a poisoned draught or do something worse. One day, she begged me to allow her to work magic on him.

"I will turn him into a beetle," Hummingbird said. "Or I can summon my animal ally to kill him." She bared her teeth. And after composing herself, she added, "If that's not possible, then let's get away from here. Copil has learned that the White Men are ready to set out for Cempoallan, and then Tenochtitlan, the day after next. Now's the time for us to escape. Why should we venture forward with them? We'll find our own way to Tenochtitlan. This man will never succeed."

"On the contrary, they are masters of death," Copil argued. "You've seen their beasts and weapons. If Hummingbird took out Cortés, another man would just rise to the top, and soon the sea would be full of their floating mountains."

Masters of death. I had to agree. It was a dark thing to admit, but I enjoyed recalling the precise moment the Mexica faced the Spaniards' horses and armor of smoky metal, the giant dogs and fire-breathing weapons. I'd heard that some of them had died of fright.

"Besides," Copil added, "I've already foreseen legions more of the White Men already on their way. If we try to run, we may find our homes have already been turned to dust."

Hummingbird's face paled, likely remembering her daughter. I hated to see my sister upset. I assured her that I had things firmly under control. "In time, I will understand their tongue, then you'll see, things will become easier. I'll have more control. You remember how good I was learning languages at the Temple, don't you?

"A new language is like a charm that needs to be deciphered," I elaborated. "Meanings of words need to be coaxed into the light. I can practically taste these new sounds in my mouth already."

▲▲▲▲

Cempoallan was set in the low-lying region of the coastal lands and was the home of the Totonacs. The people came out to silently greet us and lined the white stone road, crowding the pathways. They watched, with their eyes wide as bean pots, the mounted Spaniards passing between their gates. Cortés led the procession, followed by his officers, sitting astride their strange mounts and looking down upon the people as if they had already conquered the land. The Cempoallans had never seen such a creature before, and no doubt they believed, as I once had, that man and beast were one creation.

The clatter and tramp of armed men and horses gave way to singing, as the White Robes trailed, carrying the wooden symbol of their god on the cross. I followed with Copil and Hummingbird, along with the women of Potonchan. As we entered the gates, the crowd let out a joyful cry, and the air swelled with the sound of shell trumpets, flutes, and drums. Rose petals showered from the air and fell at our feet. Hummingbird and I looked at each other, wondering why such a fuss, though deep down, I knew the answer. Cortés must have wondered, too, for he rode back to see what the excitement was about. I caught him raising his brow, assessing the canopy of palms above my head, the crowd of servants fanning the air around me. I held his gaze briefly before turning away to allow jeweled emissaries to rope garlands of red roses around my neck.

▲▲▲▲

During my first meeting with the chieftain of Cempoallan, he asked, "Are you going to Tenochtitlan to dethrone Moctezuma?" He was so excited to meet Malinalxochitl that he nearly fell off his wicker chair. He was sumptuously dressed in white and gold and smelled of vanilla.

"No," I answered, but to myself, *Perhaps.* The seeds of a dark plan took root in my mind.

"The White Men are your attendants, are they not?" he asked.

I smiled. *Of course they are.*

It was not my intention to sit on the throne, but it would be fitting, wouldn't it? My namesake should have sat on Tenochtitlan's first throne. It would be justice fulfilled. The island city needed a ruler to mete out justice and hold men who steal and rape and sacrifice hearts to hungry gods accountable. It needed Malinalxochitl.

▲▲▲▲

The Totonacs fussed over us and gave us everything we desired. They celebrated our arrival with a feast. The banquet tables, covered with a white embroidered cloth that I marveled over, groaned beneath black-and-red-painted plates from Chalollan heaped with delicious foods. A golden web of torchlight illuminated corn cakes drizzled with wild bee honey and chía seeds, delicate tlaxcalli filled with roasted deer and quail, and meat tamalli served with the four molli sauces the Cempoallans are famous for. A dish prepared with yellow squash, apricots, and duck passed in front of me, followed by beans with epázotl. Jadestone platters and pottery presented fish cooked with shrimp, frogs prepared in a green chilli and roasted corn sauce, and a fragrant turtle stew.

The chief and I sat apart from everyone, at our own sumptuous table, set upon a dais. A thoughtful host, the chief arranged many delicacies on separate plates for me. Cortés sat silently below me, eyeing me and the chieftain with suspicion.

"Most Esteemed One, Malinalxochitl," the chieftain said, "please tell your captain attendant that I am much pleased and honored to see him and his men here, and that they may stay as long as they like."

As if he understood, Aguilar spoke up. "Tell him that the name Cortés is as respected in our lands as the name of the great Alexander, or those of Julius Caesar, Pompey, and Scipio, or Hannibal of Carthage."

I stared at Aguilar. What was I to do with this? Who was he speaking of? After thinking for a moment, I smiled at the chieftain and said,

"He says the name Cortés is as respected in the lands across the Divine Eastern Sea as that of Tlacochcalcatl and the names of your ancestors."

The chieftain beamed.

I turned the chieftain's response into the words of Chontal Maya so that Aguilar could translate for Cortés. I spoke calmly. I could feel everyone—Spaniards and Totonacs—staring at me.

After dabbing his mouth clean, Cortés spoke softly to Aguilar, who then turned to me. "Cortés says, 'I thank the chief for his hospitality and generosity. He can be certain that I shall write of his goodwill and largesse to King Carlos. The Almighty Father and all the saints in heaven are looking down upon this happy occasion and bless us all.'"

Ready to interpret these uncharacteristically polite and humble words, I turned to the chieftain. But before I could utter one word, Cortés cleared his throat in a showy manner that suggested he needed to proceed first and spoke again through Aguilar. "I would be most grateful if the chief could tell me what manner of place is Tenochtitlan, and the man, the king that rules there. I feel it is my duty, as the ambassador to the good King Carlos, to go there to meet with him."

After I interpreted what was necessary, leaving out the bit about his *duty*, the chief's brows perked up like two inquisitive caterpillars. He addressed his answer to me, saying my name again and again with reverence and awe.

"As you, oh great Malinalxochitl, already know, Tenochtitlan rises from an island in Moon Lake. Nothing else is like it in the world. There is much jade, turquoise, and gold, for the Revered Speaker prizes these above all else," he said with great seriousness. "With our guidance and protection, you will return to your city, but know this . . . the Revered Speaker and the Triple Alliance are very cruel to us," he said tearfully. "They tax us abominably and take most of our food." He gave me a sideways glance as I interpreted his words and waited for the reaction of the White Men. Cortés did nothing but nod, then gestured to the chief to continue. "And gold!" he cried. "Yes! They leave us practically no gold.

"Each year, they demand five hundred lengths of white cloth and four hundred mantles of rich design," he said. "They require fifty baskets of vanilla beans, twenty-five baskets of ground cacao, two thousand rolls of amatl-paper, and fifty live birds—parrots, herons, and hawks." He stopped to catch his breath. "And they steal our children for their sacrifices."

Cortés's nods of understanding gave way to fury as Aguilar interpreted my words.

"What did you say? They steal your children?" Cortés huffed, then jumped to his feet. His anger drew all of the Spaniards closer to him. They frowned, muttering until their discontent was a storm cloud hovering over us.

Cortés's voice rose above the others. "What ill-tempered neighbors you have, sir." A predatory gleam lit his face as he spoke on.

Niños. Los españoles. Dios. La gente. I mouthed the words I understood and claimed these victories silently. How the man loved to talk. Once he got into a rhythm, his speeches could meander for hours. I smiled encouragingly at him and the chieftain as I unlocked more and more sounds. Cortés's chatter was a small thing to put up with, so long as it got me what I wanted.

▲▲▲▲

One night, when the Spaniards were drunk from the octli they'd indulged in at a feast, Hummingbird, Copil, and I met in the shadows of a temple, where there was lantern light to see, and I filled out my plan.

"Cortés might think my name preposterous, but the people don't," I said to my friends. "They brought their tribute to Malinalxochitl, not to him. I will be the sword and shield, and he, these men, will be my army and my bait." Hummingbird's eyes widened in horror, but I continued in my dark fever. "For good measure, I will seed the story of the warrior goddess Malinalxochitl every place we go. I will tell people that the sorceress means to take what belongs to her and restore harmony and peace."

"Why not just start your own army?" Hummingbird snorted. She meant to steer me away from my plan, but her words had an appeal. I turned so suddenly that my neck flared, and I saw stars. I could see from the glint in Copil's eyes that he liked the idea, too.

"I *should*," I agreed.

Copil was quick to voice his support for me. "You'll have warriors at your beck and call soon enough," he reassured.

"It's too dangerous!" Hummingbird cried, prompting Copil to press a finger to his lips, wordlessly urging us to be quiet. He looked around furtively. I looked, too. Shadows could turn into armed men in a blink. Hummingbird continued, whispering, "How will you be able to control *two* armies? *Think*, Mali. It is irresponsible. They will turn on each other. You can't trust this man Cortés."

I turned to Copil for reassurance. He nodded and encouraged me to think boldly. Had Hummingbird forgotten my story? I thought the idea was righteous. Malinalxochitl at the head of a giant army! I closed my eyes and imagined it. Standing with my sword and shield, leading Maya, Totonacs, and White Men, preparing to confront and destroy my enemy Moctezuma.

I was puffed with my dream, though I squirmed beneath Hummingbird's hard gaze. My sister knew me well. We had studied, fought, and prayed side by side. She knew in that darkness-shrouded moment that I wouldn't back down from the idea of Malinalxochitl leading two armies. I would not be the ordinary, tragic girl the calendar priest saw in his book of divination. I could reach for greatness, just as my mother had suggested.

She shook her head and softly said, "I hope you know what you're doing."

"I do."

"You might give men false hope that it will be easy to overturn Moctezuma."

"What are you saying? I will win. The warrior-sorceress is with me, and together, we'll take down the usurper who sits on the throne."

"I don't think the High Priestess would approve of the risk you're taking."

"Nonsense. All will go well, you'll see."

I wondered aloud if Hummingbird had seen something in the prophecy stone she wore around her neck. Was it a good portent? Bad? She said the sastun had revealed nothing about me.

"Would you change your plans if it did?" she asked.

No.

▲▲▲▲

Shortly after this surge in my confidence, doubt appeared. Its bony finger poked at the edges of my dark brilliance. I felt as if I were lost inside the labyrinth again. I heard the old slave trader whisper, *You are Word— Just breathe.*

"Tell me about the House of Magical Studies," I said to Copil one day as I burrowed beneath a blue mantle. My fingers had worried the embroidered trim to loose threads, and there were holes in some places where I had been sucking and chewing on it. We were still in Cempoallan. Cortés enjoyed all the fuss the Totonacs lavished on him.

"The House of Magical Studies!" Copil had been speaking in whispers to Hummingbird when I made my request—most likely about a remedy that she thought might smooth my thoughts. He cocked his head. Even after I nodded for him to carry on, he waited, as if he could not believe that I had spoken more than one word aloud.

"Tell me." I wanted to learn. To see it through his eyes. To remind myself that this journey would lead me there, even if Cortés was the one who would take me, even if he liked to throw me against the wall now and then.

"Please," I said, and, after scratching his chin and clearing his throat, Copil began.

"The House of Magical Studies was built during the time of Ahuítzotl—Water Dog—a ruler renowned as much for his building projects as for his lust for blood.

"It stands two stories high, and marking the base are fifty-two stone serpent heads, their mouths opened and at the ready to bite the air. Much of the surface is covered with shells.

"A blind man stands guard at the entrance, his only weapons a red cloth and a broom made of white heron feathers, which he uses to clean and polish the giant disc of obsidian at his feet.

"When the moon is full, she shines upon the obsidian, but not so brightly as to offend Earth Goddess. To the casual observer, the disc appears to float above the earth. Indeed, the . . ." I heard Copil as if from far away.

My mind wandered back to Malinalxochitl's shrine and the priestesses' stories about the sorceress and her affinity for her people.

What was it the High Priestess had said? *She kept them safe from harm.* Harm. Pain. Suffering. Fray Bartolome had stories about women who had sacrificed themselves to warring rulers so that their people might live, saints tortured with fire, rope, knives, and fed to beasts because they refused to give up their love for the Son God, Jesus Christ. I understood torture.

My people had stories, too. When She of the Bell Cheeks, the moon goddess, dared to raise an army against her blood-maddened brother, he beheaded her.

I recalled these stories with the hope that they might sweep the doubt from my mind and guide me forward.

But they did something else. The tales smoothed my anger, polished it up like a blade of volcanic glass.

BOOK V

JOURNEY TO TENOCHTITLAN

We set out for Tenochtitlan in the time we called Tlaxochimaco, the Birth of Flowers, what the Spaniards plainly referred to as the sixteenth day of August, 1519. It was summer, the time of rain. Cortés and his men had been in our lands for more than three full moons.

From the jungle, we emerged onto a path that took us past fields of corn. As the days wore on, the scent of pine, cedar forests, and cool air pushed away the smells of fertile earth and flowers.

The distance between Cempoallan and Tenochtitlan was close to eighty-five of what the Spaniards called "leagues." Even though I had traveled down rivers, through jungles, and on the Divine Eastern Sea, I was unprepared for the skeletal paths etched through the mountains.

We were a great snake of men and women, nearly two thousand strong. Cortés led, of course, riding beneath the gold-and-blood-colored banner. His officers, mounted and armed, followed. The White Robes came next, then Aguilar and a group of lancers marched, and behind them wound a line of foot soldiers, pikemen, and crossbowmen. Clowns weaved in and out, juggling ahuacatl pits, seedpods, anything that caught their fancy. Then came over five hundred Totonac warriors, plus porters hauling the Spaniards' cannons and bearing baskets filled with armor and more weapons, supplies, food, and clay jars of water. The twenty Mayan women from Potonchan and the eight given by the Chief of the Totonacs walked with me. Most of the white women had stayed in the town founded by Cortés, Villa Rica de la Vera Cruz, along with fifty Spaniards, many of them sick or injured.

Cortés had taken a beautiful Totonac woman to his flowery mat, and she carried his blue banner and marched at his side. I was Cortés's interpreter and nothing more.

▲▲▲▲

As the trail climbed, mountain peaks mantled in snow rose before us. In the distance loomed Star Mountain, a place named for the sparks that shot from its crest, giving birth to stars. "Once I have my full powers, I will be able to give these people a future, one without Moctezuma. Without Cortés and this plague of men," I said to my companions as the Tlaloques beat their hammers against the mountains and called down the rain.

Mountains. Fog. Jungles. Deserts. The obstructions were many, but Hummingbird and I had learned at the Temple to look at obstacles as a chance to converse with ancestral spirits and to delve deep within our own hearts and spirit. So every mountain pass sheltered hidden caves sacred to goddesses. Every tree served as a link to the eighteen heavens. A water-starved desert held jewels like green nopales and red tuna fruits.

At every crossroads, we took extra care lest we pick up some ailment that had been left by a sorcerer at the side of the path. Sometimes we were unsuccessful.

"You say you're a sorceress, so then do something to protect us!" Cortés ordered, stomping with fury after one man exploded, another was overwhelmed by battalions of stinging ants, and another turned to stone—his eyes watching as his companions marched past him. In the mountains, many men disappeared into the mud, sucked down by the earth, which made little slurping sounds. Copil had warned me that Moctezuma might have sent Blood Drinkers to scare the Spaniards away. Or to kill them.

"They can enable scorpions and spiders to sting, so these invaders will sleep and never wake," Copil had said.

I did not want that, and even though I had not solved the charm that would unlock the full potential of my magical power, I did my best to protect everyone. And after days of watchfulness and little sleep, I became ghoulishly thin and nearly disappeared over a cliff.

Hummingbird brought me relief. I felt a great peace with her, preparing iztauhyatl and epazotl for remedies to cure fever and chills and painful swellings that afflicted the toes. She tore fresh leaves of what the Spaniards called hoja santa, ropeflower, for the small magic bag Copil wore around his neck. I replenished a small clay jar of sage tea—I liked to freshen my mouth with it—and made a tooth powder with the dried leaves.

▲▲▲▲

Ambassadors arrived from Tenochtitlan, Azcapotzalco, and Iztapallocan. They lavished us with flattery, incense, and presented gifts of jewels, gold, and embroidered cotton. Always, I interpreted.

I set a delicious feast of compliments. And lies.

"The captain general kisses the hands of Moctezuma and thanks him," began my talks to the haughty men arriving from the great city on the lake, Tenochtitlan. These Mexica lords presented gifts that surpassed all others in extravagance. They stressed to me that Moctezuma wished the White captain good health, but that due to matters of the empire, Moctezuma would not be able to meet with such an illustrious man. I understood that every embroidered mantle and feathered headdress, every collar and bracelet of gold was a symbol of Moctezuma's power. Cortés was a guest. Any well-mannered, properly raised Mexica,

Maya, Totonac would have accepted the gifts politely and returned home at a quick pace. A guest in another man's home did not keep his hand extended, expecting to receive more and more and more. It was uncivilized.

But I didn't tell Cortés this. What I said was, "They look forward to seeing you in their magnificent city. The leaders are planning a special celebration, worthy of a god, for you." I also exploited his weakness for bright, shiny things. "Moctezuma himself is overseeing the creation of a magnificent diadem, jeweled bracelets, and collars—all for your pleasure—with his personal goldsmiths."

Weaving a honeyed sweetness through my voice, I told him again and again that he was a superb leader. By now, I had mastered enough Spanish to interpret directly, leaving worthless Aguilar to stumble open-mouthed, gasping like a fish out of water. I slipped up a little, a word here or there, but my imperfections served to drive me harder in the coming days, in my quest to understand and master this man.

To all of the ambassadors, I made this pledge: "This man travels under the protection of the warrior-sorceress Malinalxochitl. Be prepared to feel the full force of her fury should you attack his followers or hinder his progress."

I saw the risk such liberties posed. I was careful. When Cortés stuck his nose in my face and promised to kill Hummingbird if I ever lied to him, I drew myself up, pulled my mantle close, and smiled.

"Put your mind to rest, Captain General. I was raised properly to speak true and mind my manners. I am just a woman, a helpmate. My voice is your bridge to help these people, to spread the peace words about your gentle god." This seemed to do the trick, though his eyes remained cold and watchful, and he mumbled something about my overfamiliarity with weapons as he stalked away. The occurrence put into my mind that another reason I needed my own army was to keep this creature's actions in check. I would dispose of him when I was ready.

So if I saw that different words might help smooth our way a little and keep our people safe, I wove them in. This took all of my concentration, abilities, and skill. I acted not as any man's mirror, reflecting the exact truth of his voice. I saw my work as something like an artist's—a mix of intelligent thought and craftsmanship. I was a nobleman, too, all polished pride and courtesy. A warrior, forever listening for danger. A sorceress, on the cusp of asserting her power.

Protect and deceive. Protect and destroy. Protect and restore. These were the pillars to my quest.

WAR AGAINST THE TLAXCALLANS

In Tzauhtlan, I was told that the Tlaxcallans were a peace-loving people, something we all hoped to be true. We would have believed anything, for we were bone weary, starving and hallucinating after our climb along flinty ridges and our descent into a barren, desolate land. The truth became plain to all of us when the Tlaxcallans attacked us in the green foothills of mountains just outside their capital city. It was a blow to the warrior and protector in me. Now Cortés's men looked to be outnumbered a thousand to one.

I stood on a hill and saw it all.

Beneath a gray sky, spread far and wide across the land, stood thousands of warriors. Many wore headpieces shaped like animal heads. Jaguars, eagles, coyotes, and owls moved as if these beasts possessed their human souls. Behind them floated a sea of banners decorated with the symbols of the war chiefs that were gathered here, and above all of them waved the sign of Tlaxcallan, a white heron.

Seeing this, I could not help asking myself, *Are we to die here?*

Every other place we'd traveled, the people had set tribute at our feet. They'd given us food and water. They'd been curious, but their words were courteous and reverential. There had never been talk of war.

I felt as if the assault were being waged against *me*.

What ignoble beasts these Tlaxcallans were!

I kept watch with my arms crossed, pacing back and forth, jumping each time the Spaniards' iron monsters blasted the air.

The first wave of fighting proceeded swiftly and fiercely. Unlike all other peoples, the Tlaxcallans were not afraid of our horses. Early in the battle, to great cries, a small force of their warriors surrounded and attacked a horse and its rider. The Spaniard escaped, but the Tlaxcallans cut off the head of the mare, thus proving to their people that the beast was not immortal.

The second wave began after ten Tlaxcallan warriors took to the field and screamed threats and danced around, miming a feast and gesturing how full their bellies were going to be after eating our flesh and sucking on our bones. It was an eloquent display. Even the most thick-skulled of the Spaniards quickly grasped the meaning.

I sent a prayer to Feathered Butterfly and to the Virgin Mother Mary, too. All goddesses deserve to be honored. I crossed myself in the manner taught by Fray Bartolome. The banner with the Holy Cross flapped in the cold air above my head, but I could not hear it. Nor could I hear the moan of the wind, or the grumblings of the men guarding me. The sound of fighting, the smashing blows of obsidian-studded swords, and the thunder of the cannons drowned out everything, except the drums whose insistent beat rose out of the ground, shadowing my heart. Again and again, a dark curtain of arrows, javelins, and darts would sweep across the sky. Then, like an avalanche of stone and fire, the Spaniards' guns and iron dragons spumed in answer, shaking the earth.

Three men guarded me. Cortés had picked the men before he left to lead the others into battle. He kissed my hand, whispered a blessing, and unsheathed his sword all in the same breath. Then he was gone, leaving me to witness death.

My tongue could not help him now. I had tried to negotiate peace, but Cortés was determined to prove that the White Men and their weapons were superior, and that his god was the stronger deity. When I went to speak with them, the Tlaxcallans had been just as obstinate, throwing insults and rocks at me.

I lifted my hand to my throat, forgetting the wound to my palm. I winced, not so much from the pain of it but the hurt caused to my pride.

"Do you see that?" Copil shouted, his eyes as large as ahuacatl pits. He clapped his hands together and studied the battle as if he were the mastermind of it.

"The White Men are magicians. Look!" He pointed. "Look how their thunder makers topple the whole file of the Tlaxcallans and the Otomí! Proud Otomí. They take a vow never to retreat. Look at them now!" His enthusiasm was a little alarming; nevertheless, I followed his gaze to the tall warriors. Their hair was shaved into bristly crests that fanned down the middle of their heads. They were naked, bodies decorated with tattoos in magical configurations meant to protect them. In one hand, they held wooden swords studded with obsidian points, and in the other, wicker shields decorated with feathers. A part of me thought it was a glorious sight.

"They say that even their women are fierce. Blue tattoos mark their skin, like the men," Copil continued. I thought of my tattoo, felt it there, beneath the edge of my blouse. "The ancients say that it was one of their noblewomen who became the first to flay an enemy's skin." He shook his head. "But the strangers' guns shatter the Otomí into the air as if they are nothing but puffs of weeds."

Behind us, one of the Spaniards grunted, as if he understood and agreed.

Though the Spaniards on the field were outnumbered, their weapons destroyed full rows of warriors without pause. The painted warriors looked confused by the noise of the cannons, the limbs and heads of their fellows raining over them.

I averted my eyes, but only for a moment.

"These Spaniards do not fight the way our people are used to," Copil said. "The Spaniards fight to the death. Better to die here than to be taken captive and feel the bite of the sacrificial knife. Look over there, at the warriors in red cone caps."

Copil leveled a jeweled finger at a fringe of Tlaxcallans on the western slope. "Do you see them?" he continued, still excited but steady. "Men who have distinguished themselves in previous battles. 'Two-captive warriors' we call them. The Tlaxcallans like to mix them in with the novices. And far behind them, those feathers there, yellow with red sticking up like sparks? The standard of a captain."

It was like watching the yellow tail feathers of a strange, giant bird. And now this bird moved toward the front line of warriors. When the smoke cleared, I could see that the feathered banner was attached to the Tlaxcallan battle leader's back by a tall woven rack of wicker.

I shuddered, feeling the breath of the Skeleton Lord as if he had risen from the Underworld and were standing behind me now.

"Do not be afraid," Copil shouted, then glanced at the sky. "I have already seen the future, and I assure you it does not end here for us. You must believe me."

But look at them! I wanted to scream. *How are we to survive this? There are thousands of them.*

If only my father had taught me more about such matters as battles and wars, perhaps then I could have understood. If only I had the sorceress's shield, possessed the magic for the right spells . . .

I fixed my mind on the calm face of Fray Bartolome. He said that there was always hope for those who followed the Almighty One. No matter the darkness, if we confessed our sins and prayed, we would find life everlasting.

Despite myself, I searched the battlefield, looking for "Malinalxochitl's warrior," the name the Cempoallan chief had called Cortés. I picked him out leading a charge, riding across the plain and beheading every Otomí who stood in his path.

"The Tlaxcallans have sorcerers at work on the field now," Copil said.

"Where?" I coughed. The cannon smoke was thick and bitter. Copil gestured in the direction of a group of black-robed figures carrying something in their hands. They placed the objects on the ground, and I saw they were incense burners. The flames began to smoke.

"Poison," Copil said. "A bark or flower of some kind. Perhaps oleander. They mean to poison the White Men with the smoke."

Just then, there was a great blast from a cannon. As the rising wind cleared the air, I saw that the sorcerers had vanished, victims of either the Spaniards' magic or masters of their own demise.

▲▲▲▲

All of the gods favored us over the Tlaxcallans that day. This was a victory in that we *survived.* After spending the night camped on a hilltop, in the ruins of a temple, we awoke prepared to confront more warriors howling for our blood. But instead of warriors came a parade of women and porters bearing gifts of food—turkeys, baskets filled with cherries, beans, and squash—and a banquet was prepared. To the merry sounds of the Spaniards' flutes and whistles, we fell upon the food and ate our fill.

"I wager you my sandals it is a trap," Copil announced, his mouth stuffed with meat, his nose and fingers blackened with soot. He wiped the grease with the back of his hand. "There is no honor in fighting an enemy who is too weak to defend himself. Not only that, they want these strangers nice and plump for their cooking pots."

Perhaps he was right, for no sooner had the Spaniards and their Totonac allies filled their hungry bellies than a wail of many conch shells split the air, followed by fierce drumming, chanting, and stomping. Assembled across the plain, far as the eye could see, was the Tlaxcallan army, moving like rows of cornstalks that had come to life in a rich man's field.

RISE OF THE NAHUAL ANIMAL GUARDIAN

Red blooms of blood stretched to the horizon.

Twenty-one days after the start, the war raged on, with soldiers fighting on top of fallen men. It was thought blasphemous to abandon warriors on the battlefield, but there were mountains of Tlaxcallans, decimated by the White Men's flesh-eating weapons. It seemed that even the gods had turned a blind eye to Tlaxcallan.

Fear kept me awake at night. *This nightmare could blow us straight to Mictlan. We could be walking the path through the first valley of the Underworld by morning.* I was on the winning side, yet I couldn't stop thinking of everything that could go wrong. I had tried to negotiate peace, but both sides were drawn to the siren's call of war.

Over time, fear brought me clarity. Then anger settled in, bringing a heat that made my skin feel like sparks of flame. It roiled my belly and made every word I spoke hot.

War is not glorious. The field of battle is a wasteland reaped of all our flowers, our fallen warriors. This is what we said and now I knew it to be true. The pageantry of the feathered banners, the whistles and drums, the clouds of incense carrying prayers to the gods seemed more like a celebration of doom than anything else. I'd been wrong to think of fighting as necessary to my cause. Something I had to shoulder through to reach my goal: Tenochtitlan.

This must end.

Looking out over the battle, I heard the mournful wail of a conch shell trumpet. The sound signaled my mind, and flashes of my life stormed through it—images of my brother, the river, shrine, and shield. I felt a subtle shifting deep inside. Not just sinew and muscle, but an uncoiling of a beastly rage living deep within my breast and ready to burst. The men who had abused and used me, the way the Spaniards regarded us as animals placed on earth to serve their every need, the humiliation of being called a goddess yet being able to do nothing—I lived it all again and again and again. And like a great serpent, the anger twisted and turned, already gorged on fury, until I could not contain it. I was ready to strike.

I heard my brother's voice within the notes of another sounding of the seashell. *Don't be frightened. You are sorceress. You've had magic since you were born. Will you claim it now?*

I knew in the next instant that I understood the meaning of my brother's words to seek the strength that awaits beyond my name and release my full powers.

I am a sorceress.

I am Malinalxochitl.

I released the fury spiraling in my chest, picked up a fallen warrior's sword and shield, and ran onto the center of the blood-soaked battlefield, weaving past mountains of the dead.

This ends now.

I lifted my arms, and without a spell to guide me, I summoned every serpent to come to my aid. The order glided sinuously over my tongue, my mouth and face framed by serpent-fanged jaws that were emerging from my head. I sensed the suppleness of silver scales, an elongation of my neck. I was nahual-animal now.

My eyes . . . it was like seeing through twin prisms. Shards of images in brilliant colors, near and far, filled my view. I stopped and turned, felt my neck stretch, then contract as I focused on *their* coming.

Crossing plains and over hills, they came by the thousands, the diamond etched and silvery greens slithering across the battlefield. They coiled around every man who stood in their way. The flat earth and mounds of grass swiveled and swayed. Even the embroidered threads in my garments breathed with life and joined the melee.

The undulating waves of open fangs caused chaos and fear. Finally, Spaniards and Tlaxcallans ceased fighting. The men laid down their swords and ran away, and without another whistle blown or drum beat to mark it, the battle ended. Men maddened with bloodlust who continued to fight and those beyond ignorance were either cut down by me or were strangled and bitten blue by my force of serpents.

▲▲▲▲

The air around me shimmered darkly. I could not feel my face or my body, just the dark whirl of malevolence still moving inside me, and it was thrilling.

As I stalked back to the camp, the White Men, Totonacs, and Maya shrank away from me. I could tell by their rounded eyes that they had seen what I did. What I was. *Good.* I had wondered if they would be able to witness my magic.

At first, Hummingbird and Copil were silent as they helped me out of my bloodstained garments and into a fresh huipilli and skirt. Out of the corner of my eye I caught the priestess nodding, a smile on her face. Copil whistled while smoothing the wrinkles from my skirt.

"The girl I found lost in the labyrinth has found her way," Hummingbird said proudly while brushing my hair.

Copil cleared his throat. "The Tlaxcallans will certainly sue for peace now. They now know that the White Men have a powerful sorceress on their side. They saw her with their own eyes!" He paused. "And once we have reached Chololan, we are practically in Tenochtitlan," Copil crowed.

I lapped up his words. Relishing the sound of *practically*, I rolled my shoulders, relieving the crick in my neck, and thought of the path ahead.

▲▲▲▲

Later that day, Copil, Hummingbird, and I went to meet with Cortés and a delegation from Tlaxcallan, which included women bearing wooden cages filled with turkeys and birds, baskets of fruit, grinding stones, and clay cooking pots. Cortés's men had cleared a space in his wide cloth house for a carpet and his strange chairs. Many of them, including the captain general, had exchanged their turtle armor for the quilted cotton vests worn by the Tlaxcallans.

It brought me joy to see Cortés with his mouth hanging open. For once, he was quiet. When he was able to spit words, they were not thankful or awed, not even fearful. He was furious. An unnatural shade of red swept his face.

He jumped up, grabbed me by the arm, and led me away.

"You are hurting me!" I shrugged him off. I still had enough strength to set him off-balance, though he righted himself immediately.

"What is this trickery?" he demanded when he thought we were too far to be overheard. His cheeks were sunken, and his hair had begun to fall out, but his diminished health didn't stop him from snarling through gritted teeth. "What demons have you unleashed from your hell?"

I took my time, brushing a lingering green serpent out of my hair. "I tried to help you negotiate peace. I begged you." I pointed outside to the field piled with dead bodies. "That is *your* hellscape. Yours and the Tlaxcallans. Never forget that."

"I don't know what you are, but that creature is"—he hunted for the word—"unacceptable!"

I shivered with delight. "I am your interpreter. And, how shall I say this? I have . . . gifts. Because of that, you can thank me later; I just saved your life and those of your men, the Maya, and the Totonacs, whom you appear to have no regard for."

"I was winning!" he snapped. He looked to grab me again, then appeared to think twice about it.

Careful. You are so close to the Great Temple, where Moctezuma sits on his throne. I softened my stance and sweetened my voice. "Yes, clearly. You are stronger. Your weapons immeasurably more powerful and deadly. Your God far superior to those of this land," I lied. I watched as he wiped the spittle from his beard with the sleeve of his yellowed shirt. "But today, you are much closer to achieving your goal and seeing Tenochtitlan and Moctezuma." How could he argue with that?

Cortés would have filled my ear with rants for the rest of the day had his scribe, Bernal Díaz, not motioned him away with his ink-stained hands. Catching my gaze, the man nodded. "Doña," he greeted courteously. "The Tlaxcallans are waiting."

With dignity, I turned on my heels and walked to rejoin our guests.

▲▲▲▲

Most of the Spaniards scurried away, but a handful stepped gallantly aside to let me pass. Their faces were gaunt and their eyes weary, yet they bowed gracefully and filled the air with their salutations.

"Doña Marina."

"Doña."

"The finest woman in all the world."

Interesting. Not one mention of the creature they'd seen on the battlefield. As if they refused to believe it or were too afraid that I might bring it back. I preferred to believe they were thankful that I had ended the war.

The emissaries bent to kiss the earth three times. One of the men, with many green feathers in his hair and an unadorned red cloak hanging limply from his shoulders, stepped apart from the others and bowed his head. In a clear voice, Red Cloak claimed that they had been sent by the great chiefs Xicotencatl and Maxixcatzin to negotiate peace.

In addition to presenting us with treasure, they placed at my feet four reed baskets filled with embroidered cloth and mantles. I welcomed the attention and acknowledged their gift with a slight nod, as if I were accustomed to this kind of display. I could not resist taking a closer look and reached down. I thought I would find cloth as beautiful as the fabric woven by the Cempoallans, but as I turned back the edges and fingered the weave of one mantle after another, I grew more and more disappointed. Such poor cloth. Not even cotton but maguey fiber.

I flicked a patch of dried mud off my cloak. Proud of myself for surviving on this godforsaken plain and for enduring every misfortune that had been heaped on my head, I looked straight into the eyes of the Tlaxcallan ambassador standing before me.

He immediately humbled himself, casting his gaze down and taking a step back. This satisfied me immensely. "Malin . . ." he sounded out, trying to mimic Cortés's name for me. Then the man jumped and corrected himself. "Malin*tzin*," he said, adding the delicate sweep of sound that paid honor to people of status.

Unmoved, I stared until he melted away. I could hear his heart nervously thumping in his chest. I looked down at my hands and clasped them together. Negotiating this peace would take skill. Calm must prevail. Tempers held in check. I was confident in my ability, trusted my old and *new* powers.

My voice was never stronger. As I saw the faces looking at me with reverence, I felt my spirit soar, as if I were about to levitate above the crowd. I was so overcome I had to breathe deeply just to keep my feet on the ground. To everyone gathered here, I already had a gold crown on my head. *Here I am, now ruling these men. What will it take for me to command an entire army?* Pride soared through me as I looked past Cortés's petulant stare. I was so close. When Cortés raised his voice and paced and moved his arms in cutting strokes, I did not smooth over his anger. Even though I had always believed that a courtly tone was best, I did not feel that way now. Perhaps the curt roughness in my voice stemmed from my impatience to press forward to Tenochtitlan. I was tired of this journey. Everyone was.

I took pleasure in watching the Tlaxcallans turn pale with fear. I not only mirrored the captain's displeasure, but I also surpassed it. My rage roared through each word. Every man listened to me, their eyes flicking between Cortés and myself, as if they could not decide whom to fear more.

Red Cloak searched my face in an effort to better understand the captain's and my discontent, but I revealed nothing. I turned to Cortés. His red-feathered cap appeared ready to take flight in the wind; he tugged it back into place as he grumbled, scoffing at the Tlaxcallans as they apologized for attacking us. They had thought we were allies of Moctezuma.

"It makes no difference to me," Cortés argued, "that you believed we were friends of Moctezuma. I offered you my hand in friendship!"

I flung these words in Nahuatl at the Tlaxcallan people. They shook their heads and wrung their hands, explaining how they had loathed the Mexica since the times of the ancients, for they were robbers and pillagers who wanted nothing more than to destroy the Tlaxcallans.

"It makes no difference to me," Cortés grumbled again, "that you are enemies of the Mexica. We"—he pounded his breast—"came in peace, not war, and should have been welcomed as friends."

His speech excited me. This talk continued as the sun charted its course across the sky. Anger inflamed Cortés and spilled naturally from my tongue.

The peoples' awe of me made me feel as though I could walk through walls. Like I was nahual-animal again. Even Cortés's men were quiet.

Oh, to hold them like that!

In that moment, I thought of my mother, of her warning me about how words would bring me shame and sorrow.

How I wished she could have seen me.

Look at your daughter now, I told myself, hoping that she could somehow hear me.

I allowed my gaze to move slowly over the faces of the Tlaxcallans gathered in front of me. Now I—Malinalli, Mali, Malintzin, Doña Marina, daughter of Jade Feather and Speaking Cloud, priestess of the Temple of the Eighteen Moons, Malinalxochitl, a sorceress in more than name—spoke for empires.

"Go back to your lords," I ordered the Tlaxcallans. "And tell them that either they must come themselves to negotiate this peace or send men with greater power. If they refuse, I, and this lord, promise that we will come to their towns and attack them."

Red Cloak blubbered, saying he would inform Xicotencatl the Elder of the words I had spoken. Cortés then shouted that the green translucent beads he was so fond of should be brought to the men to give to their leaders as signs of peace. It was his custom to give these gifts. They were pretty, but much less valuable than jade and turquoise.

The emissaries left, and that night we had plenty to eat, as the women who accompanied them prepared maize cakes, beans, and a rich stew of duck meat and turkey with tomatoes and sweet potatoes. The women fetched our water and chopped our wood to keep the fires burning and the cold away.

▲▲▲▲

We were able to breathe easier now that peace was ours. Still, Cortés and his men refused to rest without their swords by their sides, their horses saddled and ready. The wind continued to bite our bones. But I could not sleep that night. Even a warm fire and a full belly provided no relief. I tossed and turned, thinking that I might not be able to control this special power and lead the army that was gathering to serve my will. I worried myself into a fraught sleep and dreamed that Moctezuma was possessed by his animal guardian too, and the jaguar was waiting for me.

PEACE

Many Tlaxcallans took my appearance on the battlefield as a prophetic sign. It was just as Copil had said: now that a sorceress had taken up sword and shield and aligned herself with the White Men, there was no hope that the Tlaxcallans would defeat the intruders from the east. Even though it was impossible for me to tell Cortés that it was because of *me* that the Tlaxcallans sued for peace, my secret puffed me up.

In my later dealings with the Tlaxcallans, I held my chin so high it scratched the clouds.

I spoke for Cortés. I spoke for the son of Xicotencatl. On the white captain's sixteenth day of September, my words linked the two men like a well-built bridge. When my throat would dry, I had only to lift my hand, and water would be brought without delay. I could do anything now. No one would be able to stop me. Cortés was under my control, and soon I would rule. I would bring harmony and return the land to the way it should have been long ago, when Malinalxochitl was destined to sit on the throne.

▲▲▲▲

It was the month we called the Return of the Gods.

In the fog time of daybreak, as we negotiated the terms of peace, Xicotencatl the Younger, whose face was as pocked as a dish left out in a hailstorm, peppered his speech with laments as to how horribly Moctezuma and the Mexica warriors treated his people.

"All-Powerful Lady, Lord Malintzin, look at our cloaks," he said. "They are woven of maguey thread, for we have no cotton here. And no sooner do we go in search of it than Moctezuma's men are upon us, driving us back.

"Nor do we have salt. So forgive us poor Tlaxcallans if we do not prepare the finest of feasts for you."

It was then I noticed the shields carried by the young Xicotencatl's warrior guard. I studied them, while taking care not to miss any of the man's words, so I could interpret their meaning for Cortés. The shields were not of deer or jaguar pelt but of human skin. I couldn't help but wonder if any were made from the flayed flesh of a Spaniard.

My mouth felt painfully dry. I coughed, and five people jumped and brought me water in clay cups. I thanked them and drank, listening to Xicotencatl's hatred for Moctezuma and his people rumble like thunder in his throat. Such depth of feeling echoed the view of the chief of Cempoallan and reinforced the fact that not all of the people of this land were friends with the great Moctezuma.

I looked away from the young ruler's face in time to see the light in Cortés's eyes grow bright as Xicotencatl's anger spilled slowly and deliberately like honey, thick off the comb. I saw the exact moment the Spaniard's idea took hold. What would happen if he were to ask the Tlaxcallans to join his army? Would it not be better, for peace's sake, to march into Tenochtitlan with a great and united force of men?

▲▲▲▲

My talks with the Tlaxcallans continued for three days. One morning, as I prepared for another day of negotiations, Cortés presented me with forty reed baskets filled with treasures, including many embroidered cotton mantles.

"You have demonstrated very fully your desire to serve His Majesty and to give account to all the things of this land. Please accept these tokens of his appreciation," he announced with authority. He bowed to me, then in a lower voice full of bile, "We will not speak about your devil tricks for now. But mark me, lady, we will have a meeting with Fray Bartolome, in the sight of God, and talk of what transpired on the field of battle. Do you understand?" He didn't wait for a reply. Instead, he straightened, turned, and gestured toward the door to my chamber, where five women stood, their slim throats weighted down with wooden slave collars.

I moved to shrug, unaffected by his comments, but the appearance of these innocents shocked the breath from me. My fury sparked, but before I could lash out, Cortés turned on his heels and left the room. I could feel all of my fears and frustrations, my rage, taking over and twisting me. I must have appeared like a monster, for the women cringed and backed away from me.

Ashamed of myself, I rushed to comfort them, and with Hummingbird's help, I removed their collars, understanding all too well its pain and discomfort.

I gave each of them one hundred cotton mantles. "You are free to go. You can trade the valuable cloth for anything you desire," I explained.

Not one raised her gaze to thank me. They stood silently, some biting their lips. The youngest of them, who could not have been more than fifteen years, looked ready to cry.

As Hummingbird gave them maize cakes to eat and honey water, one of the women finally said that many of them had nowhere safe to go. Another cried, "How will I ever find my home? It is on the other side of the mountains." Could they stay with me?

"You must accept," Hummingbird whispered. "They will be safer here, with you."

But I needed no one's help caring for myself.

She cleared her throat, drawing my attention, and continued. "Perhaps, in time, we can take them to the Temple of the Eighteen Moons, where they can learn the ways of the priestess."

I pulled my sister into my arms and kissed her on her forehead. Yes, that was what we would do. The Temple!

Sensing that their lives were about to change again, the women threw wary glances at one another and drew closer together. Then, between sips of water, I began to tell them about the High Priestess, Rose Petal, Morning Star, and Jeweled Laughter. Smiles appeared. Heads nodded. With Hummingbird's encouragement, I told them my stories.

I felt no unease accepting the necklaces of turquoise and bracelets of gold, earrings made with white heron feathers and small red beads. One basket held elegant plates and bowls, another revealed a tortoise shell, bronze incense burners, and a soft rug made of brown deer hides. I found a mirror carefully tucked inside blue cloth. Unlike our dark obsidian mirrors, this one was as clear as a pool of mountain water. I held the mirror up, but the silvery sphere reflected nothing. I turned it and looked again, but I wasn't there.

BOOK VI

MAGIC'S PRISONER

I woke to an angry throbbing. It came from the right side of my head, as though someone were beating me with a wooden cudgel. My body ached, too, as if I had been dragged and kicked. And there was a strange, cloying smell that turned my stomach. I swallowed hard to keep the bilious stuff down.

I blinked against the contracting pain as I tried to open my eyes. There was nothing but cold, onyx darkness.

"Hello?" It took all my strength to push the word free. Shivering, I listened for a reply, which could have been as feeble as my voice. Nothing. The quiet spurred my skin to prickle, the blue tattoo to burn in spite of the cold.

Alarmed, I tried to sit. I pushed up slowly, barely able to move my head, but then my stomach whirled, and I fell back. I felt stones beneath me. I reached out and fingered their roughness. *Where am I?* Panic squeezed my chest, but I talked myself down by saying, *Look up! There. See?* And I settled, relieved that I could see little pinpricks of gray light, high above me. Over time they would turn orange, red, the gold of sunlight, and it would be enough for me to see that I was in a stone chamber with no door or opening of any kind.

Questions were all I had to attack with.

Where was I? Who did this to me? How long had I been imprisoned?

I rolled myself up, taking care of my head, which felt like a colossus, pushing my palms into the stone floor to brace myself, breathing through my mouth to ease the throbbing and nausea. I pulled my knees to my chest to rest, and suddenly my memory went flying back to the cage at the market in Xicallanco, where I had waited to be sold.

No, no, not that. I took deep breaths to calm my nerves. *Center yourself,* I heard Hummingbird say. *Breathe.* But it was a fight to keep the image of the slave trader and the feelings of anguish and terror at bay.

Then another memory. Or was it a disjointed dream from another night? A vague image of Hummingbird's nahual animal guardian engaged in a fight, protecting me. I remembered seeing the vixen and feeling the cool sweep of a dark mantle against my limbs. And there'd been a smell, sweet, like a flower. *Oleander?*

Before any memory could have a chance to settle in my bones, I tried to stand up. My legs were unsteady. My head whirled again. I thought I was going to be sick, so I reached out to find, and lean against, a wall, a corner. Finding none, I hobbled forward into the dark, holding my arms in front of me as if I were blind. Thankfully, my stomach settled. Pushing myself to confidence, I strode forward and felt my way around walls. Maybe four walls? I wasn't sure. Everything felt the same.

Then something struck me in the ankle. I cried out in surprise and felt a rush of air as a force pushed against my legs. I looked down and caught a blade of gold light before it vanished.

"Is someone there? Let me out!" I cried loudly, banging my fists against the stones, quickly regretting my actions. But again, there was no answer. After licking the gouges in my hands, I reached down and felt my way in the dark, until my fingers were able to make out a plate, a corn cake, and something wet like soup.

Something struck me again, but it was the other ankle this time. Another flash of light.

"Wait!" I dropped to my knees and stared into the light, which lingered longer now. It hurt my eyes, but I wouldn't look away. "Where am I?" My voice hung in the air, and I felt the light hesitate before it whispered a name.

"Tlaxcallan."

I heard bricks slide, and the light disappeared. I groped in the dark, looking for a crack, the opening. But I found nothing save for a folded mantle, a chamber pot.

"Who are you?" I shouted. My panic now had teeth and wanted to attack someone. I cursed a word I'd learned from Copil. I kicked at the wall, though it was half-hearted, as I didn't want to cause my body further harm.

Stirred up, angry now, my intuition nudged me to a different kind of attention. *Magic. Use your magic.* I said the charm to myself, then out loud: "I am Malinalxochitl, sorceress in more than name." I waited for the words to unlock my power, kindle a spell and set my serpent-self loose. Maybe I didn't believe in my new skill enough, I thought when nothing happened. So, I closed my eyes and imagined I was back on the battlefield—my glistening fangs, the coiled neck, snakes writhing in my hair—positioning myself, raising my arm, as if I were about to deliver sword blows. And I waited.

Nothing.

▲▲▲▲

I ripped the maize cake apart and shoved it into my mouth. It took all my will to swallow. I'd pulled the mantle over myself. The weight of it on my legs kept the darkness from eating me up. Before sitting down to see what they'd given me to eat, I had mapped out my prison. It took me twenty-four steps to walk from one wall to another. Eventually I would count four of them. All stone. I was resting my head against the wall as I chewed, keeping my gaze on the slitted openings above me to see if I could mark the passage of time. Pink light was filtering through, faintly coloring the walls. Probably morning.

Once I realized I was sealed up and could not quickly escape, it freed my mind to reason through possible explanations and nurture ideas. The obvious one: the Tlaxcallans and Cortés had locked me up, and the cell was ensorcelled with a powerful entrapment spell. I had frightened them. My animal ally had unnerved Cortés. He had been malleable, up to a point. When we were alone in his quarters in Tlaxcallan after the battle, he had called me the "Devil's Daughter." He raged while holding a crucifix and screamed, "You walk around as if you and those hideous creatures won. As if this is your army now. But it's mine. My faithful, heroic, invincible army. My men. My horses. My guns. Mine!"

The Tlaxcallans would have been accustomed to acts of magic and sorcerers undergoing transformations, so it was harder to be sure why they would need to lock me away. Maybe they were less awed and more wary. They may have been less sure of my allegiance, though anyone who knew the ancestral legend of Malinalxochitl could have guessed that I was no friend of Moctezuma's. I had planned to talk to them about joining me, supporting my army once it reached Tenochtitlan. I did not want a war. I wanted no wars. I wanted change. I wanted the warrior-sorceress, the goddess, to take her rightful place on the jaguar throne.

But maybe that's not what the Tlaxcallans wanted. What had Xicotencatl the Elder said to me at the last feast? I pictured the wrinkled face, the cavern of a mouth lacking teeth. "Moctezuma's power encompasses many nations. He can command hundreds of thousands of men to follow him onto the battlefield with no more than a day's notice. But he has never defeated the Tlaxcallans!" he'd voiced triumphantly. It sounded to me like he enjoyed their wars. Maybe he believed that Cortés was powerful enough to vanquish the Mexica. With them subdued, the Tlaxcallans would rise to power. The old man would finally rule over the enemies of his forefathers.

But what did it matter now?

I had been so close. After Tlaxcallan, all that remained in my way was the city of Chalollan and a mountain pass through volcanoes. Then we would have been in the valley of the lakes and within sight of the island city of Tenochtitlan.

Anger flared in my belly. *How dare they stop me!* All spit and spite, forgetting the ways of the Temple, I flew into a venomous rage.

I should have allowed Cortés and the Tlaxcallans to kill each other off. I should have stood quietly and watched.

I shoved the clay plate and bowl, overturning the maize cake and soup. I wasn't sorry for anything that I'd done, just hoped Hummingbird, Copil, and the Maya were all right. Thinking about my friends vanquished angry thoughts, and suddenly, I felt my body go limp. *Cortés won't hurt them, will he?*

▲▲▲▲

When the gold light turned rose, and I knew the warrior women were carrying the Sun Lord on his litter chair made of feathers to his rest, a thought bloomed, knocking the breath from me:

The legendary story of Malinalxochitl was repeating itself.

Once again, the sorceress had been abandoned by the War God, left in the dark. His name wasn't Huitzilopochtli this time, but Hernán Cortés, and he was moving toward Tenochtitlan, armed with new kinds of thunderbolts and monstrous dragon-like creatures that made child's play out of plundering and preying.

I knew how the ancient story ended—with people massacred, a son's heart cut out and thrown away. I couldn't let that happen again.

With a sudden sharp feeling of pain, I realized that this story could end the same way, if not worse. For what was more dangerous than two enemies, two men, who believed they had the rights of gods?

In my mind, I saw my father, drinking his own spittle and begging for a small morsel, as his body wasted away until it lay ashen, in a cage, with no one to mourn or weep for his loss. I saw Eagle's eager face turning from joy to panic as the jaguar bore down on him in the House of Magical Studies, nowhere to run. The cold emissary telling my mother they were never coming home. We would never hear them laugh or sing again.

And this was all Moctezuma's fault. But as for Cortés's evilness . . . I felt as if a blade were twisting inside me. Was I not to blame, too? Moctezuma had entrapped and destroyed my family. *But haven't I set the path to my own entrapment? Have I not believed that I had the rights of a goddess?* Up until now, Cortés had had my help. I'd made a pact with this devil—this was clear. But with no one to restrain him and the Tlaxcallans, no tongue to steer them away from their weapons, the bloodlust would take over, and they would destroy everything. Not just Moctezuma, but everyone, every living thing.

Now that the past had reawakened in my bones, I was quick to imagine destruction everywhere. I saw the Temple of the Eighteen Moons razed. The shield gone. I pulled at my hair and reeled back and forth between the walls, my spirit a whirling miasma of loss entwined with fear. *It is not possible. They are protected by magic. It can't happen. But what if . . .*

The Temple is in danger.

"You fools!" I shouted to my hidden captors. "You've given Cortés the power to lay waste to everything that stands in his way. He will not stop. He doesn't know how to stop." His greed for gold and fortune were his only true motivations. He talked of "saving souls," but what he valued most was his prowess as a captain and hoarding treasure. I'd seen him lining his horse's packs with gold. He hid it inside secret pockets in his garments, the heels of his boots.

Just then, I thought I felt the walls move. I went cold. Listened. The vibrations set off by my voice were loosening the stones? I felt my way around, pushing here and there to see if there was some way out. I had to free myself before it was too late. I understood the Tlaxcallans and Cortés now. I already knew Moctezuma. Someone had to stop them. Moctezuma and Cortés must never be allowed to meet.

I fought to steady myself, compose my thoughts. "Think," I said out loud. "Center yourself." I stopped and took deep breaths. "Look inside." I closed my eyes.

Immediately, I saw her: Hummingbird.

"*There you are*," she said, shimmering toward me, the image echoing a time long past in the labyrinth. My heart rejoiced to see her—such elegant steps, her dark braid with the shock of white. "*Come, I will show you the way*," she said, holding out her hand. "*You are quite close, Malinalxochitl.*" Her smile was cheery. "*You would have found your way before nightfall.*"

Startled, I opened my eyes. Long ago, she had deflated my pridefulness with these same words, but this time, I laughed.

Centered and at ease, feeling that my sister was with me in my stone prison, I knelt down and began my meditation. In this cell conjured by depraved minds, I prayed to the goddesses for help.

THE SACRED CENTER OF THE HUIPILLI

Oh, Earth Mother and Malinalxochitl, I humbly beseech you to come to my aid. Help me stop the storm that gathers in the mountains. I pledge my sword to you. I will do whatever you ask of me in payment for your help." I swallowed, sure of the next words but ashamed to say them out loud. "For too long, I allowed my dark desires to avenge my family's deaths to rule my thoughts and bond me to evil. Forgive me. Forgive this priestess and warrior. Forgive this daughter and sister. Please, I humbly beseech you to give me a chance to stop this. What has been set in motion . . . I know I can stop. Give me the strength to right the course forward. After all I have studied, all I have endured, please grant me this: destroy these barriers, so that I might prove to you that I am your ever-faithful servant."

Speaking these words, listening to their echo, spirited me back to the Temple of the Eighteen Moons and to the shrine in the forest. It was as if my prison were turning into that holy place. The air changed. The cold void receded completely. I held myself as still as possible as I watched the goddesses' images emerge out of the walls and grow into giants. I heard their oceanic breaths. Saw pink, yellow, and orange blooms the size of pumpkins exploding against the walls. Giant green leaves unfurled and tumbled around me in the air. There was the scent of earth and mud and warm corn, of sweat and roses.

Malinalxochitl's white skirt billowed in my face, and blue stitchwork inched in and out of the cotton in serpentine moves. I was too afraid to look Earth Mother in the face, but I chanced a glance at the sorceress, the real Malinalxochitl. Her eyes were edged with black soot. Small silver snakes served as crown and net to keep her churning fall of raven hair from overtaking the space. The warrior-sorceress stood high enough to reach the slivered openings in the walls, which glowed with a strange gold light that appeared to spark and fire off the obsidian shards on her shield.

I kissed the ground and noticed blue-sandaled feet, beautiful in their immensity, like the carved trunks of a rare aromatic tree. Hesitantly, I sat back on my heels. I tipped my head to see the sorceress's face more clearly.

"Malinalxochitl?" I whispered in wonder.

"I am she." Her voice was low and throaty, with the heft of confident spell casting. "I have heard your prayers, young sorceress." She leaned down from her lofty position to take a closer look at me. Her eyes were dark, amber-flecked caverns. A dark pink color outlined her lips.

I struggled to control my breath, the flutters in my stomach, my trembling hands, but I willed myself to speak. "I need your help to escape. My magic does not work here."

She laughed and looked at Earth Mother, as if to see if she'd heard me. Earth Mother simply stared. I didn't understand what Malinalxochitl found so amusing. She'd stung my pride.

"Let me say that a different way—" I began, hoping to correct myself.

"No need. You were quite clear. Of course your magic works, *sorceress in more than name*," she said a little too playfully for my taste. "I assure you," she continued. "Just think of the power you have always had, since the beginning, that which is solely yours, and you will achieve your wish." She straightened herself and sighed.

I felt as if a weight had been lifted off my shoulders. However, I didn't understand what she meant. I looked at her companion, wondering if she was going to say something to me now.

"Earth Mother never speaks. Actions are her words," the warrior-sorceress said.

As if to demonstrate, they began to stretch their limbs, causing a strong wind to whip around the confining space. I steadied and grounded myself as best I could in the buttressing gales as they spread their feet in the warrior pose, a position I knew from training with the High Priestess. I could have touched them, my hands almost within reach of them, but reasoning told me that such an act might break the spell.

And yet, how could I *not* touch them? I allowed the wind to carry me closer, and I rested my hands on their skirts. And with that connection, my life's most joyful and sorrow-filled moments appeared before my eyes, a merging of colors bright and ashen, a storm of comforting and terrifying sounds. Once again, my brother and I were playing in the marshes, then sitting with my mother, admiring the painted books. I saw my mother and me sitting in the courtyard, her gift of the turquoise necklace gracing my throat, pride jeweled with tears in her eyes. In quick sweeps, I revisited the Temple of the Eighteen Moons, solved the labyrinth with Hummingbird's help, and ventured to the special shrine that held the sorceress's shield. I heard the rushing of the Coatzacoalcos, heard Pakal Balam's deep voice, and then the sounds of that surprise attack by the river. From the sweetness of my Maya's touch to the stink of the cage in Xicallanco—I relived it all. Moments from my journey with Cortés swept before me one after the other with the fierceness of arrow shots. The first rising of my animal ally appeared haloed in light.

Even when I wanted to drop my arms and let go of the goddesses, when I thought that I couldn't bear to see or feel anything more, I held on. *This is who you are*, they seemed to be saying to me.

The chamber grew silent then, and the air stilled of all movement and flashes of light. For a moment I felt as if I were suspended inside a crystal.

Then Earth Mother, jaws snapping, shouting, tore at the walls with her bare hands. The sorceress reached out with her shield to protect me from a storm of falling stones.

▲▲▲▲

After they'd gone, I paced in the darkness. Traveling back through my life had quickened my blood. Real stones still held me fast, though the goddesses' scent lingered in my head. I took comfort in this, the visions, and in Earth Mother's attempt to break me out and the warrior-sorceress's act to keep me safe. I had prayed for their aid, and they'd come. And those fiery shards of obsidian! I couldn't help marveling again at the intensity of light captured by the shield's strange design. The High Priestess had told me a story about how, long ago, the light was strong enough to stop the sun in its path, altering time.

The shield.

The essence of a plan sharpened inside me. I needed the shield of the people's protector. I would use it to stop time and halt Cortés's progress. I would draw on my nahual again and seek help from the goddesses and do whatever else was necessary to keep the two monsters apart.

▲▲▲▲

Heart pounding, palms sweating, fingers twitching in anticipation of holding the shield located at the Temple of Eighteen Moons, I whirled around on my heels. I was ready, except there was the small matter of breaking free from my prison of stone.

Was it then that the threads in my huipilli danced? Or were they alive the entire time and I hadn't been paying attention, so used to their antics, so jaded by their magic. *My* magic. Power I'd had long before I learned the meaning of my brother's word charm. And now that I'd seen Earth Mother, entwined with living vines and flowers . . .

It was then that I knew.

Working quickly, confident beyond any reasonable person's level of confidence, I removed my huipilli and tore it so that it would lie flat, with the opening for my head at the center. I talked to the embroidery as I worked, tenderly whispering, "Don't worry, be brave now, all will be set right in just a moment . . ." The embroidery calmed as I stretched the fabric flat and gently smoothed the folds over the stones. The patterns of lightning stitched along the hem set off streaks of light so that I could see.

I knelt before my huipilli, focusing on the center, the opening. "The sacred center," I whispered to myself. "Where a woman feels safe and empowered. Center of life. Without beginning or end. Center of feelings and thought. Where all life is entwined."

I drew a long breath.

I did not have long to wait. The vines and flowers woven into the cotton sprang free and spread across the floor, working the stones, tunneling through them and prying them apart until the floor began to crack. I heard digging, twisting sounds. Their work was more silken than a hill of working ants, more ethereal than bees. With wonder, I watched the stepped patterns, the serpentine curls, how these, too, undulated, adding their strength to the efforts of the blooms and leaves. The cell's walls shook as the hole widened. The vines spread and wove their way down into an ever-widening space.

When I heard no sounds coming from the gaping hole, I thought the embroidered threads might be finished. Still on my knees, I leaned carefully to peer over the edge. The dark was beautiful. The scent of earthy green leaves, lilies, marigolds, and roses eclipsed the cold dank of mortar and rock. The vines and flowers were alive, chattering as they worked their way down. Pulling and stretching and popping as if the earth were as pliant as cloth. A happy sound.

I was dizzy with delight, a feeling I was unused to. I laughed, clapping my hands, which seemed to cast light into the shadows of my prison. I peered over again and bit my lip. *Sometimes the only opening is through darkness.* I remembered the High Priestess's words. This had to be the moment of my escape.

My heart beat loudly. Blood rushed in my ears. I waited a breath more before I made my move. Clutching the vines, I lowered myself into the flowering circle created by my huipilli, climbed down through that leafy bower that had been created for me, and left that ensorcelled place.

▲▲▲▲

The soft illumination of lightning beetles guided me. Catching sight of the bottom, I let myself drop the rest of the way. The familiarity of the paintings around me, the rich smell of earth, was unmistakable. They strengthened me. I cried out with relief, for I was back at Malinalxochitl's shrine in the forest outside the Temple of the Eighteen Moons.

With a pass of my hand, I lit the torch on the wall, casting a glow across the jaguar throne and the copper altar. Heart hammering, I turned on my heels to face the weapon I sought.

The shield was gone. My heart dropped like a stone, breaking into pieces. The dark and fear of the prison reclaimed me, and for a moment the low rumble of an owl creature's laugh sought me out. In this most blessed of shrines, I felt my hope and quest crumble to dust. *What now? I have nothing.*

I grabbed the copper altar for support. Upon pulling myself upright, I noticed strange emanations rising from the surface. Long ago, the mirror had remained cold and blank, so a part of me wanted to ignore it now. But I was no longer that girl.

Now I looked and saw myself clearly. Grimy face. Untidy hair. Naked breasts. No sword. No shield. Like a trick, my image wavered and slipped away. Flames erupted in the mirror's depths, and I saw men and women running. From what? I forced myself to face it. White Men, armed, were killing everyone in their path. There was Cortés with balls of flames in his hands, setting a city on fire. I had never had the gift of prophecy before. Was this the city of Chalollan, or Tenochtitlan? Was I too late to stop them?

I ran through the shrine, past the empty wall, the paintings, and out into the light. After time spent in the darkness of my prison, the sun's rays seared me. I cried out, covering my aching eyes. The sun was my enemy. I crumpled to the ground until the pain dulled. When I finally looked up, there they all were. Toci and the High Priestess, Rose Petal, Morning Star, and Jeweled Laughter stood together. At their backs were all the priestesses in their white blouses and skirts.

▲▲▲▲

Toci walked toward me, holding the shield. Her face showed pride, but also relief. Part of me wanted to run to her, to bawl in her embrace, but, covering my breasts with my arms, I kept my steps measured and held tight to calm. I remembered another time at the Temple, when she told me that my mother had gone away, and I'd said that I felt abandoned, that I had no family. How wrong I'd been. Here was my family. I felt the sweep of love and gratitude and the heart pull of belonging. *If only Hummingbird and Copil were here*, I thought, and then in the next instant: *I need to get back to them.* Toci, the midwife who had guided me into the world, nodded as if she could read my thoughts.

"It was prophesied in the obsidian mirror that you would come," she said, her smile wide.

She placed the shield at my feet. The weapon released an otherworldly glow in the sunlight. I knew my animal guardian would do everything it had to in order to win, but there were many people who needed this shield's protection now. My plan needed to work. My voice had caused harm. It would take ten shields and the strength of ten warrior-sorceresses to set things right.

My heart was beating so loudly, I was sure the spiny-backed caiman who encompassed the world could hear. I began to tremble and felt a cry rising in my throat.

Toci immediately closed the space between us and steadied me with her hand and voice. "My strong girl. My little dove, precious feather, my bracelets of opals and gold, come. Everything has been prepared." She paused and, turning my face to meet her gaze, she said, "We are together now. You are safe."

▲▲▲▲

Toci burned copal incense on a bed of twigs arranged on a flat stone, moving her hands to send the smoke swirling as she prayed. I sat in front of her, and she began to rub sage leaves over me, then a sweet-smelling oil followed by salt, in circles over my skin. I felt I could have jumped as high as the moon.

Toci and I were still facing Malinalxochitl's temple, with the High Priestess, Rose Petal, and Morning Star in attendance. After bidding me welcome and listening to my stories about the stone prison, the goddesses' manifestation, and the leafy passage created by the embroidered threads, the other priestesses had returned to their studies. Only Jeweled Laughter remained. The white peaks of her hair reminded me of my journey to the Underworld and how I'd nearly caused her death. My sister's embrace and gladness to see me softened the memory, but it was a time in my life I would never forget and feel content about.

The midwife had drawn a large circle in the earth at the foot of the staircase to the shrine and marked it with nature's treasures.

She pointed in the direction of a wall of trees. "North. Place of death. Fate." An eagle feather lay atop a piece of flint on a white cloth. The polished surface glinted in the sunlight. She turned to her right, where a red parrot feather and red shells lay. "East. Place of the dawn. The beginning." The wind whistled. "South. Site of promise and magic." Here was a turquoise stone. "And west," she murmured, turning again, "where the old ways die to be reborn." A clay spindle whorl and a hummingbird feather marked it.

Surrounded by these offerings, Toci washed me with water from the copper bowl that Earth Mother had forged, then slipped clean garments over my head. She brushed and coiled my hair into a braid, weaving white ribbons into the plaits.

"Now we will wait for the wind, the breath of the gods and goddesses, to join us."

I raised my gaze to the sky. The winds came in the order they had been summoned, beginning with a cold howling blast from the north. From the east came tendrils as rose-colored as the dawn, with the essence of salt. The south blessed us with warm breezes smelling of damp earth. And from the west, chattering winds filled with gold dust. Great rumbles filled the air as if far-off mountains were signaling their wish to join us.

Raising her arms out to the sides, her palms open, Toci began our prayer. "Today we breathe life, thanks to you, oh gods and goddesses of heaven and earth, sky, rivers, and seas. We bow and bare our souls before you, Earth Mother, Feathered Butterfly, and Wild Grass Flower, protectors and destroyers. We humbly ask for your shielding strength and guidance as we continue in our quest and walk the wisdom of the heart."

▲▲▲▲

Looking to the gods for wisdom is no small task, but Toci told the divine ones that my life thus far had been a journey beset by tragedy and uncertainty. I needed their help. "Her spirit and soul must be strong and steady for the work that lies ahead of her in Tenochtitlan."

After the winds calmed, Toci gathered the parrot and eagle feathers, the turquoise stone and a fistful of sage, and swept them over my body, from my head to my toes. She called for my heart, spirit, and soul to be forever strong. Her voice grew fierce as she prayed that all doubts and worries that might be fighting inside me be released to the winds.

Lightness came over me then. The stones of childhood grief and the tears lodged deep in my throat and beneath my breast disappeared.

Toci stepped out of the circle, then the High Priestess entered holding the shield and the same sword she used when we were training. I knelt before her and bowed my head.

"River Twin, sorceress in name and deed, true daughter of Earth Mother: I charge you to defend the Temple of the Eighteen Moons and to restore harmony and balance to the land in the name of the warrior-sorceress and goddess Malinalxochitl."

TRUST

It was dawn, the sky the palest pink, when I found myself ankle deep in an unfamiliar muddy marsh, surrounded by tall plants. I'd spent the evening with the priestesses, and had slept in my old, familiar chamber. Before first light, Toci had led me to Feathered Butterfly's throne room. She'd burned copal in the incense burner and, after blessing me in the name of all of the goddesses, whispered a short prayer. The words must have held magic, for just as I reached out to thank her, this marshland had replaced the Temple. Now flies and mosquitoes were buzzing around my head. I parted the grasses and reeds and stepped carefully so as not to slip and drop the sword and shield I was now responsible for. I hoped I was close to Tenochtitlan.

"You will require no guide," the High Priestess had said at the same moment that I thought to myself I wouldn't need a guide. She shook her head, reading my cocksure mind. "The mirrored surface of the shield will allow you to go anywhere." She acknowledged my surprise with a knowing smile. "Trust in the shield, and it will trust you."

Just ahead of me, I could make out a patch of cloudy green water. Ducks with emerald heads paddled in and out of the reeds. One of the birds, trailing the others, turned to watch me. I could see its feet paddling furiously beneath the water. When my brother and I were little, we talked to animals all the time, and it seemed I'd had a gift for it. It was worth a try now. "Can you please tell me where I am?" The duck tilted its head. *Look, it understands.* But then it ruffled its feathers, turned, and glided away to join the others.

I also needed to move quickly. The obsidian mirror had revealed a burning city and a confrontation between two forces on a levitating road of white stone.

I pushed on, my feet making eddies in the film of muddy water. After a few more steps, I emerged out of the thick reeds and onto the banks of a lake. Beyond the water rose the city that had haunted me my entire life: Tenochtitlan.

It soared out of the water as if an enchantment had placed it there. I had thought it would be an ugly place, squalid and suffocated by dark, brooding clouds. I was glad to see I had been wrong.

The city glistened in the rose light with temples and palaces of whitewashed stone, painted with the most vivid reds, blues, greens, and yellows. Long feather banners rose from rooftops like colorful sighs. Such marvelous words as existed in all the tongues of the world could not have prepared me for what I saw now. This was a dream breathed into being by a sacred force. It was a jeweled bracelet that had fallen from the heavens, off the wrist of a goddess. This was Moctezuma's city, I reminded myself. His center of power. Another reason to hate it. But I felt no anger. Instead, an almost rapturous disbelief.

For the first time since discovering my nahual animal guardian, I allowed myself to relax. To the east stood mountains, with two volcanoes towering above the rest, standing guard over the lake valley. There was mist veiling their peaks, and the rising dawn was turning it coral. A white causeway stretched in the distance, floating above the water. Closer to me, birds sang and flapped above the grasses. I heard the plop of frogs and the flitter of dragonfly wings. Everything sounded lazy. Even the scent of the reedy marsh encouraged reflection over action.

But not for long.

The wail of a shell trumpet pierced the air, drawing my attention back to the city. I imagined a priest at one of the temples was marking the time. The Sun Lord was advancing in his path, and now I, too, was set on mine. I heard the call of another trumpet, and it wasn't long before more followed, making me wonder if they were all announcing the dawn or raising the alarm that the Spaniards were approaching. I had to work quickly.

I scanned my surroundings. A canoe was abandoned among the reeds. My heart rose at the sight. *Thank the goddesses.* The craft was large enough to accommodate a well-off merchant and his wares. I would have no trouble paddling it to the island. I gave a cursory look to see if the craft's owner was nearby before I made it my own. After finding my balance, I placed my sword and shield carefully on the bottom of the barge. I was just beginning to paddle myself across the water, when I heard two arguing voices pierce the music of ducks, frogs, and blue flies.

"And you claim to be a magician of the House of Magical Studies? Why, you couldn't find your way out of—"

Hummingbird?

"Me? You fault me, you second-rate prophetess?"

Is that . . . Copil?

The hoarse male voice continued. "You said you had a prophecy that Malinalxochitl would be west of the Itztapalapan causeway. And when I asked you where exactly, you twitched your fingers and said, 'Over there.' So 'over there' we went, and what did we find? No one."

A parrot cackled, sounding like he agreed. *Balché.*

My friends are here! I jumped to my feet, nearly catapulting myself into the water. Righting the sloshing barge, I silenced my surprise and remained perfectly still as I waited for them to come into view. When they appeared, trudging through the low water, faces woebegone and garments muddy, I piped up, "Are you certain *no one* is here, Copil?"

Startled, they stared as if I were an apparition conjured by marsh spirits. Balché jumped high off Copil's shoulder, flapping his wings and cawing, sending ducks streaking across the water and into the sky.

"There you are!" Hummingbird cried. I would have danced at the sound of her voice and those familiar words had I not been so confined. "I told you I would find her," she said, throwing a glare at Copil, who frowned. "My jade is always right." She patted the stone around her neck, a righteous gleam in her eyes. With her skirt and mantle bunched in her hands, she strode through the muddy water. Catching sight of what I carried with me, she whispered with reverence, "The shield."

Copil, caring nothing about his garments, splashed the rest of the way toward me. He looked thinner, grayer, and he was missing a few rings. His and Hummingbird's conflict seemed to have vanished.

"I have seen strange things throughout my life," Copil said, bringing me back to my friends, "but your nahual, that army of serpents you summoned, and now this"—he gestured toward the weapons set atop a cloak stitched with white heron feathers—"I am impressed. I've heard the myths about the shield's existence, but I never . . ." He shook his head. "Your brother would be proud."

▲▲▲▲

Copil expertly steered us across the waters of Moon Lake. I sat comfortably at the center, the sorceress's weapons at my feet, with Hummingbird and Balché guiding at the front. They took turns telling me about life in Cortés's camp during these last days. I listened to their account in silence. Cortés claimed he knew nothing about my disappearance, which he referred to as "an abandonment." He'd also been wearing my jaguar pouch! At this last bit of news, Hummingbird carefully turned in her seat and shrugged off her mantle, revealing said pouch. She unslung it from her shoulder and held it out to me. I choked up seeing it again and fought the urge to look inside it.

My sister knew me well. "It's all there—the eagle feather, red shell, sliver of flint, a leaf, and turquoise necklace," Hummingbird said. "Goddess knows why he wore it. I used a spell to bring it to life and help it make its way out of that man's clutches. I've never performed such a conjuring before, but as you can see, it worked!"

I told them everything that had happened to me, focusing on the wondrous appearance of Earth Mother and the warrior-sorceress Malinalxochitl, and my reunion with the priestesses at the Temple of the Eighteen Moons. After I'd said my piece, we became quiet, but our shared happiness to be reunited was palpable. I listened to the boat glide across the water. Then Copil held his paddle still and began to speak about the horrors Cortés had unleashed in Cholollan.

"The captain general—he cut them all down." Copil's voice cracked. "He tricked them by inviting them, the lords and the nobility, and as many people as the courtyard of the Temple of Quetzalcoatl could hold. Then he barred the gates and sealed them off with his mounted dragon creatures."

I was afraid to turn to look at him. I had never seen him cry. He was one of the most fearless people I knew; the eagle had carried him across mountains and jungles to Curl Nose's palace.

"He accused the people of scheming with Moctezuma. And then the Spaniards fired their guns on the unarmed people of Cholollan. The soldiers fell on them, massacring women and children." I turned in my seat, upsetting the canoe a little, and saw tears running down his face. I reached across to place my hand on his. "People hurled themselves from the top of the pyramids. Not even the books were safe," he cried, shaking his head, "for Cortés set everything ablaze—temples, homes, palaces, and the libraries."

I had seen cities burning in the obsidian mirror, but I sensed those images were nothing compared to the horrors Copil had witnessed in Cholollan.

"It was as if the Underworld had changed places with this world," Hummingbird said quietly from the bow of the boat. "We became part of the Skeleton Lord's domain."

Copil nodded. I watched my courageous friend swipe at his eyes with the back of his hand and thought how I wished I had been there to stop it. The old me would have summoned the serpents and led my scaly followers to Cortés. I would've commanded them to attack him as I stood by, watching them coil themselves around his limbs, squeezing him to death. But I had a different plan now. There was another way to end this evil, and I had to believe it would work.

Copil squeezed my hand, startling me for a moment, and resumed paddling. I turned back in my seat to face Hummingbird, whose shoulders were set high with tension. I hated Cortés more than I ever had.

We'd gained a fifth passenger: silence.

My mind wandered and entered a dark tunnel. If only I had not agreed to become his Tongue. If only I had resisted joining him. If only I had run away. The *if onlys* descended like crows to pick at me. I wanted to tear my skin with a maguey spine.

Then, like a hand reaching out to pull me away from the sudden flare of a fire, Copil cleared his throat and asked in an uplifting voice, "What is your plan, Malinalxochitl?"

"Firstly, you must still call me Malinalli. I may be a sorceress, but I am no goddess. And I will no longer use her name to summon power that is not mine."

"Of course, Malinalli. Now, please tell us what you intend and how we can help you," Hummingbird asked.

I sighed with relief and assured them that I had given the matter a great deal of thought. A priestess of the Temple of the Eighteen Moons must always be prepared.

"My best chance of stopping these men lies with Moctezuma." Hummingbird and Copil had confirmed that Cortés was already at

Itztapalapan. "If I were to go to Cortés first, he would ignore me. My entreaty to go away from Tenochtitlan would fall on deaf ears," I explained, prompting a vigorous nod of agreement from Hummingbird.

"I can imagine it," she said.

"He would greet me, bowing with a flourish, a melting smile on his lips," I said dispassionately. How well I knew him. "Then he would ask how I'd fared, knowing full well that he—with help from the Tlaxcallans—had locked me up in a prison. He would pretend all was well between us and mask his anger over my actions on the battlefield, my failure to play my role as his interpreter." He had too many reasons now to not want me back: I was bad for morale; I had scared his men half to death; I didn't revere his God above all other deities, and most of all, Cortés hated snakes. I'd seen him squirm like a child, right in front of his men.

Hummingbird patted me, as if worried that I might be slipping too far inside my mind. "He would give you a false show of solidarity."

"He's too close to achieving his goal to let a little thing like a warning of complete annihilation get in his way," Copil sniped.

Warmth washed over me. I looked up. We were bathed in a ribbon of sunlight. "But Moctezuma might listen." I returned my gaze to the horizon. By now his spies would have informed him about what happened on the battlefield. He would be curious. I had a chance with him.

We slipped into an easier silence. The sun was cresting and the blue water sparkled as if set with crystals. Copil put his hand on my shoulder and pointed at something in the distance. "Look, Malinalli." There was an army at the far end of a causeway built over the water. The soldiers looked like puny silver ants moving on a ray of white sunlight. But looks would not deceive me. Cortés's men were menaces.

"That causeway links Itztapalapan to Coyohuahcan and Tenochtitlan," Hummingbird said, wiping the fresh mist of sweat from her brow.

"They will be at the crossroad that leads into the city when the sun is high," Copil said.

The broad avenue of white stones did not stand too far above the lake's surface. It was also broken at intervals and set with wooden bridges that could be raised to allow the water to flow freely beneath it and for the boats to pass from one side of the lake to the other. If Moctezuma had raised the bridges, Cortés would be forced to find another way to cross the lake. That would give me more time to persuade one of these men to stop.

I refocused my mind and planned my next maneuver.

My aim was a small fort that appeared to link the broad causeway to the city. "Acachimanco," Copil called it. From there I would enter Tenochtitlan. With the shield in hand, I would stop the sun, stop time. With everyone, every living thing frozen, I would move to convince Moctezuma to turn Cortés away.

There was a chance for peace; I would will it so.

I pictured myself standing between both subdued, peaceful men. The image filled me with a feeling of spiraling light. I could not leave these men to their own devices. It would have been easier for me to change the course of a river than turn away from the proud, defiant, stubborn girl that I was deep inside. The girl hungry to know everything about her namesake. Who studied and learned and accepted the path shown to her, despite every monster and nightmare.

Somehow, this is who I am. Sorceress. Warrior. Protector. This was always who I was going to be. I was a girl from the Coatzacoalcos, but I always knew what I was capable of. Life sometimes turns out the way the goddesses fated. There are twists and turns as we slip and slide along the precipices, making our way along. We can only try to avoid the chasms. It was just like my mother had said. But she was wrong in one thing: my tongue was my power, not my doom.

I gave myself over to the steady, reassuring sound of the canoe slipping through the water. It would be my last moment of true peace for a very long time.

▲▲▲▲

The clamor of the White Men could have awakened the gods. Their progress was awfully quick. No sooner had we noticed their approach when suddenly they were halfway across. I didn't think they could ever cover such a distance so easily. It was hard to ignore their stink. And the noise. Feet tramped. Dogs barked. Men shouted. Shielding my eyes from the glare, I searched for the blue-and-white cloth banner that belonged to Cortés, and the red-and-gold flag of Spain. I looked for signs of magic, too—smoke of a strange hue, a novel horde of beastly creatures or giant-sized men—thinking that the same Tlaxcallan sorcerers who had imprisoned me might be part of Cortés's army.

Even with no sign of such sorcery, their appearance was still something to behold. The horses stomped and tossed their heads. The monstrous dogs raced, sides heaving, noses raised and sniffing the air. Bridles jangled, and those decorative bells so loved by the Spaniards added to the strange, discordant music. The noise set Balché off into a fit of squawks and flutters. Copil whistled in macabre appreciation. Hummingbird and I swore oaths unseemly for two priestesses, but we couldn't master a sense of propriety now. They were moving too fast! I had yet to meet with Moctezuma.

The steadying touch of Hummingbird's hand barely calmed me. Nor was I amused by the parrot's princely strut up and onto her shoulder. I stared at the shield at my feet, glowing in the sunlight, awaiting my command.

THE JADE DIADEM

The sun was hot on the back of my neck by the time Copil steered the canoe through a break in the causeway that was near the city gates and the fort. The water had changed from a deep indigo to a shallow misty green. It was warm for the month we called Quecholli, Precious Feather. Our journey had taken us past strange, beautiful islands planted with corn, amaranth, squash, beans, sage, and flowers. I had never seen floating fields like these before.

"We must take care," Copil said as he helped me onto the causeway, "people say this place is haunted." He grunted as he pulled me up, then Hummingbird.

I did not notice anything unusual at first.

Then the sky near the gates began to shimmer with a strange luminescence. A man who did not look like any man I had ever seen before waited there. His bare skin was covered with the white paint of sacrifice. It wasn't long before another man appeared, then a woman, followed by one child followed by another, all leading a line of people out between the old gates.

Hummingbird did not even pause. "They're ghosts." She brushed off her skirt and strode toward them, leading the way. "We can handle this, follow me." Her arms were taut, tense, as if ready for a fight. The last time she looked like this was long ago at the grave site of a warrior woman.

I fell in step behind my sister.

There were hundreds of them. Some of the dead carried their decapitated heads between their hands. Others had gaping holes in their chests. All had dark, opaque pits for eyes. They moved with great ease, without ruffling the air.

The ghosts sidled close to Hummingbird and Copil, whispering, but they kept their distance from me.

"The end is near," one said, loose-jawed, his teeth clattering.

"Run! Tenochtitlan is doomed," said another, carrying a bleeding heart on her head as if it were a clay water jar. I tried to stay warrior-priestess calm, yet ready to defend myself if I had to. In the next breath I realized they meant me no harm. These restless souls were mothers and fathers, sisters and brothers.

"Save yourself," wailed a young female with outstretched arms.

Even the severed heads spoke up. Whispers rushed around me like dark streams, rising and falling—voices young and old, serious and coy, pushing to be heard.

"Come, follow us to safety," a child begged, stepping in front of Copil, holding out her hand.

Without turning to look, Hummingbird shouted, "Don't touch her unless you mean to join her, Copil!"

"I know that!" Copil muttered. "I'm a magician after all."

I tightened my grip on the sword and shield and ran the rest of the way, toward the fort, cleaving through the ghost crowds. Just then, the air erupted with the sound of a monster's beating heart, and the ghosts scattered and disappeared. It was the echo of the horses' iron-shod hooves striking against the stones. Rising with it came the tramp of marching men, the clattering and jangling of steel.

I had not a moment to spare to stop and look, for then the music of flutes and rattles sounded, and the gates opened. At least fifty Mexica noblemen wearing plumed headdresses and elaborate, brilliantly colored cloaks appeared. Beyond the gates, pyramids loomed over homes and public buildings of whitewashed adobe that edged the causeway. All the while, I was remembering what the obsidian mirror had revealed to me after I'd been awarded the shield—a meeting on the causeway between the invaders and Moctezuma.

I had not believed it, hoped the mirror was not revealing the full truth. Surely I would be able to stop these two men before this meeting took place, I had thought. I had kept my opinion to myself, knowing it was bloated with prideful longings. And now the obsidian mirror's truth was unfolding right before my eyes.

I could have faltered, but I heard the High Priestess's voice echoing in my mind, her words matter-of-fact and affirming:

The white chief will appear on the bridge of Itztapalapan, and Moctezuma will emerge from the city and stop at the fort outside the city gates. There will be throngs of noblemen, but only six Jaguar Knights and six Eagle Knights. They will be armed. Take care, for these men are trained to defend their emperor to the death. They might forsake all ceremony and protocol when they are confronted with a woman who is armed.

I could not help but smile at the idea of such a confrontation. I was ready.

But then her voice revealed something utterly surprising.

Amassed in canoes will be warriors anxious to cast their lot with the invaders and destroy Moctezuma. Among them, you will see women marked with blue insignias, bearing shields. Her voice was clear, filling me with all the grace and wonder of the Temple. *The women wait for you, priestess. They will join their power and magic to yours when the time comes.*

When the time comes. I watched Cortés dismount and accept the flowers and words offered by Moctezuma's nephew, Cacamatzin, one of the rulers of the Triple Alliance. He called Cortés "Goddess Follower," as so many other noblemen had throughout the journey. The custom irritated Cortés.

He thrust out his chest as if to push away the sounds rising in front of him. When his gesture did not mute the nobles, he frowned and tugged at his beard. Just as I knew would happen, Aguilar made poor sense of the nobleman's elegant words. He understood enough of the Nahuatl language now. Still, I winced at the mash of sounds.

"What a sorry stew he is making." Copil chuckled. "Why, even I could do better!"

I turned a glaring eye at him before moving toward Cortés.

In the way day follows night, I knew that in this moment I had to continue to be his tongue. How else would he be able to understand the meaning of the words, the meaning between the words, the meaning of unspoken words? A misjudgment, error of any kind . . . No, I would not allow that to happen. The Mexicas' survival, the lives of all the people of Tenochtitlan, the Spaniards, Maya, and the Tlaxcallans were at stake.

With a sweep of his hand, Cortés ordered Aguilar to stand back and clear the way for me. Aguilar's frown was caked with dried spit.

Cortés's eyes flicked over me. He frowned slightly seeing the sword and shield, and welcomed me in his babbling manner. "Ah, Doña Marina. How *kind* of you to grace us with your presence." He allowed his cold greeting to linger between us before speaking in a more conciliatory tone. "My thanks to the Virgin and the saints for guiding you back to us." He snapped his fingers, motioning me closer.

I did not flinch from his gaze or order. Who did he think I was? *I command serpents. I cleave pathways through the Underworld. I wield sword and shield and offer protection to the people.*

My reply was simple. And true. "Your goddess had nothing to do with my escape from your prison."

"Prison? What are you speaking about?"

"The prison in Tlaxcallan that you and the old man and his son, with the help of sorcerers, left me to rot in."

"Oh, *that*. It wasn't my idea, Doña." Sharply, as if to stab me with his stare, he leaned close. "A lot of good it did, for here you are. It appears you slithered to freedom without any trouble." He paused, waited for me to rise to his taunt. "You would be wise to ask for Her grace that she might rid you of the evil coiled within you. By my word, should I see that thing again," he threatened, reaching for the hilt of his blade, "I will kill you myself."

Satisfied with his speech, he stepped away. After a quick assessment of his men and the Mexica, he cast a nervous gaze at Cacamatzin and all the nobles gathered around, who stood waiting.

I gave the liar no reply.

Just wait. And see.

After taking a deep breath, I turned my full attention to Cacamatzin. "Oh, mighty prince! Let it be known how happy we are to meet you this day, and to finally see the city at the center of the world, Tenochtitlan."

"Lady Malinalxochitl," Cacamatzin answered, bowing his head. I took comfort hearing the goddess's name. *Let them continue to think that I am the all-powerful one.* "All has been prepared for you, my lady. Rest assured that all of your desires have been fulfilled," he said, sending prickles up my spine. "My uncle, Moctezuma Xocoyotzin, the Revered One, Lord of All, commands it. I kiss your feet and the feet of the white teotl who accompanies you."

Of course, they'd known that I was coming. His spies had been everywhere in Cortés's camp and not very discreet. His magicians and sorcerers had cast spells to try to trap us in the mountains and jungles.

"What does he say?" Cortés shouted.

"The prince Cacamatzin says that everything has been prepared for us and that he 'kisses your feet.' It is a formal greeting of welcome taught to us by our grandfathers." I refrained from telling him that the nobleman had referred to him as a sacred being.

"Ah! Well then, you may tell him that he has my permission to proceed." Cortés widened his stance and waited for the display of deference he thought was coming.

I said nothing. Cacamatzin remained steady.

"What are you waiting for, Doña?" Cortés muttered out of the corner of his mouth.

"These are words of courtesy." I smiled. "Cacamatzin kisses the feet of no man save Moctezuma."

Cortés scowled. This was not his first time meeting a person of high birth. Had he learned nothing?

I lifted my gaze to the heavens. The red-haired Alvarado, second-in-command, stepped forward and whispered into Cortés's ear. The captain's manner improved for a few moments. Then the Spaniard's focus became fixed on the crowded causeway and twin forts in front of him. His brow furrowed in concentration. He glanced at his army behind him, and as he turned back, his eyes met mine. For an instant, he seemed afraid. Rivulets of sweat trickled beneath his pinching helmet. Should the Mexica decide to attack, there was no place for his men to retreat to.

You must follow my instructions now or you will die. Listen to me.

Still, there was no point feeding his alarm, so I moved my hand to signal calm.

Soon after the last nobleman bowed, seven young men, with strands of delicate bells wrapped around their ankles and wrists, rushed out between the gates and cast rose petals at our feet. The Mexica nobles standing behind Lord Cacamatzin held themselves quietly as the men danced. They were too quiet. Most of them looked terrified. A few were looking at me curiously. But they had nothing to fear, I kept saying to myself. I would keep them safe.

Not everyone looked afraid or uneasy. A few nobles with hard stares, leaning close together and whispering, appeared desirous of causing harm.

Copil noticed them, too. He stood behind my left shoulder, out of Cortés's way. "They are allied with Moctezuma's younger brother, a man who rarely agrees with the Revered Speaker," he whispered. "We would be wise to keep our eye on them when we are in the city."

When one of the men pointed at the causeway filled with Spaniards, I wondered if they might be plotting to destroy the bridges. I looked over my other shoulder, toward the water. There were many boats filled with people. I saw the tattooed women the High Priestess had spoken of and noticed that a few of them were leaving their crafts and making their way toward me. I also noticed a curious fellow standing in one of the boats. He was covered in raggedy garments and carried a walking stick. He wore a coarse face covering, like a street sweeper who must protect himself from the dust and filth stirred up by his trusted broom. Or a vagabond. No, not a vagabond, my instincts argued, noting the way he held himself. Too proud to be a straggler.

"By the way," Copil added urgently, "the first time you speak to Moctezuma, you must kneel and say, 'Lord, my lord, my great lord.'"

I nodded, my eyes straying back to the strange figure. Copil sighed dramatically at my lack of focus. "You will not rise until he gives you leave," he said. "And above all else, you will keep your head bowed, eyes lowered, for he is a god. You must never look upon his face, to do so would bring death."

The sudden eruption of flutes and whistles, the blare of conch trumpets and pounding drums, pulled my attention back to the Mexica's reception. The mood of our richly attired escorts and of all the people suddenly changed, as if invisible hands were prodding them to stand taller.

Two long processions of barefooted princes approached us. After them came Eagle Knights and Jaguar Knights, proudly dressed in the feathered cloaks, animal skins, and helmets of their warrior class, looking as if bird and beast had swallowed them whole. These most feared warriors in our land seemed capable of felling ten men each with one swipe of their obsidian-studded swords.

"Splendid, splendid," Cortés said, smiling, though his hand gripped the pommel of his sword so tightly, his knuckles were white.

My breathing calmed as soon as the Jaguar and Eagle Knights stopped. Moving as one, they made way for four noblemen carrying the Revered Speaker on a gold litter. The Mexica immediately cast their eyes to the ground.

Out of all of the speakers of Nahuatl, I was the only one who dared to look at him.

"Is it Moctezuma?" Cortés gasped.

"Yes. It is Moctezuma," I said.

I had never seen so much gold before. Even the canopy, supported by four additional attendants, was made entirely of gold. The way the light shone upon it, the surrounding glow, made it almost impossible to look at for very long. It was as if they were carrying the sun.

I protected my eyes with my hand, and only then could I see the straight-backed figure sitting at the center. Flashes of light caught the crescent of gold that pierced his underlip, his gold ear spools, armbands, and a collar set with turquoise stones.

The horsemen around me dismounted and shoved their way forward to get a closer look. Until this moment, the Spaniards had believed that displays of great wealth and power were as numerous as flowers, and that there was nothing new that could surprise them. Now exclamations of wonder rose all around me. At first, Cortés did nothing but gape. Then he licked his lips, twitched, stepped forward and back with lustful anticipation.

Moctezuma's bearers progressed slowly in their bare feet. I moved forward to show my respect. Cortés followed me, slipping when his boot caught on my mantle.

The procession and music stopped. Two barefoot nobles advanced with censers, scenting the air around us with copal. Then two more men unfurled one cloak after another and made a colorful carpet of them upon the ground. The Revered Speaker descended from his throne in a mantle made of hummingbird feathers that fell in shimmering green waves, crowned with the jade diadem of kings. He lifted his face and closed his eyes. He had the look of a man with the power to order the heavens to come crashing down on our heads.

When he moved to walk, the nobles at his side lifted him so that he did not need to set his gold-sandaled feet upon the ground. His next steps were unaided, and yet he appeared to float.

My heart raced. Everything—every choice and event that was in and outside my control—had led to this moment.

I stepped forward and bowed, but I did not release my weapons. I was about to break all of Copil's rules.

I looked into Moctezuma's face. Darkness uncoiled inside me, entwined with a furious, vengeful heat. I wanted to rush forward and kill him. Suddenly, as if he could read my darkest thoughts, his eyes, outlined with thick lines painted gold, flashed with a look armed with blades. Then it softened, as if he knew that I would not act on those thoughts.

"Moteuczomatzin." I addressed him formally. And though I fearlessly held his stare, it was my mother I thought of in this slip of a moment, how she fretted over my manners. "I am—"

"I know who you are," the emperor said, his voice crackling. "Malinalxochitl," he pronounced, drawing out each syllable like a bow strung and ready to take aim.

I did not flinch.

He dropped his voice so only I could hear. "Have you come to kill me with that?" His lips curled into a smirk as a jeweled finger pointed at my shield.

I smiled, too. "I have come to save you," I whispered back. He acted as if I'd said the funniest thing, sweeping his hands up to his face to hide his grin and muffle his laugh. In the next instant, as I wasn't smiling or laughing with him, his face went stony. Only his eyes held life—sparks to signal that he believed he'd already won.

He turned his chin away, as if to ignore me, saying, "You would be wise to kneel, or my Jaguar and Eagle Knights will become suspicious." He spoke the truth, for these fearsome guardians had already fixed their stares on me. The air between us trembled with the tension of men on the brink of transforming into their eagle and jaguar selves. The hairs on the back of my neck stood. I sensed the horror on the faces of the watchful, rules-bound dignitaries and all of the Mexica. But I stayed as I was—on my feet.

Cortés rushed toward Moctezuma then, and to my horror, opened his arms as if to embrace the Revered Speaker. As I reached out to stop Cortés, the Revered Speaker's attendants jumped and pushed Cortés back. The Mexica people did not have to see to know that something horrible had happened. They could feel the affront—Moctezuma's shuddering recoil—and gasped.

"You must not touch him," I hissed in Nahuatl, then, realizing my mistake, I warned him in Spanish. "And do not look him in the eye."

Cortés waved his hand dismissively, then shouted at the regal figure who now stood at a distance. "So you are the ruler of this city?" Neither Moctezuma nor his attendants responded.

I took a deep breath, trying not to feel disappointed by the Spaniard's oafishness. "The teotl has strange customs," I heard Moctezuma say.

I was overcome with the need to explain the *sacred one's* abrupt manners, but when I made to reply, Moctezuma raised his jeweled fingers, and I held back. The Revered Speaker gestured to an attendant, who moved forward holding a blue cloth. My gaze fixed on the treasure on top of it—a necklace of red shells, strung with eight shrimp made of gold.

This was no ordinary gift, but an emblem of Quetzalcoatl. I watched Moctezuma place the cloth in Cortés's hands, and winced as the captain, unaware of the necklace's significance, draped it around his neck to rest over his armor. Then Cortés clutched at his plain strand of shiny beads, removed it, and went to put it around Moctezuma's head.

The Revered Speaker stretched his neck and lifted his chin as if the necklace prickled him. After a few moments, he looked straight at Cortés.

"Our lord, you have suffered fatigue," Moctezuma said. "You have endured weariness. You have come to sit upon the jaguar throne, which I have guarded for you. I—"

"What does he say?" Cortés interrupted. His voice was disrespectfully loud.

I winced, sensing Moctezuma's displeasure at this rude display. But in an effort to keep Cortés steady, I said, "Lord Moctezuma welcomes you and bestows upon you our formal words of courtesy." I intentionally kept his speech vague.

Moctezuma continued, with measured patience. "You have come to satisfy your curiosity about Mexihco. The rulers who have gone before me, Izcoatl, Moctezuma the Elder, Axayacatl, Tizoc, and Ahuitzol, protected the people with their swords and shields."

The Revered Speaker continued in his stern, formal manner, directing his speech to Cortés, not once looking at me. It was filled with Nahuatl's courtly nuances, flowery phrases meant to put his guest at ease. But this talk about the Mexica's past rulers was meant to enhance Moctezuma's stature and intimidate Cortés. I kept my voice steady, even when Moctezuma said that he had been guarding the jaguar throne for Cortés.

A smile flashed across Cortés's lips as I translated. His entire manner relaxed. "A throne? Our friends the Cempoallans offered me a throne, too. No harm will come to me here." I sensed the men standing behind us ease their grips on their swords, while I tightened my fingers around mine. Moctezuma was relinquishing his throne to no one: I was sure of that.

I felt the sting of old bruises and reached to rub my throat. I needed to be very careful.

"His ancestors maintained that you would come," I continued after Moctezuma spoke again.

His next words dropped from his lips too sweetly, like poisoned honey, setting the trap: "Rest now and take possession of your palace. Your city awaits."

I held my tongue and did not repeat this.

Monsters. I am surrounded by monsters.

The silence that followed could have held three speeches. Moctezuma and Cortés were watching me closely. Were Moctezuma someone else, I would have interpreted this statement as an expression of courtesy. But I knew all too well the horrors Moctezuma was capable of.

"Ahem." Cortés coughed. He was rocking forward and back on his heels, one eyebrow raised. I could feel his men leaning toward me, anxious to know what had been said.

I did not bend to the weight of the silence to continue.

"Doña Marina," Cortés said assuredly, "please thank Moctezuma and tell him to put his heart at ease. Make it clear to him that I come in the name of the greatest ruler in all the world and a most forgiving god. We love the great emperor well, and our hearts are contented now that we know him. For a long time, we have wished to look upon his face." He smiled. "I am here to do him no harm. We are his friends."

I heard the Spaniard's tongue slip around his bald lie and watched him remove his helmet and tuck it under his arm. He looked out over the heads of the Mexica, an expression of regal importance illuminating his face, before settling his attention on Moctezuma again. Then he leaned in closer to whisper, "Do not fear. To keep us safe, I have made plans with our Tlaxcallan allies. They number in the thousands." His grin looked so utterly evil, I had to turn away.

A man assured of his high place and the righteousness of his deeds and words, he said, "It is proper for you to think of our safety. Being a woman, you are, by nature, cautious. And . . ."

The words faded then, for I stopped listening to him.

Smoothly, trying to appear unruffled by the untruths spoken by these two men, I turned to the Revered Speaker with grace. I longed to continue to use my voice to assure everyone that everything would turn out well, that the month of Precious Feather would give safe passage to the Raising of the Feathered Banners, and that the ancient caiman upon whose back we existed would fall into a deep sleep and dream.

But I had no more words. I had seen and heard enough.

I am ready.

I took a deep breath, and with a confident sweep, I raised my arm and shield to the sky. Everything stilled as I gave voice to my charm. Immediately, the sky faded to a lukewarm blue. The air's heat cooled. So strong was the light cast from the pattern of obsidian mirrors, it stunned the sun and disabled it from advancing in its path. Malinalxochitl's shield had stopped time.

HOLDING THE SUN CAPTIVE

Every man—soldiers up and down the causeways, and all the people throughout Tenochtitlan—froze in place. Bodies came to an abrupt stop in the middle of a turn, a yawn, while scratching a nose, lifting a sword. I had reduced Cortés to a statue caught in mid-step, mid-whisper as he bent to fill my ear with more lies. His expression, like everyone's, seemed set in stone. Even the birds and fish were caught within this most masterful of all spells.

I placed my trust in the shield, and it performed exactly the way it was meant to, just like the High Priestess had promised.

But it wasn't easy, holding the sun captive. It fought me. I felt the weight of its rays, its wrath, bearing down hard on my shield, forcing my elbow to buckle, my body to bend. The light burned white and singed up my arm and braid. Just when I thought I might fall beneath its punishing force, I felt a surge of strength rise through me as all of the warrior women present in canoes and along the causeway, strong with their own magic, raised their shields high too, and together, we wrestled the sun to our will. That feeling of power! I'd felt it in my bones before, during the rising of my nahual on the battlefield at Tlaxcallan, while offering prayers to the Four Winds alongside the priestesses at the Temple of the Eighteen Moons, and while sweeping atop the pyramid of Quetzalcoatl.

Moctezuma appeared to be the only Mexica unaffected by the blast of light and the halt of time. At first, I was surprised. I watched him step to the side of a protective attendant. He must be a follower of Tezcatlipoca, the trickster god, I reasoned, making him a sorcerer as well as an emperor. Someone who possessed the powerful spells to usurp the will of mortals, even other gods.

Quick glances over my shoulders told me that the warrior women had the sun under their control. I lowered my arm and shield then. Breathed.

"A nice trick." The voice startled me, and for a moment, the sun trembled. I looked as Moctezuma approached. I could see in his appreciating stare that he coveted the shield.

"I will give you anything for it," he said.

"Order your people back into the city, close the gates, and send the invaders away from here. Use force if you have to, but no more blood must be spilled. Obey me, and it's yours." I was lying, something I had gotten good at in my years as slave, concubine, interpreter.

He smiled again, revealing teeth sharpened like a jaguar. "No. Anything but that," he said, and my hands tightened instinctively around the sword and shield.

We stood in our places, observing each other silently. His mantle fluttered and swirled, dreamlike. In the next instant, the whole of it shivered with the tiny blue-green heads of hummingbirds poking out among the feathers. The birds began to beat their wings, and a whirring sound filled the air, a fluttering soft and furious, like the sound of descending gods of wind.

I watched in silent wonder, until the embroidered threads throughout my garments stirred to life. Not to be outdone by the cloak's magic, the yellow bees and orange butterflies, the frogs and flowers, moons and stars lifted themselves free. The memory of my mother, grandmother, the priestesses, all of the women who sat over looms and spindles guiding their power and strength into lengths of cloth, washed over me.

But the most spectacular sights, the sweetest words and salutations that existed in all the known lands, could not have softened the ominous feeling building inside me.

Moctezuma turned toward Tenochtitlan, inviting me with a curl of his jeweled hand to follow him.

I looked up at the city looming before me and strode forward.

▲▲▲▲

"So, Malinalxochitl, you have come to steal my throne?"

We stood at the top of a white stone pyramid, where the winds turned his voice into a whip. I was dizzy, for in a blink he had transported us from the serpent gates that led into the sacred precinct to the top of the tallest pyramid I had ever seen. But after I took a few deep breaths, I was steady again.

"No," I replied. At one time I had considered it. It would have been fitting for the War God to lose his domination over Tenochtitlan. It was still a choice, but did I really want to sit and rule, even in the name of peace, for the rest of my life? Even if I wanted to, why would I admit it now to my family's murderer?

I pretended to study the god Huitzilopochtli's temple house, which was decorated with the sun's rays and a sacrificial stone that stood as high as my thighs. It sloped upward at its center, like the peak of a mountain. A dark smear glistened. A small earthenware brazier with monster eyes and a fanged grin stood to its left, spreading a veil of a more pungent incense to mask the blood pooled around it.

A sound caught my attention then, a soft drumbeat. However, I saw no drums, no musicians.

I dared to turn my back on Moctezuma and walk to the edge of the parapet. The soft thrumming continued as I saw, in a glance, the frozen city of Tenochtitlan spread out below me, marked with straight paths and waterways, temples and palaces, radiating away from me like the rays of the sun. Closer to me, splashes of dried blood marked the stairs. I could see it clearly: standing here, on this ledge, the priests pushing the bodies after offering their victims' hearts to the god. I felt a crushing weight against my chest. Had I been brought here to be next to die?

His voice intruded, shoving my thoughts aside. "When I was a boy, my mother told me the tale of the powerful warrior-sorceress who was defeated by Huitzilopochtli. 'It is only a story,' she'd assured. However, my priests say Malinalxochitl is much more than an old people's tale. They have been following your progress. They worry that you will rule this land one day."

I turned in time to see that he now stood directly behind me. He took a step, then another, forcing me to move closer to the edge. "Now that I can see you better, I am certain you are not the mighty being my sorcerers claim." He paused.

The hem of my mantle billowed over the lip of the stairs. One more step and I would fall to my death. Perhaps he intended to push me off to test my abilities.

As I wondered what to say or do, the eagle appeared. I heard the mighty beating of its wings before I watched it alight atop a stone owl set close to me. The Revered Speaker looked over his shoulder at the bird.

The eagle watched me for a moment with yellow eyes, then flapped its wings and released a fierce shriek as it lunged with open beak at Moctezuma. He jumped, pulling his mantle around him to shield his face. As he did, I stepped away from the edge.

The eagle circled the air above us. I looked at Moctezuma. *Here at last is my father's and brother's murderer.* I felt a hollow giddiness. Maybe the eagle will slay him, reduce the royal gaze to bloody pits.

But in the next heartbeat, Moctezuma caught my stare. "You dare to look upon me so boldly?"

I did not change my stance, choosing to let him study and take the measure of me. I imagined him thinking, *She is someone of power.* I watched while he turned his attention to the eagle, who'd returned to its stone perch. He was younger in years than my father at the time of his journey to Tenochtitlan, and of small stature, like Cortés.

"The eagle serves me," I offered in my most confident voice.

"Indeed?" The eagle raised and lowered its wings, and Moctezuma stepped back.

"It follows me wherever I go." I decided to press my point again. "You must encourage the White Men to turn back."

Moctezuma shrugged. "They are a nuisance, but they will make a nice addition to my zoo. I think they'll be more entertaining than the monkeys. What do you think? A special pavilion is being prepared for them as we speak. With salvaged timbers from their floating mountains. Next to the cages that house vipers," he said, his tongue luxuriating in the word's sound, "and crocodiles."

The thought of the scribe Bernal Díaz in a cage in the emperor's zoo sent shivers up my spine. My plan was not proceeding in a mannerly way, but I didn't panic. I had the protection and advocacy of the warrior-sorceress, the now-familiar weight of her shield in my hands. I felt emboldened to leap ahead.

With the word charm on my lips, and a spell I'd never attempted before, I transported us away from the temple to . . .

Several blinks later, after peering all around, it became clear: we were in his throne room.

I had completed a new feat of magic. Not quite what I expected—it needed a bit of adjusting—but I thought if Moctezuma could do it, why couldn't I? He was protected by Huitzilopochtli and Tezcatlipoca, but I had the tremendous Malinalxochitl, and the goddesses of the earth and all knowledge, Coatlicue and Quetzalpapalotl, safeguarding my every movement.

Moctezuma laughed, though it vibrated with disdain rather than joy.

His throne room was joyless, too, but impressive. Cool darkness caressed my skin. Torches breathed wisps of fire while rows of giant stone warriors stood with their arms raised to support the cavernous roof. Their heads bore painted crowns of green feathers. The ceiling was carved and gilded with silver. Thin panels of hammered gold hung from walls painted with murals, and feather and cotton carpets and copper lanterns shaped in the likes of beasts and birds radiated light along the black onyx floor.

"Come closer."

With a start, I looked toward the quiet slap of sandals and the brush of his feathered mantle to see Moctezuma ascend the jaguar throne. Carved of stone, the seat's feline head was turned so that it might observe all those who entered its presence. Jewels glimmered across its legs and paws.

From here, Moctezuma looked down on me and smiled through his teeth. "Come forward," he commanded.

I felt proud of my latest spell and strode with confidence across the wide room.

"Are the weapons heavy? They look heavy," Moctezuma said with mock concern. "Come, you may set them down here." He gestured to the stair below him.

"They are not heavy," I answered. But in spite of my conviction, I soon found myself bending low to set the sword and shield where he pointed, only catching myself when I felt my hand brush against the cold floor. I gasped at the might of his control and clutched the weapons close to my body.

I reached into the depths of my strength to prepare myself for the next test.

"Now, Lady Malinalxochitl, let us speak freely." His tone was like bee syrup, but I did not drop my guard. "I will send the invaders away. It will make me sad, for they would make such a good addition, but I will do it for you. I think that highly of you. Except for the dragon beings, they will stay. And their dogs! I insist on keeping those. But everything else . . ." He waved dismissively, then, leaning forward on his throne, said, "What I want is *you*. Join me." He extended his hand to me, his nails sharp and yellowed.

I jolted back, recalled the owl priest in the Underworld reaching out to me with its talons, saying the exact same words.

"I will share the jaguar throne with you. You will live like a queen. Your every desire fulfilled," he intoned, every word its own delicacy presented on a gold plate.

I backed away slowly.

"Join me. Together, you and I, the sorceress and the war god, Malinalxochitl and Huitzilopochtli, shall rule." He emphasized his words with a shake of his hand before extending it to me again. "The way it was supposed to be so many suns and moons ago. Remember?" He grinned, and it was as if he was able to see into my mind just then, for I was back at the shrine, and the priestesses were telling me her story. How Huitzilopochtli had tried to cajole her to join him. How she had wanted to believe that there was goodness inside him. "Of course you remember."

Is this what it was like for her? Her brother promising her the stars? Her resistance. Her rage?

I was not tempted; nevertheless, Hummingbird's voice came in my mind. *Be careful.*

"You honor me," I said with a slight bow of my head, "but I—"

"But?" He snatched his hand back, hunched low in his seat, and stared at me as if I was something distasteful.

I backed away a little more.

"Where are you going?" The threat in his voice was enough to make me stop. "You think you have their . . . *her* protection, don't you? That you know everything about *her*, but you don't know what you're dealing with. Gods, and I assume goddesses, are known for their unpredictable natures. Think of Tezcatlipoca," he said. "When I was a priest, I learned that the divine one is capricious and delights in tormenting man. He has appeared to me in many disguises. He was a gouty old man many suns ago, a fisher of eels, and a champion patolli player blind in one eye during his most recent appearance." He bit his lower lip and looked deep in thought. "A god follows rules unknowable to us. You would do well to mark my words and take them to heart. Your protector could change her mind. Snatch those weapons you hold so close in the time it takes you to open your mouth and utter, 'Oh, glorious goddess!'" He whined with a high pitch, contorting his body and mimicking my gestures.

Then, after a moment of silence, Moctezuma said, "I welcome these men to Tenochtitlan."

I saw the corner of his mouth slip into the slightest of smiles. He was playing a game. And he seemed pleased by my struggle to say something. It was always his intention to draw the Spaniards closer, and then pull them in, and me, too.

Moctezuma nodded to himself. "I will know their leader better. Know you better."

Did he truly believe he would successfully cage Cortés? He would soon learn the truth. I could see it: Cortés retaliating, the city exploding into flames.

Does he think he can bend me *to his will?*

My face filled with heat, and before I knew what I was doing, I was crying out, "But you cannot," lurching forward to ascend the stairs that separated us.

The jaguar throne growled, baring its teeth at me. My body froze in mid-step.

Moctezuma curled his lip. "I cannot?"

The shield began to vibrate. It was warning me. As much as it galled me to step away, I did and lowered my gaze. "Forgive me. A thousand pardons."

"'I cannot,' she says." Moctezuma shifted on his throne, and that alone alarmed me. I held my breath. "I can," he roared. "Order the Eagle and Jaguar Knights to war. Commence the rebuilding of the Great Temple at sunrise. Forbid the harvest of all fields of maize and its sale in all of my provinces. Issue warrants for the deaths of anyone I deem an enemy, if it so pleases me," he sneered.

Yes, how well I knew that. Did he remember my brother and father? How could Moctezuma sentence a boy of ten years to die?

A howl rose into my throat. My old need for vengeance was a deep, dark habit, and it took all my power to quash it so that I might speak. "The White Men's leader"—I took a breath and forced a diplomatic tone—"cannot be trusted to conduct himself with the obedience and respect owed to you and your subjects." I looked straight at Moctezuma, then pushed forward, keeping to the task at hand. "Revered Lord, the man Cortés does not deserve the honor of standing in your presence and enjoying the wonders of your city." I closed my eyes, and in that moment, I felt the bony finger of memory nudging me back to the day my brother embarked on his journey to Tenochtitlan. How his face had shone with excitement.

Then with a jolt, I remembered my brother's mysterious request. *Release my heart from captivity.* The words were so clear, when I opened my eyes again, I thought I would find him standing right in front of me.

"Are you ill, lady?" My brother's murderer was regarding me thoughtfully.

I lifted my chin. "No, my lord."

"No, my lord," he echoed, then raised his hand. "It is decided." Moctezuma turned in his throne. Slowly, his eyes passed around the room, gazing at the murals and statues, the flowers and gold panels gathered for his pleasure.

Where had I failed? How could he not see that he and the people of Tenochtitlan were in danger?

"You must send him away!"

Moctezuma stared at me. Cortés would stop at nothing to achieve what he wanted. All the pain and sorrow and death I had witnessed thus far were nothing compared to the hell that was certain to come. How was I going to protect this multitude of people? What of my army? Would my sorceress strength be enough to ward off chaos?

Malinalxochitl was as much destroyer as she was protector, wasn't she?

"I will know him. Have him. Do whatever I want," Moctezuma hissed with the last of his anger. "And I will make sure your shield never interferes with *my* sun again."

BOOK VII

OF PALACES AND SNOW

My first taste of Tenochtitlan was of snow shaved and served in a roll of stiff paper, topped with hibiscus flower syrup. It was the taste of dreams and hopes. When the Spaniards tried the delicacy, biting into it as if it were a haunch of roasted meat, the look of wonder on their faces suggested that they might be satisfied enough to lay down their weapons and live in peace. *If only it could be as easy as that—a lick of snow with the magic to turn beasts into friends.* But the sweet cold taste of hope turned to ash in my mouth. Perhaps in a different city, peace might have stood a chance. But *this* island city had been founded by the war god, after all.

The court diversions heaped on us added to my unease: feasts and hunts; entertainments with jugglers, puppet players, dancers on stilts, and poets; and ball games that symbolized the battle between the sun and the moon. I believe it was all meant to overload the Spaniards' senses and make them dumb.

Even the rose stone palace that was given to Cortés and his men was meant to seduce. A thousand of the Tlaxcallans and all of the horses were able to live comfortably with Cortés's four hundred soldiers. I do not think a single man managed to explore all of its chambers, courtyards, audience halls, fountains, and passageways. Like all royal residences, and the palaces of nobles, it was situated outside the sacred precinct. The gilded place had been the home of Moctezuma's father, Axayacatl, who had long ago joined his ancestors in the thirteenth heaven.

But perhaps the most calculating of all of Moctezuma's tactics was his order that I live apart from the Spaniards. After the speeches and banquet of a thousand plates on that first day, Moctezuma declared it unseemly for me to stay with Cortés and his men, and before Cortés could sputter a protest, twelve white-robed women escorted me to Moctezuma's aunt's palace.

Cortés turned a red darker than the little hat he liked to wear. "No! The Tongue stays with me!"

But Moctezuma insisted.

It was not Moctezuma's first strike against Cortés. The first had taken place during the journey, when Moctezuma aimed to kill Cortés with stinging ants, insatiable mud pits, and other spells. Separating me from the invaders was more dangerous, and Cortés knew it. Words were his bridge, his shield and cudgel all in one. More battles are ahead of us, my bones warned.

But I was not frightened.

I wanted to cast an illusion over the entire island. I needed a spell, an incantation that would grant me another turn at stunning the world. I could drape the island in magic and make everyone . . . What? Fall into a deep sleep so there would be no more wars?

▲▲▲▲

One day, shut in my room with Hummingbird and Copil, I told them my aim and asked for their counsel on the matter. The chamber overlooked a rose garden, with a feather bed draped in furs, and all the walls inlaid with shells and a pattern of jade-colored stones. The bathing room had its own waterfall. It was a most luxurious place.

"What of a spell from a mix of white cedar leaves, green cypress, wormwood and marsh plants, and white pine flower?" I asked.

"That cures lightning strikes," Hummingbird replied instantaneously with a shake of her head as she paced back and forth. I had told them about my meeting with Moctezuma, and though Hummingbird rarely showed fear, she did so now. Her attention turned sharply to Copil. "Will you tell her, or shall I?"

What was this? After Copil gave her a quick nod, Hummingbird stopped her pacing, and said, "This morning Moctezuma's sorcerers placed the entire city, even the lake towns, under a binding spell. It is a magic I've never encountered before."

"I've tried simple charms—like turning water into octli—but to no avail," Copil said with awe. He was sitting on the very edge of the bed, as if he was afraid of mussing it up. I nodded in understanding. Hummingbird and I had long ago come to the conclusion that Copil's kind of magic must be of a haphazard sort, for we'd never witnessed him perform any sorcery work. We didn't doubt his power, though. He had survived a journey over volcanoes, deserts, and jungles while being held aloft in the talons of the eagle. He had known my brother and told the truth of his murder. And the priestess and I were certain that Copil's friendship, bravery, and knowledge had helped to keep us alive. It was all the magic we needed.

I smiled warmly at my friend and encouraged him to continue. His face was creased with worry, deep lines along his brow, embedded into his sunken cheeks.

"I've heard that, from this day forward, even the young magicians at the House of Magical Studies cannot practice magic. No movement spells of any kind, certainly no transformations, which require a great deal of practice and skill, which, I'm afraid, I don't—"

"Copil?" Hummingbird intervened.

Copil hushed an apology.

The idea that no magic could be performed at the House of Magical Studies did sound odd. Not even a young, innocent magician could practice spell making?

"Please sit down, Malinalli," Hummingbird said. "There is more."

My attention sharpened on my friends. There were wrinkles splayed around her eyes. More silver strands in her hair. And there was less fat on Copil's bones—I'd noticed this when we were in the marshes outside Tenochtitlan—but today his garments flapped like sails. They had paid a price to follow me. Their weariness was glaringly apparent. Why hadn't I paid attention to this before?

I dropped onto a wicker chair, which creaked with my sudden weight. Copil twirled his jeweled rings. I knew this to be a bad sign.

"I feared something like this might happen," Copil said.

"What?" I leaned forward, looking from one to the other, vowing to take better care of my friends.

"When they imprisoned you in Tlaxcallan . . . after the battle," Hummingbird finally said. "When you showed your nahual-animal self . . ." She caught Copil's glance. "It frightened them, I think, the Tlaxcallans, the Mexica, Moctezuma . . ."

"Moctezuma might be afraid it will appear again." Copil's voice was firm.

"I imagine the binding spell renders the shield useless," Hummingbird said.

I had not thought of that. I would need to test it to make sure, give it some kind of task. But what, exactly?

Hummingbird walked to an alcove where white and colorful blouses, skirts, and mantles were carefully folded on racks made of polished wood. She returned with a long white feathered banner draped across her arms. As she presented it to me, Copil rose to his feet and approached.

Before I had a chance to ask, he said, "It's not just any design—this one bears the symbols of your name. See here?" He pointed to yellow five-petaled flowers and a shaft of green river grasses. Its colors were vivid and sharp. I had never seen anything so beautiful: the flowers seemed alive; the feathers shifted in the air. "We saw many like it being carried along the causeway when we entered Tenochtitlan with Cortés," Copil said.

I knew that feathered insignias were used to identify captains and their warriors on the battlefield. I had seen many—the White Heron, Smoking Water Beast, the Two-Headed Deer—on the field at Tlaxcallan.

I looked up. Hummingbird smiled softly. "We think it might be a war banner," she said quietly. "You have an army, and it is here."

▲▲▲▲

We hid the cloth away among my garments. If Moctezuma didn't want any spells cast in his city, then he certainly didn't want to see any war flags with my emblem on them. I was worried about the people who had carried them into Tenochtitlan. Were they safe? Were they here to sue for peace, like the followers of the goddess, as in the legend of Malinalxochitl I'd heard at the shrine? I asked Copil if he could make inquiries about this army.

"Be careful," Hummingbird warned him. "Don't be a hero," she said when she thought I wasn't listening.

I was afraid to let the shield out of my sight, so Hummingbird created a special backstrap made of leather and cotton, stitched with uncoiling snakes, that made it easy to carry at all times. When she pulled it across my shoulder and tugged it into place, I felt held within her protective force. Even labyrinthine palaces like Axayacatl's would not be able to hinder me now.

▲▲▲▲

One day later, still both excited and worried by the news about an army, I walked from Moctezuma's aunt's royal home to Cortés's quarters. I considered everything I knew about my army, which wasn't very much. Exactly how many people were here, gathered under my banner? The idea of it grew and grew in my mind, until doubt began nibbling at my image of leagues of men and women peacefully awaiting me. *What if they've traveled to Tenochtitlan for a fool's dream? For a girl to lead . . . ?*

I easily shrugged off the more needling questions as I arrived at the Spaniards' lodgings. The palace stood outside the snake wall's west gate, near the causeway that led to the town of Tlacopan. Cortés's soldiers had reduced the grand entranceway to a hole framed with scraps of wooden boards, completely defacing the original stone and mosaics. Standing at the ready to blow off your head was the largest of the thunder-and-fire makers. Two more of these weapons stared down from the roof terrace. After taking possession of the palace, Cortés had ordered the guns fired in a display of sound and smoke that frightened the people halfway to the Underworld. Now the palace was one of the most befouled and despicable of places, save for the White Men's encampment on the beach outside Vera Cruz.

I had to lift my skirt and bunch my green cloak in my other fist as I made my way inside and to the chamber Cortés had turned into his throne room, for I did not want to defile my garments with the piss and turds left by the dogs. In five days, the Spaniards had turned their lodgings foul. After just three days, the servants had walked out, complaining that the men were animals. The Mexica were so fastidious about cleanliness that they had built enclosed, private outposts all along the causeways for the people to use. They washed and scrubbed every paved street and road twice a day until it sparkled in the sun. Like all royal residences, Cortés's had many of these private closets, but the Spaniards refused to use them.

"You are late!" Cortés growled past the slit in his helmet when I arrived. He was all creaks and clacks, dressed in battle armor. Moctezuma had finally granted Cortés permission to visit the marketplace in Tlatelolco, and he was anxious to see it. The red-haired Alvarado, the scribe Bernal Díaz, and four others rushed to keep up with him. The only soldier to greet me cordially with a smile was the writer; the others were still wary of me, probably fearful of my army of serpents.

Our first day in the fabled city, Cortés had warned, "No magic! At the first sign of witchcraft or a snake scale, I will string you up and feed you to my dogs." He had no idea of the feat I'd already performed on the causeway. After I had released the sun, he complained of a headache, nothing more. And he knew nothing about what I'd just learned—Moctezuma had placed a hex over him, *me*, and the entire city.

He was openly hostile, but I ignored him. His moods no longer baffled me, because he was angry all of the time. I dismissed it as his fear trying to work its way out. He couldn't show it in front of his men, so this cantankerous, biting, bullying creature was what I had to work with.

I admitted that I was late. "Yes." Such a simple word. Agreeing with Cortés was often the best thing to do. I had taken a longer route, through the royal gardens and into the sacred precinct where all of the temples stood. Even after many visits and expeditions to the ballcourt to watch games and ceremonial dances, it still felt immense.

"The only reason I agreed to this living arrangement was because I was promised you would attend to me promptly at the time of my choosing," he said.

"I had a visitor this morning. One of Moctezuma's daughters, Princess Tecuichpotzin."

"Oh? Is she pretty?"

"She's a child." Sometimes the second-best thing to do was threaten him. "And if any harm comes to her, I promise I will unleash more than snakes upon your head." *I will cut you into pieces and feed you to Moctezuma's serpents myself.*

▲▲▲▲

The Revered Speaker had sent many officials and guards to accompany us. With this escort leading the way, we walked to the marketplace in Tlatelolco, Tenochtitlan's sister city to the north. It had been an independent territory with its own ruler until Moctezuma's father conquered it.

The most multi-plumed of Moctezuma's officials was a man with googly eyes. Whenever he spoke to me, his gaze would land somewhere around my feet. He carried a large decorated staff and wore a mantle so fine that I could have studied the colors and patterns for a full day and still not have caught every detail.

The entire city and outlying regions were laid out with straight walking paths and waterways. In some areas, there were canals and no footpaths, but each home still had its own access to the water. Wooden bridges connected large parts of the main avenue to other sections of the city, and these were wide, too, so people could move without jostling into elbows and stepping on feet.

We were in the middle of a dense crowd. I was worried that someone—out of fear or curiosity—might become too bold. I wished Copil was with us, but he had said there was a matter of some urgency that needed his attention.

But I need not have worried about people stepping too close to us. Everyone kept away. The Spaniards were also much subdued, so I allowed myself the luxury of enjoying my surroundings, assessing the people around me. I watched the ebb and flow of palace administrators in their colorful mantles hurrying on official business, warriors in orange cotton cloaks tied in a knot over the right shoulder, with their hair secured in a single loop in the traditional manner. I spotted the nobility, the pipiltin class, traders, and three captive warriors who wore sumptuous mantles that hung to the knees. I set my eyes on the laborers, tradesmen, and farmers dressed in simple white breechcloths and short cloaks. The women, too, were carefully dressed befitting their rank. The only ones not in attendance for me to observe were rich matrons, who rarely walked, preferring to travel even short distances by canoe.

A curt shout caused the crowd to the right of our group to part in order for a line of porters to file through toward the marketplace.

The temporary diversion allowed Aguilar to jump forward and address Cortés.

"Is there anything I can get for you, Capitán?" The man was always desperate to be useful when I was around, and I had noticed that his knowledge of Nahuatl had improved to the point that he was capable of overseeing meetings with minor officials. Cortés brushed him aside.

Cortés was quiet for a moment, taking in our surroundings. "It is impressive, this city. Our host's royal residences. Very grand. I can think of nothing like it in Spain."

"It is something to be admired," the scribe agreed.

"However . . . this morning . . . we visited a vile place. The emperor finally sanctioned our visit to see the temple of his god, Huitzil-something."

"Huitzilopochtli," I said. "It means Southern Hummingbird. He is the Mexica's war god."

"I wished you had been there, Doña Marina. But Moctezuma and his priests insist that women are forbidden from seeing it. I had to rely on Aguilar's translation."

I kept my focus straight ahead, but I could feel him incline his head to catch my reaction. And I could feel Aguilar preening.

"There were one hundred fourteen steps to the summit. Díaz counted them. Each one was splattered with blood."

"Tell her what Moctezuma said to you when you reached the top," the scribe piped up.

"Oh yes. After I climbed the stairs, your emperor said that I must be tired, to which I answered, 'Spaniards are never tired, señor.'" He laughed to himself. "The balls." He grunted, then continued. "What an abomination—the sights we saw! A giant blood-soaked idol holding a bow and arrow, with hearts sizzling in a brazier set in front of it. And there was another statue, some fertility goddess, with two snakes for a head. The devil's work. How can a man of such bearing and manners permit such a horror?"

I glanced up. Anger twisted his mouth.

"I told the emperor that he must tear down those devils and replace them with the holy cross." He leaned closer. "The next time, I will order you to disguise yourself as a boy so you can attend to me. I trust Aguilar like so." He held his finger and index finger a sparrow's beak apart, then paused and looked around. "I had the impression that Moctezuma was offended by my remarks." Cortés shrugged. "We left at once. How could I stand there in that hell? I am not finished with this. I will never allow those things to stand," he said with self-righteous fury.

I believed him. He was going to do whatever he needed to take down the idols. It would be Cholollan all over again, or something worse, unless I stopped him.

Fool. When he was standing at the top of the pyramid, he must have taken account of the surrounding land, or rather the lack of it, and noticed how vulnerable he was. With a nod, Moctezuma could order the destruction of the bridges and causeways and cut the Spaniards off from the mainland. How could this not temper the captain's anger? Alvarado and Díaz needed to talk to him. Perhaps by working together, we could get him to make plans to leave.

Without slowing his step, Cortés removed his helmet and tucked it under his arm. "I want you to talk to Moctezuma. We will go together and spread the word of God. Then he will understand the horror those figures represent."

He sped forward, giving me no time to respond. I fumed quietly to myself as he gestured at one marvel after another and made smacking sounds of delight. *You are a guest here, but you will end up in the emperor's zoo if you're not careful.*

The crowds had thinned, making it easier to see how the canals were laid out. He let out a long sigh of appreciation. "Extraordinary." He pointed. "Look, Díaz. Make note of these canals and the little clay pipes running along their sides. They are filled with fresh water from that aqueduct we saw when we crossed the lake. Chapul— What was it?" He turned to me.

"Chapoltepec."

"Cha-pol-te-pec," he sounded out. "And what does it mean? All the names mean something beautiful here."

"The Place of the Grasshoppers."

He smiled. "Now I remember. It is the source of the city's fresh water—an accomplishment equal to the Romans."

As Aguilar sprang forward with another groveling request, Cortés shoved his helmet into his hands. "Hold this." The co-interpreter was grateful for the attention.

"As I was saying before," Cortés carried on, "you must make certain he knows that I am a man of God and that I am ordered by both my king and my God to put an end to the evil practices of this land. For the good of all. His gods are false," he said with a shiver. "He has the gall to continue that abominable practice of sacrifice right under our noses. Every time I hear those drums . . ." He put his hand to his head as if his thoughts ached. "Make it clear in the way that only you can. Embellish the truth if you must."

I bristled. "That will not be necessary," I lied. I was growing accustomed to saying whatever was needed to keep the peace. And now I had an army to help control these men, deal with Moctezuma's forces, and do anything else that I wanted, I thought to myself, the image of the jaguar throne I had recently seen flashing in my mind.

Aguilar muttered loud enough for all of us to hear, "She embellishes constantly. She scatters lies like so many seeds, sowing them like an ignorant farmer who has no sense as to where they are landing and taking root."

Cortés ignored him. "The next time we are with him, I will tell you what to say, Doña. I demand change. The Almighty God depends on it. It is His will that I shepherd the people into a mighty flock of believers."

Before I could say anything, or ask what he meant by shepherds and flocks, the sound of many voices and a loud hum rose like a tidal wave, and the grandest marketplace opened in front of us. It was an expanse of space that could have contained the markets of Xicallanco, Cempoallan, and Tlaxcallan combined, with room to spare.

I gazed in astonishment, feeling weightless and giddy. Treasures from every part of the empire and beyond were before us. A colonnaded portico of whitewashed stone, beaming silver in the sun, stretched along two sides, with another side fronting water and a sturdy landing dock crowded with canoes and barges fully packed. The merchants had their wares precisely arranged and separated by clear walkways. A pyramid, almost as large as the one in Tenochtitlan, towered over the market, adjoining a white stone wall.

An exclamation of wonder escaped Cortés's lips. All his men fell under an enchantment and lost their ability to speak.

The market filled me with pride. It was as if I had overseen its orderly design and arranged the offerings of each and every tomatl, ahuacatl, and chilli all by myself. As if I had mined and carried the gold from Oaxaca, chopped and dragged the wooden beams from Tacuba, dried and carefully wrapped the pink salt from the Mayab.

Songbirds in cages and parrots on simple wooden stands were placed in one area; predator birds, like hawks and ravens, were in another, while freshly caught whole ducks and geese, ready to be plucked and cooked, had another space. Feathers, which were prized more than gold, were sold on the other side of the market, on a low platform near the feather workers and their crafts. And the furs! Large pelts of deer and jaguar to cover floors and to use as blankets were displayed with smaller offerings for making pouches and armbands.

At times I had to stop to calm myself. But then something new would catch my attention, and off I would go to explore, leaving the Spaniards behind. Why, everything needed to build a house and the items you needed to make it a home was here, in this glorious place.

"It is a market of dreams."

The voice startled me, for I thought I was on my own. But there stood Bernal Díaz, writing quill tucked behind his ear, his face shiny with wonder. He was the one soldier whose company I did not mind.

"Oh yes! And over there"—I pointed—"is where you will find fortune tellers and dream readers who will explain your dreams to you."

What might these seers tell me now? Would their words echo the High Priestess's when I accepted the sword and shield? *I charge you to defend the Temple of the Eighteen Moons and to restore harmony and balance to the land in the name of Malinalxochitl.*

A chuckle from Díaz brought me back. "I smell roasted meat."

The food stalls were on the far side of the marketplace. Tlaxcalli filled with spit-roasted venison. Pumpkin soup. Turkey stews. Maize cakes topped with fish eggs. Cups of chocolatl. Toasted sunflower seeds to munch on as you shopped. Whatever you craved, the market offered. I learned later that more than forty thousand people came to trade and barter at Tlatelolco every day.

I offered to help the scribe find paper, ink, and the quills he prized for word-making, but he said that he did not wish to trouble me, and off he went, fearlessly launching himself into the throng.

On my own again, I looked for Cortés, as it was dangerous to leave him unsupervised for too long. I caught a flash of steel and made my way toward the merchants of weapons. Some of the Spaniards drifted toward the canoe builders and the stalls of wooden oars and fishing nets. Our escorts were in a panic, trying to keep track of everyone.

When I felt assured that our guides had everything under control, I headed back through the aisles toward a series of archways where acrobats and contortionists were showing off their skills. After working my way deeper into the market, I found myself in an open square where victims of the Mexica's wars—men, women, and children—and criminals and gamblers deep in debt were being sold as slaves. I pulled back and stepped away, but I could not turn from the haggard faces and starved bodies. The wooden collars. The long poles that bound them together. Everything was for sale in Tlatelolco.

My throat tightened. I imagined the weight of a wooden collar gripping my own neck. The voice of the slave trader who had captured me on the river rumbled so loudly in my mind, it was as if he were standing right in front of me. "Wordless!" It was his name for me. "Pathetic human being!" I could smell his yellow spit.

I wandered on in search of an herbalist for something to settle the upset in my stomach. From time to time, I would hear a strange sound, a soft beating, like drums. I had heard it before. Each time, I would stop and listen. But now I told myself that it was just the music of a troupe of players, or a mix of voices. The market was so vast, and there was so much noise, that it could have been anything.

After reaching into my jaguar pouch and withdrawing a handful of cacao beans, I approached a shop draped with canopies and a display of carefully ordered clay bowls and jars. Cotton sacks and open shelves brimmed with herbs, flowers, leaves, tree bark, and rooty growths, along with all manner of creams and healing waters. The earthy smells put me at ease instantly. An elderly woman with a wreath of twisted cotton holding back her braided hair nodded and caught my searching gaze. I confided my malady to her, and she stepped away to mix a special treatment for me. In the back of the shop, I noticed the figure of a man I assumed to be her husband. His face and head were covered with coarse cloth, and a loose stole shielded his arms from the sun. A memory stirred then, of another man similarly dressed. *He was standing on the causeway?* But it quietly vanished, replaced by my thoughts of how touching it was to see the couple working and conferring together.

I watched him approach me with a clay cup of water. I was suddenly very thirsty and could practically taste the first cool sip. Silently, he offered the cup to me, but at the last minute, I withdrew my hand, clumsily upsetting a display of dried flowers and sending them tumbling. I mumbled apologies, but in truth, I don't think any words got out. I stood frozen, staring at the bold and magnificent blue tattoos encircling his wrists and arms. Feathered serpents.

I knew of only one man with such distinguishing marks as these.

"Pakal Balam," I was finally able to say.

SPRAYS OF CALLA LILIES AND ROSES

Pakal Balam took hold of my wrist. He looked over his shoulder then, and after meeting the gaze of the old woman, he led me away. We moved quickly past herbalists, feathermakers, the gold and silver workers, with me running a little to keep up. The loose stole around his shoulders had fallen, revealing more blue markings that I knew well, having traced them with my fingers and tongue. Maya symbols for sun and moon, a constellation of stars. My heart was high in my chest, beating furiously fast. The wrist he held felt on fire.

I started to cry even before he pulled me into the soft shadows of an archway. I was remembering everything: our first meeting in the dark near the warrior woman's grave, the way he sang for his warriors as we traveled down the river, the way he laughed when he caught me spying on him, and the way he cupped my body at the water's edge. The memories filled my head and lapped flicks of flame across my skin.

He drew us into scented shadows behind the flower sellers and sprays of calla lilies and roses. He turned me again and again in his arms as if afraid stillness might break us apart. When he stopped, he quickly unspooled the fabric that shielded his head and face from view. With the cloth fisted in his hand, he jutted out his chin, as if he was saying, *This is who I am now.*

I saw the jagged scar that tore from the outside corner of his right eye to his chin; another wound split his forehead in two. A swelling of healed flesh cast his face into perpetual melancholy. He stopped my hand from touching him, but I shook my head and gently continued, feeling the rough scales of his cheek, whispering, "My Maya. My Pakal Balam." His name was a burst of sunlight on my lips.

He wiped away my tears and pressed me against the wall, though not too hard, because of the shield. *Is this really happening?* I thought as his thumb stroked over my cheek. Did the goddesses send me this waking dream as a boon for the work I had done so far? Resting his forehead against mine, he breathed a small laugh, as if he'd read my mind.

"Priestess. The one the eagle follows." At the sound of that familiar voice, I felt a shiver go down my spine. Like a wind that held the promise of a hard rain. In the next moment, we laughed together softly, marveling in unison. Then no sound, no words. My mouth on his, gentle, then hard, insisting, wanting more.

We kissed in that shadowed portico most likely smelling of lilies and roses, but all I smelled was his skin—sweaty, earthy, and warm.

And then he was gone. "I will come to you," he'd promised, and without telling him about the royal palace, he slipped away.

I returned to the Spaniards, lost and in a daze. No one seemed to notice, save maybe the writer Díaz.

▲▲▲▲

Pakal Balam made his way to me that night, slipping past Lady Turquoise Star's guardsmen, I know not how. His figure separated from the shadows of my room. It was cool from the breezes off the canal and the lake beyond it. Night birds sang and night flowers released their scent. I had lit two torches so we would be able to see each other plainly. But with him standing before me, a large part of me craved the dark.

I did not know how to be with him. Here I was a priestess, a proven warrior, a nahual-spirited sorceress in possession of the goddess Malinalxochitl's shield, and I did not know who I was when I was with Pakal Balam. I think I was afraid. My body had been used by men, and though they had left no visible marks, I was scarred with shame.

We lay on the bed's fur mantle, fully clothed, and looked at each other. My Maya was leaner now, but as hard-muscled as ever. There was silver in his black hair, though he did not wear it in a topknot, like most warriors. It probably would have raised too much attention.

As I admired him for all he was, I thought that if my life should come to an end now, I would still like to be rooted to the earth with my Maya, turned into a flowering tree by Earth Mother. I didn't want this moment to end, but there was so much I wanted to know, so we bared our truths.

"After the attack, I was left for dead," he said in Maya. "I would have perished were it not for one of my men, who found me dying from my wounds in the river grasses. He carried me to safety, following the river, and on the outskirts of a village far enough away to be of no danger to us, an old woman favored by Tzapotlatenan, the goddess of healing, cared for me and brought me back to life."

I made a promise to myself that I would find this woman, to thank her. As he continued, I could see what his beautiful eyes had beheld, and I could feel a block of tears rising in my throat. He reached out and caressed my face. "You, too, have seen too much that is ugly and cruel."

I did not answer, only took his hand, which was callused and rough from scars.

I told him about the traders, the sale of my flesh in Xicallanco, all the while keeping the story loose, without too many details. I did not wish to delve too deeply into it. I did not venture into the story about the White Men. That would be for another time. But I did tell him about the goddess's shield. I had wanted to tell him about the shrine and the goddess Malinalxochitl during our journey on the river, but held back out of reverence for that holy ritual. I told him about her special temple and drew the shield into the light, so he could admire it.

As it sparkled in the torchlight, and he sighed with appreciation at its craftmanship and the careful positioning of its most telling feature, shards of obsidian caught fire from the light and reflected my gaze: a woman's face—proud and chiseled with strength, burnished by adversity, no fear in her eyes. And I saw myself clearly.

I am Malinalli.

It was enough . . . and it was everything.

▲▲▲▲

"I followed the eagle to find you," he said one night.

I was tracing his serpent tattoos. The only light a crescent moon.

"He appeared in the sky one day, then two, and I said to myself after the third time, "I know that eagle." Pakal Balam drew me closer and whispered in his deep voice, "By then I'd heard rumors of a sorceress who went by the name of Malinalli, who had been taken captive by an invading army of men from beyond the Divine Eastern Sea. She had trained serpents to do her bidding, and the snakes had attacked Tlaxcallans on a battlefield, killing all who refused to lay down their arms in peace." He held my face between his hands and looked at me so intensely that I knew he was asking me if this tale was true.

I wriggled free, turned him onto his back, and straddled him. He groaned and complimented me, smiling all the while at how deftly I had maneuvered him into a vulnerable position.

"It's true." I pulled loose strands of hair off my face and tucked them into my braid. "I did that." I nodded assertively. "You know your animal guardian, too, I imagine?" He nodded. "So you know what it's like to be in the possession of another creature, to see through its eyes," I said, happy to be able to share this experience with him. "And I have been to the Underworld," I added, arching my brow.

He was shocked by that but recovered nicely with his own surprise.

"We will have to speak of the brave Malinalli's discoveries in Mictlan at another time," he said, "because now I want to tell her about her army."

I had meant to distract him with Art of Pleasure number fourteen, but hearing him mention "my army" made me stop moving my hips, and I slid off him. He seemed surprised by the swiftness of my reaction, started to complain about it, when, on my knees, crouching next to him, I said, "They are in Tenochtitlan?"

"You know about this army?" He reached for me, but before he had a chance to lure me back, I leaped from the bed.

"Of course," I answered, pacing the room. He sat up, staring at me. "Copil, Hummingbird, and I started to spread the word in Cempoallan that the warrior-sorceress was stepping out of the mists of time to return to Tenochtitlan, and that she was looking for warriors to fight the Mexica," I explained.

"The warrior-sorceress?" he asked, perplexed.

I stopped my pacing and looked straight at him. "Yes. I told you: *I* carry her shield. I have been sent to protect and defend what is hers." As I repeated the High Priestess's story for Pakal Balam, tendrils of gold appeared with my breath. Delighted, taking it as the sorceress's heavenly approval, I lifted one delicate wisp, watching it glitter like a falling star.

Pakal Balam gasped. "You are goddess-touched, Malinalli."

The sound of my name on his lips—like a soft rain on sweet grass. I wanted him to say it again, but with panther agility, he rose and began to garb himself in his breechcloths and cloak. "If you will allow me, I will pledge my sword to you and join this army."

I watched him and had to fight against my longing to take him back to my bed. The wall that I had built around my heart after the attack on the river had melted the moment I saw the blue tattoos. Blast this talk of armies and men, all I wanted to do was look at him. Hold him.

As if he knew what was playing through my mind, my confrontation between bliss and responsibility, he put his arms around me and held me close as he kissed my hair.

"Allow you? I demand it!" I said playfully, attempting to bite his ear. But the mood that fell upon us now was heavy with seriousness, and I did not shy away from it. "I want you with me, always."

It still scared me to say this, for I had witnessed too much loss, but it was what I felt.

Whispering, teasing, he said, "I have been yours ever since I caught you staring at me over a pile of dead body snatchers."

I tried to push him away. "I was not staring!" I blushed, remembering the first time I saw him.

"You were," he said, eyes wide, smiling.

A moment later, he nodded, and his expression turned more somber. He pulled me tight to him, kissed me, then let me go. "Then we are agreed that I will join you," he said. "They are not my peoples' enemies, but neither are they entirely our friends." Pakal Balam spoke of the Mexica. "The tradesmen complain that they hold this valley and all trade in a stranglehold. They hope for change."

"As do I." Sighing, I turned away, then darted back for one more kiss. There was much that needed to be done. "How many men are here?" I asked as I slipped on my huipilli and skirt.

"Two hundred. There are two hundred more gathered in Tetzcoco and more in Xaltocan. Groups of warriors are making their way here. There are warrior women, too."

We had not yet talked about the day on the causeway when I, and the women, had used our shields to stop time.

"What of the White Men?" Pakal Balam asked. "What do you intend to do with them? I fear they are too stubborn to leave, and too stupid to see the danger they're in."

"I know. I am trying to get them away, but I'm one of the reasons they're here."

I had not told Pakal Balam about my family or the deep, dark fire for vengeance that had been burning inside me most of my life. I intended to tell him. He deserved to know everything. But right now, I needed to concentrate on solving this puzzle of careful maneuverings and alliances. I would succeed. I had to.

▲▲▲▲

During the following weeks, I spent the daylight hours with Cortés. In the deepest part of night, Pakal Balam and I would sit on my bed and look out at the garden and the water. We had moved it close to the archway that framed the view. I had decided to keep all dealings with Cortés to myself, as I didn't want anything, least of all the Spaniard, to get in my way of being with my Maya.

Most recently, Cortés had complained that I was not paying attention to my work. There was some truth to his accusation. It was doubly hard for me to stay focused on interpreting now that I was reunited with Pakal Balam. But I had vowed to myself that I would work to protect the people of Tenochtitlan, the Maya, and the Spaniards from the dangerous and selfish Cortés. And I had to keep an eye on that other monster, Moctezuma. What kind of trap might he be planning for us? I had made promises to the High Priestess, too. I carried her sword and the goddess's shield, and this filled me with a mighty strength, but was I completely infallible? In a blink, I could lose control, couldn't I? I tried not to think too much about this. But there were times during this period, day and night, when I felt as if I were juggling firesticks and obsidian knives, all while crossing a creaky bridge set above a river teeming with crocodiles.

Cortés's next decision made my juggling trick especially difficult: he ordered his men to prepare to receive the emperor. It sounded harmless, but that Moctezuma should enter such a filthy place was abhorrent to me. It would have taken hundreds of people working a hundred days and nights to clean the palace. After secret arrangements and negotiations, I informed Cortés that we were instead invited to Moctezuma's palace. I thought I would use the visit to press Cortés to admit he would be leaving Tenochtitlan soon. It was not an impulsive idea, but I should have known that urging a monster to do anything was not only impossible but foolhardy.

ON THE EDGE OF A PRECIPICE

Set no more than three hundred paces away from the Spaniards' quarters, Moctezuma's royal residence was the most splendid of all palaces in the island city. A royal official met us in the courtyard. It was a vast space crowded with skilled professionals, for the palace also housed the law courts, storehouses, reception rooms, and the workshops of the emperor's jewelers, feather workers, potters, and weavers. The administration offices were also under this royal roof, including the one responsible for informing my family about my father's murder.

Clutching the turquoise necklace around my throat, I recalled the cruel official who had brought the news, and I felt the flames of rage lick deep in my belly as guards ushered us past the alabaster pillars and up the staircase that led to the emperor's audience hall and private quarters. I took a long, deep breath. No one seemed to give us more than a passing glance, as if the presence of the Spaniards was a common occurrence.

The audience chamber inspired awe and tied up tongues. The torches and lamps turned to gold the painted walls and ceiling. The stone bench that we gathered around was set six steps below Moctezuma and his jaguar throne, the seat of authority the Mexica's war and sun god stole from Malinalxochitl. My eyes caught the lightning-fast turn of the head and snarl of the snaggle-toothed creature. A green mantle embroidered with feathers floated above the floor and around the emperor in shifting waves. On each of his arms, from wrist to elbow, gleamed gold cuffs.

I silently thanked the beast for such a warm greeting. It was the throne's custom to act up whenever it saw me, a behavior, I discovered, that made me feel all the more powerful. I settled into myself, embraced my role, and looked around without turning a muscle. Most of his court was in attendance, including his grim-faced brother, Cuitlahuac, and his cousin, Cuauhtemoc. I remembered seeing them standing on the causeway, shooting evil looks at Cortés and his men. The past months had not eased their moods. Jugglers and acrobats stood silently along the edges, waiting for a sign to perform. I saw ghosts, too—women covered with white dust, holding chisels, picks, and straps, standing all along the towering walls. They must have been the women of Chalco: I had heard a story of how these women—after the Mexica had killed all of their men in battle—had been forced to quarry, cut, and drag the stones for these walls themselves. Their eyes grew wide when we entered, and a few of the specters darted forward to get a closer look at the White Men . . . and at me. I narrowed my eyes and gave them my warrior-sorceress stare. Knowing I carried the shield tight and secure along my back doubled my courage.

Moctezuma slumped on his throne. He looked bored as he tugged on his deformed earlobe, scarred from maguey spines during acts of self-sacrifice.

The captain was feeling grievously injured for being ignored, but seeing the emperor's ears sent Cortés into a shaking rage that pitched his voice high.

"He looks like one of his bloody priests!" Luckily, the ceiling was high, making it hard to discern the squeak in his voice. His black garments and white ruff set off his red face. "Why has he been ignoring us?" He sounded more like a jealous lover than the head of an army.

I stood in respectful silence, and after observing all of the protocols, addressed Moctezuma, "Lord, my lord, my great lord," and put forth the Spaniard's questions.

After Moctezuma's response, I turned to Cortés. "The emperor has been at his palace in Chapoltepec." He had been fasting, observing rituals, and offering penance, but I did not tell Cortés this. I now kept from him anything related to the Mexica's gods. Save for this, I interpreted Moctezuma's words faithfully.

After a long silence, Cortés said, "Ask him where are his gold mines. He must be specific."

Moctezuma told me that the Cloud People in the land of the Mixtec had gold mines, which I relayed to Cortés. As soon as I stopped speaking, Cortés turned to one of his officers and ordered a search for them.

"Do you believe that is wise?" I cautioned. It didn't surprise me that he was interested in gold mines, but to go look for them immediately? To diminish his forces now was a dangerous move, but he ignored me and pushed on.

"I need a deep harbor for ships," Cortés barked, as if raising his voice would help me understand him better. Then he gestured with his chin toward Moctezuma. "Ask him where there is a deep harbor."

Part of me wanted to apologize for the rudeness. I slightly lowered my head, nothing more, while keeping my eyes on Moctezuma. When I told Cortés that Moctezuma was unsure but would be happy to send some of his men to find out, Cortés insisted on sending Spaniards with them. I thought that this, too, was a mistake, but this time I kept my silence.

"Ask him where . . ."

It had been my plan to push Cortés into talking about his departure, but the man's persistent questioning made it impossible. Despite this, I maintained an admirable level of calm.

▲▲▲▲

After the audience with Moctezuma, I tried my hand at spells that would keep the Spaniards safe while they were in Tenochtitlan. Nothing that would have raised eyebrows—simple enchantments made with everyday herbs and seeds that offered basic protections from foul water, bad food, animal bites, and stings. But the sorcery unleashed by Moctezuma's magicians repelled every charm and bit of magic. While it tested my confidence, I had only to remind myself that I was under the protection of the warrior-sorceress, and that her will was mine, to make everything feel right again.

But over the next seven days, I was repeatedly drawn to the idea of throttling Cortés's neck. Blast keeping him alive. Whenever his whines and temper and pomposity overwhelmed me, I wished I could throw him into a stone cell and muzzle him with a binding cloth. With cold determination, and drawing on every meditation and calming skill I had learned at the Temple, I kept to my task to keep everyone, even Cortés, safe.

He'd petitioned to be admitted to Moctezuma's court a total of twenty times. The emperor refused every one of them. Nevertheless, Cortés insisted that I keep pushing for an audience with the emperor, and so twice, sometimes three times a day, I walked from Cortés's palace to Moctezuma's, back and forth, taking the path that ran along the outside of the serpent wall, a route shaded by cypress and willow trees.

It was the dawn of a new morning. After walking in the sunlight, it was always a shock for me to enter Cortés's dim audience chamber. If he wasn't busy attending entertainments and ball games, making maps of the city and sampling the women who had been handed to him as easily as if they were offerings of ripe fruit, he would be here, sitting on his throne. It was just a chair, really, but one that had been embellished with a high back of cypress wood, finished with gold leaf and a flattened pillow of turquoise.

Every meeting was the same, with the scribe in a corner writing everything down on papers arranged on an overturned drum. I listened to the usual litany of complaints and the ponderous silence that always followed. And then I said the words I had been repeating every morning for the past several days.

"It is time for you to leave." As always, I pronounced each sound as if it were a precious jade, something polished and shiny to entice a light response, like, "Oh yes, of course. You are right, Doña. I will make plans immediately."

"Again with this nonsense?" Cortés shouted. "What did I tell you yesterday, and the day before that?" I refused to let him get the upper hand, looked him straight in the eye. He was the first to turn away. He pushed aside scrolls of maps and leaned back against his throne. He had bags under his eyes from lack of sleep. "We have just arrived, have we not? Besides, I have twenty of my men exploring the area, looking for gold mines and a deep, safe harbor for my ships."

We were not newly arrived: it had been months since our entrance into the city. I patiently said, "Moctezuma has pledged his alliance. He has offered his friendship to your king. And tribute. Tell me what is required, how it is to be delivered, and it shall be taken care of."

"Enough. This talk will ruin my appetite."

"You have seen Moctezuma. You have talked to him, eaten with him," I said, my voice full of encouraging wonder and astonishment. Cortés vented his frustration by swiping at the air between us, but it did not stop me. "Given everything you have told me about your king, he will be pleased with your accomplishments. It is time to go."

"Doña Marina, it sickens me to see Moctezuma use you in this way, doing his bidding to belittle our God and send us away," Cortés whined. "He is an interloper. Say nothing more."

▲▲▲▲

I was standing on the edge of a precipice. "I can feel that old crocodile stirring in his sleep," I said to Pakal Balam, referring to the creature upon whose back we all stood. Every time I appeared before Cortés and Moctezuma, I had to project confidence and calm, no matter what they said, no matter how they behaved. “No one else in Tenochtitlan has my skill,” I reminded myself out loud to Pakal Balam, who listened with exact attention, as if my words were gold. With the Temple’s teachings in mind, I told myself that I had to be “a light, a flame” and illuminate the shadows within Moctezuma’s and Cortés’s speeches. Project a patient attitude while listening to the Spaniard’s coarse tongue. And I had to do it all ever so carefully. I was here to ease tensions, not add to them. And yet . . .

Keep your sword up, shield always at the ready, I could hear the High Priestess warn.

My Maya tried to release me from the colliding forces of wills and wiles. For a few hours every day, my entire world began and ended in our bed. It was enough, until it wasn’t.

LESSONS OF THE MOON STONE

With the passing of each day, it became more obvious to me that the longer the Spaniards stayed in Tenochtitlan, the harder it would be to pry Cortés loose from it. I was sure Moctezuma was laying a trap for him, but would I be trapped by the same yoke?

I tried not to reveal my growing distress to my friends. I didn't want to add to any fears they might have already had. They were under my protection, after all. Long ago at the Temple, I had vowed to keep Hummingbird safe. Now that she was a mother, I had her child to think of. It was my fault that Hummingbird was in Tenochtitlan. She had given up her family to be with me. And Copil had risked everything to tell me the truth about Moctezuma. The magician had been a friend to my brother, probably the last student at the House of Magical Studies to see Eagle alive. These were the people I cared for most in the world. I could not fail them.

But as the days went by, my body began to betray me, eager to reveal my worries and fears. Even as I performed the simple task of braiding my hair, my fingers trembled. Hummingbird noticed it, too. After spending most of my day arguing with Cortés, Hummingbird surprised me by steering me away to a special temple. "Forget Cortés for the moment. You must see this." I'd agreed to accompany her, though I thought I would use our walk to convince Hummingbird to leave the island city and return to her child. I could not allow her to keep risking her life, as I had no way of protecting her with Moctezuma's binding spells in place. This venture had taken a toll on her. I wanted to see her reunited with her daughter, holding her, caring for her, not me.

We entered the temple precinct through the Western Gate. The size and splendor of the sacred area once overwhelmed me, but no more. The dazzle was old. I saw through the magnificent temples and butterfly colors to the shadows and to the man who ruled over it all. There were people everywhere: priests with sooty faces trailing black robes; warriors in thick-soled sandals and orange cloaks; richly dressed men and women and those in coarse cloth, running errands or going to a temple to make obeyance to the gods. One temple had a pink shell-like spiral, another an entranceway made to look like the open mouth of a crocodile. Many rose like elegant houses on platforms with stone steps, and most were dedicated to gods.

Hummingbird was familiar with my complaints about the absence of shrines dedicated to goddesses, so I assumed she was taking me to see one that I had missed. I had already found solace in Xochiquetzal's flower-filled temple, and offered the goddess of beauty, patroness of weaving, gifts of shells and embroidered cloth. At Chicomecoatl's shrine, I had dedicated prayers and placed baskets of maize and a jade snake at the feet of an elaborately carved sculpture that appeared to breathe with life. But my spirit was hungry for more sanctuaries where the force of women reigned.

"You have to go away from here. Return to Mayapan and your daughter," I implored Hummingbird as we passed a rack of hundreds of skulls, a sight that always made my stomach flip. "You have been too long apart from your child. And you'll also need to take Copil with you."

She looked at me as if I was being ridiculous. I hesitated to say more.

"Are you ordering me to go?" she asked without breaking her stride.

"Well . . ." What was I doing ordering Hummingbird? My words were coming out all wrong. The truth was, I didn't really want her to leave. But she had to.

"Don't you see? It's too dangerous for you to be here." I had to run to keep up with her. "And you know Cortés has always disliked Copil. I fear Cortés will snap at any moment." I paused, my attention veering to Copil. "So, when was the last time you saw our friend? I can't remember when I . . ." It was not unusual for him to disappear. I thought of how he went missing right after the Spaniards arrived. He had embedded himself in their camp and caused a great deal of mischief. What was he up to now?

"He told me he was going to Tlatelolco to purchase a divining crystal. He didn't like the reception you received from Moctezuma two days past. Gave him a bad feeling. Said it was time for him to 'get to work,' whatever that means." Hummingbird kept on, and I followed her lead, though I had more questions for her now that I'd heard this about Copil. She moved confidently through the crowds. People cut a wide path for us, pointing and whispering as if they recognized us as being part of the White Men's forces.

"You say 'it's too dangerous' as if we've never been in harm's way before." She shrugged. "It is a tangle," Hummingbird admitted, "a miserable web, with two fat spiders at the center, lying in wait to see who gets to be the first to tear apart their victims." She stopped abruptly, turned to look at me. "If I am not here, who will help guide you? You know my nahual ally is ever ready to protect you. I know Pakal Balam is my equal—"

"Stop. You know how much I prize your counsel." I had told her and Copil about Pakal Balam's return long ago, but hearing her doubt her importance to me made me question if that had been the right thing to do. I took her hand and turned it over in mine. "I have no greater friend than you. There is no finer warrior in all the world than you. But I *am* afraid. Tenochtitlan is not safe. It never was, but now I fear . . ."

I heard it then . . . the sound . . . like a dull drumbeat, pulsing above the dense and swirling cloud of people's voices and the constant movement of the crowd. This time, it felt close by.

"There. Do you hear that?" I leaned to the right as Hummingbird stared, eyebrows furrowed.

"Hear what?"

"That low— Listen! Like a moan, but with a steady rhythm," I said, lost inside the haunting sound. For a moment it became clearer to me than the calming pitch of Hummingbird's voice.

She turned and looked. "No, I hear nothing but . . ." She gestured to the crowds streaming around us. "Could it be a child's cry? Someone's appetite calling out to be fed?" she guessed while keeping her eye on a group of orange-mantled warriors as they stomped past us.

I waved her suggestions away. Listened. It was distinct. Pulsing.

"Malinalli, we are in the temple precinct, where there are drums everywhere," Hummingbird patiently pointed out. "A priest is probably marking off the hour of the sun. However, I don't hear anything like that now."

I turned slowly, looking all around me. Instinctively, I raised my arms to the sides, ready to fend off a threat. But when my gaze caught my friend, her head inclined, arms crossed, I knew I had gone too far.

"Maybe you're right." But I continued to glance over my shoulder as we walked on, a feeling of dread creeping through my limbs.

▲▲▲▲

Inside the temple, a cold and clammy darkness bathed my skin. Cobwebs got caught in my face and hair, and I brushed them off me, shivering, as if they were ghostly fingers reaching out to ensnare me. At first, I couldn't see anything. Hummingbird and I had had to push our way through the doors—moldy, cracked, flaking with paint—and now it seemed we had left all of the world's light behind us. A small prick of flame came into my view, and I moved toward it. The stingy glow was coming from a small brazier. The meagerness of it challenged my eyes, but in time I was able to make out statues of women, large and small, both in standing and seated poses. They were lined against the walls, pushed into the aisles. It seemed that no thought or design had been given to their placement.

"Who are they?" I wondered aloud, startling winged things that screeched and flew up in our faces and above our heads, seeking the dark.

"Who are they?" Hummingbird's eyes flashed with anger. "They are goddesses. Statues of the divine ones from all the conquered people, the lands the Mexica now call their own," Hummingbird answered, brushing feathers and bits of dust off. "And, possibly, some old idols that once stood in the city and that have fallen out of favor."

"There must be over fifty of them." They were beautiful. Many of carved, painted stone. Some decorated with mosaic.

"Eighty-eight. I've counted them. The Mexica house them like this. There is another temple stuffed with more idols of various wind, rain, and corn goddesses in another corner of the city."

I turned, taking it all in. The floor, slabs of ordinary gray stone, not something marvelous like onyx or inlaid tiles like in other temples.

"See there?" Hummingbird directed my attention to a towering idol with a kindly face, eyes of obsidian, corn cobs decorating her long plaits of hair. "From the Cloud People, I think. A corn goddess."

I hissed, angry and sickened to see the goddesses hidden away in this prison. I moved closer to the corn goddess. An artist had carved flower petals into her sash and arcs of corn leaves throughout her skirt. She was meant to be seen, meant to be honored.

Moving as one, Hummingbird and I raised our arms to our sides, and we said Feathered Butterfly's prayer for peace and transformation. We did not whisper. We were not shy. We released the words with all of our might as if they held the magic to bring them all to life.

▲▲▲▲

Back in the open air, it took time to get my bearings. I couldn't distance myself from what I had just seen. A filthy, run-down temple filled with goddesses shoved into corners, with bats and birds flying all around . . . It made me angry. One look at Hummingbird, at how she clutched the sastun around her neck, and I knew she was as distressed as I was.

"I've heard rumor of a pestilence that is afflicting the people east of the volcanoes," she said after a long moment of silence on our return to the Spaniards' quarters. "People are dying, Malinalli. The healers are mystified. Even the magicians are stunned at the ferocity of the illness. Black welts cover the body like spots on a jaguar pelt until they burst with fluid." Her words made me wince, for I could picture it clearly. "No one can explain what it is. What if this city is the safest place for me to be?"

I gave her a tight smile. Tenochtitlan was nowhere near *safe*. "Try all you like, but I'm not going to change my mind. If the rumor is true, I have faith the Temple's priestesses will learn a cure and quickly spread word of their healing knowledge. Your place is with your daughter."

We stepped into the cool shadows cast by the Great Temple, which loomed over the precinct. A commanding pyramid, taller than all the others, it had two stairways leading to two sanctuaries: one dedicated to the war god, the other to the god of rain. Giant stone serpent heads with feathered collars guarded one approach, while a pair of sleepy-eyed frogs smiled contentedly at the foot of the other. A trio of guards, armored and in orange mantles, bearing spears, patrolled the area. I felt drawn to the stairs that led to the temple of the war god. I had heard Cortés say the angle was very steep and in the same breath, brag that he had had no problem climbing the steps.

Just as I turned to investigate, Hummingbird grabbed my arm and tried to steer me in a different direction. But I'd already spotted the giant disc of painted stone set at the foot of that ascent. I was intrigued. I'd caught a glimpse of it during one of my walks through the sacred precinct, but back then I didn't have the time to take a closer look. I acknowledged my friend's protective stance, patted her hand, then moved away. What I saw next made my breath jump and heart fall. Carved into the stone was the dismembered figure of a woman, a goddess judging by her headdress, necklaces, labret, and ornamented cuffs. Then I noticed the incisions marking her cheeks: bells.

I fell to my knees. This was Coyolxauhqui, She of the Painted Bells, the Moon Goddess.

Her story roared into my head. She had fought to defeat her brother Huitzilopochtli and save the people from the blood rituals of human sacrifice. This brother brought her down, cut her to pieces.

"How did I not know about this?" I addressed my question to the air, though I knew my sister was standing at my side. I turned and could tell she was holding her breath.

She glanced back toward the guards we had seen earlier. "You have been so busy that you haven't had time to see many things here."

I looked up at the summit, and back down at the stone that had been created by Moctezuma's ancestors as a reminder that the sun war god was mightier than the moon goddess, Malinalxochitl's sister.

I leaned over the stone to make the gesture we call kissing the earth.

"What about the guards?" Hummingbird asked.

"We will honor her as she deserves."

Immediately, Hummingbird made a sound that signaled she understood and knelt down beside me. I traced sprays of old, dried blood with my fingers. I wanted to cover the goddess with my mantle. I wanted to keep vigil and pray. *Why didn't someone protect her?*

I turned my head to look at my sister priestess, hero of labyrinths and mysterious paths.

Hummingbird nodded slowly. "Let them try to move us away."

I reached for her hand. "If the goddess of the moon can be treated in this way, what hope is there for us?"

What am I saying? No hope?

The fear I saw in my sister's eyes assured me what I'd just said was wrong.

"No, wait." I shook my head and tightened my grip around her hand. "Forgive me, my dearest sister, I spoke an untruth."

I turned back to the goddess captured in stone. Her nakedness ignited a fury I felt down to my core. *No one should ever be displayed like this. No goddess, or woman, should be shown cut down in celebration of another being's superiority. And no goddess should be allowed to be shoved into a corner, out of the light.*

"The goddesses we have seen today demand that we have hope," I said. "Only through hope will we be able to move forward and protect them, protect ourselves."

A SISTER'S PROMISE

I went through my routines, applied my interpreting skills the best I could, and worked to keep all sides in a kind of perfect-imperfect balance, but the darkness I had been avoiding wanted more from me. I prayed for guidance, picturing not the warrior-sorceress or Earth Mother who had visited me in the Tlaxcallan prison but the decapitated goddess enshrined in stone.

Time grew wings, and in a blink, the Mexica and the people of the lakes were celebrating the Raising of the Feathered Banners and decorating their homes with colorful paper ribbons. There was a sacrifice of prisoners. I did not witness the ceremony, and neither did the Spaniards. The next month, the Coming Down of Waters, December, the people honored the mountains and the rain gods.

It was a day like any other. I was following a regimen ordained by the old herbalist that consisted of nourishing atoles and juice waters mixed with powders that helped soothe my stomach. Cortés's quarters reeked of the usual odors, but his throne room now bore the additional fragrances of blood and vomit. The men gathered around a large hemp bag sitting in the middle of the table.

"Look at what he did!" Cortés screamed.

Aguilar lunged and pulled the bag's tie open, revealing a black-bearded head. Its eyes were open and an opaque white. I looked away. It was one of Cortés's lieutenants, who had been left to guard the fort on the coast.

Cortés pointed wildly at the bag. "Do you see what that barbarian has done to Arguello? I swear I will kill Moctezuma with my own hands for this."

Who was he to talk of cruelty? He was behaving as if he'd never committed a vile beheading before. To the horror of the White Robes, he had performed many since invading this land.

I looked around at the soldiers gathered in the room, hoping one of them could explain what had happened. After Díaz told me that one of Moctezuma's administrators had attacked the fort of La Villa Rica de La Vera Cruz and sacrificed and beheaded the Spaniard, I felt the threads holding my hopes and plans together come undone.

The scribe continued. "The guards on the rooftop tell us that some of the bridges in the city have been removed, leaving gaps in the causeway . . ." He paused. "Trapping us."

"They are taking precautions against your allies, the Tlaxcallans," I thought out loud. *That must be it.* "There are hundreds of them here in the palace, and over five thousand of your soldier allies are scattered on the mainland, surrounding Tenochtitlan."

"I say we take the heathen hostage," the flame-haired Alvarado shouted.

Moctezuma? A hostage? They can't be serious. Is Cortés mad? Is he drunk on octli? It was outrageously impossible. But their furious faces, the way their hands reached for swords, shoved all doubts away. Couldn't they see that the minute they touched the emperor, they would die? For all my frustration with them, I did not want to see them dead.

But for a moment, I became angry, jealous even. I wanted to be the one to imprison him. *If he is to be killed, it should be by my hand.*

I masked this storm of feelings. "There's no need to be alarmed. I will talk to him," I said as if I were placating boys. "There are reasonable explanations for all of this."

But Alvarado's idea had ignited the men. They waved their swords in the air.

"We will get him now!" Alvarado roared. The men shouted in agreement. Cortés attempted to temper them.

I had to yell to be heard. "There is nothing to fear. There is still—" But it was too late. Someone, in his haste to share the news with the rest of the Spaniards, shoved me aside as he hurried from the room. I watched them from the corner. I hated hovering like this, watching their antics, trying to keep everyone steady. My fingers itched for my sword, to unstrap my shield and use them to control these men and force them to do my bidding. I didn't want the stains of more blood, more dead bodies. I certainly didn't want to kidnap Moctezuma. I wanted . . . What? Peace. A plan. Cortés gone from this land. How could this be so hard?

I shoved my empty hands into my skirt and squeezed the soft folds mercilessly. Malinalli had solved much harder riddles. Scaled mountains. Survived the Underworld. *I will think of something.* But a thought nagged: *What if the Spaniards are right, and the best course of action is to remove Moctezuma from his throne . . . now?*

▲▲▲▲

It happened so fast.

The next day, before dawn, Cortés led a group of thirty men to Moctezuma's private quarters. The emperor's shocked attendants stood silently by as Cortés strode toward them, armed to the teeth, and explained why he had to take Moctezuma hostage and move him to the Spaniards' lodgings. I was the last to enter the chamber and froze when I heard the Spaniard's words.

"Doña Marina?" Cortés turned and gestured that I approach. "Come quickly!" When I did, he pulled me even closer. "Tell my esteemed friend that he has nothing to fear, for we will honor him in all ways."

My legs were shaking. I could feel Moctezuma watching my face as I listened to Cortés's next words. I could feel the weight of the spells that had been conjured to make me weak. When the Spaniard finished speaking, he refused to let me go. I turned to the emperor. His eyes were dark and menacing. I interpreted calmly, then leaned closer so that only Moctezuma could hear me. At any moment, an arch of his eyebrow could send us all to the top of the pyramids to have our hearts cut out.

After a long moment of quiet, after gesturing to attendants that his blue mantle needed to be retied, he looked up at me.

To my surprise, he behaved as if he had been expecting this. "My councilors will never allow it," he said simply. "The jaguar throne is here, in this palace."

I lowered my eyes for a moment. "I know." Then I thought of my father and my brother. Did I really want Moctezuma to live?

As if he could sense my dilemma, the emperor laughed. For a moment, I felt everyone in the room knew what I was thinking.

Moctezuma waved his jeweled hand. "Take one of my sons and two of my daughters as hostages in my stead."

I blinked. He would barter his own son and daughters away? I turned and presented Moctezuma's idea to Cortés, but I knew what the Spaniard would say.

▲▲▲▲

It became so quiet that you could have heard a thorn from a nohpalli drop. Moctezuma consented to go with us and made all of his explanations to his advisers, guards, and priests. Then, beneath a gray sky, his nobles carried him on his royal litter to the same royal dwelling that housed Cortés and his men, the dwelling that had once been

Moctezuma's father's, following the same path I had been taking back and forth between the palaces. The people—merchants, porters, and priests on their way to the marketplace and temples—gaped at the procession. But no weapons were raised in protest. No words were said. There was just a terrifying silence.

▲▲▲▲

Once the jaguar throne was carried over to the freshly painted and gilded chamber on the second floor, the emperor continued the work of the empire. It had taken twenty hulking men to move it on a special dais and hundreds more to transform Moctezuma's personal rooms with feathered wall hangings, carpets, caged songbirds, gold idols, and Moctezuma's perfumed wives and concubines. One of the first of Moctezuma's possessions to be moved was the special cedar-and-gold screen that shielded him from the court's view when he ate.

It was all smiles and games at first. They were all great gamblers. Cortés appeared to have a talent for winning patolli games, until I realized he was cheating. Moctezuma was aware of the deception. The Spaniard taught the emperor betting tricks involving dice someone had carved from black onyx. But soon the merriment became strained. Cortés would laugh, and the emperor would laugh harder. Moctezuma would bet a few gemstones on a play. Cortés would bet twice that and more. This was the way of things for two months, until the tension became so great that the air turned green with hatred.

▲▲▲▲

I was well acquainted with Moctezuma's habits and the workings of his court, so on a morning when I knew he would be alone, I hurried along the passageways to his chambers.

I found the emperor sitting on his throne, his jaguar-spotted cloak shifting around him in a wind that I could see the effects of but not feel.

The torchlight, though feeble, was enough to give a dull shine to the chains around his wrists and ankles. Shadows clung to the red-painted walls. A chocolatl cup and a tobacco pipe were set near him. The chamber was stark compared to his usual awe-inspiring surroundings, but at least it was not dusty and cobwebbed, like the temple of fallen goddesses.

He looked me over slowly and grinned.

I tensed, feeling my mouth go dry.

"Are you here to gloat? Tell me, why does the earth not swallow you up?" he said. "In your attempts to take my throne, you sow nothing but pain and anguish, Malinalxochitl."

"I do not want your throne."

"Keep saying that, and maybe you will believe it." When I did not respond, he tried worming his way through my wall of confidence. "You will not be rid of him, or me, so easily." Moctezuma looked away. "However, the white captain will never have my throne. My priests have seen into the future, and they tell me that he will never rule here. You, on the other hand . . . they cannot explain, with any certainty, what is to become of you."

His eyes flicked over me, and it was like being pricked by a comb of needles.

I refused to be afraid. Suddenly he rose to his feet and moved toward me, lurching unsteadily, dragging his chains and a Spanish iron lock as large as a human heart. I took a step back, and he smiled again.

He stopped when he was close enough to touch me and leaned in to whisper, "If there is nothing binding you to this place, then come with me, Malinalxochitl. We can escape, you and I." He shook the chains that tied his wrists. From the look on his face, you would have thought it was a noise as delicate as the tinkling of small bells. "I know a way," he said. "I learned many secrets when I was a priest. And the magicians at the school taught me things, too." He smiled slyly. "My nahual, *my* animal guardian, protects me. I have nothing to fear. Come with me." There was an urgency to his words. "We will start a new city. Bring order and balance, the way it should be." His voice soft and intimate, his gaze still heavy and dark, daring me to refuse.

I was not tempted, but at the word *nahual* my spirit creature hissed deep inside me. I felt surprise and comfort. *The spell his sorcerers placed over the city must be weakening.*

I turned my back on him and walked away. When he howled, the force of his anger blew out all of the light and nearly knocked me down. "You are an abomination," he screamed. "You are an embarrassment to your people and to this land. You are lost, Malinalxochitl, and you will be remembered for the pain you caused."

His insults followed me through the palace, nipping at my heels like a band of toothsome creatures called up from the Underworld.

▲▲▲▲

"This is the first and last time Moctezuma and I will ever be in agreement, but he's right, you must escape," Pakal Balam said to me after I'd told him about my meeting with the emperor. I had just finished applying a calming remedy to the angry scars across his chest. There was a single torch glow, but the moon was full, and the night sounds from the palace garden were rising and falling gently. I acted surprised, but I really wasn't. I knew this moment would come. I knew by the way my quietly strong Maya had been clenching and unclenching his hands, and by his pacing, that he was set on getting me out of there. The way we clung to each other at night hinted that a separation was forthcoming. But on this particular night, I pressed my body so tightly against his that I thought *maybe* we would melt together into one perfect omnipotent, fearless, marvelous, enchanted being. Much had happened to me, so why not this?

Never. It could never happen as long as I was the goddess's shield.

I got up from the bed and draped myself in a huipilli that fell to my knees. The Maya found me staring out into the garden.

“I cannot leave. Not now,” I said. “Nothing has changed here. The people, everyone, they need my protection.” I was still trying to reconstruct the hope that I felt on the day I had stopped the sun. But to be truthful, I felt a great unsteadiness. Moctezuma’s howls had upset me. How could I say this to Pakal Balam?

“The White Men are doomed.” My Maya’s eyes were fixed on me, his jaw tight. “The people are getting restless—those who live here and the ones waiting for you. Some think Moctezuma will take action. If not, then his cousin Cuauhtemoc will. That one will raze the city if he has to, to rid Tenochtitlan of the White Men.” When I looked away, he took a gentler tack. “When the time comes, we will fight, I swear to you. But I need to take you away from here now.”

“No.”

“Your shield cannot make them go away, Malinalli. It cannot stop Moctezuma from moving forward with whatever trap he is plotting. The embroidered threads will not be able to aid you here. There are limits—”

“No,” I said more firmly. Protecting the people was but one of the many promises I had made to myself. I also had to find the source of that strange sound, solve my brother’s mysterious words, and go to the House of Magical Studies. I had been avoiding it, not out of fear, but because . . . I was not ready to face it yet.

Pakal Balam walked away and reached for his breechcloths and mantle.

Is he leaving me? I wanted to rush to his side, but I held myself steady, save for my voice. My words spilled, spiked with anger. “Where are you going? Back to the soldiers?”

“The forces gathered along the lake require a firm hand.”

“But—”

“Have no fear—”

I cut him off, asserting myself, “I *have* no fear.”

He took a deep, patient breath. “I meant, I will be your eyes and ears on the mainland. I will prepare—”

"But your place is here. With me." I heard the strident desperation in my voice and turned away. *Get hold of yourself.*

"I must go," Pakal Balam insisted gently. "I will be watching. Waiting for your sign." He kissed me then . . . on my forehead. It happened quickly, as if he was afraid a deeper kiss would lead to his not going. But he did go. I dropped onto the bed, all feelings hollowed out of me, save one: I'd been abandoned. Again.

▲▲▲▲

I don't know how long I slept, but when I woke up, the dawn light was just beginning to thread its way across the sky, there was an overturned bowl of what smelled like octli on the bed, and Pakal Balam was gone.

I was hoping that I would find him tangled in the soft white mantle. That his leaving was just a dream.

But it wasn't a dream. It was as real as what happened the next day: Cortés announced that the emperor had surrendered and relinquished all control of his empire and accepted the King of Spain as his supreme lord and master. I had been feeling alone and confused, but now it was as if someone had come up from behind and given me a good shove. The news jolted me into a bruising level of alertness. *I* had not interpreted a conversation of this importance between the two men. How could such a talk occur without me? Had Cortés assigned Aguilar to take my place?

Days later, Cortés sentenced the Mexica official responsible for Arguello's beheading and all of the man's attendants, even his sons, to a barbaric death. They were mauled by the Spaniards' dogs, then chained to stout poles and burned alive in the sacred precinct. The people of Tenochtitlan were invited to watch. Hundreds of bodies pressed shoulder to shoulder. Hundreds of eyes looked toward the platform where a silent emperor sat with the jade diadem of authority on his head. The entire Mexica world heard their Revered Speaker's silence give way to the sound of whipping flames, exploding bodies, and sizzling fat.

Then Cortés ordered the removal of the statues of the gods of war and water, and all of the other idols, from the Great Temple. Using ropes, thick mats, greased planks of wood, and wooden rollers, hundreds of priests carefully lowered the statues to the ground, then carried them away on litters, never to be seen again. Copil, Hummingbird, and I were horrified and tried to stop them with our magic, calling on disappearing charms, immobility spells, hexes of last resort learned at the Temple. And in answer, the air vibrated with colorful patterns and haloes, but even the threads stretched half-heartedly to come to my aid. I felt my animal-self hissing in vexation to find itself trapped deep within me. I could feel it trying to uncoil, but then a countering sensation would pummel it back and then reach to squeeze my throat. Hummingbird wrestled for control of her vixen creature, which appeared, then disappeared from one moment to the next. And Copil's rings flashed and smoked, the starry pattern across his mantle blinking like thousands of sleepy eyes. But the force of Moctezuma's binding spell held us fast. Hummingbird and I bore the indignity of struggling against invisible chains as constricting as the heavy manacles choking Moctezuma's wrists and feet. The people fearfully bore the indignity of witnessing their gods being replaced with a new one. It was a dangerous silence. But it was soon drowned out by cactus spines in the thousands raining from the sky.

THE HOUSE OF MAGICAL STUDIES

I should have attached myself to Cortés's side but I could no longer think when I was around the Spaniard.

Sprays of red roses and carnation petals covered the ground where I walked, though I was too distracted by an incessant sound to tread lightly around the delicate displays arranged for a ritual. I thought it might be coming from the temalacatl stone in the sacred precinct, where one-to-one combats were waged against prisoners of war. A quick turn of the area told me it was not.

There was a heaviness to the air. A prickling rain began to fall. It was as if the idols that had been removed were grieving over their homelessness. I walked armed with both sword and shield. I trusted no one save Pakal Balam, Hummingbird, and Copil.

That soft thrumming . . . Was it coming from the belly of an Underworld beast, warning that it was time for it to be fed? Time for me to go? Was it just a lone priest marking the movement of the sun, like Hummingbird had said? Whatever it was, I was determined to learn its source.

Standing in the middle of the temple precinct, I closed my eyes and listened as intensely as I could.

North. It was coming from the north.

My legs suddenly seemed to have a will of their own. When I finally stopped, I found myself standing in front of the place I had longed to see all my life, the House of Magical Studies. It was set far from the temples, in a gloomy site patched with mist.

I drew a shaky breath and slowly exhaled.

My brother and father were once here, perhaps right where I am standing now.

I remembered playing with my brother in the clearing near the giant stone head and watching him sweep his imaginary sword, shouting, "Follow me, sister!" I saw my father hunched low and drawing maps of our land on the dry earth. This was how he explained the world to me, and our place in it. I felt my heart opening to the past and became filled with such longing that I could barely stand.

Suddenly, a hulking figure appeared at the entrance. "Who is there?"

Alarmed, I drew back. But seeing that his hands held nothing but a red cloth and a broom made of heron feathers, I stopped my retreat.

The man's eyes were pale white, a sightless stare rimmed with scars and gobbets of sagging skin. I remembered Copil's story about the guard who protected the entrance to the House of Magical Studies, chosen not for his strength but for his ability to keep the pathway clean. The guard could *hear* specks of dirt and dust as they fell and would sweep them away before they had a chance to deface the polished circle of stone.

Today, the obsidian mirrored a churning gray sky. It appeared unblemished, even though rain fell, and bits of paper and dried leaves circled everywhere.

"Who is there?" he yelled again. He raised his chin and cocked his head in a way that brought chills up my spine. I had witnessed warriors blinded by blood flowing from their head wounds behaving this way.

"I am Malinalli," I announced. "The river twin, the monster slayer, sister of the magician Eagle, sorceress in more than name, warrior-priestess of the Temple of the Eighteen Moons who is under the protection of

Malinalxochitl." The more I said, the prouder I became, and yet I wasn't sure I would be able to proceed inside.

I cleared my throat to remove the irritation clawing at me. "Might I, with your permission . . . ?"

"Enter, please! The sister of Eagle, the sorceress, is always welcome. Alas, there is no one here to greet you save I. They have all gone into the mountains, to the Caves of the Ancestors, to complete an initiation ritual," he said.

I hesitated to step on the stone, for the surface was so deeply dark that I thought I might be swallowed whole and disappear. I yearned for a stick so that I could test for stability. After taking a deep breath, I set off in short, fast leaps across the obsidian.

Safe on the other side, I peered into the dark maw of the school, brushing my hand against the surface of the shell wall, pricking my finger and drawing blood.

"I will await you here." And with that, the blind caretaker turned back to his post.

I wiped the rain from my arms. As there were no torches to light the way, I proceeded carefully, descending deeper. It smelled of earth and damp. I had to crouch to protect my head. The sounds of shifting dirt and slithering creatures merged with my footsteps. As I was thinking that a little light would be good, a flame burst in a simple lamp affixed to the earthen wall. When another flame flickered bright, followed by another, I quickened my step. I hoped to find signs of my brother's life. That here on this mound of pressed earth was where he sat, and over there, by the clay bowl, and near the curve in the wall, was where he ate and slept. I wanted to follow in his footsteps. Learn the magic that would bring him back to life. Learn more regarding his death.

My mind filled with darkness, then a brooding unease that I was long familiar with. My younger self had wallowed in such moods, but I shook it off now. As the firstborn, I should have been the one to attend the school. My brother might still be alive now, the Spaniards nothing but a bad dream. How I'd hated my brother for being allowed entry. A childish feeling, for he'd introduced me to and shared a world of magic and spells, the secret charm that released my power. And now I was a sorceress in my own right.

The path wound on and on, and the walls began to widen, moaning as if the action of making room for me hurt. I reached a sunken chamber where the walls were faced with stone. Someone had chiseled symbols, but I did not recognize them. I moved my hand over the signs and wondered if my brother had done the same.

Spread out in front of me were two rows of earthenware cups, with brushes next to each place, along with white ribbons and yellow kernels of corn. Some of the bowls and settings were overturned and looked out of place, as if they had been knocked over.

Deeper in the chamber I found baskets filled with white cloth and short black cloaks. There were scatterings of crab shells, matted furs, and snakeskins. Stacks of lava-stone bowls, like the one I had found in Eagle's pack after he died, were shoved in a corner. So fiercely was my heart beating, I could hardly breathe. I wiped my eyes with the backs of my hands as I kept looking for . . . something, anything, a clue that might reveal what it was I needed to do now.

Perhaps it was because I wanted so much for something to happen, that nothing did. I had vowed to come to Tenochtitlan so that I might solve the mystery of my brother's words, avenge his and Father's deaths, and here I was. No one could deny that I was a brave daughter and sister, close to fulfilling my vow. And yet there was no triumph. I was not proud. There was an army of Spaniards and Tlaxcallans in Tenochtitlan, and we had left a path of destruction in our wake. Thousands of people had died. I wanted to think that I had saved lives, too, but all I could summon now was an unfathomable feeling of loss.

I stood still so long the roots of dark-worshipping plants reached out to claim me. Then the earth shifted again. An opening revealed itself as the stones and earth parted, filling the air with deep-throated rumbles and a chilling, keening sound. The cave seemed to want me to move forward, so I did. I slipped off my sandals. The deep shush of flowing water turned my skin cold. I continued on until a river stopped me from venturing farther. I remembered that much of Tenochtitlan rested on top of an underground lake. Were there caverns like this one all over the island?

The dark surface rippled like a snake's skin as I knelt to peer into the water's depths. I don't know how much time passed before there was a flash of silver light in that inky murk. The light grew strong and steady enough to catch my reflection. As my face melted away, another image took shape: a young boy's face. The surface of the water danced, marking him clearly—round dark eyes the same as mine, black hair, a quiet smile. *Eagle!*

I felt the rising of the sun and the moon and all the stars, and for a moment joy lifted me off my knees into levitation. *My brother lives!* This was no simple illusion or dream. I was sure that I had only to reach out my hand and my brother would be there, alive again.

"Sister!" The sound rippled through the water and washed over me in blessings of grace that banished the cold away. I felt him—he was nearby. I was certain of it. Perhaps he'd been able to protect himself with his magic after all, and he was here, waiting for me. Then, also carried by the water, the elusive thrumming that I had been drawn to since I entered the city.

I followed the river deep into the earth. The walls continued vibrating with that incessant sound and tried to distract me from my joy. Instinctively, I reached for the sword slung on my back and my shield. Armed, I continued to follow the river through a maze of tunnels and chambers. One was so small and tight, I was forced to crawl forward on my hands and knees, but I did not let go of my weapons. The High Priestess would not have advised that.

The vibrations became so loud and forceful that I thought my blood was pulsing to its rhythm. It was the strangest sensation. Even the river at times, where there was a glimmer of light streaming through the rocks, looked red.

The noise was getting frighteningly, maddeningly close. At least I was back on my feet, though feeling my way through the dark of twisting passageways. It reminded me of the labyrinth.

I swallowed back the bile that rushed hot into my mouth. Warm sweat trickled down my spine. I bit my lip. *Where are you, Eagle?* The blind guard at the school's entrance must have known about these tunnels. Why hadn't he said something? Warned me? Guided me a little?

I thought the river would lead me to the center of the underground caverns, but instead I felt like I was walking in circles. I had not marked my route, so there would be no way for me to find my way back out. The ground sloped, and I followed it. The path climbed, and I scrabbled like a crab. I was struggling for air.

How I hated mazes.

Just breathe. All will turn out well.

So when the tunnel finally turned into another chamber, I shouted my good fortune. By now I hardly noticed the sound. I *was* the sound. It was in me, under me, above me. When I saw the offering table in the middle of the cave, I ran to it, greedily breathing the fresh air circling through the space. It was set high, like the one at the Temple of the Eighteen Moons, but this one was made of blackened stone, charred, with veins of gold. It supported a magnificent dome of crystal that cast a brilliant pink corona of light.

But unlike the Temple, this place had a foul odor. I slowed my steps and peered into the shadows until I found the culprit: smoke curling out of the belly of a stone owl, where two hearts sizzled.

A wave of nausea rolled through me. *What kind of place is this?* Tightening my grip on my sword and shield, I moved closer to the crystal, magnificent and casting sparks throughout the chamber. I could feel sweat beading on my face, my pulse racing, but I kept going until I stood in front of the transparent pink dome and the treasure it protected.

It was beautiful and terrifying. I knew at once what I was seeing: a red pulsating heart, moving in time with the sound reverberating throughout the room. The rhythm seemed to be driving the movement of blood in my veins.

Time stopped for the second time in my life, and then it threw me back to when I was a child, seeing the House of Magical Studies through my brother's eyes. How close he felt to me in those moments. How afraid I'd been for him when the jaguar appeared. *Release my heart from captivity.* I dropped my sword and shield and grasped the crystal between my hands. This was what my brother wanted me to find.

I turned the dome, mesmerized by the heart's insistent beating, the music of life, and all at once, I had to fight back tears. As I told myself not to cry, the warrior-priestess in me sensed someone, hidden deeper, behind the owl. I froze. I knew it was Moctezuma before I saw him. But what was he doing here? He was supposed to be locked in chains and under Cortés's guard.

"Soooo," Moctezuma said, drawing the word out as if he were pulling it out of his throat. "You have finally arrived, sister of the magician Eagle." He paused, blinking his dark eyes. "You look pale, practically dead."

I ignored his last remark but believed it a good thing he knew I was the twin. One less matter we needed to discuss.

The emperor's dark and tattered robe moved like wisps of smoke. His face was painted with the black-and-blue stripes of the War God, and he wore an eagle lip plug and gold ear spools. When he fixed his penetrating gaze on me, I felt something primitive surge between us. He moved his head, the gesture more owl-like than human. It reminded me of the priest I had vanquished in the Underworld.

"You're supposed to be locked up in chains," I said.

I glanced down at my hands. My fingers barely grazed the dome but were stiff as claws. I tried to calm myself a little, lest I break the crystal.

The sorcerer nodded back and forth. "I am there, and I am here. In chains and free. Two things can be true at the same time, do you not think so? What a stupid mob these strangers are. Look at what they have done to this land. And now look at what they have done to you, poor, poor Malinalxochitl. Or should I call you Malinalli now?" He grinned, and I felt as if he was trying to imagine me unclothed. "Or Doña . . . How do the White Men say it? Malina?" he said, struggling with the sound. "Here you are, serving them . . ." He tsked. ". . . when they should be serving you, or, better yet, serving *me*."

At the sound of my names, bats erupted from the shadows and shot from wall to wall, swooping low over my head, sparking a dry laugh from the magician.

"But it doesn't really matter, as you are a thorn in my side just the same. The people are all worked up because of you, ready to leap to your banner and fight me.

"I hear they call you a goddess? *Pfffft*." His eye followed the bats. "Now, if your brother were standing here, he would have combated them with a spell. Or used them to strike back at me." His voice echoed throughout the chamber, surrounding me with his insulting words. I wanted to slap him for even thinking about my brother. Or did he believe I would turn into a puddle at the mention of him? That grief would overwhelm me? Not so, most Un-Revered Speaker of the Mexica.

Breathe.

"Move away from there, you treacherous woman. Humble yourself before me! And then you may come talk to me." With a sudden twirl of Moctezuma's hand, the jaguar throne appeared before us. It sized me up and growled low in its throat. I stayed right where I was, wondering how quickly I could reach down for my weapons. "What? You would ignore me?" Moctezuma complained incredulously. "You would not treat Copil like this, or Hummingbird," he said, smiling behind his hand and dirty fingernails.

What did he mean by that? What were Copil and Hummingbird to him? But I made no move or gesture in anger. Cortés's manners, or lack of them, had made me accustomed to provocations mouthed by monsters, and yet I felt a surging swell of disgust rise in me, ready to bite.

Wait.

"Let the crystal go," he commanded.

When I did not obey him, he growled low, the sound vibrating up through my soles and body. His face was like a thundercloud, and in the next moment, he became something else. I watched him transform himself, assume various guises in quick succession, beginning with Huitzilopochtli, wearing a massive headdress of hummingbird feathers, then the god Tezcatlipoca, one side of his head encased in a laughing mask and the other side with a frown more diabolical-looking than sad. He ended with Xocolalt, the god of hunting, antler-headed and brandishing a giant bow with a notched arrow dripping blood, before becoming Moctezuma again. I became dizzy watching him turn from god to god, but I never let go of the crystal.

"What a stubborn thing you are. Act as you wish, but know this—I have come to help you. Just say the word and I will destroy these invaders. Or . . ." His smile twisted, baring yellow teeth. "I can help in another way." The folds of his mantle moved excitedly. He raised his arm to his side, flipped his palm up, and unfurled his long fingers, revealing a clutch of seeds, pods, and dried petals. Gold stars swirled around the seeds and petals in his hand. I followed the arc they made. "After such an arduous journey, you must long for peace. Here it is." He thrust his hand toward me. "A bit of water is all it needs. One sip and you will be reunited with your brother."

His eyes seemed to grow larger the longer I looked at him. I gulped the air and made it mine. I smelled the dankness of the earth and the rot of the emperor. I heard the beetles and scorpions push at the dirt around my feet. I tasted blood where I bit my lip and saw Moctezuma's eyes grow wide and his shoulders swoon.

Listen.

"I know you miss him," he said, turning the words over with his tongue as if they were delicious. "And you have suffered so much. Come." He motioned at me with his free hand. "Come and be with your brother."

I am priestess trained and guardian of the shield, you monster.

"Enough with the games." Moctezuma rose into the air with a whoosh, and the throne vanished. He drifted back and forth in the air above me. "How long are you going to hover over that thing? Your brother's heart." I could not mask my surprise at hearing that, even though I already knew it was true. "Oh, so you *are* surprised? How young you are. They should have taught you better. Priestesses." He spat the word like something rotten. "They should have taught you how *not* to be taken captive and locked up in a stone cell. Such an easy spell."

No. What is he saying? "It was you?" And suddenly, I was back in that place, feeling the walls closing in on me. At the shock, I nearly let go.

He laughed, and even the cavern rumbled, though it did not muffle the heart, which was still beating, its rhythm pounding through my blood.

"You thought it the work of the Tlaxcallans, didn't you? And that fool Cortés," he trilled, floating above me in a sick sort of ecstasy. He landed with a thump, frothing the earthen floor. "No." He shook his head. "I needed to stop you from coming to Tenochtitlan.

"Your brother's heart is the source of sustenance and life for the city. It's the young ones, who don't know what kind of magic they're capable of, that make the best hearts. Your brother was one of the most talented magicians this land has ever seen. Foolish to allow his prognostications about my demise to reach my ears, but he was the best. I had to have him," he said, sidling up to the crystal and looking at it adoringly.

A sharp pulse passed through me then, sizzling my fingers. He was trying to loosen my hold, but I held on.

Moctezuma stepped back. "To keep his heart company, to lend a pleasing quality to the air, we burn good, strong specimens alongside him. In this case, because of you . . . Well, you left me no choice . . . your friends . . ." He pulled aside a thick draping of cobwebs, exposing the dead, hollowed-out bodies of Copil and Hummingbird.

"No!" The rage of a thousand Malinallis flamed inside me, and once I started screaming, I found I couldn't stop. The sound of my fury stabbed me all the way to my core and loosened the sinuous serpentine creature that rested there. I let go of the crystal and, miraculously, it slid back into its place. I reached down for my sword and shield, moving in a flash, surprising Moctezuma with my speed and readiness to do him harm.

He turned agilely on his feet, producing his own sword, set with blades of obsidian like shark's teeth. I stopped screaming then. I needed to save my strength so that I could kill him.

"I will feed them to my animals," Moctezuma said, whipping his cloak off, exposing his tattooed chest and mantled loins. "Later. When I am finally finished with you!"

Before the last word fell from his mouth, I was repeating the words to my charm, hoping that the enveloping spell spun across Tenochtitlan would break now. It must have, because as he turned into his nahual animal, I rose into my power, my serpent-self.

Moctezuma dipped his head as if he meant to rub his ear against his shoulder, and that's when I saw the dull flash of long, sharp teeth. A ridge of tawny, black-spotted fur swept across his face and throat.

"Your stubbornness must be a family trait," the half human and half beast said.

I stood perfectly still, feeling my head and face becoming enveloped by the carapace of scales and fangs. My eyes grew and narrowed to slits. The vengeance and anger that had been building inside me over the years uncoiled throughout my body and girded me in invisible armor.

"Why could you not stay away!" he shouted.

"Kill me, then," I fired back at the man-jaguar pacing back and forth in front of me. I felt Eagle standing armed and at the ready by my side. "Just like you killed my brother and father."

The beast stopped. "Put you in a cage?"

And the evilness of his admission made me gasp, for I never thought he would ever admit this out loud to me. And for him to shove the deed in my face? I surprised myself by nearly laughing. *Of course he would. Why would I ever believe otherwise of a monster like him?*

"I am thinking of something far worse for you, little goddess," Moctezuma snarled. "I sent magicians and sorcerers after you. I destroyed your home. But you are a persistent creature." The beast reared back on his hind legs, towering over me. "And now it is *you* who have brought this scourge of white worms to my land. You gave these creatures a voice."

I hissed, vowing to end this now. I raised my shield, and the flash of the obsidian mirrors embedded throughout the design must have startled him, for he cried out as if he'd been struck. We lunged at each other then, and I swung my sword the way I'd been taught by the High Priestess, batting him away one moment, moving in on the attack in the next, using my shield to protect and direct the pink light emanating from the crystal into his eyes.

But just when I was about to deliver the fatal blow, I held back. Would this bring more darkness, or light? Was I ready to plunge this sword, kill him, and live in a dungeon wrought by vengeance forevermore?

Before I could realize an answer, shadows in the tunnel sprang to life. The emperor roared as something grabbed me from behind, lifting me off the ground. I uncoiled swiftly and bit my attacker in the thigh with my fangs, eliciting a scream of horror and alarm. But instead of letting me go, the man kicked me toward another soldier, who put his booted heel on my scaly green neck, stopping me. The cavern filled with Spaniards, and the distraction was enough to reintegrate my nahual ally into my body. It was no longer a threat. But my transformation back into my warrior-woman self so startled my second assailant that it gave me time to land many forceful blows and reduce him to a groveling heap.

I shoved him from me and backed away as Cortés and his soldiers circled Moctezuma like a pack of coyotes. The beast part of him was gone now, too, so it was the man Moctezuma who stood at the center. Though completely vulnerable, he appeared calm.

I watched, waiting for him to summon the might of his ancestors and the gods to destroy Cortés. And me. I clung to my shield, heard the shift of falling rocks and turned just as one of the soldiers stepped forward and struck Moctezuma, and one by one, they stabbed him to death. I crumpled to the ground and yelled at them to stop, but they did not. Steel swords as long as my arm slid and hacked into his body. The cave rang with unspeakable sounds. I caught Cortés standing among his men, his face flush with excitement. Something like terror moved into his eyes, but by the time he noticed that I was watching him, a different expression had fallen into place. It was the exultant arrogance of my land's defiler.

Suffused with brutish strength, I jumped to my feet and flew across the chamber, toward the crystal. I heard Cortés shouting, ordering someone to catch me, but by the time someone with a sword dripping with the emperor's blood could reach me, I was throwing off the crystal dome and holding my brother's beating heart in my hand. To the sound of shattering glass, I ran as if the Spaniards' hounds of hell were after me. Even when a real threat appeared, and Moctezuma's skeleton henchmen came swarming down the river, I could still feel the dogs snapping at my heels.

SOMETIMES THE ONLY OPENING IS THROUGH DARKNESS

I flew past the blind guard at the entrance to the House of Magical Studies. The sun was on my face, but I felt no warmth. Blinking through tears, gritting my teeth against the shudders that intended to take me apart, I kept my brother tucked against my body and moved quickly, winding through the crowds that had gathered to witness a procession. Until I remembered the ritual was a yearly enactment of the war god fighting the moon goddess. Brother against sister. The sun out to defeat the moon for sky power and supremacy of the hearts and minds of the people.

I stumbled into an alcove. Stopped. Leaning against a wall for support, I looked down at the heart I was cradling against my chest. It was not beating now, but it glowed like a ruby. It colored the air with the rich tang of copper and the sweetness of roses. It halted all breath, made me feel that I was holding the center of the world, the most hidden, fragile core.

I slammed my shield hand against the wall. The weapon shuddered, and I felt pain throughout my body, but I did it again. And then I kicked the stones, my mind shattering into a thousand pieces. So this was my fate? To lose my brother . . . again? To hold his heart in my hand? To see my friends butchered? I lurched as my stomach emptied itself of everything I had eaten. I stood there shaking. All of them had been sacrificed to keep Tenochtitlan alive. In that moment, I could have prayed for peace, prayed for help. But why? Why bother now?

I slid down the wall. I felt dead to nearly all sensations save for one: fury. Anger because I felt no relief that Moctezuma was gone. Anger that the gods and goddesses must have deemed his murderous acts to have merit. Anger that everything I had worked for—peace—appeared to be coming undone. Once, I had believed my quest, my whole purpose, was to kill him. That exacting vengeance would make everything right. That it would force change. If I had to embrace darkness to bring his death about, then so be it, I used to think. I could not live with that murderer walking the earth. But now that he was gone, I felt . . . nothing. And it enraged me.

The shrill sound of a whistle shook me out of my spiraling stupor. It sounded four more times. Then the drums began. I did not have to look to see what was happening; all I had to do was listen to the onlookers standing nearby to know that the warriors were entering the precinct and performing a slow circle dance in front of the Great Temple. Dressed in their Eagle and Jaguar Knight costumes, designed to terrify enemies and honor the sun god. Stomping their ocelot-skinned and eagle-clawed sandals on the carpet of flowers. The ringing of their gold ankle bells. And then I overheard someone say that a woman was approaching them from the opposite direction, ". . . and she's wearing a feathered headdress, gold jewels, with bell-shaped tattoos on her cheeks." She of the Painted Bells. The moon goddess. "She carries a painted shield that shines, and a sword."

A ritual to mark the battle between sun and moon. I closed my eyes and tried to stem the tide of my ever-widening outrage. Who was going to strike her down first? Then there came a cry too strange to be a flute. It came again.

"¡Mueran!" Let them die.

I jumped. Still cradling the heart, I peered around a corner and saw flashes of silver light. A group of Cortés's soldiers darted through the crowd, making their way toward the musicians. Metal breastplates, helmets, and swords sparkled in the sunlight. The soldiers surrounded the dancers and musicians, and when the cry came again, the Spaniards fell on the men lost in the music and the dance.

The body never forgets the tremble in the air that precedes war.

"No, no, no, no, no."

I didn't know what to do, and yet I felt a protective sweeping force gathering within me. *The Spaniards must be stopped.* But in the next instant, I was sobbing and looking down at my brother's heart. *But I can't leave. How can I leave you now?* No. It was impossible. To let go of him? I wanted to carry him with me forever.

The blast of the Spaniards' firesticks set off more screams for help. I squeezed my eyes shut and tried not to listen, tried not to care. I willed them all to go away and leave me alone with my brother. *Just let me have him for a little while more.*

I sheltered the red jewel that had once beat inside my brave and magical twin for as long as I could. Shaking, I placed my brother's heart down, whispering "I'm sorry" over and over. Like a balm to my wound, the High Priestess's words came to me, *Never forget who you are.* And then Hummingbird's voice, *They know your power.* And my brother Eagle—I felt his words in my bones, *You are sorceress in more than name.* Then a pack of terrors resurfaced—the stench of the slave cage, the cold of the stone prison, the sour bloodiness of the owl statue's belly. Like a dagger to my chest came the murderous horror of being handed to strangers as if I wasn't worth anything. The thundering majesty of my bravery and my shield stopping time. Flashes of my past mixed with my present, with intimations of what was coming for me, all whirling and binding Wild Grass together. It was as if I carried my own book of divination inside me, sacred only to Malinalli.

I launched myself into the air and ran toward the Spaniards, my sword drawn, shield in place, ready to protect the women and children from the menace that I had guided to Tenochtitlan.

▲▲▲▲

For heartbeats, I was the painting on the wall at Malinalxochitl's shrine come to life—the running warrior-sorceress, with her shield raised. I was another creature, too. My hands were beginning to shimmer green. I felt the undulation of smooth scales against the inside of my belly, and the light in my eyes was breaking into prisms. But I worked to keep my nahual in check. I wished this test to proceed differently.

Either people were paralyzed by the Spaniards' attack or not fully aware of what was happening. Some cursed me as I urged them to take shelter and move out of the way of danger. The closer I got to the Spaniards, the more harm I wanted to inflict on them. The soldiers were striking the hands off the drummers. They hacked arms and split open chests, thrust pikes and spears into the dancers and onlookers gathered nearby, until blood stained the petals and stone. Severed heads spun through the air and hit people in the stands.

I ran and struck the armored men down with a burst of speed that was goddess-made. It wasn't courage alone that drove me. It was deep terror. I'd always known this could happen. I had to protect the women and children, the helpless, from whatever monsters I encountered.

And there were many, because the Spaniards' Tlaxcallan allies appeared then, painted for war, and added their voices to the roar tearing through the precinct. They wielded flint-studded swords and cut down everyone standing in their way.

The whole world was screaming.

As if my body were accustomed to this savagery, my feet moved quickly, finding purchase on stairs, moving around falling and flailing bodies as people pushed and tried to get away. I shielded them as best as I could. Then, above the fury, a single order—*Destroy them all!*—rang out like a thunderbolt and stopped me.

I looked up. Gunmen and crossbowmen were on the rooftops of the surrounding temples, and even the palace of Axayacatl, shooting their weapons of death indiscriminately.

I paused to catch my breath, even as the air split with the rush of loosened arrows piercing their targets with dull moans. I was sure to die if I remained there, but I no longer cared about dying.

I ushered as many people as I could to safety. Some men were as frightened of me as they were of the armored Spaniards, perhaps more. With my white huipilli bloodied, my hair a nest of vipers from the wind and explosions, and my flesh-eater of a sword and strange obsidian-mirrored shield, I knew I must look like a nightmare terror made flesh. The women, on the other hand, were not so afraid, for many followed me eagerly, and a few took up fallen weapons to fight alongside me. Perhaps I reminded them of a different time, when women ruled from thrones. Seeing them made me wonder where my army was.

I had only a moment to think about Pakal Balam before the Mexica descended in torrents to save and defend their Eagle and Jaguar Knights. They came stomping, chanting, and waving spears, calling for all of the Spaniards to come out and fight like men. They shot flaming arrows and set fire to Cortés's palace. Their magicians let loose their spells and conjured headless corpses and cadavers to appear. An entire force of dead men, the skeletons I had seen on the river beneath the House of Magical Studies, shuffled through the temple square, killing everyone, including the innocents of the city. The screams muffled the slaughter.

I was not afraid. I kept to my work, shielding women and children who had come to the temple square to admire a spectacle. A religious ritual practiced since Malinalxochitl's defeat. I muscled my way past the work of sorcerers: giant scorpions, crab creatures, and walking corpses. I had seen worse. But the anger, still building inside me, was a new sensation. It was more ravenous and destructive than anything I had felt so far in my short life. More than anything else, I was angry at myself. I had not achieved peace. I knew that none would be reached this day, though peace was what Toci and all of the priestesses expected from me.

▲▲▲▲

The moon rose full and proud. I crawled over dead bodies to get to the Great Temple. I knew without much reflection what I had to do next. *But will it be enough?* I did not pause until I was standing atop the great moon goddess stone. I screamed with all my might, unleashing the rage that ran through my flesh and heated my blood. *Sometimes the only opening is through darkness.*

"I warned you!"

My voice. My magnificent voice. I lifted my arms, shield and sword, and summoned the serpents that glared at me from every corner of the precinct, all of the fanged-tooth vipers carved into the bases of the temples. The dying sun and rising moonlight danced across the green-white-and-gold-painted snakes, some with feathered crests and bejeweled eyes of white-and-orange coral. I was lucid and sure. I had not long to wait.

The snakes quaked to life. The monuments grew, pounding the earth as they reared and coiled and bared their fangs in gruesome hisses. Their undulations broke stairways apart and catapulted the temples of the war and rain gods to the ground. The fifty-two serpent heads that decorated the House of Magical Studies answered my call, too, demolishing the magicians' place that had refused to teach girls.

But it wasn't enough. Even with stones falling all around me, setting off explosions and geysers of smoke, I could still hear Cuitlahuac, Moctezuma's successor, ordering his forces to resume the attack. I could hear the sorcerers conjuring new skeleton armies, and Cortés, the valley's latest usurper, directing his men to take what gold they could and flee across the causeway to Tlacopan.

I did what I had to do and raised my shield, and through the power of the moon and a waning sun, I stopped time again. Every soldier, stone serpent, and conjured beast froze.

I was not alone. I felt the basalt and cypress wood goddesses from the sad and dusty temple house, and She of the Painted Bells, Earth Mother, Malinalxochitl, and Hummingbird standing beside me. They were all stretching their limbs and at the ready to see me bring down everything that had been built to contain them, subordinate them, control them.

Breathe. But don't wait.

I moved forward, searching my mind for the words that would move two men to see the world as I did. Would the Mexica's new tlahtoani help me create a city of peace? Would Cortés? There was only one way to find out.

EPILOGUE

The light was rose gold. It was always so at this time of day, morning, the earth stirring awake, the sun slipping into view, and me with a broom in hand, sweeping. It was the festival season we called Tititl, your end of December and beginning of January, when we celebrated the push and pull of the world's forces—past and present, war and fertility, life and death. A sun and moon period that lifted Cihuacoatl, Snake Woman, the Toltec earth mother, fierce warrior and goddess of midwives, to the place of honor. For me, the season symbolized the long breath of renewal we must take before starting a new plan. An inhalation filled with hope. Chaos might be all around, but with every breath, every shush of my broom, I could feel myself getting stronger. Sweeping made me powerful enough to stretch my mind back to the death and strange rebirth of Tenochtitlan.

To begin, how was I to know that a new beast was ready to rise up against me? Evil made flesh with five heads. Instead of negotiating with two men, I would be saddled with dealing with all of them—Cortés, Cuitlahuac, Cuauhtemoc, Xicotencatl the Elder, and Moctezuma's powerful priest, half eagle, half ocelot—and not a single one of them would be interested in peace.

But that's what happened. It *almost* made me wish Moctezuma had still been in power.

After I had returned the light to the moon and had soothed the stones back into their temples, lies about me spread like green pond scum over fetid water.

"The people's protector, her magic, was defeated, and Cortés won. What the serpents started, Cortés finished." "The warrior-sorceress charmed with serpent powers was beheaded by Huitzilopochtli." "All of the goddesses were banished to a cave in Malinalco." "A woman who called herself Malinalli was killed by exploding shards of volcanic glass."

The stories were never-ending. But for those who were truly concerned about me, the truth was not hard to seek out:

Cortés had me hunted down and carried out of Tenochtitlan. How had I allowed this to happen? I still had some of my magic then, the threads would sometimes come to life for me, but I'd lost my connection to my nahual animal guardian. Perhaps I had used up all of my power the day I conjured the stone serpents to life. Even docile green garden snakes had paid me no mind. My charm, I had been horrified to learn . . . just words. And then, less than a year later, Cortés had me carried back in a coffin with a window cut just right so I could watch the Spaniards destroy the city.

The final death blow came in our month Fall of the Plum Fruit, also known as the Great Festival of the Dead. It was your year 1521, August 13, a day beloved by the Spaniards because it was the feast day of Saint Hippolytus, the patron saint of horses. To the victor went the riches of the empire, including my son, Pakal Balam's son. Cortés believed the boy was his. I did nothing to disprove his claim, though you had only to look into his amber-gold eyes to know he was not created with the Spaniard's seed. The boy's proud and unflinching stare told you he was Maya. Chapolin, I called him. I wanted him to take his place in this Mexico City Cortés was building, even though the new noblemen and clerks from his revered Spain would end up throwing the conquistador out of the city, and someone named Inquisitor would burn many of Cortés's men at the stake during the quemadas.

Before Cortés took my son away from me, I taught the boy how to survive. How to live atop the crushed stones, sacrificed hearts, and marsh grasses, in this city that was once the marvel of the world, a dream breathed into being by a sacred force, a jeweled bracelet fallen off the wrist of a goddess. I needed him to witness the new arrivals, those pale men armed with steel swords and women wearing wide skirts. To be aware of the takeover, the shocking carelessness and greed. To listen as they argued and shouted, and used the sweat of the survivors to work the soil, plant cotton and tobacco, and build new roads. To feel the terror and horror of what had happened years ago in his bones. What mother wants that for a child? To subject him to all of that? Shouldn't I have shielded him? The mother in me, the priestess, the girl who loved her mother's painted books and the warrior, needed him to know the truth so that what befell Tenochtitlan would never happen again.

I raised my voice to make a difference. Conquistadors and Spaniards new to the city shouted strange words and shook long sheets of paper covered with their spidery crawl of symbols in the survivors' faces, claiming ownership of great sweeps of land. There were many translators now, but a few of the Mexica noblemen and women would only talk through me. They continued to believe my voice was all-powerful. "Malinalxochitl," they insisted on calling me, as if I were the goddess nursing a revenge plot against the latest invader. I think more than a few of them prayed that I would turn back into a serpent. Some brought me things, mostly rabbit pelts and feathers. I did my best to guide them. I did what I could for the farmers and the feather workers, the artists and the traders. Often my help was not enough to fend off someone's grubby, greedy hands. As word spread of my failures, the people stopped coming to me. I united myself with a Spaniard, and the goddesses blessed me with a daughter. For her protection, I named her María, after the Virgin. She loved the bustle of the city, the shield flowers and tasseled corn plants with feminine faces that decorated the Spaniards' churches. She revered the scent of candles. For me, it was the smell of death, while copal incense conjured goddesses, feathers, and bells.

It was strange, and marvelous, how the city was not as conquered as people thought. Some Mexica warriors continued to fight, unleashing sprays of arrows at unsuspecting backs. There were tales of blue-tattooed women attacking the soldiers who were rebuilding the aqueduct, and of phantasms of animals—giant lizards and vultures—dragging and carrying away grown men. The ghosts of Cuitlahuac and Cuauhtemoc shadowed all those who were sent by Spain to rule. Skeletons skittled freely, dressed in velvets and silks and hats the size of ships.

For years, I stayed. I felt I had to look at what I had wrought. Live in that early hell I had a hand, a voice, in creating. People pointed at me. Treated me like a curiosity. There was enough ridicule to make me think of the little girl with the big name who was bullied and teased, but I never felt that way for long. They still feared me, though. And depending on my mood, I liked that people kept their distance, looked away, crossed themselves in the manner of the four directions whenever I turned their way. Another reason I remained . . . My heart insisted that Pakal Balam had survived the battles. I was sure I would find my Maya waiting for me again on the far side of the city walls, near the fort they once called Acachimanco.

But there was only one place for me now.

By the time I returned home, Cortés had left for Spain—with my son—and María was enchanted by the Spaniards' city and her silks and her heeled leather boots. At the Temple of the Eighteen Moons, I tended to my chores, like sweeping the steps of Quetzalcoatl's temple, and fulfilled new roles. Jeweled Laughter led us now. The High Priestess was struggling after battling the pestilence of the smallpox. With their blessing, I now taught sword fighting, and Yucatecan, Chontal, Nahuatl, and, with no trepidation, Spanish. I had learned that it was good to speak many tongues and understand the rhythms of words: to raise your voice, to be a knower of things.

I have found peace in the labyrinth, not because I relish solving it but because I have discovered that this is where I feel closest to Hummingbird.

I have returned the shield to its rightful place on the wall in the shrine set in the forbidden forest, where it waits to be held by a new warrior-sorceress with the heart to continue the fight, the magic to change the world.

AUTHOR'S NOTE

This novel is a work of fiction based on the real woman who interpreted for Hernán Cortés and Moctezuma from 1519 to 1521. She has come down to us as Malinalli, Marina, and Malintzin. Indigenous leaders believed she was the goddess Malinalxochitl. But the name that has stuck to her is La Malinche.

The first time I heard this name, it sounded bad. I didn't know who she was. When I was older and read Bernal Díaz del Castillo's *The Conquest of New Spain*, I became mesmerized by her. How did she end up becoming Cortés's interpreter? She was eighteen years old—so young! How did she feel to be standing between Cortés and Moctezuma, at the center of colliding worlds? Her mastery of languages alone impressed me, a shy Mexican American woman. I became obsessed with her. This is a woman who is reviled to this day in Mexico, labeled the whore/traitor completely responsible for the Spanish conquest of Mexico. She's been cast as Eve, a treacherous, conniving woman. I sensed a story. I was wary of historical accounts told from a predominantly male point of view.

Though she became the voice that bridged these two men, there is very little information about her life. There are no writings in Malinalli's voice. In the absence of her exact words, I immersed myself in books on women's roles during the precolonial period and Díaz's account of her. I researched the mythology of gods and goddesses of ancient Mexico and reacquainted myself with the monuments and artifacts at the Museo Nacional de Antropología in Mexico City. But even after filling index cards and notebooks with research, I had to give my imagination space. I will admit that giving myself permission to let go was hard. But it excited me as well. In the end, I let my characters and the story I was weaving together guide me. I leaned into magnificent Mesoamerican myths and the magic these stories spun to tell my tale.

NAHUATL PRONUNCIATION

Nahuatl is a beautiful language. There are a few basics that have helped me better understand and appreciate its beauty.

Nearly all Nahuatl words are accented on the next-to-last syllable. Such as Me SHEE ka for Mexica.

Vowels:

a = ah

e = eh

i = ee

o = oh

uh/hu = w

Consonants approximate English, except in the following cases:

c followed by an *i* or *e* has the sound of *s* as in song

x and *xh* sound like the English *sh* as in shake

z sounds like the English *s*

qu when followed by *e* or *i* is pronounced like a *k*

hu is pronounced like the *w* in will

tl is a soft, single sound made with the tip of the tongue against the teeth while pronouncing *l*

tz is a single sound, like the *ts* at the end of cats

ACKNOWLEDGMENTS

I began exploring and writing this novel twenty years ago. But perhaps I truly started on the day my parents took the whole family to the Museo Nacional de Antropología in Mexico City in the late '60s. Standing in the Mexica Room during that first summer visit, looking up at the serpent-skirted Earth Goddess Coatlicue, planted the seed for this book. I am forever thankful to my parents for their love and for sharing that museum and all of the wonders of Mexico. And I can barely put into words my love for my sister, Adela, and brothers, José, Ed, and Paul, the best life companions.

This manuscript has taken many shapes, and its earliest readers have included my sister, Adela Langrock; my niece, Isabelle Langrock; and dear friends Gretchen Effler and Jim Biery. Each one of them made me feel as if I were engaged in a noble pursuit, and for that magic, I am eternally grateful.

To my Barat College sister Donna Vitucci, who sat at my side until I completed my application to the artist residency program at Ragdale . . . thank you, my dearest D.

My husband, Bruce Hatton Boyer, kept me steady, and his wisdom, patience, and love nourished me on a daily basis throughout the pursuit of this endeavor. Thank you, Bruce, for honoring me with the space and time I needed to follow Malinalli.

Most crucially, there was a special group of readers whose support, notes, and encouragement helped to make this novel possible. For over twenty years I've endlessly learned from every one of the talented writers in my writing group: Michele Weldon, Pam Todd, Arlene Malinowski, Teresa Puente, Marja Mills, Elizabeth Berg, and Nancy Horan. No matter where we gathered, whether it was in someone's dining room, the Oak Park Library, or online, they read, critiqued, and enthusiastically ventured back in time to Mexico with me.

My agent, Mariah Stovall, at Trellis Literary Management, has been fearless since the first moment I reached out to her. Her grace and editorial skills kept me focused, while her unwavering spirit encouraged me to reach for the stars.

My editor, Michelle Herrera Mulligan, always knew what this book meant to me. I owe a profound debt of gratitude to her for her time and editorial expertise. Beginning with our first conversation, I felt instantly connected, understood, and seen. Most importantly she encouraged me to seek my unique vision for this story. For her patient guidance and unwavering enthusiasm, mil gracias. And to the entire Primero Sueño Press team, notably assistant editor Yezanira Venecia, and the Atria team, including Erica Siudzinski, I offer my deepest thanks. You are among the most thoughtful and supportive people I have ever met.

A special note of gratitude to the librarians at the Newberry Library and the Museo de Antropología in Mexico City—each visit felt like a homecoming to me.

In the end, it was that summer day in Mexico City that I remember as if it were yesterday. I see us gathered outside the Museo with the colossal statue of the Rain God Tlaloc towering behind us. Pride radiates from my father for we are standing in the country of his birth, my grandparents' homeland, set to encounter the greatness, creativity, and power of Mexico. It was a journey back into time. But for me it will also be the day time stood still, giving me the chance to catch up to my spirit and soul.

ABOUT THE AUTHOR

Veronica Chapa is an author, essayist, and award-winning copywriter with a master's degree in advertising from Northwestern University's Medill School of Journalism. She lives in the Chicago area with her husband.